LADY LAVENDER

Samantha Lin

to Maria,

Jenny and Melody,

and

all the Regency Lovers

VOLUME I

would be practical to gather all your artwork in one part of the house, in a space for you to draw and paint as much as you wish. Do consider it, dearest Ellie.'

Marcus's proposal was a lot less daunting than his wife's and much more appealing. The very notion of having rooms in Thornleigh Abbey dedicated to her work made her smile.

'I will, my dear brother. Thank you.'

2

AUBREY CHARLES BEAUMONT, the 7th Viscount Sutton, read the letter for the third time. It was a rather plain letter, full of the usual civilities, written in the steady hand of a gentleman to whom Sutton had been introduced, but with whom he had no previous correspondence. It was, in some ways, a bold and presumptuous letter, addressing Sutton so directly without any established understanding. It was from Mr Earlwood in Darlington, Hertfordshire, whose home was sixty miles away from Bellevue Park, the Sutton family seat – not a long distance to travel for friends, but a little too much for mere acquaintances.

Yet, it was a remarkable letter, solely for its inclusion of a name most dear to Sutton: James Graham.

Lieutenant James Graham: his childhood friend who, through the years, had become his closest friend; an energetic, good-natured man of four and twenty, now serving in the British Army. A few months earlier, Graham's estranged elder brother had passed away without a proper will, leaving the Graham family inheritance open to claim. However, Graham's time with his regiment, his growing kinship with his fellow soldiers, and his previously fraught relations with his family, all left him unwilling to inherit what was rightfully his. Instead, Graham had remained in the army, intent on working for a promotion rather than buying a commission. Not long after his decision, the army rewarded him for his merits, and his battalion was transferred from its billets in a Hertfordshire town to a location as of yet undisclosed to the public.

It was a move that both disappointed and concerned Sutton: disappointed because he had hoped Graham might return to the childhood house close to Sutton's own estate, and concerned because of the army's continued campaign against Napoleon in the Peninsular War. Patriotic as he was, Sutton did not relish the thought of losing his dear friend to an unnatural, untimely death.

He glanced down at the letter, once again trying to discern its meaning. It was possible Mr Earlwood was simply offering his friendship in Graham's absence; Mrs Earlwood had been close to the Grahams in her youth, and the family had indeed spent time with Graham while he was stationed in Darlington, during which Sutton himself had made the Earlwoods' acquaintance. He knew Mr Earlwood was fond of Graham, and it was entirely possible that Graham spoke about his own bond with Sutton. Few of Sutton's own circles knew Graham well, and even fewer held military aspirations; Mr Earlwood, while having no sons himself, might be acquainted with those who had enlisted. Perhaps the gentleman's invitation was nothing more than a heartfelt gesture.

But there was another possibility, the thought of which made Sutton's temper flare. The Earlwoods had three daughters, two of whom were at an age where an association with a viscount would be very beneficial indeed. In his five and twenty years, Sutton had been lured into the courtship dance more than he could recall, and certainly more than he would have liked. The viscount had no misgivings about his numerous connections with the fairer sex – indeed, he was very fond of harmless flirtations – but he was also sensible about the reputations of the parties involved. He never had any wish to ruin a lady's reputation by account of an imprudent dalliance, and, after inheriting the viscountcy, he guarded his own name and title even more closely. There were important lessons to be learnt from some of his previous entanglements, and Sutton had no wish to be caught in an unfortunate trap now, especially when Graham was indisposed to provide counsel.

Yet, from Sutton's few exchanges with Mr Earlwood earlier in the year, he had sensed nothing shrewd about the gentleman. It would be most impolite to respond to Mr Earlwood's generosity with unfounded suspicions. Sutton's own wariness revealed more about *himself* than the gentleman's intentions, and he had enough common sense not to be ruled by prejudice. Indeed, Sutton knew the secret to happiness lay in maintaining genuine relationships, and that one could never anticipate where these relationships might start. Graham had taught him that, and Sutton was not foolish enough to dismiss the lesson.

A quick consultation of his calendar and appointments, some mental calculations and adjustments, and he was all but ready. The harvest would begin in two weeks, which was plenty of time for Sutton to accept Mr Earlwood's invitation and stop by London before returning to Bellevue Park. If Darlington proved to be a bore, he would rejuvenate himself in the great capital of England.

His decision made, Sutton pulled out a fresh piece of paper and picked up his pen. He would pay his visit to Darlington with all due courtesy, and with all necessary caution.

3

WITHIN THREE DAYS of Ellie's quiet declaration at dinner that she was amenable to having her own space for her paintings, plans were made, discussed, and finalised, sending the usually quiet halls of Thornleigh Abbey into a bustle of activity. As the small parlour had unofficially become Ellie's work area, and as it was in proximity to the rather neglected west library and reading room, Marcus noted it would be sensible to cement that wing for Ellie's artistic purposes. Unlike the main library with its in-built shelves, the secondary room contained bookshelves that could be easily removed, while the books themselves could be redistributed amongst the other rooms in Thornleigh Abbey. The west library was to become an exhibition space, the attached reading room Ellie's own drawing room, and the small parlour Ellie's permanent art studio. Kitty remarked that the southerly aspect of the wing, combined with the large windows in all its rooms, would provide plenty of natural light, while the small staircase in the west wing, with its easy access to Ellie's living quarters, made the entire section perfect for her needs.

It was amongst this disarray that Ellie now sat in the formal drawing room with Kitty and her childhood friends, who visited Thornleigh Abbey every week or two. Kitty sat on the large chaise between Miss Mary Earlwood and

Miss Phoebe Ingram, and had in her lap a large brown and white cat that had adopted Kitty and taken residence in Thornleigh. Mary, the eldest of three Earlwood daughters, was a vivacious lady of three and twenty whose high spirits and enthusiasm often matched Kitty's. Meanwhile, Phoebe was more reserved, though she was rumoured to have a quick temper, particularly when provoked by her fiancé Mr Tom Winslow. Indeed, Kitty had regaled Ellie with tales about the bickering couple's courtship, which had, for a time, drawn many raised eyebrows and muttered comments along the streets of Darlington.

While Kitty, Mary, and Phoebe took the larger chaise, Ellie was seated beside Harriet, the middle Earlwood sister. The two young women were similar in age and disposition, and both preferred quiet company to the lavish dinners and balls that seemed to enchant many others of their age. It had taken half a year of polite companionship before, at a picnic during which their company became particularly jovial, the two young ladies found themselves conversing at length for the first time. Not long after, they began to call on the other, spending as much time in conversation as in companionable silence while they read or drew together.

Presently, while Kitty, Phoebe, and Mary discussed the Prince Regent's latest exploits, Harriet glanced at Ellie with a small smile and asked, 'Have you had any more news from Mr Richard?'

Ellie nodded. 'There was a letter from him last week, along with sketches of his new companions. He's been keeping busy and learning new drills – he speaks very highly of his new regiment. I miss my brother, but I think he's very happy where he is.'

'I'm glad to hear it. I very much admire Mr Richard's enthusiasm.'

'He does possess that in abundance,' Ellie replied, smiling. 'He wrote separately to Marcus, much to my relief.'

'Oh, that is excellent news! It must have been terribly difficult to watch them quarrel.'

Ellie nodded again. 'Richard oughtn't have concealed his intentions to enlist, and Marcus oughtn't have opposed the decision so violently – I don't know what would've transpired if not for Kitty's intervention. And now with Richard away, only Kitty's presence keeps Thornleigh from becoming dull.'

The two ladies regarded Kitty, who was regaling a piece of gossip with particular relish. 'And what of your garden landscapes? Are they almost ready?'

'Not quite.' Ellie paused to find the right words. 'Lately, I've been fascinated by what autumn brings. With summer ended, the parks and ponds mist over – I so love looking at that lovely in-between state of water that's not water. Even when we're indoors, the light is softer, mellower, and falls so gently upon the rooms, and objects, and people. It's as if all the shapes and colours of the world are trying to coax everyone to prepare for the coming winter.'

Ellie gave her friend an apologetic smile. 'I don't suppose that makes much sense.'

'It does,' replied Harriet. 'I would very much like to see your new pieces when they're ready.'

The young woman was warmed by her friend's encouragement. 'What of your Celtic cushions? Have you finished the final one?'

Harriet shook her head. 'I've not had the chance. Papa has invited a friend to stay at Dunnistone, and there has been too much to do around the house.'

When the other ladies had finished exchanging their news, Phoebe asked for everyone's attention, which was readily given.

'We have chosen a date,' Phoebe said after another round of tea was poured. 'Tom and I will be married in October.'

Kitty stopped scratching her cat's ears and clapped her hands in delight. 'Oh Phoebe, how marvellous!'

'How were you able to keep from announcing your news for so long?' asked Mary. 'I would have burst with the excitement!'

Ellie and Harriet voiced their congratulations, which Phoebe accepted with gratitude. 'Ours has been such a long engagement,' she said, whose engagement preceded that of Kitty and Marcus. 'We kept delaying our nuptials after Papa's accident, but the doctor believes he's made a full recovery.'

'Of course,' Kitty said, more softly this time. 'It's wonderful Mr Ingram will be there on your special day.'

Phoebe reached over to take Kitty's hand. 'I'm sorry your dear father wasn't there on yours.'

'Thank you.' Kitty shook off her melancholy. 'But Mama was there, and she was *thrilled* – and her joy was no doubt doubled by Christopher's timely letter, and knowing she could quit England's climate once I was married.'

Mary and Phoebe laughed. 'How is your mother finding Italy?'

The butler chose this moment to enter. 'Pardon the interruption,' he said, bowing. 'The easels have arrived – shall they go in the parlour or the small library?'

'Has the library been cleared?' asked Kitty.

'Yes ma'am.'

'Oh!' said Kitty, delighted – there had been several bookcases to move earlier that morning. 'Well then, where would you like them, Ellie? Your painting room or the exhibition hall?'

Ellie blushed at the newly ascribed names. 'The…latter, please.'

The butler bowed, while Mary looked to Kitty with renewed interest. 'The exhibition hall? You said you were carrying out some simple refurbishments, not rearranging Thornleigh Abbey itself!'

'Refurbishments *are* part of the process,' Kitty said sheepishly, glancing up at Ellie. Mary, with her unparalleled astuteness, immediately caught on.

'Ellie's holding an art exhibition! *That's* what all the "refurbishments" are about! And the easels – of *course*! Why didn't you say so?'

'It's not yet been decided,' Ellie replied meekly. 'It would be lovely to have a space to paint and to keep my paintings, but to have an *entire* exhibition… That would be excessive.'

Mary's expression softened. 'You are, without a doubt, one of the most talented artists I know. I don't claim to be an expert in such things, but when I look at your paintings, I feel inspired – which is not my usual response, mind you. You inspire me to see the world in a different way – and that, I think, is a rare gift indeed.'

'I agree,' said Phoebe, who was the most sensible of the group. 'I am particularly partial to your watercolours – they are so unique, and simply exquisite. I don't believe I've seen anyone use colours the way you do.'

'And your pencil sketches,' Harriet added in her quiet voice. 'I didn't know drawings without any colour could have so much depth. Even Papa, who has little interest in the arts, was struck by the sketched portraiture you did over the summer.'

Kitty nodded. 'Your work speaks for itself, dear Ellie. Even if you do not wish to hold an exhibition, I hope you will allow us to see your finished paintings on occasion.'

The cat in Kitty's lap meowed as if in affirmation, much to the ladies' delight.

'Of course,' said Ellie, blushing from the unexpected praise. She tried to envision an intimate group of her family and friends gathered for an evening, where her paintings was just one of many topics of conversation, and found she did not balk at the idea. She looked up at Harriet, and found courage in her friend's smile. 'When the new rooms are finished, you are all welcome to the…exhibition.'

Her hesitation was not lost on her friends, who seemed to understand precisely what Ellie needed. Mary, who had a penchant for social gatherings and had helped organise Ellie's debutante ball, was the first to speak.

'Dearest Ellie, the only requirement for an exhibition is having something to exhibit – and you certainly have many splendid paintings to share with us all. And if you wish to mark the occasion with a little extra – perhaps dinner, followed by some light entertainment – then we could certainly arrange that. You need not concern yourself with anything beyond your artistry.'

The ladies voiced their agreement, easing the last of Ellie's uncertainty. As the older women discussed the particulars, Ellie turned to Harriet, who gave her friend an encouraging smile.

'I think it will be a wonderful evening,' said Harriet, her voice soft yet sincere. 'And if you ever find the attention too overwhelming, I'm sure Mary or Kitty would be delighted to draw it away from you with a song or two.'

'Thank you, Harriet.'

She found her friend always knew just what to say, and there was no need for any more words.

4

IT BEGAN TO rain a few hours into his journey, and by the time Sutton arrived at Dunnistone House on the following day, the viscount hoped he would not be rueing his decision. Since this was a route Sutton seldom travelled, he had stayed overnight at an unfamiliar inn that, while it provided all the necessary amenities, had none of the hospitality to which he'd become accustomed. What would have usually been considered a minor inconvenience was exacerbated by the incessant downpour that dampened both his boots and his spirits. At times like these, his long legs aching to leave the confines of his jolting carriage, Sutton wished for nothing more than to be at home, the fire crackling in his studio, a paintbrush in one hand and a brandy in the other.

Nevertheless, Sutton maintained his composure and was nothing short of poised as he stepped out of the carriage. He was received by Mr Earlwood, whose jovial greeting drew a smile from the viscount.

'Lord Sutton, it is such a tremendous pleasure to welcome you back to Darlington!' The two men shook hands, and Sutton was surprised by the older gentleman's sturdy grip. 'I hope the unfavourable weather has not hindered your journey too much – but ah, let us go inside and make you comfortable!'

'Thank you, Mr Earlwood. You are most kind.'

They entered the manor while the staff worked quietly and efficiently around them, carrying Sutton's two portmanteaux and leading the carriage and horses to the stables. Everyone from the butler to the footman had a pleasant air that warmed Sutton as much as being inside the charming country house.

When they had reached the staircase, Mr Earlwood asked, 'Would you like to stop by your rooms first, or shall we go to the drawing room now for some tea?'

Sutton indicated his preference for the latter.

'Splendid. This way, Lord Sutton.'

The drawing room favoured comfort over style, an ethos Sutton suspected extended to the rest of Dunnistone House. As they settled into the plush, slightly worn chairs, Sutton was nothing but grateful for this reception.

'Now, if memory serves,' Mr Earlwood said once the tea and biscuits had been served, 'you visited Darlington earlier this year, when our friend Mr Graham – ah, I mean to say Lieutenant Graham, though that will take some getting used to – when Lieutenant Graham was billeted here.'

'Yes, I believe it was for much of the past winter, and some of spring. I have been long acquainted with Colonel Watson, since before our mutual friend joined the army, and I daresay I took undue advantage of the good colonel's hospitality.'

Mr Earlwood smiled. 'I'm sure Colonel Watson thought no such thing, and both he and Lieutenant Graham were happy for your company. Speaking of the latter: what an achievement! I cannot recall the last time I knew anyone who enlisted as a gentleman volunteer and was subsequently promoted on merit alone.'

'Indeed,' replied Sutton. 'Most of my acquaintances – some who purchased commissions in the army of navy – were quite disbelieving when I informed them Lieutenant Graham had earned his place.'

The viscount sipped his tea, deciding not to mention he had offered to sponsor Graham on more than one occasion, or that his exasperation at his friend's constant refusals was now replaced with admiration.

Mr Earlwood let the silence stand a little before asking: 'How is he faring?'

'Rather well, I think – or so he writes.' Remembering Graham's latest letter, Sutton smiled and shook his head. 'He's taken to his way of life, and to his new role and responsibilities. I've no doubt he's found his calling, but...'

Mr Earlwood waited for Sutton to finish his sentence, but the viscount let the thought linger, a little embarrassed to have spoken so out of turn with a man he barely knew.

'Has he written to you?' Sutton asked instead.

'Twice, since leaving Darlington. He mentioned you in his last letter, and expressed his concern that you might make a hasty decision to relocate to Essex prematurely before his next posting is finalised.'

Sutton's lips curved into a thin smile. 'Did he ask you to intervene, Mr Earlwood?'

'Not at all,' the gentleman replied, unaware of the viscount's growing discomfort. 'I hatched the plan entirely by myself – I do believe it would be prudent to await news of Lieutenant Graham's permanent station.'

Before Sutton could be irritated by Mr Earlwood's meddling, the older man said softly: 'I've had two sons, both taken from us in their infancy. If they'd lived long enough to enlist, I would wish to be as close to them as possible – even if that meant standing beside them on the battlefield.'

This revelation surprised Sutton, whose more aristocratic acquaintances generally considered it vulgar to venture into such subjects. However, once Sutton registered the magnitude of Mr Earlwood's words, his previous judgements about the gentleman wavered.

'Lieutenant Graham often visited us while he was in Darlington,' Mr Earlwood continued. 'Mrs Earlwood and I knew him as a child, and were very fond of him – it was good of him to call on Dunnistone House when he was first billeted, and he returned so often that he felt like part of the family.'

'His combination of enthusiasm and kindness is unmatched,' said Sutton evenly.

'Indeed. He and my eldest daughter got on exceedingly well – I suspect she saw him as the brother she's never had.'

17

Graham had mentioned his fondness for Miss Earlwood. 'Forgive me if I have misremembered,' said Sutton, 'but you have three daughters?'

Mr Earlwood nodded. 'Mary is two and twenty, Harriet is eighteen, and Lettice is nine. I would be delighted to introduce them at supper – if Mary and Harriet make it home this evening.'

The mention of an introduction made Sutton bristle – he had no intention of giving consequence to unmarried ladies – but the gentleman's easy manner gave him pause. Sutton allowed his curiosity to take hold, and said: 'You seem simultaneously relieved and irked by their possible absence.'

'Well, I am glad you might be spared Mary's talk about the upcoming event, but I would be disappointed if they forgot their manners, knowing we have an esteemed guest. But ah, now I am forgetting myself, blabbering on like this! The girls are childhood friends with Mrs Marcus Ashcroft of Thornleigh Abbey, and have been there the past week. Are you acquainted with Mr Ashcroft?'

'I've not had the pleasure.'

'His sister, Miss Eleanor Ashcroft, is a talented young artist with a very impressive output. My daughters are helping to arrange a permanent exhibition for Miss Ashcroft's growing collection, and are planning an informal affair for its launch in two days.'

'Is that so?' asked Sutton, keeping the scepticism out of his voice. His experiences with the world of art had shaped his opinion that, while having one's works featured in an open exhibition was a commendable feat, organising a dedicated space for a single artist was a declaration of either genius or vanity – and never both. That he had never heard of Miss Ashcroft did not stand in her favour.

Mr Earlwood, oblivious to Sutton's thoughts, continued with enthusiasm. 'Ah yes, now I recall Lieutenant Graham praising your artistic endeavours – you might like to attend the exhibition!'

'I would hate to be an imposition,' said Sutton.

'Nonsense! I shall ask Mrs Ashcroft if there is room for one more – let's hope we won't inadvertently upset the seating arrangements.' Mr Earlwood paused, suddenly remembering himself. 'That is, if both you and Miss Ashcroft are amenable. She is a very sweet young lady and extraordinary with a brush, but a little timid. Oh dear, I hope I have not spoken out of turn – Mrs Earlwood would be quite right to give me a talking to if she finds out.'

Sensing his host's embarrassment, Sutton said, 'I would be quite content either way. I have fond memories of Darlington, and look forward to being reacquainted with its charms.'

'Ah yes, very good – we can certainly accommodate that.'

The matter settled, the two men moved on to other subjects, and it was not long before they were called for supper. As Mr Earlwood had foreseen, his daughters were dining at Thornleigh Abbey – an absence that did not trouble Sutton, who spent much of the evening trying to ascertain if the older gentleman had any ulterior motives in hosting a viscount in his humble home.

5

MARY, HARRIET, AND PHOEBE returned to their homes on the eve of the exhibition, leaving the three Ashcrofts to enjoy their first family supper in a week. It was a quiet and relaxed affair, with only the slightest hint of melancholy when they toasted to one another's health and to Richard's eventual homecoming. Knowing her other, more spirited brother would disapprove of any 'mawkish dawdling', Ellie looked away from Richard's empty seat and set aside her concerns about his new position in the British Army. Instead, she focused on the present exchange between Marcus and Kitty, which concerned the naming of the newly refurbished rooms.

'That won't do,' Marcus said, when Kitty suggested 'Paintings Galore'. 'Too ungainly in sound and sentiment.'

'"Easels Emporium?"'

'Good gracious, are you planning to open a shop, my dear?'

Kitty waved off the comment, then smiled. '"Eleanor's Corner?"'

'That would have been the perfect name for Ellie's nursery wing,' replied Marcus with a chuckle. 'How about the "Artist's Wing"?'

'Oh, I like that! What do you think, Ellie?'

The young woman blushed. '"Artist" is perhaps a little too… Well, I don't believe it's the appropriate term for me.'

'How do you mean?'

'Sir Thomas Lawrence is an artist. Mr William Turner is an artist. I am…not.'

Kitty scoffed, as if personally affronted. 'Nonsense. You have an artist's eye, hands, and skill – that makes you every bit an artist as those gentlemen.'

Marcus placated his wife with a simple touch. 'Ellie, do you like the name?' he asked gently.

'I do,' she replied, her voice softer than usual.

'Then let the three of us, and Richard, call it the "Artist's Wing". The rest of the world can know it as "Miss Ashcroft's Wing".'

Ellie nodded. 'Thank you. I shall aspire to become worthy of the title.'

'Well then,' said Kitty, 'shall we try out Ellie's drawing room?'

They left for the new set of rooms and settled in the chaises. Marcus poured some sherry for them, while a footman brought out the last of the Gunter's confectionery box, a souvenir from Marcus's most recent London trip. Ellie was enjoying a lemon jelly when a note arrived from Mr Earlwood. Marcus read it, then said:

'Mr Earlwood has been hosting a guest from Cambridgeshire – Viscount Sutton of Bellevue Park. He's in Darlington for a few days, has an interest in the arts, and would like to attend Ellie's exhibition tomorrow, if she has no objections. Mr Earlwood apologies for the late notice, and assures us Lord Sutton would not take offence if we do not wish to be introduced.'

'A viscount who won't be offended by his social inferior refusing an introduction?' Kitty asked, amused. 'I would be tempted to exclude him, if only to test his claims.'

Kitty's light-hearted tone and mischievous smile told Ellie she was not serious, though Ellie thought someone like Lord Sutton may not appreciate the jest.

'I have heard of Lord Sutton,' Marcus said, 'but we belong to different clubs – I believe he's a member of White's, or Brook's. From what I know, he's well-respected, and does indeed have a passion for the arts.'

Ellie nodded. All the guests to tomorrow's exhibition were close friends, and none of them had more than the usual interest in paintings. To have in attendance someone with knowledge and experience was both a thrilling and terrifying prospect.

'Since Lord Sutton is in Darlington for a short visit,' Ellie said slowly, 'and since there is plenty of room left at the dining table, I don't see why we should not extend him the invitation.'

Her words were calm and measured, and did not reflect the apprehension Ellie felt. Marcus, however, saw beyond her composed exterior and gave her a gentle look.

'Very well. I shall write to Mr Earlwood immediately.'

When this was done, and a footman sent to deliver the note to Dunnistone House, Kitty and Marcus decided to retire for the evening.

'I shall stay a little longer,' Ellie said, kissing them both goodnight.

With her brother and sister-in-law gone, Ellie was free to take a turn around the rest of her wing at her own pace. She went about the rooms with a candle, lighting just enough sconces and candelabras to see her surroundings. The combined efforts of Kitty, Phoebe, Mary, and Thornleigh's staff had transformed the dusty, neglected secondary library into a spacious area where Ellie's best paintings were now thoughtfully arranged. A connecting door led Ellie to the familiar sanctuary that was once the parlour in which she did most of her work, but was now solely set aside for her artistic purposes. Although her friends had left the room untouched, it nonetheless felt different, imbued with a gravitas Ellie had not noticed weeks ago.

This had been her studio for as long as she could sketch, where Ellie set to paper what she saw with her eyes and felt in her heart.

In the subdued light, Ellie surveyed the drawings and paintings at various levels of completion. Here, she saw the sketches of Kitty, whose features she knew so well that she did not require her to sit for a portrait; there, her first oil painting, which had taken her much cajoling last year before she was granted permission to work with such unladylike materials; and there, the series of rainy-day watercolours, which she had only begun a mere fortnight ago.

Pride swelled in her chest, strong and unexpected. When had her leisurely hobby grown from the seeds of her fancy into a tangible collection, ready for display? When had she set aside her reservations about sharing her passions, and agreed to exhibit her most revealing self, the very essence of Eleanor Ashcroft?

She took a deep breath, inhaling the scents of paints and oils that no amount of airing had been able to clear. With small steps, Ellie made her way to the door that separated the inner sanctum of her studio from the outer realm of her exhibition room. Here, leaning against the doorframe and standing on the edge of both worlds, Ellie took in the sight before her. And then, as with the softest fluttering inside, Ellie allowed her imagination to take flight.

She saw visions of Thornleigh Abbey tomorrow evening, when the great hall would be filled with flowing dresses and sharp waistcoats. Only glimmers of the newly-polished floors would shine, covered as they would be by an assortment of fine shoes, while the chandeliers lend their glow to the jewels resting on ladies' bosoms, and the chains from gentlemen's pockets. The dining room would be shining with the finest silverware, the table laden with dozens of dishes for each of the evening's three courses, and Harriet, seated beside Ellie, would remark on Mrs Nancy's unsurpassed skills. Afterwards, when the thirty-five pieces Ellie had selected were available for perusal, Kitty would flitter amongst the guests and provide anecdotes about some of Ellie's recent works, while Marcus, who was not fond of large gatherings, would converse with some of his closer friends, eyes bright with pride. Mary and Phoebe would stay off-centre and discuss topics other than the arts, while Harriet would set aside her own anxieties, and remain steadfast by Ellie's side. And occasionally, when the longing for Richard's presence became too strong to ignore, Ellie would reach for her own necklace and find her father's emerald ring, the only heirloom the late Mr Ashcroft had left for his illegitimate son, and the only parting gift the soldier had given to his dear sister.

'There will be no prospect of matrimony where I'm going,' he had said, sliding the ring off his finger.

'And there will be none here, either,' Ellie had protested.

Richard's smile had been sad as he took his sister's hand and curled her fingers around the ring. 'This is for when you're sad, or scared, or excited about sharing your latest painting. I might be far from home, but I'll always be your brother, and I'll always be praying for your health and happiness, my dearest sister.'

She had removed her own ring, ignoring her brother's protests. 'I know my mother was not fond of you, but this has been mine longer than it's been hers. I wish to leave it to your safekeeping, and so I shall.'

Ellie reached for her neck chain now, finding solace in the token Richard had left for her. She tilted her head upwards and closed her eyes, envisioning both her beloved brothers in the roomful of people who would soon occupy her space. The figures solidified in her mind's eye – Kitty's chestnut curls, Marcus's gentle smile, Richard's red uniform – and Ellie felt herself begin to relax. The first threads of clarity, the onset of shapes and colours and possibilities, the exhilarating edge between the real and the imagined – *this* was what she loved about creating her own art; this sweet, untarnished prelude to pencil or brush.

Ellie straightened, holding close to her this wondrous transformation, this intimate painting only she could see, and might one day bring into the world.

6

SUTTON HELD THE unwavering belief that in order to understand an individual's disposition, one must observe them for a lifetime in polite society – or for a day in their natural habitat. After three days at Dunnistone House, Sutton saw enough of the Earlwoods to challenge his previous caution. Mr Earlwood, with his amiable nature and eagerness to engage in all manners of conversation, had clearly found the perfect complement in Mrs Earlwood, who, while more reserved than her husband, possessed kindness and good sense in equal measure. All three daughters had received Sutton warmly, imploring him to recount his numerous adventures with Graham and listening with fascination when the viscount spoke about his own interests. Sutton soon discovered Miss Earlwood had the vivacity of her father, Miss Harriet the acuity of her mother, and Miss Hannah – insisting with utmost seriousness for a nine-year-old that Sutton address her as 'Lettice' – the agreeableness of both. Indeed, the youngest daughter had acquiesced when, upon wanting to attend Miss Ashcroft's exhibition in a new dress, she was met with Mrs Earlwood's firm reiteration that none of the girls were allowed more than three new dresses each year, and, besides, Lettice's collection of her sisters' outgrown gowns meant she had thrice more choice. Although Mrs

Earlwood had seemed a little embarrassed about the incident unfolding before their guest, Sutton could only admire how she had handled the delicate situation, even as he found the family's reduced circumstances unsettling.

More unsettling than the Earlwoods' situation – one shuddered to think of having fewer servants than the fingers on one hand – was the heartfelt and easy affection displayed by every member of the family. Sutton was not accustomed to such an environment; his own parents had never uttered a word of endearment to him or each other, interested only in Sutton's survival into adulthood. *Their* obligations had always been to the family line and titles – and they had told him as much with words and actions alike. Indeed, it was only after his older siblings were lost to illness, and Sutton became the only heir, that he was afforded every luxury he wanted, including adopting Graham as his playmate – perhaps the only kindness his parents had shown him.

The viscount had formed the firm opinion that love and affection were reserved for friends, not family; one had the power to choose the former but had no say in the latter. It was thus perplexing to Sutton that the Earlwoods could be so happy to spend their days with one another.

He was still contemplating this mystery when they took Sutton's carriage and horses to Thornleigh Abbey for an exhibition he didn't particularly wish to attend. The viscount was happy to accept the Earlwoods for the time being, but he was wary of what might transpire at such a gathering. It would not be the first time Sutton became an instrument used to improve another's social standing.

His first impression of the Ashcrofts stood in their favour: the party was met by well-presented footmen, while two groomsmen, their manners sturdy and assured, attended to Sutton's horses. The viscount often judged a master by his servants, and these men reflected well on theirs.

When the party entered the manor itself, Sutton was welcomed by a spacious and tasteful hall that was grand in scale yet intimate in décor. He took in the interior's pleasing combination of masculine and feminine touches: the halls had soft colours with strong lines, and the portraits that towered above them were brightly painted and lit. While Sutton preferred darker palettes, he was nonetheless drawn to the radiant centrepiece, a double portrait of a gentleman and his wife that captured their joy and mirth.

'That painting of Mr and Mrs Ashcroft was completed the past summer from one of Miss Ashcroft's sketches,' Mr Earlwood commented at his side. 'I've known Mrs Ashcroft since she was in the cradle, and this painting certainly does justice to her exuberance.'

After Lettice was sent to dine separately with the other children, Sutton followed the Earlwoods to the drawing room. Their hostess approached them as soon as they were announced, her eyes and smile even brighter in person.

'Mr and Mrs Earlwood, it is so lovely to see you both!'

Mr Earlwood kissed her offered hand, and replied, 'Nothing would have kept us from Miss Ashcroft's exhibition!' He then turned to the viscount. 'Lord Sutton, please allow me to introduce Mrs Ashcroft.'

Sutton bowed to Mrs Ashcroft's curtsy.

'Thank you for your generous invitation,' he said evenly, noting the conversation had dimmed since his entrance. 'Your home is lovely.'

'Thank you – but I'm afraid I shall have to redirect your compliments.' Mrs Ashcroft's eyes glinted with mischief. 'By family decree, I have been barred from making any decorative choices – and for the best, I might add. I hear you have a very keen eye yourself, Lord Sutton.'

'It comes and goes with my fancies,' he replied.

'Well, I do hope you'll take a fancy to tonight's exhibition.' She brightened when a tall gentleman approached their group. 'Lord Sutton, I hope you will allow me to introduce my husband, Mr Ashcroft.'

'A pleasure, Mr Ashcroft,' Sutton said with a formal bow, which the gentleman returned in kind.

'We are pleased to welcome you to Thornleigh Abbey,' said Mr Ashcroft. He had a calm demeanour that put Sutton at ease. 'Mr Earlwood has told us a little about your artistic pursuits, and I would love to know more.'

Before he could reply, they were interrupted by an older woman.

'Ah, Mr and Mrs Ashcroft, this is all spectacular, if I may say so myself! And Mr and Mrs Earlwood, I hope the girls have been behaving! Oh my, are we making introductions?'

Mr Ashcroft bowed at the woman. 'We are pleased to see you this evening,' he said. Sutton caught a flash of exasperation from Mrs Ashcroft. 'Lord Sutton, would you kindly oblige us in another introduction?'

Sutton had no wish to be acquainted with the woman, but reminded himself he was here at Mr Ashcroft's invitation and Mr Earlwood's recommendation. It would be perfectly within his rights to walk away – and leave the manor altogether – but that would speak as much of *his* manners as the woman's. Sutton gave Mr Ashcroft a small nod.

'Lord Sutton, please allow me to introduce Mrs Norris.'

'Mrs Norris,' said Sutton, keeping his voice neutral.

'Ah, Lord Sutton – how lovely. Pray tell, what are you a Lord of? I was talking to Mr Digby when you were announced and didn't hear your full title!'

'The Sutton viscountcy of Bellevue Park, Cambridgeshire, ma'am.'

'So well-mannered! The boys in Darlington could learn a thing or two from you, Lord Sutton – except Mr Digby, of course, for he's the very paramount of virtue. Have you been in Darlington long? Is this your first time visiting?'

It took great effort for Sutton to remain civil. 'I was in Darlington earlier this year to visit some of Colonel Watson's soldiers. One of them, Mr Graham – who has just become lieutenant – is a good friend of mine.'

'Mr Graham?' There was some surprise in those two words, which the older woman tried to hide. 'Now I support our soldiers as much as the next person, but it is quite inconvenient that they are occasionally billeted in Darlington. I suppose there's no choice – we *are* one of the home counties, unlike Cambridgeshire – but it does get quite rowdy, you know. All that drinking, too – my late Mr Norris never touched a drop, God bless his soul, and neither does Mr Digby, come to think of it. Do you drink, Lord Sutton?'

'When the occasion calls for it – and tonight is certainly one of them. Do excuse me, Mrs Norris.'

Sutton bowed and left, hearing Mr Earlwood make his apologies before joining the viscount and suggesting they find Mr Curtis, who would sit beside Sutton at dinner. Sutton acquiesced, though he did not trust his temper – he might have to leave after all, if Mr Curtis proved to be an imbecile.

They soon found Mr Curtis, an austere gentleman who seemed to share Sutton's current temperament, and exchanged the customary courtesies before Mr Earlwood was called off elsewhere.

'Well, Lord Sutton,' Mr Curtis said once they were alone, 'you are giving quite the impression of being here under duress. Shall we attempt to remedy it with a pleasant topic to discuss? Books, horses, the weather – the choice is entirely yours.'

'A generous offer,' Sutton replied, still rather vexed, 'but is this distraction for my benefit or yours?'

Mr Curtis raised an eyebrow. 'I don't see why it couldn't serve us both.'

The viscount paused at Mr Curtis's refreshing honesty. Mr Earlwood had done well in facilitating this introduction.

'I daresay I'm curious,' Sutton remarked. 'You appear to be under as much "duress" as I am – what brings you here?'

'The insufferable duty of friendship and providing, as they call it, "moral support".'

This time, Sutton fought hard not to smile. 'Insufferable, indeed.'

'A personal sentiment unrelated to Miss Ashcroft's works themselves,' Mr Curtis added. 'In fact, her artistry deserves my highest commendations.'

If Sutton had read the gentleman correctly, Mr Curtis was not one to dispense such praises liberally. 'And who might this young lady be? I have only been introduced to Mr and Mrs Ashcroft thus far.'

Mr Curtis looked across the room, landing on two women on the other side. 'I assume you are acquainted with Miss Harriet Earlwood. The lady beside her is Miss Ashcroft.'

There, smiling shyly next to Miss Harriet, was a pale, freckled, unremarkable young girl, ruining her fine gloves with nervous wringing. She was entirely out of place at her own celebration, rousing both Sutton's pity and disappointment.

'If I have learnt anything,' Mr Curtis said quietly, 'it is not to judge too quickly. Now, I hope your curiosity has been sufficiently satisfied to make a choice: books, horses, or the weather?'

After deciding on a subject that could be as personal or detached as the conversationalists wished, Sutton and Mr Curtis discussed horses for a good ten minutes before dinner was announced, and the viscount temporarily parted with his new acquaintance to escort Mrs Ashcroft to the dining room.

7

WHEN THE LAST guest was finished with the final course of sweets, creams, and puddings, Kitty announced the commencement of the exhibition. Ellie, who had been silently reciting the Kings and Queens of England for most of the meal, followed Kitty's lead, the words from her friends and family washing over her like water.

As they approached the Artist's Wing, questions formed and bubbled in Ellie's mind, ready to spill over in a stream of embarrassed tears. What would her guests think of her paintings? What would she do if they disliked the fruits of her long, languishing labours? What if her acquaintances simply pretended to enjoy the art in Ellie's presence, only to whisper afterwards about the foolish arrogance of Miss Eleanor Ashcroft?

Her thoughts were halted when someone took her trembling hand, giving it a gentle, reassuring squeeze. Ellie looked up to see Harriet, sweet and gentle Harriet, her eyes warm, her smile small yet steady.

The wordless gesture worked wonders. Ellie's last steps towards the exhibition room became measured and sound, her breaths equally calm. The rest followed easily: once in the room itself, the two young women stood on one side, allowing the ladies and gentlemen to make their own way to the paintings. Low murmurs grew to a pleasant buzz of conversation, and Ellie soon felt the familiarity of her situation: tonight was merely another social gathering where she and Harriet found themselves in a corner to observe the merriments rather than partake in them. Ellie looked at Harriet to point out the parallels, but the amused glint in her friend's eyes told her Harriet had come to the same conclusion. Ellie smiled, her stance and fears softening.

Before long, Mr and Mrs Earlwood approached the two ladies, their presence bringing further comfort to Ellie. She had spent many hours with the Earlwoods since Kitty first introduced them, and Ellie had become fond of their gentle and unassuming nature. Indeed, Mr and Mrs Earlwood, who were both happy and loving parents, had treated Ellie like their own daughter, offering her tender encouragement and practical advice alike. For Ellie, her eldest brother embodied authority, her other brother constancy, and her sister-in-law vitality, but Mr and Mrs Earlwood offered a hitherto novel abundance of unassuming affection that stemmed as much from their wisdom as their disposition.

Ellie smiled and curtsied to the pair. 'Mr and Mrs Earlwood, thank you both for coming this evening, and for being so patient with any disruptions caused by Mary and Harriet's absence.'

'My dear, it is entirely our pleasure,' replied Mrs Earlwood. 'Mr Earlwood and I wished to be the first to congratulate you on your wonderful achievement – you possess a rare and unique talent, and it warms my heart to see its recognition tonight.'

Mr Earlwood added, 'And we are delighted to see some landscapes of our gardens. I thought I recognised that arrangement of tulips and hyacinths!'

Flushing with pride, Ellie could only utter words of thanks.

'But I believe we're keeping you from your other guests,' Mrs Earlwood said. 'Congratulations again, my dear, and we hope you'll enjoy this evening – you certainly deserve it!'

Not long after the Earlwoods started taking another turn about the room, Mr Curtis approached them, imposing as ever in his distinctive green waistcoat. While Ellie initially found the saturnine gentleman intimidating, her opinion was softened by his frequent visits to Thornleigh Abbey and her own brother's high regard of him. She knew much of Darlington had not treated the gentleman kindly, and often wondered how many of them saw the caring heart hidden beneath his constant sarcasm.

'Miss Ashcroft, Miss Harriet,' he said with a perfunctory bow. 'I congratulate you on your accomplishments.'

'Thank you, Mr Curtis. I hope you have enjoyed the paintings.'

'To the best of my abilities.' There was a brief pause before he continued. 'Miss Ashcroft, I will speak plainly: I greatly admire your discipline and persistence, without which you would not have produced such a large quantity of work. I hold no partiality towards any single painting displayed tonight, but I commend you for the quality of your overall collection.'

While this was far from lavish praise – which neither Ellie nor the rest of Darlington would expect from Mr Curtis – the honesty of his words and the essence of his approval were not lost on Ellie, who replied with a genuine smile:

'That is very kind of you, Mr Curtis.'

'Kindness has nothing to do with my appraisal,' he replied, though his usually acerbic tone softened.

Ellie hid a smile. A thought occurred to her, and she gathered her courage. 'Mr Curtis, might I trouble you for a favour?'

'That depends on the favour – though, naturally, I will endeavour to assist if it's within my abilities.'

'My brother Richard had always insisted on naming my paintings, but he never managed to do so himself. Would you perhaps help devise some of those titles? You are such an accomplished wordsmith, sir.'

The gentleman gave a small, rare smile. 'It would be my pleasure, Miss Ashcroft, if you do not mind waiting. I'm returning to Yorkshire next week for two months at least, but I will write to your brother about a convenient time to call, perhaps in November.'

'Of course,' replied Ellie. 'I hope you enjoy your time in Yorkshire.'

'Thank you. One day I shall convince your brother to visit. I may have finally met my match in a gentleman with little interest in travelling.'

After Mr Curtis's departure, Harriet, who had always been a little afraid of the gentleman, turned to Ellie with wonder. 'What a remarkable exchange that was – and with Mr Curtis, of all people!'

Ellie's answering smile widened as she saw Phoebe approach with her fiancée, Mr Winslow. The young man lavished praise on Ellie's achievements, while Phoebe, having shared her enthusiasm when helping organise the exhibition, now remained more reserved with her compliments. One by one, the residents of Darlington stopped by, with Mr and Mrs Worthington, Mr Digby, and Mrs Stevens arriving in quick succession. Shortly after, Mrs Norris approached them, spending most of the time commending both ladies on their choice of attire before launching into a general appraisal of modesty, while the accompanying Miss Woods praised the soft lighting and warm colours of Ellie's garden landscapes.

With each conversation and gesture of goodwill, Ellie eased into a more comfortable state. When Ellie had spoken with most of her guests, Harriet, who wished to examine the paintings again, left to take a turn about the room. Ellie watched her friend join Kitty and Mary, and felt joy and pride swelling in her chest. During all the hours and years she'd spent on her private passion, Ellie had never imagined her creations would be admired by so many. It was emboldening, and a little intoxicating.

Her heart full, Ellie smiled when she saw Mr Earlwood returning, this time with a gentleman beside him. Even without an introduction, Ellie deduced from the man's confidence and attire that this was none other than the viscount.

'My dear Miss Ashcroft,' Mr Earlwood said, 'allow me to introduce the Viscount Sutton, from Cambridgeshire. Lord Sutton, this is Miss Ashcroft, our talented artist of the evening.'

Lord Sutton gave a measured bow, which Ellie returned with a curtsy. 'Miss Ashcroft, it has been a pleasure.'

For the next few minutes, he and Ellie spoke at considerable length about the recent weather, the Hertfordshire countryside, and the architecture of Ely

Cathedral, which was in walking distance from Lord Sutton's estate. Though their conversation remained polite and impersonal, Ellie noticed a sharp intelligence in his dark, steady gaze, and she became more than a little curious about his artistic appraisal.

When they had exhausted their lists of their favoured English cathedrals, Mr Earlwood gave a small chuckle and said: 'I am a creature of habit, and St Albans suits me perfectly fine – and has the advantage of being only eight miles away. But alas, I'm sure you both wish to discuss your craft in depth – please excuse me, Miss Ashcroft, Lord Sutton.'

Mr Earlwood nodded to them both and walked away to join his wife. In his absence, Ellie's proximity to Lord Sutton seemed much more intimate. She became keenly aware of the viscount's striking physique: his defined jaw was softened by a white silk cravat, tied in a stylish knot, and his rich curls, which almost appeared black, framed his intense features.

'You have produced and assembled an admirable collection,' Lord Sutton finally said, his voice measured. 'Congratulations, Miss Ashcroft.'

'Thank you,' replied Ellie. The viscount was very different from what she'd expected, and Ellie felt daunted under his scrutiny. But Ellie straightened herself, drawing strength from the very existence of this exhibition, and of the Artist's Wing. 'Lord Sutton, I do not often have the pleasure of discussing art with those who share my interest. As much as I am heartened by the constant encouragement from my family and friends, I have long yearned for the perspective of another artist, such as yourself. While I understand we are a little more than strangers, I trust and value Mr Earlwood's opinion, and I would value yours – and your honesty – equally well.'

Ellie took a steadying breath and refrained from avoiding Lord Sutton's gaze. He seemed unimpressed when he replied: 'Surely, your art instructor would be qualified to offer an opinion.'

'He was dismissive of me and left over three years ago for a more lucrative position.' Ellie touched the ring on her neck chain, smiling at a memory. 'It was my family who encouraged me to continue my work.'

The viscount was silent for a long moment, his eyes unreadable.

'Very well – I shall be honest with you.' He paused, and the lines around his mouth deepened. 'But I shall only do so if you understand my criticism is well-intended. I have no interest in causing offence tonight.'

She had hitherto never conversed with anyone so direct and self-assured, and Ellie found she admired his tenacity. 'Of course. I had not thought otherwise, Lord Sutton.'

His lips remained tight, his words controlled. 'Then let us begin with your portrait – specifically, the one of Mr and Mrs Ashcroft with their horses.'

Ellie nodded. He was referring to the oil painting wherein Marcus held the reins to his favourite horse while gazing up at Kitty, who was mounted on her own mare. The scene was inspired by a joyous spring afternoon shortly before Richard left for the army, when the family of four picnicked in the nearby Rowan's Edge. She had lain awake that night, trying to savour her memories, before deciding the next morning that neither pencil, charcoal, nor watercolour could capture what she wanted. Presently, she was afraid Lord Sutton would deride her choice of medium and lecture her on oil painting being a solely masculine pursuit.

'I was rather taken with it,' Lord Sutton continued. 'You have produced a great likeness of Mr and Mrs Ashcroft, and captured their high spirits. However, while I enjoyed the sentiments behind the painting, I found its execution sorely lacking. The colours are muddy and mismatched, revealing an inexperience with brush technique, and, indeed, the most basic principles of oil painting. I suspect you've received little or no instruction on how to use the medium.'

Rather than being dismayed by the viscount's astute criticism, Ellie sighed in relief, agreeing wholeheartedly with his observations. He had made no mention of Ellie's impropriety in working with an unladylike substance; even Richard, her staunchest supporter, had hesitated at her idea to try oil paints.

'I admit I have been too ambitious with oils,' Ellie replied. 'It has not been a year since my brother Marcus first allowed me to try them, and I know I have learnt a great deal since then – though I can undoubtedly benefit from further instruction. We have been trying to engage a suitable tutor, but the best ones are not willing to teach me oil painting.'

Lord Sutton scoffed. 'Not willing, or not able? At least your family has no objections to your interests.'

'Do you disapprove?'

'Hardly. Who am I to prevent anyone who wishes to spend hours inhaling noxious fumes and ruining their wardrobe with every accident? I'm certainly not one to speak.'

Ellie could envision Lord Sutton scowling at a stained shirt, and smiled at the image. 'I've taken to borrowing Cook's aprons – she's not yet remarked on their mysterious disappearances.'

'A fine idea,' replied Lord Sutton. His mouth softened slightly.

Feeling more at ease with the viscount, Ellie said, 'Might I ask what you thought of my watercolours?'

She watched, fascinated, as the viscount became serious once more. 'They display a much firmer grasp on technique. Yet you appear to have only painted what's expected of you, not what you truly *want* to capture. Your output is commendable in its quantity, but it nonetheless remains singular in derivative subject matters: the same vases, flowers, landscapes. All too pretty and perfect – not at all to my tastes.'

His final words hung over them. For as long as she could remember, Eleanor Ashcroft had been enveloped and protected by those who loved her, and by a constant stream of encouragement. Presently, even as she felt the heavy hurt in her chest, Ellie nonetheless found his behaviour refreshing, like the cold wind that kisses her cheek when leaving a warm house on a winter's day.

Ellie lifted her head and embraced the criticism with all the gentleness of her nature.

'Thank you, Lord Sutton, for your honesty. I know I have so much to learn about art – indeed, I suspect it will be a lifelong journey – and I would like to think I can only improve hereafter.'

The viscount nodded. 'I hope you are not disheartened by my opinions. There are many who think highly of your work, as evidenced by the wealth of compliments you have received tonight.'

Lord Sutton's attempt to mitigate his criticism made Ellie smile. 'While I am grateful for those compliments, I value your judgements more, as they have given me much to ponder. Might I enquire about your own art?'

'I'm working on several grand pieces – the sublime simply sings to me.' He straightened as he spoke, and the change in light brought Ellie's attention to a small scar above his left eye. 'I look forward to resuming my work next week. When working with oil paints, one must wait long enough between sessions for the canvas to dry completely, and there's no better way to prevent a premature session than a trip to London – or Hertfordshire, if you will.'

Ellie coloured a little. She had known it would take time for the paints to dry, but it had been quite unsettling to discover precisely how long.

'It's a common mistake,' Lord Sutton said, sounding sensible rather than kind. 'Our reliably grim weather does not help our cause.'

'I rather like the rain,' Ellie replied. 'I believe I will be perfectly content to paint fruit bowls and vases in the coming months.'

'Ah, Miss Ashcroft, perhaps you should seek superior subject matters and observe your surroundings with fresh eyes. If you wish to improve in your craft, you must begin to see the world in a unique way. It is possessing that distinct perspective that makes one an artist.'

'I fear I must disagree,' she said softly. Ellie did not wish to contradict the viscount, but she was even more unwilling to remain unheard. 'We all view the world in a slightly different way – and by your definition, every living being is an artist. I think... I believe that, above all else, an artist cannot merely perceive, but must *create*.'

Ellie had stopped taking note of their proximity during their discourse, but now, in the ensuing silence of her defiance, she was once again attentive to Lord Sutton's arresting features: his strong jaw, his striking nose, the scar that bisected his left brow, and his deep, hazel eyes, that seemed to seek her very soul.

'Miss Ashcroft,' he began, his voice rich and soft. 'That is indeed quite an observation.'

Before Ellie could ascertain precisely what he meant, they were interrupted by Kitty.

'Ah, there you are Ellie – and Lord Sutton. Refreshments are being served in the drawing room, if you wish to join us.'

'Thank you, Mrs Ashcroft.' If Ellie had thought the viscount formal and distant earlier, he was now inaccessible. He gave them both a small bow before departing.

When he was out of earshot, Kitty said under her breath: 'Why thank you Lord Sutton, for your exceptionally kind offer to escort us to the drawing room. Your manners are faultless.'

'He isn't so bad,' replied Ellie. 'He's in an unfamiliar environment, and his only acquaintance is Mr Earlwood – and barely so, from what Harriet told me. He had no reason to attend, or to be so honest in his appraisal.'

Kitty was suddenly concerned. 'Was he unkind?'

'Not at all.' Ellie reassured her sister with a smile. 'It was quite lovely speaking with him – I could learn a lot from Lord Sutton.'

'In that case,' Kitty said, linking her arm with Ellie and walking to the drawing room, 'I will endeavour to hold a better opinion of the viscount.'

8

SUTTON'S IMPASSIVE MASK almost slipped when he entered the drawing room, which contained the softest furnishings and most inviting seats he had seen. Too often had he spent evenings in flamboyant aristocratic homes that reflected the vulgar tastes of their owners, and, while Thornleigh Abbey's dining rooms and halls had been pleasant, it was the drawing room that embraced all who entered. He concluded from his brief exchanges with Mrs Ashcroft that the mistress of the house did not possess a keen aesthetic eye, and he suspected it was the young Miss Ashcroft who was responsible for achieving the fine balance of elegance and comfort. A large fire glowed in one end of the room, hearty and welcoming, while the flames dancing above the candelabras and sconces brought out the refined furniture and tasteful wallpaper. There was a modest pianoforte near one corner, and a number of portraits dotted the walls, smaller and more intimate than the stately depictions in the main hallway.

As he sat down on a plush couch, Sutton's attention turned to the central portrait taking the pride of place above the hearth: a young man, no more than a boy, was wearing a soldier's uniform with a certainty and pride that belied his years. In the daylight, the portrait would appear formal yet understated, but the flickering firelight lit the laughter in his eyes, bringing the boy's mirth and affection to life. The painting reminded Sutton of Graham, and, not for the first time, he longed for his friend's presence. With Graham, he could dispense with all the airs and façades expected of him and be perfectly himself.

Sutton was still pensive when Mr Earlwood and Mr Curtis joined him, the older gentleman offering him a glass of port. The viscount accepted it and listened to the men's discussion. He had appreciated Mr Curtis's company and conversation at dinner, and their brief exchange on the topic of education now evolved into an extended discourse centred on the separation of classes and sexes in a learning environment. Mr Earlwood admitted he had no strong opinion, and it was not long until Mr Curtis asked about Sutton's stance on the matter.

'As with most things,' replied Sutton, 'my opinion would depend on the situation. While I have no objections against allowing boys and girls from all walks of life to sit in the same schoolroom, such a notion would be difficult to put into practice.'

'Why is that?' asked Mr Curtis.

'There are simply far too many external factors to consider: the location of these lessons, the responsibilities of the children and their parents alike, the inclinations of individual students – not to mention the instructors, and the very content of the lessons themselves. It is a young gentleman's civic duty to read the radical tracts supporting the American Revolution and the Reign of Terror, but it is another matter entirely for a farmer's son to develop dangerous ideas about his natural rights.'

Mr Curtis spoke with a thin voice. 'Do you believe these natural rights do not exist for a farmer and his son?'

'Not at all – only that the *status quo* has resulted from centuries of steady progress and should not be disassembled overnight. Small steps are far more effective than rash leaps, for citizens of all classes; before sitting their children side by side, the gentleman should learn to plough his fields and the farmer should learn to maintain his accounts.'

Mr Curtis nodded with some reluctance, though the deep frown lines remained etched in his face. Sutton felt a rush of compassion for the older gentleman; Mr Curtis seemed a perceptive and virtuous man, and Sutton suspected his sullen countenance spoke not of any personal shortcomings, but of an unfortunate lack of affection and joy in his life. Sutton wondered if he himself might have sported a similar scowl had Graham not befriended him.

His sympathy aroused, Sutton politely remarked, 'I would very much like to think that, with the aid of many careful and considerate steps, your vision might one day become a reality.'

'Thank you, Lord Sutton.'

As Mr Earlwood enquired after the school of which Mr Curtis was the benefactor, Miss Earlwood, Miss Ingram, and Mr Winslow began a lively discussion about how to make use of the pianoforte, concluding with Miss Earlwood at the keyboard while Miss Ingram and Mr Winslow sang a hearty duet. The rendition was jarring to Sutton, who had a great appreciation for fine music. Among his circles were connoisseurs of Bach, Haydn, and Mozart, men and women who owned several instruments and played them exceedingly well. In *those* circles, one behaved with more dignity, treating music with due reverence and respect – or, at the very least, with more skill. It took the viscount all his control to stay in his seat and *not* make his way to the pianoforte to demonstrate a correct interpretation of the sheets.

Of course, these thoughts were swiftly followed by Sutton's own remonstrations. He had held these beliefs – and often expressed them – for five and twenty years, and they had done him no favours in acquiring friends. When Graham was only a gentleman volunteer in the army, Sutton could count on his stalwart companionship throughout the year, so long as Sutton himself was willing to be displaced, which he often was. Now that Graham was a regular part of his regiment, Sutton could not afford to affront new acquaintances, especially if they had been welcoming and attentive hosts without any discernible ulterior motives.

So, given his station and situation, the viscount chose the only reasonable option: pour himself another glass of port.

When he sat down again, Sutton observed his surroundings, once more appreciating the room's décor. His gaze fell onto Miss Ashcroft. The young lady sat at her brother's side by the fire, holding herself with far more ease than earlier. She smiled at her favourite songs and clapped enthusiastically at the end of every performance. Every now and then, she would reach for her necklace and play with the ring that hung from the chain. Never once did she move towards the pianoforte herself. Indeed, Miss Ashcroft seemed perfectly happy to leave the spotlight she had held all evening, and now gave the impression of not wishing to return. The vitality and intellect he had witnessed earlier during their conversation, the assertions of her mind and spirit, had all but disappeared. Miss Ashcroft was once again another unremarkable lady he would soon forget.

Sutton gave a soft sigh, and waited for the evening to end.

9

WHEN ELLIE ENTERED the morning room well into the next day, the sun was making a rare appearance, sending its rays through the stained windows to create delicate patterns on the floor. A small breakfast was already set out for her, and the lack of the same at Marcus and Kitty's usual seats indicated they would take their meal upstairs. Ellie thanked the footman when he pulled out her chair, again when he poured her tea, and a third time when his services were no longer required. The young man bowed and left Ellie to take her breakfast alone.

The sounds of cutlery and crockery, quiet as they were, echoed in the otherwise empty room. In the aftermath of festivities, Thornleigh Abbey was once again silent, reminiscent of the long days and nights after Richard left for Eton and Cambridge, before Kitty entered their lives. Her sister-in-law had been a blessing in every way, breathing laughter and cheer into the very foundations of Thornleigh itself. One evening, when Marcus was still uncertain about the nature of Kitty's regard, he had indulged in a rare bout of nostalgia, recounting to Ellie the blissful years of his short youth, long before Richard and Ellie's time, when their father doted upon the late Mrs Ashcroft and the young Marcus. Ellie had known from the tone of her brother's voice that he wished to create the same happiness with Kitty – and in that moment, when Marcus admitted the strength of his own affection, Ellie had felt, for the first time in her fifteen years, the pangs of loneliness.

Happy as she was that her dear brother had found a companion – and happier still when Kitty became a permanent addition to their lives – Ellie discovered, slowly but surely, the difference between solitude and loneliness. Solitude was the misted meadows of autumn, the turning of pages before a crackling fire, the heady scent of fresh paint threading through the handkerchief tied around her nose; loneliness, its lesser and greater sibling, was the unspoken and unspeakable universe between Mr and Mrs Ashcroft that precluded her, the quiet sadness of husband or wife when the other was away, the unrelenting ticking of a clock in a sunny room.

For most of her life, Ellie had befriended and embraced solitude; now, she must learn to be called on and embraced by loneliness.

The memory of Lord Sutton's forlorn, retreating figure returned to her, and a curious sensation swelled within Ellie's bosom. Despite his eloquence and poise during their conversation, it was this final image of the viscount, silent and uncertain, that lingered. He had arrived with the Earlwoods and was a stranger in Hertfordshire – Ellie had been so wrought with nerves the previous evening, she had not questioned the viscount's presence any further. Now, after the nourishments of sleep and breakfast, Ellie wondered whether Lord Sutton had indeed felt welcome amongst an intimate company of strangers. Above all, she reproached herself for seeking the comfort of her own family upon entering the drawing room, instead of ensuring Lord Sutton was pleasantly engaged. He had bestowed on her the thoughtful and critical evaluation she had always longed for, but Ellie had offered nothing in return.

Although Ellie had not spent much time in society, she knew the boundaries of acceptable behaviour for ladies like herself, and, more importantly, understood the finer points of etiquette that challenged the lines without crossing them. It would be scandalous to write to Lord Sutton directly, but penning a letter for her brother to include in his own missive to the viscount would be perfectly tolerable. She would have to explain her reasoning to Marcus, but, given how delicately and fastidiously she would phrase the contents, Ellie doubted her brother would refuse her request.

Her heart set, Ellie rang for the supplies to be prepared, and left the breakfast table for her writing desk.

That afternoon, Ellie found herself under her favourite oak tree in Rowan's Edge, sketching Kitty and Marcus with their horses. Kitty, who always relished a ride, had suggested the impromptu excursion on account of the sun's presence; the days were growing shorter, and soon, it would be uncomfortable to stay outdoors for extended drawing sessions.

Presently, Kitty and Marcus were astride their horses and gazing out at the scene before them. Although their backs were turned to Ellie and they were some distance away, Ellie could still hear snatches of their conversation, frequently punctuated by Kitty's laughter. Ellie's own lips were curled into a smile as she sketched, knowing she could work at her leisure and not be concerned about her subjects becoming skittish.

Immersed in her drawing, Ellie did not notice anyone approaching until Marcus turned around his horse and broke Ellie's concentration. As her brother made a comment to Kitty, Ellie became aware of the newcomers' voices.

They belonged to Mr Earlwood, as pleasant as ever on his chestnut gelding, and, to Ellie's surprise, Lord Sutton, dark and imposing on a grey horse.

She thought of the letter she had written that morning and the request she had yet to make to Marcus, and felt the beginning of a blush. Ellie smoothed out her dress and gathered her thoughts while the men dismounted and made their way towards her.

Mr Earlwood and Lord Sutton reached her first. 'Miss Ashcroft,' the older gentleman said, 'how delightful to see you today! And my, what a drawing – it is coming along quite nicely!'

Ellie curtsied and waited for Marcus to join them before replying: 'You are too kind, Mr Earlwood – these are just some early sketches. We wished to take advantage of the fair weather while it held.'

'A sensible plan.' Mr Earlwood bowed to Marcus, then raised his voice to address Kitty, still seated on her mare some thirty feet away. 'Mrs Ashcroft, would you care to join us?'

'Thank you, but no,' she shouted back. 'If I lose my pose before Ellie is done, I'll never hear the end of it!'

Ellie ducked her head, mortified by her sister-in-law's candour. When she thought she'd reached the heights of her embarrassment, Kitty spoke again, just as loudly:

'Lord Sutton, you are reputed to have an eye for such things – how are Ellie's sketches coming along?'

If the viscount was disconcerted by Kitty's behaviour, he did not show it; on the contrary, Lord Sutton seemed calm, almost bored, as he offered Ellie a bow.

'May I, Miss Ashcroft?'

Ellie nodded, her heart beating erratically at what the viscount might say. Marcus, having sensed her discomfort at garnering unwanted attention, started enquiring after the Earlwoods.

She could not discern the precise quality of Lord Sutton's voice when he asked, after a long pause: 'Miss Ashcroft, is this the result of a day's work?'

'Half an hour at most,' replied Ellie uncertainly. 'We only set out at two o'clock, and Kitty insisted on some other positions before this one.'

This time, Ellie heard the curiosity as the viscount gestured to her sketchbook and repeated: 'May I?'

She nodded again, and watched as Lord Sutton picked up the book from her easel and turned back the pages. Something flashed in his expression – if Ellie were better acquainted with the viscount, or with the world at large, she might have thought it was longing.

'These are good,' he finally said. 'Your studies of the figure on horseback and your framing of the landscapes are all quite sound.'

'Thank you, Lord Sutton. I am…fond of Rowan's Edge, and have used it as a backdrop as often as I can.'

'Even the day after your grand exhibition opening?'

There was a hint of derision in the question, but Ellie was not quick to take offence. She found the viscount's behaviour peculiar and wondered what might have caused such a response.

Gathering her courage, Ellie said: 'It was Kitty's idea. It's impossible to keep her indoors on a fine day, and she's very fond of Rowan's Edge, too. I had thought to try working with oils again, after your advice yesterday, but Kitty offered a better alternative. I have the rest of the colder season to stay inside and paint.'

'Do you draw every day?'

Ellie nodded a third time. Her art was not often met with such intense interest, and the viscount's manner was a little intimidating. Yet, Lord Sutton was standing close enough for Ellie to hear the genuine curiosity in his question. When she looked up to respond, the air shifted between them and Ellie caught a trace of his scent, woody and warm.

'For the past five or six years,' she said, her own voice softer than usual. 'I enjoy it immensely.'

Lord Sutton considered this. In the afternoon light, Ellie thought she saw his eyes soften.

'Your dedication is admirable,' he said, returning the sketchpad to the easel. Then, in a low voice: 'Last night only exhibited a small portion of your talent, Miss Ashcroft.'

Having only caught the first remark, Mr Earlwood said: 'Indeed, Miss Ashcroft is an admirable young lady! Ah, what a drawing – and it's practically finished. Miss Ashcroft, do you still need the poses?' Ellie shook her head, and Mr Earlwood yelled once more: 'Mrs Ashcroft, you may return to us now! Miss Ashcroft is done with her sketch!'

A sound of relief came from Kitty's direction before she brought her mare around and dismounted. As Kitty exchanged proper greetings with the gentlemen, Ellie glanced at the viscount. All evidence of his previous sentiments was erased, his expression impassive once more. His conversation became cool and stilted, and when they parted ways twenty minutes later, Ellie knew only she had seen past Lord Sutton's composed demeanour.

10

SOON AFTER HIS sixth birthday, Sutton's father had impressed on him the importance of spring and autumn. Winter and summer, with their extreme conditions, were ill-suited to any contribution on a landowner's part, but the two transient seasons of planting and harvesting were vital to the continuing prosperity of Bellevue Park and its 8,000 acres. As a little boy, Sutton had cared little for these sombre lectures in his father's study, longing instead to play outside like other children; as a youth of thirteen, having just inherited the Sutton viscountcy, he wished for nothing more than to indulge in his new position without bearing any of the responsibilities. It was his mother's death three years later, during his last term at Cambridge, that cemented the reality of his situation. Without the late Dowager Countess to oversee the estate on his behalf, the task fell solely to Sutton. He had never received any affection from either parent, but they had left him a centuries-old legacy, along with hundreds of mouths to feed. His own singular aspirations were of little consequence in light of these obligations, and, as the seasons changed year after year, Sutton continued to take on his rightful role.

This autumn, upon his return from Darlington, Sutton embraced his duties with much fervour, throwing himself into the proper management of his lands and estates. His undivided attention to such matters and the long hours spent outside, rain or shine, alleviated some of the listlessness – and, dare he admit, the *ennui* – that had plagued him after Graham's departure, and, more recently, after the unexpected exhibition in Darlington. Indeed, Sutton was so intent on exhausting his mind and body that, on one occasion, he physically assisted with the harvest, earning a few scratches across his hands and along his arms. The pink marks evoked fond memories of Sutton's childhood games, and while Sutton was not so uncouth as to make a habit of these coarse contributions, he certainly accepted the merits of occasionally rolling up one's shirtsleeves for fear of dirtying them in the fields.

And so, it wasn't until Sunday – his fifth day back in Cambridgeshire – that Sutton had fulfilled his biannual duties. He spent an hour at the pianoforte with a new Beethoven sonata, another in the chapel, and several more in his art studio, the last of which only served to aggravate his mood. It was thus with a short temper that, soon after dinner, Sutton entered his study to contend with the small pile of personal correspondence that still required his attention. He and his steward had devised a system for sorting his mail, and while Sutton remained prompt with the essentials, he was sometimes guilty of neglecting less important matters.

As predicted, most of the letters in this final pile were from those he had met only once or twice before. One missive, however, caught his attention – from Mr Marcus Ashcroft of Thornleigh Abbey.

He opened the envelope and found a small note.

Dear Lord Sutton:

I hope you will not find me presumptuous in writing to you thus. My sister has penned some thoughts regarding your attendance at her exhibition, and, given she writes of matters beyond my expertise, I hope you will not find me imprudent in sending you her words directly.

On my part, I wish to thank you once more for your gracious company. I hope your journey home was suitably pleasant and uneventful.

Yours, &c,

M Ashcroft

The main letter, penned by none other than Miss Ashcroft herself, was presented in such a delicate script that Sutton had no trouble imagining the writer's dainty hands as she held her pen.

Dear Lord Sutton:

I wish to thank you once again for your time, company, and conversation at the exhibition yesterday evening. Your words have given me much to consider; you have introduced me to a range of possibilities concerning art and aesthetics. I must, however, confess I am still a little uncertain about what constitutes supreme art, both in your view and – if I have understood correctly – in a wider, universal perspective. I would be much obliged if you might kindly share your position, or, as I do not wish to take up any more of your time, direct me to another source. My brother is always amenable to expanding Thornleigh Abbey's library, and any recommended titles would be most appreciated.

Wishing you the very best for your current and future endeavours, I remain your humble servant, etc, etc,

Eleanor Ashcroft

P. S. I had not anticipated meeting you again in Rowan's Edge. I would be very much obliged if you have any suggestions on how I might improve my figure or landscape studies.

He read the letter again, trying to make up his mind about its contents. He had not expected such a heartfelt and insightful letter from Miss Ashcroft, nor her brother's permission to send her words to him directly. Sutton had been confronted with his own artistic shortcomings when he attended the young lady's exhibition, but he had hidden them well. Now, after receiving Miss Ashcroft's bold and sincere letter, Sutton was reminded once more of how his art was *contrived* and *mediocre*.

Yet, even as those unbearable words echoed in his mind, Sutton remembered their encounter in Rowan's Edge. He had studied Miss Ashcroft long before she was aware of his approach: the young lady had been relaxed, content, and utterly in control of her craft. Sutton had never seen a woman

52

sitting so comfortably in front of an easel, her day dress simple and tasteful, her hair a little tousled. Even her timidity, which returned during their conversation, had only sparked his curiosity – and now, with the arrival of her letter, Sutton could only concede he was intrigued by Miss Ashcroft.

Putting down the missive, Sutton rang for his steward.

'Allen, the Ashcrofts from Thornleigh Abbey, Hertfordshire, are henceforth correspondents of the highest priority.'

'The highest, sir?'

Allen's tone carried a hint of surprise, though the clarifying question was well-founded: only a few, close companions belonged to the category.

'Yes, Allen.'

The steward nodded, but before Sutton could dismiss him, a footman entered, this time carrying a tray.

'Sir, a letter from Lieutenant Graham has just arrived.'

Sutton hid his excitement behind an approving nod. 'Very good.'

The viscount did not wait for the men to leave before opening the letter.

My dearest Aubrey:

Mr Earlwood wrote last week that you had accepted his invitation to Darlington, but I've not had word from him since. How was your trip? Was the weather favourable for a hunt or two? I find the grounds some of the most pleasant in the country. Were you introduced to some of Darlington's other residents? How are the Earlwood sisters? I await news of your adventures!

Now, I expect you've returned to Bellevue and are busy with the harvest, but when you're ready for another journey, perhaps you'll consider crossing over to Essex. I'm pleased to announce we've now found a permanent station in the Colchester Garrison. Huzzah! Our daily drills, training, and other duties have increased substantially since moving into the barracks, but you are always more than welcome to visit.

Your dashing redcoat friend,

JG

P. S. Any sightings of Lady Lavender?

Sutton had started calculating his departure upon seeing 'Colchester'. With as much dignity as he could muster, Sutton strode through the hallways, searching for his staff rather than summoning them, issuing rapid instructions to all he crossed. Within mere minutes, word had travelled that Lieutenant Graham had been permanently relocated to Colchester, and the viscount would be visiting him post-haste. The required arrangements were carried out efficiently, with the portmanteaux packed, horses harnessed, and a skeleton staff selected.

Before the sun had set, Sutton was on his merry way to Colchester and Graham.

'Aubrey, you look like a dirty, wet dog!'

Having just swung off his horse, Sutton grinned at this greeting, removed a soaked glove, and shook hands with his oldest and dearest friend.

'And so we finally resemble each other once more,' he retorted brightly. The rain had ceased earlier, but Sutton nonetheless grasped this opportunity to bemoan his ill fortune. 'It only took riding through the night in this ghastly weather to do the trick – I don't imagine I would've paid you a visit if you'd been stationed further afield.'

Graham gave Sutton's horse an affectionate pat before it was led away. 'A night of riding, or of being carted about in your carriage? There is a distinct difference, my friend.'

'Neither is as comfortable as remaining put in Bellevue. In any case, I don't know how you manage to complete even a quarter of your exercises under such conditions – I hereby opine that one should only be required to dirty one's hands when the climes have struck the perfect balance between rotten and radiant.'

Graham laughed. 'We'll make a soldier of you yet. I take it you've settled in suitable lodgings?'

'Suitability is a subjective notion, but I daresay Allen has outdone himself in finding a quaint house on Priory Street to rent for the year.'

'A year?' Graham's initial surprise quickly turned into mischief. 'Heavens, are you reconsidering joining us after all?'

Sutton glared at his friend, earning himself a slap on the back. They started walking towards the garrison, passing a number of soldiers on the way. Some of the men had been acquainted with Sutton during previous visits to Graham's postings, and they nodded at Sutton in greeting.

'How are you finding Colchester so far? Regretting your decision to relinquish your inheritance? Ely is marginally less awful this time of the year.'

Graham's smile only widened. 'Why, yes, I have also missed you – I am very pleased you are here now.'

'We can't have Lieutenant Graham grumpy and broody,' replied Sutton with a shrug. 'Especially now he has a platoon to lead.'

'Do mind your manners, Lord Sutton; it isn't polite to accuse your innocent, inferior friend of your own shortcomings, few as they are.'

The statement was made with mock sternness, but held enough truth for Sutton to pause ever so slightly, his affection for Graham suddenly swelling in his chest. This was precisely why Sutton held his friend in such high regard: Graham possessed unmatched insights into Sutton's character and was forthright in expressing them, but he was also unduly compassionate, embracing Sutton's foibles as much as he admired Sutton's strengths.

Knowing this, Sutton relaxed completely in a way he could only do with Graham. 'I have more than a few shortcomings,' he said sincerely. '*You* are the superior in all areas that truly matter.'

They had reached the main compound, which looked every bit as severe as Sutton imagined.

'This is rather bleak compared to your billet in Darlington,' said the viscount.

'Indeed – Darlington now feels like a distant dream. But there is much to do here, not least in regards to training and discipline. I've not been here a week, and I feel I've been pushed beyond my limits several times over.'

As they sat on a bench just outside the building, Sutton studied his friend more carefully, seeing the slight changes that initially escaped his notice. Graham's posture was more rigid than before, and he seemed to be favouring his left side. The ribbon that tied back his dark blonde hair had seen better days, and there were shadows under his eyes that spoke of early mornings and late nights. Yet Graham's eyes were as playful as ever, his smile as bright.

'Perhaps Colonel Watson should be working you harder, since you're still very much upright, wearing that perpetual grin.'

The said grin widened again. 'I'd welcome the challenge! I've never felt so alive, so full of energy!'

While Sutton admired his friend's enthusiasm, he could not comprehend it fully. The viscount enjoyed an extended hunt and a difficult bout of fencing just as much as the next self-respecting gentleman, but he preferred spending the rest of his time on other, more refined pursuits.

'I've been training several new recruits,' continued Graham. 'It's been quite an education for all involved. The army's extensive rigour and discipline are new to most recruits, and being on this side of the fence gives me a new appreciation for my superiors. How I would love to lecture my younger self!'

While Graham spoke, Sutton studied his friend's movements, focusing on his uneven posture. He gestured to it now. 'Are you being treated for that?'

'Oh yes, I'm fine, thank you. I was careless and bested during drills yesterday – a new recruit delivered an impressive strike, and now I'm sporting an even more impressive bruise.'

'And so the student becomes the master,' said Sutton, a little quietly.

Graham studied his friend for a long moment, causing Sutton to look away. In a gentle voice, the lieutenant asked, 'What's on your mind, Aubrey?'

'Is my art any good?' He hadn't intended to be so blunt, but now the topic was broached, the viscount couldn't help continuing. 'Is it really "contrived at worst, mediocre at best"?'

'You know I am exceedingly unqualified to comment on the subject,' his friend replied softly. '*You* are the one with an unrivalled passion for art.'

'But not the talent.' Sutton sighed, feeling quite sorry for himself. 'And would you agree with Livingston? Is my art nothing but *contrived* and *mediocre?*'

Graham placed a hand on Sutton's shoulder. 'My friend, I refuse to indulge your self-pity and misery. Neither am I willing to become yet another of your obsequious acquaintances. We both know you've always loved art but were never serious enough for a lifelong devotion – so what *I* want to know is what on earth has sparked these glum musings.'

Sutton sighed again. 'While I was in Darlington, I was introduced to a young artist who hosted her own exhibition – has Mr Earlwood written to you?'

'Not yet, but I expect he will include it in his next letter. Go on.'

'She is very young – no more than sixteen or seventeen – but she is...' Sutton faltered, caught between his honesty and pride. Another sigh, and he succumbed to the former. 'I suspect she is much better an artist than *I* ever was at her age.'

Graham nodded thoughtfully. 'Do you think she would be benefit from some instruction?'

'Undoubtedly,' replied Sutton. 'Alas, given her sex and background, the very idea of achieving any artistry – or any pursuit beyond the accepted accomplishments of a gentlewoman – is an exceptionally delicate matter. Her family was uncommonly supportive at the exhibition, but with the exception of myself, all the other guests were close friends and acquaintances. I suspect her guardians would not be so welcoming to excessive visitors outside their immediate circles.'

'Indeed. But your understanding of this young lady's position and of art itself – not to mention your own position – makes you uniquely equipped to broach the subject with her family. I'm certain you will be able to offer advice without overstepping.'

Sutton silently agreed, while several possibilities started forming in his mind. He acknowledged and respected the paramount importance of a young woman's reputation, and he was confident any suggestions or introductions he might make would be acceptable to Mr Ashcroft. Yet his pride held him back. How long would it take for Miss Ashcroft's output to surpass his? How long, for her to realise the *contrivance* and *mediocrity* of his own works?

'Aubrey, don't get too caught up in your thoughts. Trust your instincts – they've served you well these twenty odd years.'

Sutton looked up at the lieutenant, whose good nature was infectious. 'James, you are much kinder and wiser than you let on.'

Graham smiled. 'Perhaps – but you are the much better dressed. Come, let's go inside – there are several portraits you might enjoy, including one of the Marquess of Wellington himself.'

Sutton nodded, his heart swelling with gratitude. 'Lead the way, my friend.'

11

ELLIE MADE NO attempt to conceal her delight when, after a fortnight's absence, Harriet arrived at Thornleigh Abbey for an afternoon of tea, cakes, and conversation. In anticipation of Harriet's arrival, Ellie had discussed the menu at length with Mrs Nancy, the family's cook who had fed three generations of Ashcrofts. Ellie's own appetite had been unpredictable during her childhood, exacerbated by a series of continual illnesses, and Ellie knew better than most never to take these simple pleasures for granted. Together, they planned and created enough delicacies for a large group.

When Harriet entered Ellie's new drawing room where the dishes were charmingly laid out, she all but gasped at the sight.

Ellie smiled as they both took their seats around the laden table. 'I wanted to have something lovely prepared for your visit, as it's been so long since we've had the afternoon to ourselves. There's plenty more in the kitchen, so I thought we could take some baskets around the village tomorrow.'

'Yes, let's do – that is wonderfully kind of you.'

After they made their selections, Harriet brought up the foremost topic on their minds.

'I'm sure you've heard this countless times by now, but I thought your exhibition was marvellous. Even though I'd seen most of your work, displaying them together as you did was just splendid.'

Recalling how Harriet's presence had alleviated her distress throughout the night, Ellie said: 'I couldn't have done it without you, dear Harriet. I was so nervous throughout dinner – I can hardly remember any of the ordeal. It only seemed to get worse from there on, and I was afraid I would cause a scene!'

'Perhaps we remember the evening differently. *I* was terrified when Mr Curtis approached us in the exhibition room, but you were so confident and collected!'

'Mr Curtis has become a familiar face here, and he's always treated me as an equal.'

'Does he really dine here often?' Harriet grew thoughtful at Ellie's nod. 'When Mr Curtis first took up residence in Bradley House, so many people said unkind things about him. Mary was particularly horrible – she still makes the occasional quip.'

'I know he doesn't have many friends,' Ellie said softly, 'but I had not known the general opinion was so much against him.'

'Your brother was acquainted with him well after Mr Curtis had made his patronage of Lampton School known. When he first moved to Bradley House, Mr Curtis appeared so dour and spoke so harshly that the townspeople kept their distance. I don't doubt the reputation of his sharp tongue, but...'

Harriet took a deep breath before continuing.

'It saddens me to see him so alone. He reminds me of myself before I met you – everyone knew me, but no one made an effort to understand me. Even though no one avoided me, few actively approached me. So I suppose I can understand how unhappy Mr Curtis might be, and the thought saddens me greatly.'

'Dear Harriet, you are good and kind.'

The other girl looked down. 'And rather silly, too.'

'Kindness is never silly,' Ellie replied. 'If the world were half as kind as you, dear Harriet, then there would be much less unhappiness.'

'Thank you,' Harriet said softly.

They both helped themselves to some more delicacies.

'How are your sisters?' Ellie asked after they'd shared their appreciation for Mrs Nancy's chocolate cake. 'It's been some time since I've properly spoken with Mary, and longer still since I've spent time with Lettice.'

'Truthfully, I don't know what to make of Lettice lately – she's been very temperamental and difficult to appease, despite our best efforts. Mama and Papa are concerned, but Anna assures us Lettice is just going through "the passing phase for every strong-willed young lady". I honestly don't know what we'd do without Anna, bless her.'

'It mustn't be easy for you,' Ellie said, sympathetic.

'Some days are better than others, but no one knows when Lettice might decide to throw a tantrum. One evening, Papa admitted to me – rather quietly, mind you – that he's grateful at least *one* of his daughters has never been a handful.'

A small smile tugged at Ellie's lips. 'I can't picture a nine-year-old Miss Harriet Earlwood running amok and dirtying her petticoats at every turn.'

'Nor I, of a younger Miss Eleanor Ashcroft.' Harriet lifted her teacup in a toast. 'To not being a handful.'

Ellie echoed the words, and they sipped their tea together. She was warm and content, luxuriating in this quiet, uninterrupted afternoon with her closest companion and confidante.

Harriet peered into her teacup before continuing. 'Mary has also been acting strange – lost in her own world, smiling to herself and gazing into the distance. When Kitty visits, they excuse themselves or talk in hushed whispers – I think Mary has found…an admirer, I suppose. It's even more suspicious when Mary and Kitty start talking loudly about Phoebe's upcoming wedding every now and then, as if to distract me from their real purpose. Mary never shares her innermost thoughts with me, but it mustn't be easy for her – she has more than her own reputation and happiness to consider.'

Ellie heard what her friend had left unsaid. Entering into matrimony was essential for the three Earlwood girls, but it was not a burden Ellie had to bear. A few years ago, before Ellie could fully comprehend its implications, Marcus had informed her of the small but comfortable fund Ellie would inherit should any ill befall her brothers. She was also fortunate in having developed an intimate friendship with Kitty, who would never send her away from Thornleigh Abbey.

When Ellie spoke again, she did so very carefully. 'Whatever the outcome, I wish Mary every happiness, just as I wish the same for you, and for Lettice.'

'Thank you, Ellie. Sometimes, I know not the shape of my own happiness, nor how to attain it.'

Ellie took Harriet's hand. 'You are not alone in this, dear Harriet.'

She was about to ring for another pot of tea when the butler entered with a bow.

'Excuse me, Miss Ashcroft, Miss Earlwood – Mr Ashcroft has asked me to bring this letter to you. He also wishes to inform you he and Mrs Ashcroft have gone riding, and will be back for supper.'

'Thank you, Mr Wilson,' said Ellie. She waited for him to leave before studying the elegant script. 'I don't recognise the hand.'

'Oh?' Harriet peered at the offered envelope. 'It bears your full initials and all the particulars of your address, which is mighty formal – perhaps it's in relation to your artwork?'

Ellie turned over the letter, where the wax insignia, curiously positioned not to seal the letter, was also unfamiliar.

'It's from Lord Sutton!' said Harriet. 'Lettice asked about his signet ring when he stayed at Dunnistone, and he was kind enough to explain. It's rather curious he would write to you directly.'

Ellie blushed at the insinuation.

'But I'm sure Lord Sutton is nothing short of proper,' Harriet added hastily. 'Besides, the letter has not been sealed – an invitation for your brother to peruse and approve its contents, one would assume.'

Taking in Harriet's assurances, Ellie unfolded the page and read aloud the words within.

Dear Miss Ashcroft:

I hope this note finds you and your family well. Thank you for your own kind sentiments, which your brother included in his last letter – I do hope I am not being imprudent in replying to your letter in the same manner. The question you asked has no simple answer, or, indeed, a singular answer – I doubt your very statement of "supreme art" would go uncontested, much less any speculations about a universal perspective. I regret that I, a mere man, am unqualified to satisfy your query.

However, my own interests in art has led me to collect a number of volumes on the matter, and, if you are so inclined, it would be my pleasure to invite you and your family to peruse my library in Bellevue Park. If you do not wish to travel sixty miles to leaf through pages, perhaps you might like to see the artworks in my personal collection. I also recall your partiality to Ely Cathedral, which is but five miles away, should you wish to visit. I have written to your brother about the invitation – wherein I will enclose this note – so I hope you will not consider this indecorous, but rather, my goodwill towards a fellow artist. I wish you the very best for your current projects, and I remain faithfully yours,

Aubrey Charles Beaumont, 7th Viscount Sutton

'What a generous invitation,' Harriet said after Ellie had finished reading the letter. 'How will you reply?'

'I'll have to speak with my brother at supper,' replied Ellie. The hours until then seemed a little long, but she brushed away the uncharacteristic thought. 'If he consents, I would very much like to go. We could see the Cathedral and stop by Cambridge and the colleges. I think Kitty might like to visit, too – she was quite curious about St. John's after Marcus and Richard spoke about their time there. All I have are Richard's sketches of Cambridge – I would very much like to make some of my own.'

'And it would be lovely to make the journey before winter sets in.' A note of excitement entered Harriet's speech. 'Oh, Ellie, Lord Sutton speaks of his collection – I wouldn't be surprised if it includes some works by the Masters you so admire!'

Ellie's heart quickened at the prospect. 'Do you think it might? Did Lord Sutton mention anything while at Dunnistone?'

'He wasn't very talkative, but I do remember him speaking of his collection when Papa enquired – and now you shall see it for yourself!'

'I can only imagine what wondrous works he'll have – oh, I must tell Richard!'

Harriet smiled and helped herself to another slice of cake. 'How is Richard? Has he settled into Colchester?'

'He has – he's sent some sketches with his last letter. They're mostly of regimental livery – he knows how much I love those details.'

Ellie rose to fetch the sketches, and the two friends admired them at length.

After returning from their long ride, both Kitty and Marcus were in high spirits at supper. 'We found some mushrooms at Rowan's Edge,' Kitty said as soon as they were seated, 'but Marcus was adamant about leaving them be. Quite a shame, really.'

'It would be most unfortunate to fall ill from one of the poisonous varieties,' her husband replied. 'Perhaps Mrs Nancy could accompany you next time you decide to forage – she possesses an admirable amount of experience in that regard.'

Kitty gave a playful pout. 'Are you suggesting I'm neither admirable nor experienced?'

'Far from it, ma'am. However, since Mrs Nancy would be working with any procured mushrooms, she might have specific requirements in mind.'

'Touché, sir,' replied Kitty with a smile. 'How was Harriet's visit?'

They spoke about Harriet and the Earlwoods during the first course, and it was only after the second course was served that Marcus asked Ellie:

'Have you read Lord Sutton's note? His letter came with the morning post, but I only saw it shortly before we went riding.'

'I have,' replied Ellie softly. 'His invitation is most generous.'

'Indeed.'

Ellie nodded, a little flushed. Even with Marcus's knowledge and consent, it felt improper to correspond so intimately with a man who was not one of her brothers. Now, she did not know how to express her desire for Marcus to accept the invitation. After what seemed like a prolonged moment, Ellie managed: 'His collection must be quite remarkable.'

This was indication enough for Kitty. 'Then we must see it,' she said. 'We don't have any engagements until Tom and Phoebe's wedding in late October – do we, Marcus?'

'I believe not. Shall we stop by Cambridge on the way?'

Both ladies answered in the affirmative, which settled the matter for Marcus, who promised to write to Lord Sutton on the morrow. Their conversation turned to the familiar topic of Richard's most recent letters about his new station and regimental life, but it was not until they sat for coffee in the drawing room that Ellie's quickened pulse began to settle.

12

His housekeeper was too professional to voice her displeasure at her master's unnecessary involvement, but Mrs Jennings still regarded Lord Sutton with the same thin lips and furrowed brows as when he, at the age of seven, had brought home a stray dog. Resisting the urge to duck his head in remorse, Lord Sutton said, 'A little more to the left.'

The footman complied and looked to their master for his appraisal. Sutton scrutinised the depiction of horses he'd moved into the rooms intended for Miss Ashcroft, and studied the space between the painting and the cream curtains.

'A bit more to the right,' he said. 'The balance must be perfect.'

As the footman adjusted the frame, Sutton avoided Mrs Jennings' gaze, which had grown steadily more impassive over the last few days. As the housekeeper of the Bellevue House, Mrs Jennings possessed both an intricate knowledge of its daily management and a refined taste for its furnishings and décor – a combination of talents Sutton had called on since receiving Mr Ashcroft's letter. However, while the viscount's keen eye had served him well during periods of refurbishments, his immaculate attention to detail and commanding presence now proved difficult. Few other guests had managed to disturb Bellevue Park before their arrival, and in all the years since Sutton became lord of the manor, Mrs Jennings had never seen him focus so much attention on a singular apartment.

'Now, my lord?' asked the footman.

Sutton frowned. 'No, that won't do. Try the other one.'

Mrs Jennings issued the instructions while Sutton paced into the adjoining dressing room and bedroom. The apartment, known as the Calliope Rooms, had been decorated in soft tones that reminded Sutton of Miss Ashcroft's gentle nature. Meanwhile, the rooms contained some of the largest fireplaces in the house, a detail he thought the young lady might appreciate. The only item missing was the perfect painting to replace the garden watercolour he had removed yesterday, which he felt was too tame and uninspired. Sutton would never admit it to anyone – and only a few would be aware of it, given his careful nonchalance and practised indifference – but he simply thrived on praise. He knew Miss Ashcroft would make the usual compliments, but this time, Sutton wanted more than polite commendations; this time, he longed for the sincere approval of one who appreciated aesthetics as much as he.

When he returned to the sitting room, Sutton smiled at the large oil painting of the sea, its waves a bold and vibrant statement. He had picked out the piece from his personal gallery this morning and was afraid it would be too gloomy for the Calliope. He looked at Mrs Jennings for her opinion.

'The painting has a certain weight to it,' she said. 'I wouldn't like to see it in the Prospero or the Highlands, but it serves well here, sir.'

'Very good,' Sutton replied. 'Thank you, Mrs Jennings.'

The Ashcrofts arrived a little before midday in a chaise and four, and Sutton went out to greet them at the carriage ring. He noted with great satisfaction that Grove, his faithful butler, had held the footmen to impeccable standards, the Sutton family crest crisp and distinct on their spotless livery. Sutton had often stood here to welcome new guests to Bellevue Park, and he almost managed to convince himself there was nothing different about receiving the Ashcrofts today.

When their carriage came to a stop, Mr Ashcroft disembarked, helping his wife and his sister before bowing to Sutton. 'You have a beautiful home, Lord Sutton, and your grounds are very fine indeed. We very much enjoyed the ride in.'

'I am pleased to hear it,' replied Sutton. He addressed and bowed to each guest in turn. 'Welcome to Bellevue Park, Mr Ashcroft, Mrs Ashcroft, Miss Ashcroft. Please do make yourselves at home.'

The ladies curtsied, and the Ashcroft patriarch spoke for them all. 'Thank you, Lord Sutton. We are very much obliged.'

While the staff tended to the horses and portmanteaux, Sutton led his guests inside the house. Mr and Mrs Ashcroft paid their compliments, but Miss Ashcroft remained silent, her eyes wide and bright.

'Your home is simply magnificent,' Mrs Ashcroft said when they walked through the great hall, lined with Grecian and Roman busts and sculptures. 'Bellevue Park is quite possibly the most spectacular residence I've had the honour of visiting.'

Sutton struggled to keep his smile from showing – it certainly would not do for his new acquaintances to mistake pride for vanity. 'You are very kind, Mrs Ashcroft. Bellevue's lands date back to 1689, when His Majesty King William the Third created the first Viscount Sutton for Charles Beaumont, the 5th Earl of Beaumont, in recognition of my ancestor's services during the Glorious Revolution. The house was constructed in 1701, but the staircase and the upper floors weren't completed until the mid eighteenth century.'

They reached the end of the great hall, which intersected with the three others. These four hallways formed a cross, and held at their heart a double spiral staircase, its white stones radiant in the sunlight.

'Truly beautiful,' Mrs Ashcroft murmured. 'I was impressed by Thornleigh Abbey when I first beheld it, but I daresay Bellevue Park is altogether incomparable.'

'Thornleigh Abbey boasts the familial warmth made possible only by its residents,' Sutton said graciously.

'And Bellevue Park the dignified grandeur made possible only by the test of time.'

It was Miss Ashcroft who spoke, her voice soft yet determined – the first words she'd uttered since her arrival.

'I am humbled, Miss Ashcroft,' Sutton said, bowing once more. When he straightened and studied the young lady more carefully, Sutton saw hints of weariness.

'Forgive me – I am keeping you from your rest and refreshments.' A silent look was all it took for the footmen and housemaids to approach. 'I hope you will find your rooms satisfactory. There is tea in the salon when you are ready.'

While the ladies opted to follow the two housemaids to their rooms, Mr Ashcroft chose to remain with Sutton. The two men proceeded to the salon and sat by the large windows with their tea. Mr Ashcroft was polite, reserved, and appreciative of Bellevue Park at just the right amount. He was a few years older than Sutton and held himself with the quiet assurance of a gentleman who knew himself and his place in society. His blue eyes were calm and perceptive, but they had lit up in his wife and sister's presence. This was a man who was happy in his situation and wanted for nothing – and Sutton envied him a little for it.

Feeling a need to know the family better, Sutton enquired about the Ashcrofts' journey from Darlington. He wasn't surprised to hear they had stopped at Cambridge.

'My sister has heard many tales of St John's College,' explained Mr Ashcroft, 'and she was delighted to see the buildings for herself.'

'Cambridge is a lovely town,' agreed Sutton. 'I was at King's myself. Did you visit the Chapel?'

'We did. Miss Ashcroft has recently taken an interest to gothic architecture and she was very impressed indeed.'

Mr Ashcroft listed a few other landmarks they had visited during their sojourn in Cambridge before the conversation turned towards London, discovering they shared some mutual acquaintances, and were both members at White's.

'I have visited perhaps once in the last year,' Mr Ashcroft admitted when Sutton expressed his surprise. 'While I enjoy some aspects of London, I prefer to keep my trips as short as possible – I am much more partial to the country.'

'Of course,' replied Sutton, who did not share the sentiment. Graham had once made a similar pronouncement, which baffled Sutton for several years. Eventually, the viscount conceded the bustling town wasn't suited to every taste – and after that came an even more unsettling revelation: that he might have developed a stronger preference for home had his childhood been filled with warmth and affection.

They rose when the ladies returned, lovely and fresh in their finer dresses. 'We were speaking of how the leaves have begun to turn,' said Mrs Ashcroft once they were seated. 'The grounds must be quite a sight in autumn!'

'Perhaps we could go for a ride tomorrow,' Sutton offered. 'We could head into Ely, if you have not yet been.'

'We have not,' replied Mrs Ashcroft. 'I know Ellie wishes to sketch the cathedral, and it would be good to stretch our legs.'

'Then I shall make the arrangements,' said Sutton. He knew the oft-mentioned building held great appeal for Miss Ashcroft and took the opportunity to satisfy his curiosity. 'Miss Ashcroft, may I ask why you are so interested in Ely Cathedral?'

The young lady, who was sipping her tea, gently placed her cup on her saucer and gave a small nod.

'I love the symmetry of English cathedrals,' she said, still a little timidly. 'I find it all very pleasing.'

It was a simplistic and childish answer, and Sutton nodded in response, strangely disappointed. But Miss Ashcroft was not yet finished, and her voice, when she resumed, had grown in strength.

'What I love most, however, are the discrepancies. The symmetry is but an illusion; the imperfections are what can tell the living stories of each building – and I find that breath-taking.'

Sutton felt his own breath catch, and could only nod again. Earlier, he and

Mr Ashcroft had set aside the best seats for the ladies: chairs offering the superior vantage of the gardens, bathed in the right amount of sunlight; now, as Sutton watched Miss Ashcroft take another sip of tea, her pale, freckled skin kissed by the sun, he was quite certain his seat offered the most pleasant view.

If Mr Ashcroft noticed Sutton's intense gaze upon his sister, he showed nothing of it. Instead, the gentleman said, 'Lord Sutton, we would be delighted to go riding tomorrow. Thank you once more for your hospitality.'

'The pleasure is all mine,' Sutton replied automatically. Reminding himself of the role he must play, he continued: 'Since the day seems promising, would you like to take a turn about the gardens? Alternatively, you are all very welcome to peruse my art collection – I would be delighted to accompany you either way.'

'Thank you,' said Mrs Ashcroft. A look passed between her and Miss Ashcroft, and Sutton caught the younger woman's small nod before Mrs Ashcroft continued. 'A walk would be most wonderful.'

Outside, they were greeted by a soft autumn sun and the cool air that promised chilly months ahead. Sutton led them towards the main gardens, while Mrs Ashcroft paid compliments to her apartment and enquired about its history.

'Ah yes – the Arabella Rooms are among the favourites in Bellevue Park. They are named after my great grandmother, who had quite the artistic eye and a particular penchant for subdued pastels. In addition to redesigning several suites and rooms, she also repurposed one of the private gardens to incorporate a range of delicate blossoms. Miss Ashcroft, your rooms – the Calliope – was also one of her designs.'

'They are very pleasing,' replied she in her soft voice. 'I especially admire the painting in the sitting room.'

A gentle warmth swelled in his chest, along with a flutter of pride. His concerted efforts had not been in vain!

'That is one of Mr Turner's earlier "experiments" during his visits to Bellevue,' he replied. 'He, of course, was unhappy with the result, and had intended it for his fireplace. I convinced him my fireplace would suit just as well – without clarifying I meant *above* and not *in* it. I don't think he's quite forgiven me for the oversight, but I have given Mr Turner my word his painting will never leave Bellevue.'

Miss Ashcroft's expression was one of astonishment and awe, which lasted until they reached a crossroads. Sutton stopped here, and said to the group at large: 'Here are the formal gardens. There's a labyrinth and an orangery to the left. To the right are the flower and vegetable gardens, the chapel, and the small brewery. There's also a private area in the East Wing with a rose garden, though I'm afraid there's not much to see at this time of the year. There are grain fields at the other end of the hunting grounds, and a mill and larger brewery by the river.'

After a general consensus to walk through the formal gardens, they set off again, with Sutton and Miss Ashcroft at the front of their party. Behind them, Mr and Mrs Ashcroft enjoyed their walk in silence, and around them, the birds sang their afternoon song.

Eager to resume his conversation with Miss Ashcroft, Sutton said: 'You have a keen eye for colours. Do you have any preferred palettes?'

'I am most comfortable working with soft, chalky colours,' replied the young lady, 'but I am most captivated by the bold and vibrant. I think I would like to experiment with richer colours one day, but...' Here she hesitated with a wisp of wistfulness. 'Such an exercise is beyond my capabilities.'

'Nothing is beyond anyone's capabilities if they have the perseverance – which I believe you do, if your exhibition is any indication.'

'You are too kind,' she replied. 'You were correct in suggesting, back at Thornleigh Abbey, that I still have much to learn. I'm certain your own talent greatly exceeds my own.'

Offering her a small bow, he said, 'If I have learnt anything in my artistic and intellectual explorations, it is that there is no limit to the pursuit of knowledge. I, too, have a great deal to discover – perhaps we might even learn a few things from each other.'

She gave him a small, sweet smile, and it was not without difficulty that Sutton directed the conversation to a less daring topic.

'Miss Ashcroft, Mrs Ashcroft, are you partial to any particular flowers?'

'I'm afraid my uncanny ability to destroy any plants under my care has contributed to my impartiality,' replied Mrs Ashcroft. Having entered the main garden, they were surrounded by at least twenty species of flora.

'I share that uncanny ability,' admitted Miss Ashcroft. 'But I am quite fond of wildflowers. When we were children, my brother and I – my other brother, that is – we loved picking them, and would often bring them back to the house.'

'You have another brother?' asked Sutton, feeling a little foolish. He had not enquired into the Ashcrofts, and now added, 'Please forgive my oversight – I did not mean to exclude him from my invitation.'

There was a slight pause before Miss Ashcroft answered. 'He joined the army two months ago, so you could not have known. His name is Richard, and he's almost a year older than I.'

At her soft words, Sutton recalled the portrait in Thornleigh Abbey of the young redcoat, blazing with spirit and sadness. 'Miss Ashcroft, I hope you'll be kind enough to forgive my assumptions once again, but is it his likeness that hangs above the fireplace in your drawing room?'

'It is,' she said, surprised. 'Before he left, I convinced him to sit for the portrait in his uniform – I like to think Richard is at home with us in some way.'

This discovery brought on a number of peculiar feelings, making it difficult for Sutton to distinguish amongst them: admiration at Miss Ashcroft's obvious talents, epitomised in the portrait; bewilderment at her decision to exclude her best work in her exhibition; shame for affording her such little credit upon their first meeting; longing for a similar portrait of Graham in his drawing room; fear of being unable to do his friend justice; and awe and wonder at Miss Ashcroft, and the desire to unravel the mysteries of this unremarkable yet extraordinary young lady.

But the viscount simply cleared his throat and said, 'My closest and dearest friend, who is a brother to me, is also in the Army.'

Miss Ashcroft slowed her pace and turned to regard him more fully, a world of understanding in her soft, sincere eyes.

The atmosphere had turned, and Sutton led the small, silent party to the garden's open rotunda. The four of them sat down amongst the autumnal colours and reflected on their newfound connection.

It was Mrs Ashcroft who broke the silence. 'Let us not brood unnecessarily,' she said. 'Richard writes about enjoying the challenges of his new life and his fondness for his new comrades. Lord Sutton, is your friend similarly happy in the army?'

'Without a doubt,' Sutton replied with a smile. 'I was in Colchester just last week to visit his regiment, and while he's found the responsibilities of his new rank demanding, he was in very high spirits indeed.'

'Colchester?' Mr Ashcroft asked. 'Is your friend with the 5th Foot, under Colonel Watson?'

'He is. Where is Ensign Ashcroft stationed?'

'The very same! What a coincidence.'

Sutton broke into a smile, knowing he would have much to write in his next letter. 'My friend, Lieutenant James Graham, has been training the new recruits in his platoon – perhaps your brother is among them.'

'Quite possibly,' replied Mr Ashcroft. 'Did you have a good opinion of Colchester?'

Sutton detected the gentleman's unspoken concern. Knowing the sentiments all too well, he did his best to assuage those fears. 'Ever since Lieutenant Graham joined the army several years ago as a gentleman volunteer, I've visited several of the towns and barracks where he was stationed. The Colchester Garrison is the most well-equipped by far, and while it may not offer a range of home comforts, I, for one, am glad that my good friend has been granted lodgings there.'

Mr Ashcroft nodded in thanks, and an understanding passed between the two men. The atmosphere shifted once again, returning now to the pleasant calmness that marked the beginning of their walk. Mrs Ashcroft directed the conversation back to the garden's various specimens and launched a series of queries about the surrounding plants. Sutton was happy to oblige, though his own knowledge was not extensive. However, the party soon discovered, much to everyone's surprise, that Mr Ashcroft's horticultural expertise was the most superior of their party.

The ladies retired to their rooms after a hearty dinner. Miss Ashcroft was particularly apologetic, insisting she did indeed wish to view Sutton's art collection and was extraordinarily grateful for his generosity. Sutton reassured her in his gentlest manner that he never once doubted her sincerity and gratitude, and that they had all the time in the world to peruse artistic delights, an activity best enjoyed in daylight when one was well-rested. Though he kept his observations to himself, Sutton had noticed Miss Ashcroft was almost entirely silent during dinner, and that she looked pale in her elegant periwinkle evening gown. He was sorry to bid her goodnight, but would be sorrier still if she took ill on his account.

As both men were not yet ready to retire, Sutton invited his guest to take a drink with him in the small drawing room where he and Graham had spent many long evenings. This was one of Sutton's private sanctuaries, favouring warmth and comfort over the sweeping grandeur of the formal rooms, and it had been many years since a newcomer had stepped through the door. But with Graham now leading a different life, Sutton saw the virtues of forming new friendships. There was much to be admired about Mr Ashcroft, who had been courteous to Sutton without flattery, and who, more importantly, seemed a most devoted husband and brother. Sutton's own parents had been indifferent to each other and none of his siblings had survived into adulthood; the viscount rarely saw a family as happy as the Ashcrofts, and he found himself wishing to know them more intimately.

Keen on making a good impression, Sutton resolved to be on his best behaviour and selected the best bottle of dry sherry.

The two men settled in front of the fireplace with their glasses. Mr Ashcroft took a sip, remarked on it approvingly, and then asked, 'How long has

Lieutenant Graham been in the army?'

'Two and a half years. He's developed quite an attachment to his regiment.'

Sutton briefly thought about the extent of this attachment, and how his friend had forsaken the Graham inheritance and heritage in order to remain with the army. While Sutton would not have made the same choice for himself, he had begrudgingly come to respect Graham's decision.

'Lieutenant Graham has spent some time in Darlington,' Sutton continued. 'He introduced me to Mr Earlwood when I visited the lieutenant earlier in the year. So long as my friend is stationed in Great Britain, I will endeavour to call on him as often as possible.'

'Hence your recent journey to Colchester,' said Mr Ashcroft.

'Indeed. Since the 5th are to remain there until next summer at the very least, I've rented a house in Colchester about a mile away from the garrison. You and your family are more than welcome to make use of it, should you wish to visit your brother.'

Mr Ashcroft appeared surprised at this, much to Sutton's delight. 'That is very generous of you.'

'Please, don't mention it.' Then, more quietly, Sutton said, 'I understand the difficulties of having your nearest and dearest in the army during these troubling times.'

The other man studied the pale liquid in his glass. 'I was far from supportive when Richard first joined the army; that he did so without my knowledge did not help his cause.'

Sutton bit back his questions and nodded in silent encouragement.

'When I was young, the British Army was a group of undisciplined vagrants – gamblers and drunks who enlisted for meagre wages and a roof over their heads. Even after the reforms, I thought very little of the army. If not for Mrs Ashcroft's actions at the time... I shudder to think what irreparable rifts might've resulted.'

'Actions?' Sutton asked before he could temper his curiosity.

'She found Richard – who had disappeared after our disagreement – and convinced him to return to Thornleigh to have a proper discussion with me, or, at the very least, to say goodbye to Ellie. Naturally, both her and my brother's actions caused quite a scandal in Darlington, but it is wholly in my good fortune that Mrs Ashcroft is exceedingly resilient to slander.'

'Ah, the unbidden power of words,' remarked Sutton, who had his own conflicting ideas about gossip. It provided an excellent source of entertainment, but crossing a thin line could destroy one's reputation and, by extension, one's livelihood.

Mr Ashcroft took another sip of his sherry. 'In addition to Lieutenant Graham, are you acquainted with anyone else in the Armed Forces?'

'A few – unavoidable during our times, I suppose. I met the Marquess of Wellington on several occasions when I was younger.'

Sutton rose to refill their glasses, his thoughts turning to Graham and the men from the 5th he'd befriended over the years. Even if Sutton did not have his viscountcy and responsibilities to consider, he doubted he would've had the courage to seek a lifestyle which required such sacrifices.

Returning to his seat, Sutton remarked, 'I have the most profound respect for the men who continue to serve and protect our country.'

'As do I,' replied Mr Ashcroft. He said nothing further, but his grim, downcast eyes revealed all. In this moment, Sutton realised perhaps he had some wisdom to offer the older gentleman after all.

'It is difficult when our loved ones are placed so close to danger,' Sutton said carefully. 'But I, for one, am humbled to call such an honourable and noble man my closest friend – a friend who often reminds me, in no unclear terms, that his decision to remain in the army reflects highly on the ones he wishes to protect.'

There was a measure of silence while the meaning settled over Mr Ashcroft. 'Thank you, Lord Sutton. I am much indebted to you.'

Sutton simply nodded in response, thinking how he was, in turn, much indebted to Graham.

13

ELLIE AWOKE AT DAWN, and, since she knew sleep would not return, the young lady rose and stretched in front of the still-glowing fire in the bedroom. She had been greeted by its enthusiastic flames after supper last night and welcomed its warmth now. The clock on the mantelpiece told her it was just after six.

Wrapping a dressing gown around herself, Ellie entered the adjoining sitting room, where she startled the young housemaid tending to the fire. They exchanged quick, embarrassed words, before a lady's maid was sent up to help Ellie dress. This woman was older and calmer, and informed Ellie that breakfast had been laid out in the morning room if she wished to venture downstairs, but she was equally welcome to dine upstairs if she so wished. Ellie considered this while her stays were secured. When the thick curtains were pulled open, she took a moment to admire the soft autumn sky, the rising sun painting the horizon pink.

'Thank you,' said Ellie when she was properly attired. 'I would be much obliged if you could direct me downstairs.'

They left her rooms, and Ellie delighted in the sight that greeted her: the first light of day filtered through the windows, settling over the age-old stones like a gentle blanket. At the heart of Bellevue Park lay the double spiral staircase, the light from its domed top casting intricate patterns on the steps and columns, bringing a smile to Ellie's lips.

She took her time descending to the ground floor, enjoying the look and feel of the grey stones. The staircases were built such that, while they were separate and started on opposite ends of the hallways, they provided the illusion of being intertwined. If two people were to take a different entry point on the ground floor, they would see the other's ascension till they reached the very top without ever intersecting. Ellie found the very notion fascinating and longed to see how the staircases would work in practice.

She was still marvelling at the architecture when they reached the salon and the lady's maid withdrew after a silent curtsy. A little lost in her musings, Ellie took two steps into the room and stopped, startled.

Before her was Lord Sutton, seated by the window, absorbed in a book. Dressed in a navy ensemble, the viscount was sprawled across the chair in a carefree manner that might've bordered on inappropriate were this not his home, at an hour when he clearly hadn't expected company. The Lord Sutton she'd seen was prim, proper, a touch passionate, and wholly an English peer; the Lord Sutton before her now was languid, striking, with a mass of black hair, still damp and slightly curly. Ellie felt a sudden, inexplicable urge to run her fingers through his hair, and immediately blushed at the thought.

Ellie was so entranced and embarrassed that she did not notice a footman approach, and almost jumped in fright when the man asked, 'Ma'am, do you have any requests for the kitchen?'

She looked up at Lord Sutton to see his surprise intensify into sharp interest, before dissolving into cool composure. Feeling more than a little foolish, Ellie mumbled an unintelligible response, wishing she had remained upstairs instead.

To both her relief and further embarrassment, the viscount marked his page, rose to his feet, and greeted Ellie with a deep bow.

'Good morning, Miss Ashcroft. Did you sleep well?'

'Yes, quite,' was all she could manage.

'I'm glad to hear it.' Then, to the footman: 'Some tea for Miss Ashcroft – the Lapsang, and make it strong.'

With unparalleled poise, Lord Sutton gestured at the small table with its setting for four, pulled out a chair, and remained patient until she sat.

'If I recall correctly, you prefer your tea strong, with two sugars, and a dash of milk,' he said. At her nod, Lord Sutton brought her the sugar bowl and milk jug. 'May I get you anything to eat?'

He was still standing as if he were waiting on her. Ellie's flush deepened, her naturally small appetite nowhere to be found. 'Thank you, but please don't trouble yourself any further.'

Ellie felt the viscount's gaze on her, but said nothing when he went to the serving table and filled a large plate with an assortment of pastries and cold cuts. Upon returning, Lord Sutton set the food between them, took the opposite seat, selected a piece of toast, and began buttering it on his own plate.

His movements were so natural and unassuming that Ellie started to relax. The footman returned with her tea, and her hands did not shake much when she prepared it to her liking. She took a small sip and welcomed its rich, smoky notes. This was nothing like the tea from yesterday afternoon, which had been light and refreshing; this was hearty, and tasted of faraway mountains and roasted pines. It warmed and strengthened her enough to speak.

'Please forgive my intrusion,' she said, struggling to meet his eyes. 'I had not thought... I had not expected...' She swallowed. 'I am usually the first to rise.'

'There is nothing to forgive, Miss Ashcroft – I myself am a poor sleeper. Please, do treat my home as your own.'

Lord Sutton's soft words were beyond those of a polite and gracious host, and his hazel eyes deepened beyond measure. Not understanding the intensity, Ellie looked away and reached for the ring on her neck chain, her heart pounding to an unknown rhythm. But even more unsettling than these novel sensations was her sudden desire to raise her eyes again, to discover for herself the very essence of Lord Sutton.

As she studied her porcelain teacup, the viscount took a bite of his toast. He continued with his breakfast, carrying on without speaking. Ever so gradually, Ellie began to calm once more, until she chose one of the pastries he had selected earlier.

She took a small bite, then followed it with another. 'This is one of the best pastries I've had the pleasure of enjoying,' she finally said.

'That is high praise indeed, Miss Ashcroft.' Lord Sutton's smile and easy manner loosened some more knots in her stomach. 'I will pass on your compliments to the pastry chef. Please, do help yourself to anything you like, and do not refrain from requesting any of your personal favourites. We'll do our very best to accommodate.'

'Thank you, Lord Sutton – I suspect I am forming new favourites as we speak.' She offered him a small smile and finished her pastry before choosing a second. The viscount watched her, and she would not be surprised if her preferences were relayed to the kitchens by luncheon.

After a few minutes, Ellie gathered her courage again and asked, 'Might I enquire as to what you were reading?'

'Plato's *Republic*,' he replied. 'Are you familiar with it?'

'I've not read the volumes myself, but I know some of its concepts.'

'I assume you're referring to Plato's stance on art and aesthetics?'

Ellie nodded. 'Our art instructor, Mr Hill, was…a fervent advocate of classics.'

'Oh?' Detecting her hesitation, Lord Sutton asked: 'Do you mean he was a stuffy snob with no business instructing young ladies?'

Ellie laughed at this unexpected comment and relaxed at Lord Sutton's smile. 'Precisely. He also made it very clear that instructing me and my brother Richard was beneath him – even at the start, when my brother and I were all but eight.'

'I'm surprised Mr Ashcroft didn't send him packing.'

'Oh, Richard and I kept the details to ourselves. We only told Marcus about Mr Hill's true nature after he'd left shortly after I turned fifteen – to join a baronet's family in Warwickshire, no less. Marcus was furious about how Mr

Hill had treated us.'

'I can only imagine,' Lord Sutton said, his confusion evident. With his brows furrowed, Ellie could see more clearly the small scar above his left eye. 'Why didn't you and your brother tell Mr Ashcroft earlier?'

Ellie took another sip of her tea, fortifying herself. 'Mr Hill never thought much of me, but he tried to teach Richard everything he knew, which I do believe was a considerable amount. But Richard never had the time or patience to paint – he loves sketching everything in sight and is exceedingly good at it, but he would lose interest after ten or fifteen minutes. When Mr Hill first taught Richard how to paint – of course, at that time I wasn't allowed to use anything but pencils – Richard's work was so abysmal and Mr Hill's reproach so scathing that we almost decided to ask Marcus to find us another instructor, only we didn't wish to trouble Marcus. It had taken the good part of a year for Marcus to find Mr Hill – all the others left after a few weeks, or even a few days. Poor Richard was in such low spirits, and he's one of the happiest people you'll ever meet. Wanting to help, I took one of his sketches and turned it into a watercolour. I had watched and listened enough during our lessons that the result was passable – certainly better than poor Richard's attempts. At our next lesson, Mr Hill saw my painting and, thinking it was Richard's work, began complimenting him on his sudden improvement. My brother was delighted to have tricked Mr Hill, and I was thrilled to have my work lauded for the first time. We maintained the deception for the next five years, and we never revealed our secret to Mr Hill.'

Lord Sutton had remained attentive throughout Ellie's anecdote, which she had never relayed before – that was always Richard's role. She knew her own retelling was lacking her brother's embellishments, but Ellie was pleased she had managed nonetheless. The viscount's warm response provided her with further encouragement.

'That is quite extraordinary,' he said, all admiration. 'Do you still collaborate with your brother?'

'Yes – many paintings from the exhibition are made from his sketches. He includes sketches in his letters, too. Sometimes he sends only sketches – Kitty is quite fond of trying to decipher any news from those. I owe a great deal to my dear brother.'

The viscount smiled, a small curve of his lips and quirk of an eyebrow that Ellie was coming to recognise as the private side of Lord Sutton. 'Ah, but all those paintings, with all the right colours and the right brushstrokes – and some hastily applied oils – all of those are *your* doing, Miss Ashcroft.'

The warmth started in her stomach once more, spreading lazily throughout her body until she felt it in her fingertips.

'Thank you,' she replied softly, keeping her eyes fixed on his. 'Thank you, Lord Sutton.'

They remained that way, joined by an inexplicable intimacy, until they were interrupted by the butler bringing Lord Sutton a letter. Both caught off-guard, but still warm with delight, Lord Sutton thanked the man while Ellie looked out the window at the promising day.

'My apologies,' Lord Sutton said once the tray had been set down. 'It is from Lieutenant Graham – any letters from him are to be brought to me immediately.'

'There is no need to apologise,' said Ellie, admiring the viscount's deep regard for his friend. She tipped her head towards the tray. 'Please don't allow my presence to keep you from reading the lieutenant's letter.'

Her offer seemed to put Lord Sutton at odds. 'Would you mind terribly? I have no wish to be rude, particularly when in such delightful company...'

He trailed off, uncertain. But Ellie, who had anxiously awaited news from Richard at every turn, could empathise all too well.

After a quick survey of the room, she said, 'Might I take a better look at the wonderful paintings here? I'm rather fond of the alpine landscape and would very much like to study it more closely.'

'Yes, of course.' His eyes took on the same intensity as earlier, his voice the same depth. 'Thank you, Miss Ashcroft.'

Nodding, Ellie stood from her seat and walked to the painting in question while Lord Sutton broke the letter's seal. She could neither name nor explain precisely what had passed between them after her unexpected intrusion, but

Ellie was quite certain they had reached a level of understanding she had hitherto not experienced. For those few, precious heartbeats, a veil had lifted to reveal what lay beneath their usual reserve, and they both wordlessly accepted what they saw.

The thought made her smile once more. She studied the bold strokes of the depicted mountain, and wondered what it might be like to see the snowy peaks for herself.

The quiet and unexpectedly pleasant morning adopted a new tune as noon approached, bringing with it Kitty and Marcus. As she exchanged greetings with her brother and sister-in-law, Ellie realised she had hardly missed their presence. Earlier, the viscount had shared parts of Lieutenant Graham's letter, which, to Ellie's delight, included some passages praising the hard-working new recruits of the regiment, though none were mentioned by name; afterwards, the two fell into a lengthy discussion about art, starting with landscape paintings and seamlessly moving onto matters of portraiture, working with oil, and the increasing status of watercolours. So absorbed was she that Ellie scarcely noticed the time pass, and had all but forgotten her initial reservations that very same morning.

Lord Sutton, however, let nothing slip his mind. After ascertaining Mr and Mrs Ashcroft had broken their fast upstairs, and then waiting for the ladies to change into their riding attire, the viscount led them to the stables. To their delight, the midday sun had held its own against the scattering of clouds. They walked at a leisurely pace, enjoying the hues of yellow and orange around them.

When they reached the stables, Lord Sutton said, 'The stable master and I have chosen these horses – I hope they will be suitable.'

They were each paired with their mounts, and Kitty expressed her pleasure about her mare while Marcus nodded appreciatively at his own steed. As a groom helped Ellie with her light chestnut gelding, Lord Sutton said to her,

'This is Sunshine – a befitting name for one of the gentlest creatures I've ever known. His line has been with our family for generations, and you will not find a sweeter or more patient creature.'

'Thank you, Lord Sutton.' Ellie stroked the horse's golden mane, thinking she could brush his coat for hours on end. 'He's beautiful.'

As Lord Sutton proceeded to introduce Kitty and Marcus's horses, Ellie and Sunshine followed the groom to the mounting block. While she had a fairly decent seat – thanks in no small part to both Marcus and Richard's interests in riding – Ellie preferred gentler horses to the more spirited types her family favoured. Lord Sutton's selection perfectly suited Ellie's temperament, and she said as much to the gelding, stroking his neck and complimenting his mane.

When all four riders were ready, they set off at a walk on the scenic, southern road leading away from Bellevue Park, taking the time to admire the stretches of cultivated parkland belonging to the estate. The viscount introduced them to a few landmarks, and Ellie was particularly fond of the mill that happily did its work by the stream.

Soon after leaving the estate, they switched to an easy canter on the main road to Ely. Lord Sutton had assured them the ride would take no longer than fifteen minutes, which Ellie thought a perfect length of time to enjoy herself without tiring. She was also very pleased with Sunshine's smooth gait, and the comfortable seat made no time of the trip itself. Not far in the distance, Ely Cathedral's magnificent spire rose from the meadows.

As they approached Ely and slowed their pace, Marcus, who had been riding beside Kitty, brought his horse next to Ellie. The two siblings rode side by side, taking in the looming view. From the first time Marcus had accompanied Ellie to visit Hatfield House back in Hertfordshire, they had decided to take in all novel scenes together. Despite the considerable changes in their lives over the past year, her brother was now at Ellie's side once more.

'Alright, my dear?' he asked, voice soft and gentle.

'More than alright,' she replied, just as softly. 'And you, dearest brother?'

Ellie saw the pure pleasure in his eyes as Marcus looked upon the green pastures, the grazing sheep, the formidable cathedral, the other two riders in their small company, his wife donning the magnificent blue riding coat he'd gifted during their early courtship.

'I'm splendid,' he said.

Up at the gate, Lord Sutton stopped to exchange words with a young man. From what she could gather from the conversation, it seemed that shortly after their arrival yesterday afternoon, Lord Sutton had sent word to the Dean, requesting an audience at the Cathedral. Furthermore, Lord Sutton had arranged for a picnic to be sent from Bellevue's kitchens, along with some sketchbooks and pencils should Miss Ashcroft wish to draw the cathedral.

If Ellie was surprised by Lord Sutton's foresight and consideration, she certainly wasn't alone; Marcus, who had noticed as much as Ellie, commented softly, 'Our host is most generous and gracious.'

Thinking back to their exchanges this morning, Ellie couldn't agree more.

It was just after they'd exchanged farewells with the Dean and his family, complete with a promise to return, that Ellie felt the first touch of heated dizziness. She blinked it away, attributing her light-headedness to the day's excitement, and resumed her conversation with Kitty. By the time they'd left Ely and were cantering back to Bellevue Park, however, Ellie's discomfort had grown unduly, until she struggled to see clearly or to keep her seat. Sensing a change in his rider, Sunshine slowed to a walk without any prompting.

The next wave of faintness struck without warning, and Ellie slouched forward, wrapping her arms around Sunshine's neck. She was not unfamiliar with these dizzy spells, which were frequent in Ellie's childhood, but it nonetheless took all her concentration to keep breathing. She could barely register her situation – her head was too light, her limbs too heavy.

When a gentle hand lifted her cheek from Sunshine's mane, Ellie saw her brother, pale with worry.

'I'm sorry,' she managed, 'I feel rather ill... I'm sorry – I don't mean to cause trouble...'

Vaguely, she heard Marcus's quick discussion with Lord Sutton, before her brother helped Ellie off her horse and onto his own stallion. Safe within her brother's arms, Ellie allowed herself to be carried away, too disoriented to speak again. In her final consciousness, Ellie wondered how Sunshine would get home, and why Lord Sutton had ridden away in another direction.

14

IT WAS THE perfect autumn afternoon, the likes of which inspired poets and painters, muses and musicians – but Sutton barely noticed. Galloping at full speed, he passed the trees, fields, and farmers reaping their bountiful harvests – and all he saw was Miss Ashcroft, slumped over Sunshine, limp and lifeless and swallowed by her very own clothes. When she was carried off her horse, her arm had hung about her side, bare and white. The image remained with Sutton, heavy and thick, making him sick to the stomach as he sped back towards the village.

When he dismounted outside his physician's home, Sutton tripped and almost fell, catching himself at the expense of the stable boy who'd come to assist. Quickly regaining his balance, Sutton thanked the boy and handled him the reins, immediately making for the door. The physician, who had undoubtedly heard Sutton's arrival, recognised the viscount's urgency and was donning his coat.

'Mr Shepherd,' Sutton said without preamble, 'a young lady has been visiting Bellevue and has taken ill while riding back to the house. Her brother has taken her back to the house – please, Mr Shepherd, tend to her.'

The physician nodded, relaying quick instructions for his kits to be brought. When he asked for his horse to be saddled, Sutton gestured to his own.

'My horse is ready.'

'Yes, thank you,' the physician said without delay, bringing his saddlebag kit and attaching it securely. He swung himself up, adding, 'Lord Sutton, I will tend to the lady to the best of my abilities.'

He was off, galloping towards Bellevue Park, leaving Sutton impatient and waiting for another horse to be readied. Suddenly bereft of activity, Sutton paced the courtyard, paying no heed to the uncertain maid and stable boy lingering by. He glanced at the stable where the groom was adjusting the saddle and bit; it took Sutton all his discipline to refrain from taking on the task himself. It was not the fear of impropriety that stopped him, but rather the knowledge that his interference would only hinder the groom's efforts.

No more than five minutes had passed until the horse was ready, but it felt like five minutes too much. A word of thanks to the groom and stable boy, and Sutton was astride once more, racing back to Bellevue Park and his ailing guest.

Climbing the staircase two steps at a time, Sutton paid no heed to anything other than reaching the Calliope, where he was greeted by Mr Ashcroft in the sitting room.

'She has developed a slight fever,' the gentleman said in a low voice. 'She has been fatigued on her journey – it may have led to the fainting spell and fever. The physician says she is not in any immediate danger, but would like to keep her under observation.'

Sutton released a small sigh of relief before composing himself once more. 'I am glad she is unharmed.'

'Yes, indeed. We are much indebted to you for your hospitality, and for obtaining a physician so quickly, but I must also apologise for the inconvenience we have caused.'

'Please, let us not speak so at such a time,' Sutton replied rather abruptly. 'My only concern is for Miss Ashcroft's health, and my only wish is for her quick recovery.'

'You are too kind, Lord Sutton.'

The bedroom door opened, and Mrs Ashcroft and Mr Shepherd emerged. Sutton nodded to the physician, whose hair was still dishevelled from his hasty journey.

'Lord Sutton,' the physician said. 'I have given Miss Ashcroft a tincture to help soothe her nerves and another to lower her fever, but what she needs most is rest. Keep the fire in her rooms high at all times, but open the windows every few hours during the day to keep the air fresh. We must ensure she does not catch a cold.'

He paused, glancing between Mr Ashcroft and Lord Sutton. Seeing this as his cue, Sutton said, 'Thank you, Mr Shepherd. Mr and Mrs Ashcroft, do excuse me – I have some business to attend to in my study.'

Having given the physician leave to speak with the Ashcrofts in private, Sutton made his way downstairs. A small measure of hurt throbbed in his chest, though he knew it was unwarranted – he was barely acquainted with the family, and was certainly not privy to the intimate details of Miss Ashcroft's health. Yet, Sutton had hoped…

The viscount shook his head, admitting to himself he knew not what he had hoped. Focusing now on what he *did* know, Sutton sought Mrs Jennings, who, though he suspected had already instructed the household to care for Miss Ashcroft, patiently listened to her master speak.

'We must have some chicken soup prepared,' he said, after he'd relayed Mr Shepherd's instructions. 'And those fruit tarts – Miss Ashcroft mightn't wish for any at the moment, but they must be ready when her appetite returns.'

Mrs Jennings nodded, 'How shall dinner be served, sir?'

'In the small dining room,' he replied after some consideration. Any of the larger rooms would be distasteful under the circumstances. 'The full three courses will do.'

On his way to the study, Sutton stopped a footman and said: 'Wait for Mr Shepherd outside the Calliope – send him to my private study.'

When Sutton finally entered his sanctuary, he closed the door behind him and sagged against it. The nervous energy that had been driving him dissipated as quickly as it had been conjured, leaving him weary and bereft. Only hours ago, Miss Ashcroft had caught him off-guard when he was luxuriating in the quiet beauty of the early morning, not expecting to have company. When their eyes met for that brief moment, he had seen in her countenance so pure and intense a longing that had him reacting in kind. There, wearing a lilac dress and kissed by daylight, Miss Ashcroft had stood, oblivious to her own radiance.

But now, the very same woman was taken sick, small and pale and frail. The image of her limp body returned, and it took Sutton all his strength to propel himself away from the door and stumble to his chair. A cold sweat broke all over, and Sutton could do no more than close his eyes and wait for it to pass.

He was still in the same position when a knock on the door and a faraway voice announced Mr Shepherd's presence. Sutton straightened and called in the doctor.

'Lord Sutton,' the physician said as he entered, taking the seat Sutton had indicated. Mr Shepherd, who had been the family's main physician from before Sutton was born, neither commented on the younger man's appearance nor enquired about his connection with Miss Ashcroft.

'Thank you for lending me your horse,' he said instead. 'I apologise for the uneven gait of your replacement – the poor creature injured his leg months ago and is perhaps too old to make a full recovery.'

Sutton vaguely recalled his borrowed ride's uncomfortable seat, but he'd been too intent on the journey to consider the cause. Now, he felt a little ashamed of his single-mindedness, and knew he had been too demanding of the doctor's horse.

'You will have a new horse within the week,' Sutton said by way of both apology and thanks. 'And do let me know if you require any such replacements in the future. Having a fast and reliable steed is crucial for your vocation.'

'You are most kind, Lord Sutton.'

Etiquette dictated that he enquire no further about Miss Ashcroft, but Mr Shepherd, who was under Sutton's employ and patronage, understood the viscount's unspoken concern.

'I will return tomorrow morning,' he said, which brought Sutton some relief. The doctor would not leave if Miss Ashcroft was in any immediate danger. 'In the meantime, I will procure some medicines that will assist in the lady's recovery and to boost her general constitution.'

'Thank you, Mr Shepherd. Do speak to Mrs Jennings before you leave – we have detained you from dinner, and a basket has been prepared for you.'

Sutton grew calmer after the physician's departure, which he took as a confirmation that Miss Ashcroft would indeed be well. His appetite slowly returned, and Sutton took a few long, deep breaths before leaving his study for the small dining room.

He found Mr and Mrs Ashcroft already seated, speaking in low voices and holding hands. They both straightened upon his entrance, and Sutton noticed Mr Ashcroft withdrawing his hand from his wife's. This small gesture, even more than their shared gazes and whispers, made Sutton feel like an intruder to their intimacy.

'I'm sorry for keeping you waiting,' he said, maintaining a neutral tone. He sat at the head of the table and felt like an interposer in his own home.

The Ashcrofts, however, were full of warmth and gratitude. 'Lord Sutton,' said Mrs Ashcroft, 'we are terribly sorry to impose on you thus. You have been such an attentive host, and are so very kind to send for your doctor – we are greatly in your debt.'

'Please, let us speak no more of it,' Sutton replied. 'Miss Ashcroft's recovery is of the utmost importance, and you are all welcome to stay at Bellevue Park as long as is necessary.'

Mr Ashcroft's relief was visible. 'Truly, we are much obliged, Lord Sutton.'

The first course was served, and the party of three ate in relative silence. Their thoughts were on the missing fourth member of the group who connected them all.

'I hope you'll forgive my candour,' Sutton finally said, unable to leash his concern any longer. 'Has Miss Ashcroft suffered from such afflictions before?'

There was a moment of hesitation before Mr Ashcroft set down his fork, regarding Sutton with serious, unreadable eyes. The viscount felt he was being measured and judged and, as Mr Ashcroft's expression shifted, Sutton knew a decision had been made.

'Yes,' Mr Ashcroft said quietly. 'My sister has never had a strong constitution and would tire easily from even the shortest excursions. It was only in the past two years that she has appeared to gain some strength – but even so, it took her several months to recover from her most recent chill.'

Sutton nodded, taking in the full weight of this meaning. But Mr Ashcroft was not yet finished.

'My sister may be soft and mild in her treatment of others, but she is hard on herself, and more stubborn than you could imagine. Too often, her illnesses escalate because she dismisses her discomfort, or does not speak up – she is more concerned about "causing trouble" than her own health.'

The words brought back the vivid image of Miss Ashcroft slumping on her horse, sending Sutton's heart racing once more. If he had not thought long and hard about her disposition and decided to pair her with the soft and gentle Sunshine; if another, faster, less sensitive steed had borne Miss Ashcroft...

Mr Ashcroft softened. 'I am grateful for your friendship and hospitality, Lord Sutton. It is not in my nature to seek new acquaintances, but I am very fortunate to have met you.'

Struck by these words, Sutton could only nod in acknowledgement, breaking the gaze he and Mr Ashcroft had been holding. An understanding had passed between the two men and, were he not concerned about the lady convalescing upstairs, Sutton would have recognised its significance. As it were, Sutton remained quiet for the rest of the meal, allowing Mrs Ashcroft to lighten the atmosphere with her comments about the dishes. The viscount pondered the two truths he now faced: he was powerless where Miss

Ashcroft's fragile health was concerned, and he was powerless to cease caring.

As Mr Shepherd had predicted, Miss Ashcroft's fever broke the next day. It was soon concluded that her fainting spell had indeed resulted from general fatigue and was not the prelude to a more serious ailment. Regardless, both the physician and Mr Ashcroft erred on the side of caution, and thus, Miss Ashcroft was primarily bound to her bed and her rooms, taking short strolls in the gardens when the sun made its appearance. Sutton, however, was otherwise preoccupied when Miss Ashcroft left her rooms, and attended his long-standing appointments. He had not expected to entertain the Ashcrofts for longer than a week, but the family did not begrudge his absence – they, too, understood this time of year was crucial for the tenants and famers who worked the land.

Indeed, he had barely seen her since that wretched afternoon. If Mr and Mrs Ashcroft weren't so fierce and constant in their love for the young woman, Sutton may have found an excuse to breach the unspoken rules of proprietary that held together his society. As it were, Sutton paid Miss Ashcroft his highest regards by lavishing upon her the finest care and attention through Bellevue's staff, and, equally, by respecting her privacy during her convalescence. Consequently, the more Miss Ashcroft recovered and regained her strength, the more agitated Sutton became.

Since Mr Shepherd had instructed Miss Ashcroft to avoid any unnecessary exertion where possible, Sutton had also insisted she dine upstairs, removing the formalities required for dinner. Mrs Ashcroft doubled as a bedside and dining companion, but Mr Ashcroft continued to take his meal with Sutton in the small dining room. The conversation was generally light and of little consequence, and though the two gentlemen had only a few common interests, they bonded over their shared values and virtues. Nonetheless, there were several occasions when Sutton felt Mr Ashcroft remained only under obligation, if anything could be surmised by the faraway look that entered his eyes. But Sutton took no offence, instead admiring the strength and depth of the older gentleman's brotherly affection.

And so, the viscount concentrated his efforts on preparing a small art exhibition in one of Bellevue's neglected galleries, which hitherto held the portraits of distant and minor relations. After some deliberation, the portraits were moved to join the Curiosities in the West Wing and replaced by the most treasured items of his collection, which Sutton usually kept in his private chambers, or in the rooms where he himself painted. He found it surprisingly difficult to part with the Rembrandt in his antechamber, until he remembered Miss Ashcroft's unadulterated delight at the mere thought of seeing an original.

Outside of arranging and re-arranging his art collection for Miss Ashcroft's viewing pleasure, Sutton also found refuge in his correspondence with Graham. He had written to his friend about the situation, omitting no detail save his innermost, incomprehensible feelings. Judging from Graham's response, his friend required no explication – in this, Sutton suspected Graham understood him better than he did himself. Prior to Miss Ashcroft's unfortunate incident, Sutton had also enquired about Ensign Richard Ashcroft, to which Graham replied in the affirmative: the new recruit was, by a happy coincidence, assigned to Graham. In his latest letter, Graham expressed his wish for Sutton to visit Colchester soon, adding that Ensign Ashcroft was keen to make his acquaintance if the viscount permitted it. Not once had Sutton verbalised how terribly he missed his friend, but Graham, bless his heart, read between the lines and wrote the words in Sutton's stead.

On the same afternoon Sutton had received this very letter, Mrs Ashcroft sought him in his study and informed him Miss Ashcroft was feeling well enough to join them for dinner. A cloud lifted at these words, and, as soon as Mrs Ashcroft left, Sutton rose to consult his chef and his valet.

15

AFTER FIVE DAYS of bed rest, broken only by short walks in her coarser daywear, Ellie welcomed the delicate material and craftsmanship of her lavender evening gown. The maids who attended her were gentle and deft, and, despite the slight ache in her body, Ellie enjoyed the sensation of silk against her skin and pins in her hair. Yet, unlike others of her situation, Ellie was not well disposed to hide her uneasiness behind such fineries. She was aflutter with nerves, and even Kitty's enthusiastic greeting in the sitting room was not enough to dispel her discomfort of having inconvenienced so many.

They made their way down the stairs and entered a small dining room where the gentlemen were already seated at a round table. Ellie relaxed a little at the intimate furnishings, so alike in atmosphere to the second dining room in Thornleigh, and was further comforted to see the dinner table stripped of all but the essentials. Only a week prior, she would have surmised that formalities and extravagance defined Lord Sutton's character; now, as the two gentlemen rose and bowed at the ladies' arrival, Ellie conceded she was mistaken in her initial impression.

She and Kitty curtsied in response and were directed to their seats: Ellie was flanked by her family, and she sat opposite their host. She glanced up just before Lord Sutton took his own seat, and saw the soft smile curl around the viscount's lips.

'Miss Ashcroft,' he addressed her, then paused, allowing his deep voice to reverberate throughout the small room. 'How are you feeling?'

'Much better, thank you. I hope you will accept my gratitude for your kindness, as well as my apologies for being such an imposition.'

'The former I shall gladly accept, but let us hear no more on the latter. We are all glad you are well, Miss Ashcroft.'

Kitty expressed her agreement, and Ellie looked down to hide her flush. Noting this, Lord Sutton addressed Ellie's family. 'Mr and Mrs Ashcroft, I hope you'll find tonight's meal palatable – we have strived to achieve a balance between the humble dinners from the last few days, and the richer fare that might trouble delicate appetites.'

'You are very modest to label those previous dinners "humble", sir,' said Kitty, who had regaled with Ellie the abundance of food served at Bellevue.

The first course of white soup, fish, poultry, and sweetbreads was served, and Ellie took particular liking to the soup, which was so delicately flavoured that she almost requested another serving. The fish was cooked and seasoned to perfection, and the boiled chicken so soft it melted in her mouth. Ellie could hardly keep up, but she soon saw that no expectations had been made of her. Indeed, as the evening progressed and the tablecloths were changed, the company eased into conversation about the weather, the country, the latest particulars of the Prince Regent, and even some news about Richard, who was not only one of Lieutenant Graham's subalterns, but also one of the most promising. Kitty and Lord Sutton exchanged the most words, with the occasional remark by Marcus; Ellie, who always preferred to listen and observe, felt no need to say more than she wished tonight.

After dessert was laid out, an assortment of fruits, biscuits, cakes, trifles, and even ices, Lord Sutton addressed Ellie directly once more. 'I received a letter from the Dean of Ely this morning, Miss Ashcroft. He sends his regards and wishes you a quick recovery.'

The news that the Dean had heard of her unfortunate incident diminished the joy of her lemon ice, but only a little. Lord Sutton, who noticed this, continued casually:

'The Dean's wife called a few days ago, wishing to speak more with you about your drawings, when Mrs Ashcroft relayed to her you were unwell.'

'Oh, I thought I'd mentioned her visit,' Kitty said, quite embarrassed. 'Forgive me, Ellie – it truly slipped my mind.'

'She rather admired your sketches of the Cathedral,' Lord Sutton said, 'and would gladly welcome you back to Ely at any time.'

'That is very kind of them,' replied Ellie. She did wish to return to the cathedral and produce a few more sketches for a larger canvas piece, but Ellie had caused enough trouble as it were, and was only just sufficiently recovered to sit at a relaxed dinner. But though she left the rest unsaid, Ellie felt the weight of Lord Sutton's scrutiny even as he moved on to another, related topic.

'Miss Ashcroft, if you feel inclined, I was wondering if you might wish to peruse some of Bellevue's art collection?' Ellie glanced at Marcus, whose easy demeanour told her the viscount had discussed the proposition with her brother. 'It is also perfectly understandable if you wish to undertake the endeavour at another time,' he added, this time with a little flourish. 'I shall await your command, whichever you choose.'

Ellie took a moment to consider. Her limbs were a little heavy, but she attributed it to the usual effects of a satisfying meal rather than any excessive fatigue. In fact, after her period of bed rest, Ellie suspected another gentle stroll – within the sheltered hallways of Bellevue Park, no less – would do her more good than harm.

'May we, dearest brother?'

They rose shortly after Marcus's consent and were led further into the East Wing. Lord Sutton offered Kitty his arm, and Ellie and Marcus trailed behind. Softly, her brother asked: 'Ellie, you will let me know before you have the chance to over-exert yourself?'

She nodded in earnest. 'I will – I promise.'

When they reached the gallery, Lord Sutton announced: 'I am pleased to present to you some select pieces from my modest collection.' He bowed deeply, and when Ellie saw the mischievous glint that belied his words, she hid her own responding smile.

Her amusement quickly faded when she entered the long antechamber and saw, with her very own eyes, the dozens of paintings that were perhaps Lord Sutton's most prized possessions. Three chandeliers were supplemented by a number of candelabras and sconces, lighting up the gallery as if it were day. And oh, the paintings! Ellie's eyes drank in these offerings, darting from canvas to canvas, barely resting on one item before indulging in another. Time stood still, and yet, it also escaped her – there were so many treasures to devour, but only one pair of wide, excited eyes.

She was so struck with awe that Ellie hardly noticed her companions until her brother obstructed her view, and placed his warm fingers upon her forehead.

'Ellie? Are you quite all right?'

The young woman blushed, remembering the trouble she had so recently caused.

'Yes, I'm fine, thank you. This is all just…extraordinary.'

At this, Lord Sutton said, 'I recall having a similar reaction to Miss Ashcroft upon first viewing the works of Leonardo da Vinci and Michelangelo.'

If his intention had been to calm, Lord Sutton's words had the opposite effect. 'You have seen those in person? Oh, Lord Sutton, *truly*? What were the originals like? How were you able to access them?'

'Perhaps that's a tale for another day,' he replied softly, though his eyes were as warm and rich as she had ever seen them. 'Mr Ashcroft, may I show your sister around the room?'

Had Ellie not been so preoccupied with the paintings around her, she would have registered the innocuous question as a request for permission, and a prelude to something more. And when her brother consented, Ellie did not see the look that passed between the two men, nor the significance of Lord Sutton's proffered arm.

'Miss Ashcroft,' he said, his voice taking on the same quality as when she first arrived at dinner, and when, in what seemed like an age ago, she had stumbled upon him at breakfast, leisurely and languid.

Ellie placed her gloved hand in his and felt Lord Sutton's warmth through the delicate silk.

'Lord Sutton,' she said with a softness that had nothing to do with timidity. 'I am honoured to see your collection.'

True to his word, Lord Sutton took Ellie around the room, introducing her to each individual piece before allowing her the time to observe it with all her care, admiration, and passion. After seeing the first dozen or so, Ellie noticed the artwork had been organised by neither time nor place, but by subjects and themes which underwent subtle developments as they progressed. They had begun with stills of fruit, containing an enviable number by Dutch masters Ellie had only dreamed of seeing. Gradually, they moved onto larger, more open areas, leading towards the grand, sweeping landscapes that made her heart skip and her breath catch. She was particularly struck by a somewhat disproportionate but nonetheless wonderful painting, which Ellie recognised as one of Mr Turner's lauded works.

'I could introduce you, if you'd like,' Lord Sutton said. 'Just don't mention the painting in your room – he's still quite sensitive about its existence.' Overwhelmed with wonder, Ellie could only nod.

And then, there were the grand, magnificent pieces depicting warfare, which aroused murmurs of appreciation from Marcus and Kitty behind them. While she wasn't personally fond of these larger, more visceral pieces, Ellie appreciated their artistry and how they evoked feelings she had kept hidden. When they stopped at a depiction of Napoleon, Ellie turned to Lord Sutton for the first time since the tour, surprised, confused, and a little hurt.

'He was not always as he is now,' Lord Sutton said, answering her unspoken question. 'Beethoven wrote a symphony for him, but after Napoleon crowned himself emperor, the maestro scratched out the title page and changed his dedication to "the memory of a great man".'

'And how the world now suffers from his excessive ambition,' Marcus added.

To Ellie's relief, the representations of conflicts and warfare only numbered a few, and they soon moved on to the idyllic pastures and past-times of the Renaissance. She admired these greatly, and marvelled at the familiar names inscribed on the frames.

A little further on, Ellie was struck by a series of oval paintings with mythological figures that would be considered risqué had they not seemed so allegorical. Seeing no plaque introducing either the works or the artist, Ellie enquired after them.

'Ah yes – Antoine Watteau's *Seasons*.'

She could not help but gape at his response. 'Antoine Watteau? His *Seasons*? The *lost* series of the four seasons?'

'I suppose they have been considered lost,' he said, almost teasingly, 'but I see you have now found them.'

She was full of questions – positively brimming with them – but his light demeanour was nonetheless grounded by patience, and Ellie knew she had all the time in the world to ask him. For now, she only wished to confirm one thing, though she was quite certain of the answer.

'May I return to see these again?'

Lord Sutton nodded, catching the firelight in his hazel eyes, which now had a spark of their own. 'As often as you wish, Miss Ashcroft.'

'Thank you, sir.'

They were nearing the end of the exhibition, and Ellie felt the fatigue return to her. Seeing this, Lord Sutton led her away from the Watteau and to the doorway instead.

'Perhaps that should suffice for tonight,' he said, ever so gently. 'I have many other pieces that might interest you, but we could save those for another day.'

She longed to see everything in Lord Sutton's collection at this very moment, but knew such a desire was both unreasonable and unconducive to her recovery. Slowly, the company of four walked through the corridors and reached the grand staircase, stopping at the foot of the stairs. The past hour had already surpassed Ellie's dreams, and, judging from Lord Sutton's words and behaviour, she was indeed welcome to return as often as she wished.

'Thank you, sir,' she repeated, not knowing how to express the depth of her feelings. But Lord Sutton understood. As he passed her hand back to Marcus, Ellie saw his unmistakable affection.

'Goodnight, Mr and Mrs Ashcroft.' He bowed, a sweeping gesture that encapsulated the pride, the flourishes, and the kindness of the man. 'Goodnight, Miss Ashcroft.'

It was not until much later, when Ellie was drifting off to sleep, that she wondered why Lord Sutton had not shown her any of his own works.

She was still considering her observation when she rose the next day. The fires had been stoked, and a lady's maid helped Ellie with her toilette. When she was properly attired, Ellie left her rooms, eager to broach the subject with Lord Sutton. She smiled as she descended the double spiral staircase – the sun was hidden by clouds this morning, and the dim light that filtered through the domed ceiling shrouded the heart of Bellevue Park in mystery.

Ellie had just taken a few steps from the first floor when she noticed Lord Sutton had done the same from the opposite staircase. She felt the illusion of the double spirals as much as she saw it – there, across from the hollow centre of the staircases, the viscount descended, surely, steadily, and entirely out of her reach.

He noticed her presence almost instantly. Ellie could not discern his expression from such a distance, and she was vaguely disappointed before it occurred to her he could not see her clearly either. She studied him: the bold lines of his striking figure and the mass of black hair that framed his features. His conduct was everything she had expected from a viscount, yet his character surprised and intrigued her. She longed to learn more about this man across from her, yet she was afraid of her own longing.

The illusion held till the very end: they descended at the same pace, but their paths never crossed. It was not until they both reached the ground floor and circled around the staircase before they met again. By then, Ellie was a proper young lady once more, and he, the charming and obliging host. They bade each other good morning and made for the breakfast room where her family was waiting.

Ellie kept her thoughts to herself all morning and made no requests until luncheon after the table had been cleared and the tea and pastries brought in. Ellie chose a fruit tart and casually asked, 'Lord Sutton, I hope you'll forgive my candour, but I was wondering if you might be willing to share some of your own paintings? I am quite keen to see them.'

'Why yes, of course.' She noted a flicker of hesitation in his response. The viscount picked up his tea and nodded at Ellie's plate. 'Perhaps when you are finished, if you so wish?'

Ellie beamed. 'Yes – I would be much obliged. And these are lovely – I daresay I have been quite spoilt.'

Her brother smiled at this. 'It is good to see your appetite has returned, dear Ellie.'

'Mr and Mrs Ashcroft, would you like to join us? I confess my own paintings pale in comparison to those of the great masters', but you are welcome to judge for yourselves.'

While Ellie wondered about the veracity of this admission, Kitty said: 'You are too kind in assuming I have the capacity to make such judgements, Lord Sutton. It is a very generous offer, but I fear your talents will be wasted on me.'

'Then perhaps you might wish to accompany us to the adjacent rooms,' the viscount offered. 'My grandfather was very fond of horses, and his collection of equine paintings is near the gallery.'

'Ah, that does sound fascinating,' replied Kitty.

The matter decided, the party ventured into the west wing, which Ellie understood to house the viscount's private quarters. She wondered how many other guests had been invited to this part of the house.

They stopped down a corridor and entered different rooms.

Although Marcus and Kitty were but a few feet away, Ellie now felt a sudden proximity to Lord Sutton. She became keenly aware of his presence: his even breathing, his woody cologne, his measured footsteps. The room was full of paintings and sketches, all in various stages of completion – this, too, alerted her to the sanctity of the room and her position as the trespasser.

'Miss Ashcroft,' he said, the hesitation returning once more, 'here are my meagre offerings. The ones on those two walls are finished – but many are not…what I'd hoped them to be.'

Bemused by the viscount's sudden uncertainty, Ellie focused on the paintings before her. She studied the canvases he had indicated – and felt more than a little perplexed.

Perhaps Ellie had unfairly requested to view the viscount's own work after she had spent hours gazing upon the masterpieces in his private collection; perhaps her esteem and expectations of the viscount had simply been too high. What she saw – what Lord Sutton had created – was a collection of paintings that surely belied the viscount's excellent tastes.

She glanced at Lord Sutton and saw a flash of emotions she would not have ascribed to the viscount: apprehension, fear, and the smallest tinge of hope. For a moment, Lord Sutton seemed like a young boy, desperate for an elder's approval – but the moment passed as the viscount straightened, his countenance steady and controlled once more.

Having glimpsed a part of the viscount Ellie was sure he rarely shared, she now chose her next words very carefully.

'Lord Sutton, I greatly admire the subjects you have chosen,' she said sincerely. 'All your paintings are so very grand, and full of so much passion and dedication.'

The viscount gave her an amused smile. 'I doubt I was as dedicated as you, Miss Ashcroft.'

'That is very kind,' Ellie replied, flushing a little. She looked upon the paintings again, searching for compliments, her hand reaching for Richard's ring hung about her neck.

She settled on a large canvas depicting a ship caught in a storm. The colours the viscount had chosen made it very difficult to discern ship from sea from sky, but they had brought out the ferocity of the waves.

'This is mightily intimidating,' Ellie said. 'I am particularly in awe of the waves – I really feel I might be swept away by them at any moment. You have really captured their power.'

When Lord Sutton didn't respond, Ellie continued with the next painting, depicting a large battle scene filled with knights on their horses. The canvas was taller than her, its width perhaps twice her arm span. Yet, despite its impressive size, the knights and horses had skewed proportions, and the overall perspective was jarring.

Ellie swallowed. 'This one is so large – I can't even imagine how you accomplished it. And the battle itself is so...*chaotic.*'

She turned her attention to another painting: the nine Muses, their features quite disproportionate. 'And this one – each Muse is so...distinct. Your portrayal is nothing but...*unique.*'

The viscount scoffed, and Ellie caught him shaking his head. 'Miss Ashcroft, you are too kind. Let us be honest with each other: I am a dreadful "artist" who does not deserve the designation.'

The admission was not easily made, and the viscount's resignation pained Ellie. 'Don't be so cruel to yourself,' she said firmly. 'You are a passionate, accomplished artist who has experimented with numerous subjects, and who possesses exceptional tastes. Any deficiencies you see in your own work is simply part of the process – we *all* see our own deficiencies, but we must learn to overcome them with our patience and perseverance.'

Lord Sutton chuckled this time, his rich baritone resounding in the room. 'Ah, Miss Ashcroft – I believe *you* are the accomplished artist here, and with such wisdom, too. I never had much patience or perseverance – and, unlike your brother Mr Richard, I never really had the talent, either.'

She opened her mouth to protest, to defend him from himself, but Lord Sutton touched her arm lightly, the warmth of his fingers seeping through her sleeves. 'Truly, Miss Ashcroft, thank you for being so kind in your assessment.'

He removed his hand and bowed to her, in every way that was proper for a gentleman. But his hazel eyes, flecked with warm amber, beheld Ellie with an intensity that was decidedly ungentlemanlike.

And she, in an equally unladylike manner, stored what she saw in the most secret recesses of her heart.

16

SUTTON REMAINED IN the driveway for a full ten minutes after the Ashcrofts' carriage had left his sight, paying no heed to the light raindrops that gradually soaked his coat. He was starting to feel the autumn chill, but though Sutton knew there was a fire and fresh clothes waiting for him inside, he was reluctant to step back into the house. Ever the steadfast butler, Grove stood a little behind him, wordlessly waiting for as long as necessary. It was not unprecedented for Sutton to behave thus, staring into the distance after a guest had departed, but this was the first time he'd done so for anyone other than Graham.

If this anomaly were to be mentioned, Sutton would have stated that he was simply gathering artistic inspiration. Yet it would be a half-hearted denial, as his mind replayed the last few exchanges with the Ashcrofts: the family's heartfelt gratitude for his hospitality; Mr Ashcroft's concerns about Ellie's health for the journey back to Hertfordshire; Mrs Ashcroft's contemplation of accepting Sutton's offer to extend their stay; and, most vividly, Miss Ashcroft's polite but firm refusal, citing their extended impositions and Mr Shepherd's declaration of her recovery. Mr Ashcroft concluded by once more inviting Sutton to Thornleigh Abbey, but this promise of returning the Ashcrofts' visit was little consolation to his sunken spirits.

When Sutton returned inside, his morning coat left droplets of water on the marble floor. In the absence of his new companions, the grandeur of Bellevue Park was heavy rather than homely. He climbed the staircase to his chambers, bathed, and dressed. Despondency covered him like a thick winter blanket, and he did not even try to shrug it off. His current state was not unfamiliar; under these circumstances, he settled for what usually followed.

'Send for Mrs Evans,' he instructed before proceeding downstairs to his studio. Knowing the woman would arrive in three quarters of an hour, Sutton took his time in preparing his work space and sharpening more pencils than required. But as he laid down one pencil and picked up another, he could not divert his eyes from the paintings he had shown Miss Ashcroft. They called to him, echoing Miss Ashcroft's attempts at praise, until all he could see in his previous pride and joy were the very flaws she had left unspoken.

He rose to remove the offending canvases. When a footman announced Mrs Evans, the viscount enlisted his help in manoeuvring the final piece, much to his guest's astonishment.

'Why, Lord Sutton, I am fond of that shipwreck! How has it offended?'

He bowed, she curtsied, and they settled into their respective chairs.

'Mrs Evans, it seems our tastes have diverged since we last met.'

'Temporarily, I hope – else it would be a terrible shame indeed.'

The viscount let out a long sigh.

'My, we're in quite a mood today,' she said, a little playfully. 'Will it be dour portraits today?'

'Always the temptress, Mrs Evans,' Sutton replied drily. 'No – I want to try some sketches to the shoulders. By the window, if you please.'

The atmosphere shifted at his command, and Mrs Evans rose to her feet, sitting on the stool as instructed. 'Hair?'

'Up, for now.' Sutton moved to his artist's seat and scrutinised the scene before him. 'Turn your head a little to the left, please. No, that's too much – yes, there. And look up. Yes – just so.'

He picked up his pencil and notebook and started on the sketch, becoming quickly absorbed in his work. Mrs Evans remained perfectly still, her golden curls darkened by the clouds outside. The two shared a long and colourful history, complete with the occasional disagreements that arose from clashing tempers, but Sutton had always admired her professionalism and her unsurpassed ability to hold poses for inordinate lengths of time. Her intelligence and wit he considered fortunate additions, and there were times when Sutton considered Mrs Evans one of his confidantes, if not a friend.

'Hair down now, same position,' he said, when the first sketch was done. 'A little more to the right – there.'

They worked for an hour or two, during which the constant scratching of Sutton's pencils and his occasional orders served as the only sounds. His mind drifted to Miss Ashcroft more than once – how would the light transform her features? might she ever give him the opportunity to find out? – but he promptly reminded himself of his present occupation. Mrs Evans's countenance and figure were of perfect proportions, and Sutton was fortunate she was such a willing subject.

After half a dozen sketches, Sutton rang for tea and, after a long look outside, for the candles to be lit. The rain had developed from a mere drizzle to a steady downpour, and he chided himself for not insisting more strongly that the Ashcrofts delay their departure for a more reasonable day. But Mr Ashcroft was a sensible man, and Sutton suspected the family would take lodgings at the inn where they were to change horses. Sutton was no longer their host; it was no longer his responsibility to ensure Miss Ashcroft would not catch a chill.

A servant's return with refreshments brought Sutton out of his reverie, and, upon remembering Mrs Evans's presence, he was faced with the altogether disconcerting knowledge that he had been caught in a moment of complete distraction. The viscount was in no mood for any of Mrs Evans's usual teasing remarks, but to her credit – and his relief – the lady was perceptive enough to recognise his solemnity.

She helped herself to some tea and sat on the chaise she usually occupied during breaks. 'A penny for your thoughts?'

'Just the one, for my considerable observations? That hardly seems fair.'

'Threepenny, then.'

Sutton smiled. 'I shan't be deceived, ma'am – empty promises will not induce me to reveal my innermost feelings.'

Mrs Evans reached into her pocket and tossed a small item at Sutton, who caught it despite his surprise. Opening his palm, Sutton looked down at the guinea and broke out into laughter.

'I expect my change at some point, sir.'

Still chuckling, Sutton nodded, turning the coin in his hand. That he and Mrs Evans inhabited separate worlds made it easy to speak to her – that she had modelled for him for seven years, and kept his confidence for the last five, ensured his words would not be repeated elsewhere.

'I recently received some negative – but not altogether incorrect – feedback about my art.'

'And do you hold his opinion in high regard?'

She was not unintelligent, and her assumption about the critic's sex revealed more about their world than her own bias. Sutton did not correct her, not wishing to expose himself more than necessary.

'No, not at first. But now...' Irked at the direction of his thoughts, Sutton stood, marking the end of that discussion. 'Are you quite finished with your tea?'

Mrs Evans, who had been privy to worse moods than this, simply took another biscuit. 'Not quite, Lord Sutton. You are always so patient with my indulgences – thank you.'

Now bristling with irritation – and more than a little ashamed of his ill manners – Sutton strode to scrutinise his sketches. He frowned at what he saw: the pencil work, while rough, was significantly lacking in passion and purpose. Even in this preliminary, most basic stage, Sutton could see the precise criticism Miss Ashcroft had the ability to perceive and the integrity to express.

'Uninspired drivel, indeed,' he muttered, setting aside the papers and picking up his penknife, though he was not lacking in sharpened pencils.

Readying his instruments was usually a calming exercise, but today, Sutton worked hard to keep his temper in check; he almost shook from the effort to remain gentle with his tools.

The small tinkle of porcelain told him Mrs Evans was done with her tea, while the soft rustling of skirts alerted him to her presence. 'Perhaps you require some inspiration, sir?'

He looked up to see her unlacing her corset, her expression impassive and professional. Sutton doubted this change of wardrobe would have much effect on his deficiencies, but it had been a while since he had practised his life drawings. When it came to the form, Mrs Evans was by far Sutton's favourite subject, and he had always welcomed the exercise.

'Perhaps I do,' he said without much enthusiasm. 'In the usual place, then.'

Mrs Evans had shed all but her chemise and was about to pull it over her head when Sutton stopped her.

'Leave it on. I want to try something different.'

She obeyed and went to recline on a seat in the studio, fashioned for this exact purpose. Mrs Evans was neither modest nor embarrassed, and simply waited for Sutton to finish sharpening his pencils and provide further instructions.

When he was done, Sutton observed the woman with a critical eye. She had been the subject of countless studies, but Sutton had never thought to draw her partially clothed. Indeed, he knew her body well, both professionally and personally, and had long considered it flawless: a full bosom, a soft and round belly, and voluptuous hips. The thin chemise hid most of her curves, but Sutton liked the way it hinted at them. He usually gave specific, almost pedantic instructions, but Sutton was satisfied with how she had arranged herself.

'Just like that.'

The woman quickly hid her surprise and remained perfectly still, save for the gentle rise and fall of her chest. He took a long moment to decide how to approach the sketch, but when he reached his conclusion, Sutton worked quickly, barely pausing for his own breath.

The sketch took half the usual time to complete, but Sutton was loathe to stop. 'Raise your left arm. Look down. Yes – there.'

He continued in such a fashion, the tip of his pencil scratching against the paper and leaving behind its imprints. When one pencil became too blunt for his liking, Sutton roughly set it aside and replaced it with a fresh one, never missing a beat in his drawing. Such a frenzied session was rare, even for one as passionate and intense as himself, and Sutton relished in the blood pounding through his body, gathering at his fingertips. But as he drew Mrs Evans in different positions, it became obvious that Sutton's eyes and mind were at odds: while the woman in front of him was sun-kissed and full-bodied, he was haunted by images of the exact opposite, of pale skin and a slim figure. He tried to dismiss the confusion, but his work suffered nonetheless, diminishing in resemblance to Mrs Evans until he knew not what – or whom – he was drawing.

He stopped somewhere in the seventh or eighth sketch and sagged in his seat from defeat. When Mrs Evans, still in her state of her undress, rose and poured him a drink, Sutton gratefully accepted, only now aware of his own thirst. But when she placed a hand on his chest and started sliding down, Sutton caught her wrist before it could reach his waist.

She withdrew from him, inquisitive. They had shared a mutual understanding about their relationship upon their first personal encounter, a few months after the death of a farmer husband who left her with two babes and no means to feed them. Sutton had agreed to become her patron, giving her a generous annual allowance for her continued modelling, as well as the occasional personal service. They would terminate the agreement at either party's discretion, and would not begrudge the other for doing so; on the contrary, they each encouraged the other to enter matrimony favourably, with Sutton facilitating the introduction of suitable candidates, and Mrs Evans providing her honest appraisal of the few ladies the viscount had considered courting.

It was an arrangement that suited them both, and in the years since its establishment, Sutton rarely turned down a personal proposition.

'Perhaps another time, sir?'

The viscount looked at the woman with whom he'd had the most longstanding dalliance, feeling nothing but goodwill.

'Perhaps,' he replied, and they both knew his words to be untrue.

17

AFTER TWO DAYS of travelling in the rain, the dark stones of Thornleigh Abbey were a welcome sight indeed. Their trip home took longer than expected, owing to the abysmal weather and the additional care they took with Ellie's health, favouring the hearth at several inns when the downpour seemed unending. Fortunately, these precautions paid off; Ellie was only a little tired upon their return and had a hearty appetite at dinner. Indeed, Kitty exceeded Ellie in her fatigue, and the older woman barely finished the first course before retiring for the evening.

And so, it was with great contentment that Ellie now sat in her favourite chaise in front of the drawing room fire, looking through the letters that had arrived during her absence. Marcus was beside her with his own correspondence, a glass of port next to him. Ellie had received a dozen odd letters, mostly from other residents of Darlington – she suspected those contained further congratulatory words about her exhibition. There were two thick letters from Harriet, and, to Ellie's joy, one from Richard.

Richard's letter was dated three days ago, when Ellie had just left Bellevue Park.

My dearest sister:

I hope you are now comfortably settled back home and are being sufficiently fussed-over by Maria, Mrs Nancy, and Mrs Rowley. I expect that, with their constant care and attention, you will soon become twice the size I remember when we next meet.

In all seriousness, my dearest sister, I do wish you would take better care of yourself. The contents of our brother's latest letter were gravely concerning, and I had considered applying for a leave of absence under the circumstances. You, who know your own limits more than anyone else can surmise, are so infuriating in your stubbornness – and still you insist on pushing yourself beyond your abilities. I can hear your huff of denial as you read this, but we are no longer children, my dear sister, and we must bear some responsibility for our own actions.

My time in the Army has influenced the latter sentiment, and I hope you will forgive me for being so forthright. While my days in the Regiment are long and often leave me bereft in the evenings, I could not be happier about my decision. The last time I had felt a semblance of this camaraderie was at Cambridge – but while university was full of schoolboys receiving some sort of education, the Regiment is rife with men who, for the most part, wish to be here to serve their country. Our names only mean as much as our efforts, and I find it altogether a breath of fresh air.

There I go, writing at length about a subject tedious to most. I have enclosed some studies of the barracks, which I hope will make up for my rambling. I miss you terribly, dearest sister – your kind and gentle soul is the only thing lacking in my new home here. Please do take care of yourself, and I greatly anticipate seeing you sometime soon.

I remain your loving brother,

Richard

It took Ellie considerable restraint to remain seated in front of the fire and not move to the writing desk tucked away in a corner of the drawing room. But Richard's concern echoed in her mind, and Ellie settled for re-reading the letter and studying his sketches instead, savouring every detail from her dear brother. She was well-accustomed to his playful and cheerful disposition, but there was a note of genuine happiness in his words. How she wished to know more about his daily life and activities, about his strenuous schedules, about his new friends. About Lord Sutton's friend, Lieutenant Graham, whom Richard had not yet mentioned, but about whom Ellie wished to enquire.

Most of all, her own happiness swelled in response to Richard's admissions. She had been the first to express reservations about his decisions, but was now the first to accept that her brother had finally found a place to call his own. Richard, who had walked in the shadow of Mr Marcus Ashcroft, was no longer held back by his past. It made Ellie question her own previous, ill-informed notions of what occurred within the army, and, in doing so, gave her yet another reason for wishing to visit the Colchester barracks.

The clock struck ten, and Marcus gave her a knowing look. Rather reluctantly, Ellie left her correspondence on the writing desk for tomorrow, kissed her brother goodnight, and headed upstairs. As she climbed the stairs, passing the family portraits that brought back memories of Bellevue Park's grand collections, Ellie's thoughts became clarified. She wished to attempt some depictions of the army, focusing not on the blood and warfare, nor the honour and glory, but the simple camaraderie and friendship that had so affected Richard. It was an unsuitable subject matter for a well-bred young lady, but, emboldened by her experiences over the past fortnight, Ellie set aside her reservations.

Perhaps Lord Sutton was right, after all – perhaps Eleanor Ashcroft needed to test her boundaries and paint not what others desired of her, but what she desired for herself.

It took Ellie the entire morning to write her letters, and it was not until after Kitty left to join her friends for afternoon tea that Ellie had a moment alone with her brother, taking their own tea in the parlour. Kitty had left in a flurry of excitement about Miss Ingram and Mr Winslow's upcoming nuptials, and while Ellie enjoyed her sister-in-law's enthusiasm, she nonetheless welcomed the peace following her departure.

Once the siblings were alone, Marcus turned to Ellie. 'How are you feeling?'

He had asked the same question in the morning, but that query had been directed at her physical health; now, he gestured at what lay deeper.

Ellie looked into her brother's blue eyes, so different from her own grey ones, and allowed the words to flow. 'I am feeling so many things, my dear brother. I am happy for Miss Ingram and Mr Winslow, and excited for Kitty, whose enthusiasm is simply contagious; I am relieved for Richard, who has settled so well in the army, but I am concerned, because the days are getting shorter, and the long nights cannot be without difficulties. Perhaps I am being singularly selfish in wishing to have Richard back at Thornleigh, where we spent the warmer days picking wildflowers in the meadows, and the colder ones playing cards and charades in front of the fire. I know we are no longer children and it is now our time to bear certain responsibilities, but...' She paused and drew in a long breath. 'Forgive me – I don't know what's taken a hold of me.'

'Ah, my dearest Ellie.' Marcus's eyes were warm, full of the same pride she saw at her debutante ball and her exhibition. 'You have grown into a fine young lady, Miss Eleanor Ashcroft – a little verbose, perhaps, but fine nonetheless.'

Ellie couldn't resist pulling a face. Marcus laughed, and it was not long before she joined in.

'But what of yourself?' he asked when they had settled down. 'How are *you* feeling, for yourself?'

She thought of all the wonderful new things she had experienced since her exhibition, and especially of their time in Cambridgeshire.

'I have had this longing,' she said, slowly and softly, 'for something...more. I long to learn more, paint more, explore more – but I do not know how to do it, or even where to start. I long to be overwhelmed by the tremendous amount of knowledge out there – but I do not know where I can find such a place. Even when I was awed by Lord Sutton's private collection, I knew it is merely a small portion of what is out there. Oh, how I long to see for myself the paintings and sculptures on the Continent that have survived thousands of years! The more I see of the world, the more am I dissatisfied with my own lack of experience and understanding; and every day confirms my belief that what I *think* I know forms only a small portion of how much *more* there is to learn.'

Her feelings became too much, and Ellie required a moment to compose herself. Marcus waited patiently, showing none of the disapproval she had feared.

'Those longings frighten me,' she continued. 'I do not enjoy travelling for long distances, and I am anxious and reserved in the face of strangers. I know not how to attain what I wish for, and the truth of my own inadequacies saddens me. Perhaps Mr Hill was right – true art belongs to the domain of men.'

'Mr Hill was *not* right,' Marcus said fiercely. 'Not about "true art", not about your talents, not about many things. I'm sorry I misjudged his character.'

Ellie managed a small smile. 'Please don't be – Richard and I had become experts at fooling everyone, especially Mr Hill. And *you*, dearest brother, had all these responsibilities thrust upon you, not least having to look after Richard and me. I'm grateful you found us a knowledgeable art instructor. Though Mr Hill was unaware of it, he taught me how to think for myself, and how to collaborate with Richard – I wouldn't change any of that for the world.'

Marcus placed a hand over hers, needing to compose himself before continuing. 'Dearest Ellie, I am proud of you beyond words. I hope you'll indulge me in answering one thing: do you wish to pursue art beyond a lady's accomplishment, and with the rigours of a professional artist?'

It was a question that pained her brother to ask and was discomforting for Ellie to answer. Yet when she set aside the various reasons and reasoning, the apprehension and fears, her answer was pure and simple.

'Yes. I don't know how, or if it will be possible, but yes. I do wish it.'

Marcus inhaled deeply. 'I will be honest with you, Ellie: I have many reservations about your choices. But if I am to learn anything from my reaction to Richard's decision last year, it is that I cannot allow my prejudices to determine your future. You are determined and talented, my dear Ellie, and

I will support you to the best of my ability.'

He paused for another moment.

'We have friends who might be able to assist in your journey,' he said. 'I will write to them for their advice.'

'Thank you.' Marcus still had his hand upon Ellie's, and she turned her palm up to give it a gentle squeeze. 'You are the best brother one could have.'

She had hoped her words and gesture would convey both her gratitude and her understanding of his dilemma, and, judging from the way Marcus's eyes misted again while he smiled, he had felt every sentiment.

VOLUME II

18

NOT A WEEK after the Ashcrofts had departed and Sutton had his encounter with Mrs Evans, the master of Bellevue Park set out for London alone. The skies had cleared a little in the interim, but the few days of rain were a prelude to autumn – the chilly season had well and truly set in. His journey south was littered with autumn leaves, which always took him by surprise year after year; the shift appeared to take place overnight, with the lush summer greens replaced with the oranges and yellows, fluttering against the north wind.

He arrived at his townhouse in time for afternoon tea, but Sutton was restless, finding fault at every turn. The rooms weren't properly aired, the fires not warm enough, the tea too weak, the sandwiches without flavour. His arrival had been unannounced, even to his skeleton staff, and though the viscount knew he would be ashamed of his temper once he had calmed a little, he did not hold back his displeasure.

After he finished reprimanding his butler, Sutton asked for his correspondence and became more morose upon finding nothing in the tray of cards and letters from the last week. The Season itself would not start until after Christmas, and Sutton had given no notice of his visit, but his pride was wounded at this perceived slight. He was Lord *Sutton*, and his London visits were *always* accompanied by copious invitations and engagements. Had his absence from town over the last month rendered him irrelevant? Was he forgotten by the droves of thespians and philanderers whose palates changed with every season? Would he be reduced to seeking the company of men who had once called on him with great fervour?

No – it would *not* do. He would spend a few hours at White's – an ample amount of time to announce his arrival in London – and see what other entertainment arose in the evening. His resolution steeled him, and Sutton rang for the valet to dress him.

Before he went upstairs, the viscount poured two glasses of brandy and drank a generous amount of his own, leaving the second glass untouched in the morning room.

It was for his butler, who would understand the apology.

Well into his fifth brandy, Sutton found it difficult to refrain from overtly disagreeing with his companions. He had been warmly welcomed by his artistic circle convening at White's this afternoon, but despite the familiar comforts of the viscount's favourite gentlemen's club, Sutton was far from appeased. A significant shift had occurred within Sutton these past few months and he no longer found the present conversation appealing.

'In my opinion,' Mr Byrd was saying, 'Mr Turner's latest works do not defy the conventions enough. If an artist finds himself bound by any limitations, whether societal or personal, then he loses the right to call himself an artist.'

The Baron Marchand nodded with a severity that was almost comical. 'Indeed, sir. For what is an artist, if he is not challenging the status quo?'

'An imitator,' replied a third, a Mr Gulliver.

Mr Byrd shook his head gravely. 'And an imitator might as well call himself a philistine,' he said.

'But what about the beautiful or pleasing?' asked Lord Marchand. 'Isn't good art something that can also be enjoyed?'

'*Anyone* can enjoy the beautiful,' Mr Byrd replied with much vitriol, 'but only a select few can recognise and understand the very *soul* of a work – and that, my friends, is hardly visible to the masses.'

Sutton couldn't help but scoff at this, and the gentlemen's attention turned to him.

'Do you disagree, Lord Sutton?' Mr Byrd asked. 'You've not said much on the topic – I, for one, would very much like to hear your opinion.'

In fact, Sutton had not said a single world since they began their discussion on aesthetics, and, had he not drawn the men's attention, Sutton would have been perfectly happy keeping his opinion to himself. Even now, he didn't wish to voice his thoughts, not for the fear of causing offence and controversy, but because he didn't wish to waste any more of his time with these imbeciles.

'I disagree on more than one account,' he said, in too ill a temper to be more diplomatic. 'Who are you to judge what is beautiful, what is worthy, what has *soul*? Who are you to judge what the *masses* see and don't see?'

Mr Byrd bristled at this and opted to pit his superior years over Sutton. 'I have developed, over my considerable lifetime, the knowledge and skills to make these distinctions. The masses, while they might be able to appreciate the occasional pieces of art, nonetheless lack the breeding required to distinguish true art from what's simply pleasing – and often soulless.'

'Are you suggesting that a thorough understanding of art, and the ability to make any related judgements, are wholly dependent on breeding, *Mister Byrd*?'

The older man stilled, and Sutton saw he had hit the mark. Were he in a more gracious mood, Sutton would have followed up his cutting remark with something more light-hearted, but as it were, he had tired of Mr Byrd's pretentious manner and was angry at himself for not having noticed such behaviour years ago. Swirling the brandy in his glass, Sutton sat back leisurely to wait for a response.

'Lord Sutton,' he began, instantly acknowledging Sutton's status, and, by extension, his own defeat, 'your query veers too close to the epistemological for me to answer. I concede my knowledge can be quite limited in this regard.'

Sutton nodded and straightened his waistcoat. 'Gentlemen, I'm afraid I'm presently unfit for such intellectual discussions. I bid you goodnight.'

He rose and left, indifferent to the muttered remarks behind him.

Sutton made his customary visit to Savile Row the next day, and allowed himself one more engagement in the evening, this time by attending dinner at Mr de Lancie's. A gentleman with both the means and appetite for society, Mr de Lancie spent far more time in London with his aunt and sisters than at his family seat with his parents. Indeed, on the few occasions when Mr de Lancie ventured into the countryside, he and his entourage more often than not wound up in Bellevue Park. Sutton always welcomed Mr de Lancie's visits, and received an equally warm welcome in the gentleman's London lodgings.

'I'm so pleased to see you,' Mr de Lancie said when Sutton entered the drawing room. 'How long has it been – four or five months? What brings you to town – and what has kept you away so long?'

The viscount accepted a glass of sherry. 'You know – this and that. I'd read about Brummell's latest styles, but I wasn't much impressed in person.'

'And a real shame too,' agreed Mr de Lancie, who was loosely acquainted with the dandy. 'Our poor Beau – I don't think he's ever recovered from the incident. I hear Prinny's blacklisted anyone who still favours Beau.'

Sutton scoffed, all too familiar with the Prince Regent's antics. 'I don't suppose the War has done anything in Brummell's favour.'

'No indeed.' Mr de Lancie sighed, shaking his head. 'In truth, I've been struggling to navigate the fine line between austerity and extravagance. I may think Prinny's spending habits are deplorable, but I myself often indulge in the very same manner.'

'Your awareness does you much credit,' replied Sutton. 'Besides, no one can fault you for finding ways to nourish your soul.'

The gentleman smiled. 'Well put, my friend. On that note, have you been playing anything for four hands? I've been drawn to them since some friends played two Mozart keyboard duets. Köchel 381 and 497, if I remember correctly.'

Sutton replied that he had not.

'They're both quite extraordinary, if a little old-fashioned. Herr Beethoven has also composed a few – I've managed to track down a few sheets of some variations he published ten or twenty years ago. Would you care to join me sometime?'

'I'd be delighted. At Bellevue, perhaps? I suppose it's time to acquire a second pianoforte – for I know you certainly won't.'

Mr de Lancie laughed, not at all embarrassed about his vocal disdain for the modern instrument. 'I would give you mine, but all the modern music requires gradual changes in dynamics so I've no choice but keep at least one pianoforte. Whatever happened to good old terracing?'

'We could play them on your Baroque keyboards – though who knows to what effect.'

'So long as Herr Beethoven doesn't find out we're abusing his compositions,' Mr de Lancie said with a smile. 'I'll order another copy of the sheets and send them to you. Are you in London long this time?'

'I think not. I intend to visit Graham in Colchester soon, and return to Bellevue thereafter.'

'Shame – there are some soirees next week you might enjoy. How is the old chap? Not yet regretting his decision to refuse his inheritance?'

'He's been promoted to Lieutenant – all on his own merit, mind you – so I'd say he's never looked back.'

Mr de Lancie's amazement made Sutton feel proud of his friend. 'He must be the first lieutenant I know who did not purchase his commission. My goodness, I doubt I'd survive an entire week there.'

'You and me both.'

'Do give him my best,' said Mr de Lancie. 'I hope to see him again soon, either in London or Bellevue.'

This exchange proved to be the highlight of Sutton's evening – not long after Mr de Lancie went to attend to his other guests, Sutton was ambushed by a young man he'd met once previously, and whose enthusiasm in their conversation was far disproportionate to their level of acquaintance. Not wishing to offend any guests who weren't his own, Sutton could only nod politely and make the occasional remark, all the while waiting for the man – whose name he didn't quite catch the first time round, and didn't ask for after a good length of time had elapsed – to recognise his faux pas and leave Sutton in peace. Unfortunately, the man interpreted Sutton's noncommittal responses as stoic encouragement, and thus, Sutton endured the assault for three quarters of an hour. He could not remember being so relieved as when dinner was finally announced.

He was seated between Mr Seymour and Mr Finch, neither of whom he had offended in recent memory. Since Mr Finch was speaking to his other neighbour, Sutton nodded to the man on his left and formulated the appropriate words.

'Mr Seymour, it is a pleasure to see you again. Is your family well? How has Mrs Seymour taken to Kent?'

'Very well, thank you. And you, Lord Sutton? What brings you to London this time?'

'Mr de Lancie's dinners, of course.' His light quip was opportunely timed, for their host had taken his seat and the first course was brought in.

After starting on his soup, Mr Seymour said, 'I believe the last time we spoke, you were in the midst of obtaining some early Caravaggio sketches. What was the result of your quest?'

'Ah yes, those elusive wonders!' Sutton was surprised the other man had remembered. The two men had not spoken in almost a year, but the viscount now recalled Mr Seymour had proven himself a connoisseur of the arts. 'I traced them back to Sicily and was able to acquire a couple at a rather hefty sum.'

'Congratulations on your acquisition. Have they lived up to your expectations?'

'Quite. It's extraordinary to see the sketches that preceded his early masterpieces.'

'Yes, indeed,' said Mr Seymour, with an indifference Sutton found wholly unsuitable to such discussions. 'However, I myself am much more partial to later Baroque works, which are considerably more developed and sophisticated.'

'Is that so?'

'Why, of course. Later Baroque works on the whole contain technique and artistry far superior to their predecessors – a detail not lost on you, I am sure. Just as the Ancient Greeks learnt how to differentiate the mediocre from the excellent, so too has our age inherited a fine eye for detail. I, for one, am honoured to be reviving these sentiments.'

Mr Seymour continued on, but Sutton had stopped paying attention. While he did not disagree with the gentleman's sentiments, the viscount thought the repeated assertions pompous and distasteful. Sutton had been long acquainted with this brand of excessive posturing and arguing for argument's sake, but he no longer found the exercise appealing.

It wasn't until the tablecloths were changed twice more that Sutton was able to extricate himself from the conversation, which Mr Finch had joined since the second course. The exchanges had been so full of airs and graces, and so completely devoid of a fruitful discussion, that Sutton found himself quite irritable by the end of the meal. Having endured till dessert, the viscount turned down the offer of brandy and made for their host.

'Mr de Lancie,' he said, 'thank you for a delectable dinner, but I'm afraid I must take my leave.'

'Of course – another engagement this evening?'

An image of a glowing fire and a glass of port in his study flashed in Sutton's mind. 'Something of the sort.'

His friend nodded with a tell-tale smile. 'It was good to see you, my friend. I'll have those sheets sent to Bellevue, but do call again if you decide to remain in London this Season.'

'Likewise, Mr de Lancie. Thank you for your hospitality.'

His despondency, alleviated by his walk home in the cool autumn night, set in again when he reached his townhouse just past nine o'clock. The evening had just begun for the *Ton*, but Sutton felt no inclination to partake in any of the available entertainment. The purpose of this trip had been to regain some inspiration and to lift his spirits, but his senseless ennui had only worsened in face of society. There was nothing he wanted to do, and only a few people he truly wanted to see – and they were not in London.

He had barely warmed the fireplace in his townhouse, but Sutton was now determined to set out for Colchester at dawn. It mattered not that the army would be busy and Graham indisposed for the most part. Sutton would happily volunteer and assist the barracks in any capacity, and he would not be deterred.

19

MR AND MRS TOM WINSLOW'S wedding date was marked by incessant rain, but the newlyweds hardly seemed to notice. After the ceremony finished, the wedding party and guests made the short journey from the local Darlington church to Mr Winslow's house where breakfast was served. There was barely any room between the tables, even with the adjustments made to the dining and ball rooms to accommodate the Winslows' family and friends – it seemed all of Darlington's residents were invited to celebrate the happy union.

Fortunately for Ellie, the Ashcrofts were seated with the Earlwoods and Ingrams. Mr Ingram was looking a little pale but was otherwise in good spirits, while Mrs Ingram wore a lovely green gown for the occasion. She had exhausted her own handkerchief in church and had to borrow Kitty's during the wedding breakfast.

It was not until around noon that Ellie and her family had the opportunity to approach the newlyweds and congratulate them directly. While Kitty paid Phoebe many compliments about her dress and hair, Ellie curtsied to Mr Winslow.

'Congratulations on your nuptials,' she said. 'I wish you and Mrs Winslow all the happiness in the world.'

'Thank you,' Mr Winslow replied, a twinkle in his eyes. 'Though I'm sure our days wouldn't be without the occasional bickering.'

She smiled meekly at this and ducked her head. On the few occasions they'd met, Ellie had been taken aback by Mr Winslow, whose sarcastic remarks and exaggeration often veered towards the buffoonish. His previous altercations with Phoebe had left the poor woman more than a little injured, and Ellie could not understand how Kitty thought the pair well-matched.

Having heard Mr Winslow's declaration, Kitty said, 'Please do invite me to adjudicate during the said bickering sessions.'

Ellie's smile became a little forced while the other three laughed outright. Unlike Kitty, who had been childhood friends with the bride and groom, Ellie – and the rest of Darlington – had only witnessed the courtship from a distance. Kitty had alluded to the part she played in their eventual engagement, but Ellie had not enquired into the details, nor had she questioned her sister-in-law's involvement. Now was certainly not the time to begin such unpleasant musings; instead, Ellie drew out the small gift she had prepared for the newlyweds, feeling rather nervous about its reception.

Recognising Ellie's discomfort, Kitty remarked: 'Ah, Ellie has a gift for you both.'

Ellie held out the small package in her hands. 'It's just a little something I thought you might like,' she said softly.

'Thank you, Ellie,' said Phoebe. She unwrapped the small package, removing a picture frame that was clasped together. Phoebe opened it gently and gasped in delight at the likeness of the new husband and wife in each side of the swivel frame.

'Oh, Ellie, this is beautiful!'

Phoebe held it out to Mr Winslow, who regarded it with wonder. When he spoke again, his voice was as solemn as when he had exchanged wedding vows.

'Miss Ashcroft, you are extraordinarily gifted. Phoebe and I will treasure this – thank you.'

Ellie's smile was no longer forced as she curtsied and said, 'You're very welcome, Mr and Mrs Winslow.'

The party exchanged a few more congratulations before Phoebe said, 'Ellie, I know I'm asking a great deal of you, but I would be much obliged if you would prepare some portraits for us all, especially for my dear Papa. If you do not object, I would also like to compensate you for your time – or for your paints, at the very least.'

These last words were uttered both quickly and quietly, and both women blushed at the implications. On the one hand, Ellie was extraordinarily pleased about having received what could be rightly concluded as her first artistic commission; on the other, the introduction of compensation was a base concept that would certainly offend her eldest brother, if Mr Ashcroft discovered the conversation. Yet Ellie understood Phoebe's wish to show her gratitude, and while Ellie herself would never attach any monetary value to her work, she liked the idea of proper recognition under the correct circumstances.

'I am very humbled by your suggestion,' she said slowly. 'I am also very fond of your gardenias – perhaps you might be willing to part with some of them, to add some light and colour to Thornleigh? I would like that very much.'

'Yes, of course!' The last trace of embarrassment disappeared from Phoebe's countenance. 'That is a fine idea – thank you, Ellie.'

As Ellie and her family bade the newlyweds farewell, Mr Digby began approaching the couple. He was wearing a yellow coat both ill-fitting and too bright. She was too far to hear his words, but Ellie nonetheless found his idiosyncrasies and cheerful attire endearing.

20

COLONEL SAMUEL WATSON, the commanding officer of the British Army's Fifth Regiment of Foot, regarded Sutton with a severe gaze that made him feel like a small boy. During their previous acquaintance in Darlington, both Sutton and the Colonel had been mutually respectful equals who both understood that Graham was their common factor. Even when Sutton accepted the Colonel's invitation to lodge at Birkenbridge House for several weeks, the viscount had been acquainted with the man behind the uniform.

Now seated across the Colonel's imposing desk in a room filled with maps and missives, Sutton came to appreciate how a uniform could change a man. Prior to leaving London, the viscount had hastily written to the Colonel about his intentions to volunteer at the barracks, feeling rather pleased with himself at his generosity. But in the presence of the Colonel's silent and severe assessment, Sutton could only hope his letter had not contained anything overly foolish.

Just when Sutton considered aborting his mission and apologising instead, the Colonel broke his silence. 'I understand you and Lieutenant Graham share a very close bond.'

'Yes, sir. We are practically brothers.'

'And I understand you and Lieutenant Graham also share some common interests and leisure activities.'

Sutton nodded and, realising the implications, replied more solemnly, 'Yes, sir.'

'It is not in my power – or my prerogative – to prevent you from remaining close to the barracks, especially as you have acquired your own accommodation. But while *you* bear no formal obligations to the British Army, the same cannot be said for Lieutenant Graham. Indeed, the situation on the Continent remains in flux, and every Regiment across the country is preparing for an upcoming campaign.'

The truth left Sutton quite chastened. 'I understand, sir.'

The Colonel gave him another long look. 'I have no doubt you do, Lord Sutton. Nor do I doubt your intention to volunteer here. But more than that – and I hope you will forgive my frankness – it is your financial or material contributions that would prove the most useful. The soldiers need to be fed and clothed, and there is only so much His Majesty's coffers can provide.'

Sutton nodded, all too familiar with the issue. When Graham first joined the army, he had been appalled and saddened by some of the disparities between the rich and poor. As every officer was responsible for acquiring and maintaining his own livery, the pecuniary differences were visible amongst soldiers who had, for the most part, set aside their backgrounds. Graham himself had seen his fair share of cold winter nights, until Sutton, who could not sit idly by the fireplace while his dearest friend suffered, commissioned and sent Graham the finest woollen livery he could find. But Graham had been upset by what he saw as unnecessary charity, and the two friends had partaken in one of their most serious arguments.

But these current circumstances were entirely different; the current issue was about neither Graham, nor Sutton, nor their respective pride, but a company of officers and their new recruits who were doing their utmost to protect and serve their country. Sutton refused to watch the men freeze through another winter, and he was certain Graham felt the same. And if the lieutenant had any qualms, Sutton could refer them to the Colonel.

His decision made, Sutton retrieved his calling cards and borrowed one of the Colonel's pens. 'Here are my steward's details. Please relay the specifics to him – he will see to it.'

'Thank you, Lord Sutton.' The Colonel softened, and Sutton glimpsed the man behind the uniform. 'We are all grateful for your generosity.'

'It is entirely my pleasure.'

Colonel Watson nodded, and looked at his pocket watch. 'It's still the luncheon hour – I believe Lieutenant Graham will be in the mess hall.'

Heeding the dismissal, Sutton tucked away his card case, rose, and bowed to the Colonel. 'I will not distract the lieutenant from his duties, sir – you have my word.'

Sutton located the mess hall with no great difficulty, and found his friend at a table across the room. He made his way to Graham, nodding to a number of officers who responded in kind and paid the viscount no particular attention. While his well-travelled and slightly unkempt appearance had done him no favours with the Colonel, it served him well here.

Graham saw him a little before he reached the table, joy and surprise lighting the lieutenant's face. 'Heavens, I did not expect to see you so soon!' Graham exclaimed. 'What brings you here?'

'The company, of course.' Sutton nodded at one of the men he recognised. 'Lieutenant Hammond, it is very good to see you.'

'Likewise, Lord Sutton,' said Hammond.

Sutton waved a hand at this. 'Perhaps we should dispense with such unnecessary titles and refer to one another as equals.'

Graham grinned. 'Does the Colonel know you're here?'

'I wouldn't dare intrude without his permission.'

'Rightly so. But before we disregard decorum completely, perhaps a few introductions are in order?' Graham paused briefly, and Sutton nodded his assent. 'Lord Sutton, I'm pleased to introduce you to Lieutenant Fielding, Ensign Smith, and Ensign Ashcroft. Gentlemen, this is Aubrey Charles Beaumont, the 7th Viscount Sutton.'

If Sutton had not known of Ensign Ashcroft's relations, he would have easily passed by the younger man in a crowd; now, Sutton saw past the man's different colouring from his siblings and noted the familiar set of his jaw and a certain brightness in his eyes.

'It's a pleasure to meet you all.'

The other men responded in kind. Then, without further preamble, Ensign Ashcroft said: 'Lord Sutton, I know you have shown the utmost kindness to my family, and for that, I am in your debt.'

While this impassioned declaration was not altogether appropriate for two new acquaintances, Sutton approved of the young man's tenacity and, more importantly, his sincerity. This boy was most certainly related to Miss Ashcroft.

'I am honoured,' Sutton said, keeping his tone light, 'but you ought not indebt yourself so quickly – especially since, as you may have learned from Lieutenant Graham, I am wont to call on my friends at the most inopportune moments and cajole them into abandoning their posts.'

As soon as the words left his lips, Sutton worried he had gone a little too far, too soon – but his apprehensions were assuaged when Richard Ashcroft laughed and the other men followed.

'It's quite true,' Graham said, still chuckling. 'I've often found myself unceremoniously dragged to a hunting trip or an art exhibition without any prior arrangement, or any say in the matter.'

'I don't think I care much for either,' the younger man said, wrinkling his nose and sparking another round of laughter.

This launched a discussion of the men's personal interests, the more experienced officers advising on how to maintain some of life's pleasures despite their long days and nights in the regiment. As agreed upon, they disposed of formal addresses thereafter, referring to one another by surname only. Sutton, who had inherited his father's auxiliary titles since birth and had equated the absence of his title with either familiarity or rudeness, was at first taken aback by his name being passed around so easily amongst his company. His mind understood the advantages of this new address, but it took his instincts a little longer to register the same.

The time passed by quickly, and it was not long before the small group parted ways. Before they left the mess hall, Sutton invited Graham to drinks and conversation at his rented Colchester house in the evening, which his friend happily accepted. Sutton left the barracks in high spirits, intent on providing instructions to his steward and staff at Bellevue Park. He expected to remain in Colchester for a few weeks at least, and he intended to make the most of his time here.

It was almost eleven when Graham arrived at Sutton's Colchester house and was shown into the drawing room. The viscount had spent his evening reading some manuals for officers of the British Army, and was so engrossed in the book that he had left his drink mostly untouched. When Graham's arrival was announced, Sutton rose to pour a second glass for his friend.

'What are you reading? And is that gin?' Graham asked by way of greeting, while he shook out his messy hair and deftly retied it. Sutton offered the glass and held up the book. 'Ah yes, the good Baron de Rothenburg. An excellent source of drills, with some very useful tips for the uninitiated.'

They sat opposite the fire, with Graham on the left and Sutton on the right. This was their unspoken positions, and though everything else about the drawing room was unfamiliar, the two friends made the space their own.

'How would you rate the *Regulations* now that you've gained some experience with the permanent regimental life?' asked Sutton.

'Quite acceptable. You've reminded me – I ought to find copies for all the new recruits.'

Sutton took a sip of his gin and grimaced.

'Too rough for your refined tastes?' Graham sampled his own glass and emerged unscathed. 'This is much better than what we have – we ought to roughen you up a bit if you truly intend to remain in Colchester for the time being.'

'Then I have yet another reason to pray for the war's conclusion.'

Graham laughed outright, eliciting a smile from the viscount.

'And you've yet to try our meals,' Graham quipped. 'Your delicate sensibilities will have you packed and away in Scotland before the rest of us can queue for seconds.'

'I do happen to consider haggis a delicacy, if you must know,' replied Sutton mildly. 'But I shall remember to keep the finer drinks from you, given you sorely lack the ability to appreciate them.'

'I appreciate your collection very much indeed,' Graham said, eyes twinkling, 'but I am also happy to drink the dubious substance we poor soldiers can afford.'

'Well then, please help yourself to the bottle, and to the dozen or so tucked away in the cellar.'

He rose briefly to ring for a servant, requesting a bottle of brandy he had brought with him from London. This new glass Sutton drank with great relish.

'Now this, my friend, is a proper drop.'

Graham gestured to the first bottle. 'How did you come by a dozen of this?'

'The housekeeper has relations working at the local distillery – the Hull Mill, I think it's called. I thought it wouldn't hurt to try.'

'The Hull only built a distillery a year or two ago – we both know you prefer your spirits aged to "perfection"!'

Sutton shrugged. 'The housekeeper was very persuasive.'

'Which I would believe, if you were one so easily persuaded.' Graham shook his head, a smile on his lips. 'For all your aloof exteriors, my dear friend, you have a heart of gold.'

The viscount waved off the compliment. 'I'd thought becoming a lieutenant would cure you of such nonsense – especially after such a long day. I take it you must be up early?'

'Oh yes – we start drills at six in the morning and usually head for bed at eleven or twelve in the evening. But you know, I still admire the constitution of our mutual acquaintances who can play cards until seven in the morning and rise at noon to prepare for the next party. Military training is nothing compared to *those* exertions.'

'Your admiration is much misplaced,' Sutton said, rather severely.

'Is that so?' There was twinkle in Graham's eyes. 'Is your sudden arrival in Colchester due to a certain level of…disillusionment with the *Ton*?'

Sutton scoffed. 'Mere "disillusionment" is putting it far too politely. I might even have to concede that you were right about London society.'

'Now now, let's not say anything you'll regret in the morning.' Graham softened. 'London's loss is my gain. And for what it's worth, I think it very noble of you – not only for coming to aid us, but also for speaking with the Colonel instead of…'

'Instead of just milling about?'

'Precisely.' With cheek, Graham added, 'Though you have undoubtedly made "milling about" quite an art form.'

Sutton allowed himself a small smile. 'Naturally. But do let me know if you need any provisions – not just for the army, but for yourself.'

The lieutenant glanced at the small pile of logs beside the fireplace and looked knowingly back at Sutton. 'Now that you mention it, winter *is* almost upon us, and firewood doesn't chop itself…'

And here, finally, Sutton laughed, letting the tensions uncoil from his body. His friend grinned and added another log to the fire before refilling their glasses.

When the lieutenant had settled back in his chair, he said: 'I received news from my cousin – the one with the Graham inheritance. He seems to be handling the estates well, and has made the effort to visit the tenants personally. The more time passes, the happier I am about my decision.'

Sutton nodded, neither disputing nor agreeing with his friend. The viscount could not deny his friend had found his calling, but he still needed to accept Graham's new responsibilities and priorities – none of which involved Sutton.

As if sensing his rumination, Graham turned away from the merry fire and studied the viscount carefully. 'How are you?'

'I don't know,' Sutton replied honestly. 'I am conflicted, and restless, and there is no written manual to offer any assistance. Most of all, I am uninspired. Everything I create is mediocre at best. It would be pitiful were it not so insufferable.'

Graham nodded in sympathy. He took another sip of his drink. 'Any sightings of Lady Lavender?'

Sutton gave Graham his best glower. 'Not now, James. It's bad enough you include that in every damn postscript.'

The lieutenant turned to face Sutton, his expression patient and kind. It was enough invitation for the viscount.

'I feel powerless, James. So much is beyond my control – I cannot find peace anywhere in this wretched world.'

'Yet you decide to rent a house next to one of the largest barracks in Great Britain,' Graham said gently. 'It seems the peace you seek can only be found here.' Graham placed a hand upon his own heart.

Sutton's low grumble was his only response.

'My dear Aubrey, you are always shouldering burdens that are not yours to carry. Your authority and responsibilities start and end in Bellevue – even there, you cannot command the sky or the soil. But you *can* command yourself, my friend. Find a way to assist the war effort, spend time with us lowly soldiers, keep an open mind – there's no need to burden yourself with anything else.'

Sutton sighed softly before rising to refill their glasses once more. The two men sat in silence for a quarter of an hour, watching the fire together. There was no need for anything more; this comfortable companionship was precisely what Sutton needed.

Graham rose to leave when the clock struck half eleven. Sutton followed suit, picking up the book he had set aside.

'Take it for the new recruits,' he said. 'I'm pretty much finished.'

'I will. Thank you.'

Sutton walked his friend to the entrance, already a little forlorn. Nonetheless, he bowed to the soldier with much exaggeration. 'Goodnight, Lieutenant Graham.'

'Goodnight, Lord Sutton. I'll see you in the morrow.'

Sutton watched his friend leave, and stood watching long after he had left.

21

IN THE MONTH following the Winslows' wedding, Mr Ingram visited Thornleigh Abbey a total of eleven times for his portrait sitting. Mr Ingram proved pleasant company, content to read his book and allowing Ellie to work in silence. The initial sketches were quickly made, but transferring them onto a canvas proved more challenging. Ellie initially struggled with the colour palette. She associated everyone in her close acquaintance with a principal colour, which darkened and lightened according to their moods: Marcus was tawny, rich and warm and comforting; Richard was amber, steady and bright; and Kitty crimson, assertive and bold. She did not know Mr Ingram well enough to form her own conclusion about his colours, and it was Kitty who finally imparted some advice in her typically blunt fashion: Phoebe was partial to pinks and yellows, and this portrait was for her new home.

Once these crucial decisions were made, the painting quickly took shape and form. Outside, the days grew shorter and colder; inside Ellie's corner, she used her brushes and paints to capture one of Darlington's most beloved figures. She would soon be applying the finishing touches, and there would be time enough for the canvas to be framed and presented.

But even as she dedicated herself to Mr Ingram's portrait, another work, half-formed yet persistent, lingered in Ellie's mind. Amongst her piles of papers, hidden from sight, were the ideas of a scene she had pieced together from the various sketches Richard had sent her. The final image was vivid every night, but became elusive in the light of day: an image of soldiers on the eve of battle, bent over a fire, their bodies hunched from the cold, their jaws set with determination. It was an image that haunted her, filling the gaps between the sheets Richard sent to her, pulling at her heart. She had never been so struck with a desire to paint; she had never felt so bewildered about having to begin.

So Ellie's sketches lay in its pile, growing steadily into the last autumn days, waiting for Ellie to gather the courage and set a blank canvas onto her spare easel while she busied herself with another work.

Her routine broke in the last week of November when a letter from an unfamiliar name arrived at breakfast. They had been discussing Ellie's upcoming birthday, for which she only wanted a small gathering, when the morning mail arrived. Ellie turned the letter in her hands, curious about its contents, yet feeling quite obliged to pass it to Marcus at the other end of the table. She was still deliberating when Kitty, who noticed the young woman's consternation, peered across and said:

'Who is Mr A. N. Livingston of Piccadilly? Do we know anyone from Piccadilly?'

His attention piqued, Marcus folded away his newspaper. 'Ellie?'

She could not prevent the blush that crept into her cheeks, though she was not guilty of any indiscretions. 'I don't recognise the name or the hand.'

Ellie held out the letter to Marcus, who gave her a considered look before declining. 'It may pertain to your artwork,' he said quietly. 'The letter is yours to open.'

Her fingers were a little unsteady as she broke the seal, but her voice was firm when she read aloud its contents.

Dear Miss Ashcroft:

I hope you do not find it discourteous of me to contact you thus. I am a private agent based in London, and I currently represent over twenty artists, some of whom are ladies from respectable families. I have received high commendations of your work from a respected acquaintance, who informed me of a private exhibition you held in September. After making enquiries amongst my peers and colleagues, I have found your work is hitherto undiscovered.

As the collection, evaluation, and promotion of art – especially the works of lesser known artists – lie within my professional interests, I write to you to obtain permission to see your works in person. I would be more than happy to oblige if you do not wish for your identity to be made public, or if you wish for one of your family members to meet me in your stead. I consider it a personal and professional duty to treat these matters with the strictest confidence.

I enclose here my card and a list of references for your perusal. I look forward to hearing from you in the near future.

Yours sincerely,

A. N. Livingston, Esq.

There was a second page with at least a dozen references, and Ellie noted some familiar names. She held out both sheets to her brother, not quite managing to meet his eyes.

Kitty, however, did not hold back her pleasure. 'This is most wonderful news, dearest Ellie! Oh, a private agent with an eye for art – and a representative of other ladies such as yourself! Most wonderful news, indeed! Don't you agree, Marcus?'

'It is indeed,' replied Marcus. 'I would have preferred if Mr Livingston wrote to me directly, but I applaud his foresight in providing those references. I know three of these gentlemen and I will write them promptly.'

Ellie gathered her courage to look at her brother. 'You are not displeased?'

Marcus gave her a small smile. 'As I've said, I would have been more pleased if he had addressed me instead – but that is beside the point. This is excellent news for you, dear Ellie, and I shall support you every step of the way.'

'Thank you, dearest brother.'

'In the meantime, you might wish to consider the options of either meeting him yourself or assigning your proxy.'

Ellie had already decided. 'I wish to meet him, either with you or with Kitty – or both. I do not know what will come of this, if anything, but I would wish to explain my works and answer any questions he may have.'

Her brother nodded while Kitty enthusiastically offered to chaperone.

'I suppose we are finished with breakfast, then?' asked Marcus playfully. 'I know *I* have several letters to write.'

Kitty folded away her napkin. 'Oh yes, let's get to it. I've been meaning to write to Mama – it's been a few weeks since I last heard from her and Christopher.'

'And I'd like to share the news with Richard,' added Ellie. 'I'm aware nothing may come of this correspondence with Mr Livingston, but I think he'll enjoy the news.'

Marcus nodded. 'Of course. And if these references are in agreement about Mr Livingston's good character, then I see no reason why you can't respond to him directly.'

Their purpose decided, the Ashcrofts left the breakfast room for the adjoining parlour, where they settled at their respective writing tables – a rare occurrence, given Kitty was not the most fastidious with her correspondence and Marcus often conducted his from his study. The thought of all three spending their morning in this fashion made Ellie smile.

When they had barely sat down, Kitty interrupted the silence thus: 'I wonder which of our mutual acquaintances informed Mr Livingston of Ellie's exhibition.'

'That is indeed a mystery,' replied Marcus.

Ellie voiced her agreement, then focused on the task at hand. She had written to Richard almost daily since autumn began, the words sometimes spilling forth faster than her hand could comprehend. But there was something different about this morning as she started the letter with her usual greetings; an image of the unnamed soldiers around the fireplace came to her mind, unbidden. It remained just long enough for Ellie to know precisely what she wanted in her final sketches – a task that required Richard's assistance.

She set to work with her news and her request. Her nib tinkled when she dipped it in the ceramic inkwell, a sound echoed by her brother and sister's pens. Soon, the parlour was filled with the soothing scratching of pen on paper, which continued well into the morning.

22

WHEN SUTTON FIRST befriended Graham many years ago, the two boys spending the better part of their days climbing trees and skipping stones, the viscount would not have thought it possible that their friendship would land him in a foreign part of England, taking luncheon with hundreds of men from various – and sometimes dubious – backgrounds, in a mess hall where notions of table settings and service were altogether discarded. He would not have thought it possible that he, the 7th Viscount Sutton, would be developing an easy camaraderie with boys and men who, had they met outside the peculiar sanctity of the Colchester Garrison, would have passed his notice.

Yet here he was, listening to Ensign Smith from Shropshire regale them with a childhood tale about his peddler family; here, enthralled by Lieutenant Fielding from Cumbria, whose broad vowels and dropped consonants brought out the vivid ruggedness of the Pennines he described; and here, Sutton himself, explaining exactly how he was able to provide the regiment with his own barley and corn, to an audience that looked as if *he* were the outsider.

He held onto his illusions of grandiosity for precisely two days before accepting he *was* indeed the outsider. It was only due to the officers' respect for Graham that they welcomed him into this different world. While Sutton considered himself an eloquent speaker amongst his own peers, witty enough to hold his own, he was often speechless in this new company. Graham, on the other hand, born a gentleman's son and experienced in navigating Sutton's circles with much grace, also endeared himself to those below his station whom he treated as equals. Graham could listen to Lieutenant Fielding dissect Thomas Paine's philosophy just as easily as he listened to Ensign Smith divulge intimate details of his first private conquest. Indeed, while Sutton bristled at these uncouth discussions, unable to decide whether radical thoughts or bawdy descriptions should offend him more, Graham saw no need of making these distinctions. Sutton found himself constantly humbled, his esteem for his friend continually rising.

One soldier who particularly caught Sutton's attention was Ensign Richard Ashcroft. While the other men might exhibit their tempers or lewdness from time to time – and Sutton himself was no exception – Richard never spoke an ill word. Even after vigorous days when the combination of rain and mud dampened Graham's spirits, Richard shared naught but gratitude and good cheer, drawing attention to all their blessings. After a particularly challenging day, Sutton had returned to his private lodgings with an extra measure of guilt, knowing he would rest in luxury while the men serving his country were only afforded a few short hours in cramped quarters.

Sutton was still mulling over the subject at luncheon the following day, and did not notice Graham and Richard until they had pulled out their chairs. The two men greeted Sutton warmly, and the viscount noticed an extra spark in Richard's eyes.

'Ashcroft has been in exceedingly good spirits all morning,' Graham said when they were seated. 'He insisted on waiting till luncheon so he could share the cause with you.'

If Sutton was pleased by this insistence, he made no show of it. Instead, the viscount smirked and said: 'Out with it, soldier!'

Beaming, the ensign said: 'Well, in short: I received a letter from my sister this morning, and she bears some excellent news!'

The words sent his heart into an unexpected tumble, taking him much by surprise. He barely registered the glance Graham cast his way at the mention of Miss Ashcroft, his attention so completely fixed on Richard.

'Oh?' He kept his voice as neutral as possible, though his next words betrayed his thoughts – and his heart. 'Are matrimonial congratulations in order?'

The brief silence that followed made Sutton feel like a small boy caught with his breeches down. He began to colour, realising exactly what he had said – along with the unambiguous implications – and mentally cursed himself in all the languages and inflections known to him.

To Sutton's relief, Richard neither questioned nor acknowledged his forthright and ill-mannered interest in Miss Ashcroft, and only smiled, saying: 'Not at all – my sister is far too occupied with her art to concern herself with such mundane matters! In fact, her news pertains to her art: she's been contacted by Mr Livingston, an agent from town, who heard about my sister's private exhibition and now wishes to see the works in person. My brother knows very little about the art world, but Mr Livingston has provided him with a list of references for his perusal. If all goes well – and I see absolutely no reason why it wouldn't – Ellie will have her work assessed by the first professional! Of course, she was very subdued in her letter, but I know she must be thrilled!'

As Graham offered his congratulations, Sutton grappled with the thoughts that followed the ensign's revelation. Mr Livingston, one of the most respected art critics in the whole of England, had contacted Miss Ashcroft directly and requested to see her works; Mr Livingston, who represented the likes of Mr Turner, who was responsible for the careers of a few privileged and talented artists, wished to assess Miss Ashcroft as a potential client; Mr Livingston, whom Sutton had once invited to Bellevue Park, and who had uttered those despicable words that taunted him still…

Sutton swallowed twice and waited for Graham to finish speaking.

'Please give Miss Ashcroft my most heartiest congratulations,' the viscount said. 'It is an unparalleled honour to have caught Mr Livingston's attention. If your brother requires any additional assurances, do let him know I not only vouch for Mr Livingston, but also commend him as having the keenest eyes in his profession.'

These words sparked some recognition in Graham, who had been with Sutton when Livingston visited Bellevue, and who had subsequently been privy to Sutton's foul mood afterwards. Thankfully, Graham kept this discovery to himself, and only added, 'Ah yes, I do remember meeting Mr Livingston once – he does indeed have an excellent reputation. Miss Ashcroft must be quite the extraordinary young lady.'

Richard grinned. 'She is, indeed.' Then, after a pause: 'I was wondering if you could offer some advice on a topic I've been pondering for a while… I know it's not been long since I've joined the army, but do you think I could perhaps be granted some leave?'

'That will depend on the nature of your request,' Graham replied. 'Apart from the annual allowances – which you have not yet accrued – the Colonel does consider special requests for leave. Your behaviour has been exemplary so far, and I'm sure you have good reasons for your request – I would be happy to endorse you, if you'd like.'

The ensign's smile softened, as did his voice. 'Thank you, Lieutenant Graham – your support means a great deal to me. I've not seen my family for almost six months, and I miss them terribly – especially my sister. She's turning seventeen soon, and I would like to surprise her on her birthday.'

'You are a wonderful brother,' Graham said, no doubt thinking about his own unhappy relations. 'Miss Ashcroft is very fortunate to have you.'

The ensign looked a little sheepish. 'Not always – I've certainly dragged her into a fair share of trouble.'

At this, Graham tilted his head towards Sutton. 'Just as this one here has dragged me into a fair share of the same.'

'Your recollections are amiss,' Sutton replied. '*You* were the one who always insisted; and *you* never had to contend with a furious nurse. She thought you were the sweetest boy on earth – if only she'd known you were responsible for ruining half my wardrobe!'

'Don't blame me when *you* were always the grouchy one, never showing any humility. *I* always knew to give her my best smile.'

Sutton grumbled. 'She gave you sweets, that time I fell off the tree.'

'That time *we* fell off the tree, when *you* insisted we pick those apples.'

'I got five lashes, but you got *sweets.*'

Richard's soft chuckling grew into hearty laughter, and he wiped at his eyes. 'Oh, how you two bicker like brothers!'

Sutton allowed a small smile to show, realising how much better he felt compared to only moments ago. Graham had remembered Sutton's grievances with Mr Livingston and had done his best to lighten Sutton's mood.

'I think my sister would like you both very much,' the ensign said. 'And she might realise that my "boyish antics" are not so uncommon after all.'

'And I would very much like to meet Miss Ashcroft,' Graham replied, his smile warm as he looked at Richard, 'but I'm afraid I must remain in Colchester.'

The younger man nodded in understanding, though a sliver of disappointment flashed across his face. He recovered quickly enough, saying: 'That's a right shame. I suspect our mutual friend isn't quite so open in your absence.'

'I do have a reputation to uphold,' Sutton said, tilting his head in a caricature of the privileged peerage.

Richard laughed softly. 'Nonetheless, might you wish to join us at Thornleigh? I know my brother wishes to return your hospitality, and I'm certain my sister would welcome your esteemed artistic opinion.'

He thought back to their last conversation, where Miss Ashcroft displayed her far superior instinct where art was concerned. His hesitation was becoming too long to be polite, and Sutton was grateful when Graham interrupted.

'If you do decide to go, could you call on Mr Earlwood on my behalf? I'd very much like to send him a few bottles of the local gin – yes, Sutton, the one you can't stomach. I've written to him about it, and it would mean a great deal if you could convey them in my stead.' Then, with much cheek, 'Besides, despite any protests otherwise, you must be itching to swing by London, if only briefly. Colchester has nothing remotely resembling Savile Row.'

There was no denying that, though Sutton did have a few choice words to say about Graham's choice of gin, which launched a friendly argument about the spirit. Soon after, the trio was joined by Lieutenant Fielding and Ensign Smith, who were from another platoon and had just finished their shift.

'You've beaten us again,' Lieutenant Fielding said, his voice rough. 'Smith, you'd best be quicker next time with your firearms – you can't let Ashcroft get the upper hand every time.'

Ensign Smith was far from chastised. 'I assure you, Lieutenant, I always take my time with my firearm – it's how the ladies like it.'

A few weeks ago, Sutton had choked on his stew at a similar innuendo. Now, the viscount merely said: 'More matter with less art, if you please.'

Both lieutenants guffawed at this while Richard rolled his eyes. 'Poor Master Shakespeare would be scandalised to hear your interpretation, Sutton.'

'I'd like to hear *your* interpretation,' Ensign Smith interjected before the viscount could devise a suitably witty remark. 'What have you been doing with *your* firearm, Ashcroft? Set it off yet in Colchester?'

Richard, who never participated in any banter about the gentler sex, laughed a little too loudly in response. 'No, not in Colchester.'

'How about before you joined the army? What are the girls like in Hertfordshire?'

Sutton saw Richard glance at Graham, and, sensing the young man's growing discomfort, said: 'I imagine quite similar to the girls in Shropshire, Smith. Now, our Ashcroft here is a gentleman – and alas, I doubt he can be persuaded to kiss and tell.'

'A shame,' Lieutenant Fielding replied. 'Fortunately, *I* am no gentleman, as you very well know!'

The conversation soon devolved into this explicit topic, and it was to Sutton's great relief when he heard the bell signalling the end of the luncheon hour. The men rose, ready to resume their duties.

'Thank you, Sutton,' Richard said quietly before they parted. 'I have no inclination to contribute to such discussions. Now, Thornleigh: I'll speak to the Colonel tonight and write to my brother if permission is granted. Oh, I do hope I'll be able to go – I'd so love to see the surprise on my sister's face!'

Sutton nodded, straightening his waistcoat. As he began his stroll back home, Sutton tried to envision the look of delight on Miss Ashcroft's face at their arrival. He found he liked the image far more than he dared to admit.

23

EVERY MORNING AFTER the arrival of Mr Livingston's letter, Ellie watched her brother as he attended to his breakfast correspondence. It was not until the third day that Marcus looked through his letters and remarked: 'Ah, here are two of Mr Livingston's references.'

Before Ellie could respond, she was presented with her own letter tray. There were three envelopes: from Richard, Phoebe, and, rather unexpectedly, Mr Curtis.

'It appears you'll also be quite preoccupied,' her brother said, wearing a small smile.

A little puzzled, Ellie held out the third envelope. 'This is from Mr Curtis.'

'So it is indeed! Mr Curtis had a few questions about your art I couldn't answer, and I saw no harm in him writing to you directly.' His smile softened. 'You've become quite sought-after, my dear.'

Kitty, who had not received any correspondence, picked up the day's newspaper and refilled her tea. 'While you two tend to your serious business, I shall undertake the equally serious task of remaining informed about the latest fashions and scandals.'

The sky outside was the same, dull grey, but it was warm and cosy in the breakfast parlour. Ellie refilled her own tea and decided to read her letters in the order of familiarity. Seeing Richard's penmanship always set her heart at ease; this time, she noticed his strokes had become less refined but more assured.

My dearest sister:

What capital news about Mr Livingston! Your letter had me grinning like a fool all day long, and I was subject to much teasing throughout – but though some of my new friends here know very little about art and aesthetics, they congratulated you nonetheless. Many of the men have mothers and sisters who work as hard as their fathers and brothers – they found it peculiar when I relayed to them our society's disdain towards young ladies who possess their own minds and skills. I confess I am a little at odds with these two vastly different worlds I inhabit, but what I do know for certain is how pleased I am that your talents are finally being recognised.

Sutton was present when I relayed the news to Graham – that is, Lord Sutton and Lieutenant Graham – we are not bound by such ranks and titles in our leisure time, and I have slipped into a habit that might seem crude or disrespectful for your gentle ears. In any case, Lord Sutton was there in the mess hall – he's made a habit of sharing the midday meals with us, and sometimes joins us for supper – he's also been providing us with much better fare than the standard Army issue, for which we are all tremendously grateful – oh dear, my thoughts carry me away far more quickly than my pen. Lord Sutton is acquainted with Mr Livingston's reputation, and speaks highly of the man – by now Marcus may have obtained his requested references, but I suppose another guarantee can't hurt – and Lord Sutton has vouched for Mr Livingston's character. In fact, he considers Mr Livingston one of the most accomplished and well-connected agents in Great Britain, and believes that his endorsement could singularly launch your career. Now *I* know nothing about such matters, but after all the time I've spent with Lord Sutton, I can vouch for *his* character.

Your name also came up during a conversation with another friend, Ensign Smith. We were discussing winter chills and remedies, and I mentioned how you have always found the cold weather difficult to endure – I hope you don't mind. Smith has a younger sister who suffered a terrible bout of illness when she was ten – she was bedridden for weeks and almost claimed by our good Lord. The Smiths are a family of sheep farmers, so when she was fully recovered, she was slowly put back to work to help with birthing lambs and the like – but only for short lengths at first.

She gradually increased her time spent outside until she became stronger than even *before* her illness. Smith thinks your general constitution might also improve after taking up light walking every day regardless of the weather – he thinks it would be much better for your health than remaining inside for the fear of falling ill. Now we are not physicians here, but perhaps you might find some of this advice helpful, provided you are warmly dressed before heading outside – you were lamenting about not wearing your cerulean cloak much, so now might be the time to put it into good use.

Please do take care of yourself, my dearest sister, especially with winter coming so sharply upon us. I send you all my love, and remain your loving brother,

Richard

P. S. As requested, here are sketches of my new friends. I have included several of Lieutenant Graham – he has such pleasing features!

Her brother's words brought great comfort to Ellie; she wished to write back immediately to express her gratitude for the advice and her excitement about Mr Livingston's upcoming visit, but the other two letters beckoned. After a quick glance at Marcus and Kitty confirmed they were both still absorbed in their reading, Ellie opened the letter from Phoebe.

Dear Ellie:

Words cannot express the depth of my gratitude, or my apologies for having missed you when you and Kitty called yesterday. The portrait of my father is even better than I'd imagined – you have captured him perfectly.

I thank you again, though words will never suffice. Tom and I look forward to seeing you next week for our first sitting.

Yours &c,

Phoebe

Smiling, Ellie opened the third and final letter.

Dear Miss Ashcroft:

Your brother has no doubt informed you of my intent to contact you. In short, I have been seeking the opportunity to convene with you about your artwork and offer my assistance in naming your pieces. I understand you may think this unnecessary, or that your opinion on the topic has changed since your exhibition, but I am at your disposal if you still require my assistance. Your brother has invited me to dine at Thornleigh on Thursday, and you and I could discuss your works prior to our meal, if that should suit you.

I await your response, and remain yours, &c,

Demetrius J. Curtis

Ellie looked up at her brother, who had finished reading his letters, and asked: 'Is Mr Curtis dining with us tomorrow? He has offered his assistance in naming my paintings.'

'Is tomorrow Thursday? I've quite lost track of the time… He must be back from Yorkshire.'

Kitty laid down her paper, her interest piqued. 'What did Mr Curtis say?'

'Mrs Ashcroft,' said her husband, a smile in his voice, 'may I remind you that *I* am the one you have married, and am thus deserving of your every loyalty?'

'You may. And may *I* remind you, Mr Ashcroft, that such loyalty entails chastising one's husband for forgetting to inform his family of any company at dinner? Mr Curtis has his dietary preferences, and I don't intend to be scolded by Mrs Nancy for failing to inform her.'

Marcus had the decency to look sheepish. 'You are quite correct, Mrs Ashcroft – I am duly chastised.' When his wife returned to her paper, he asked Ellie: 'How do you feel about Mr Curtis's suggestion?'

'It is an excellent idea – and I think it very generous of Mr Curtis to offer his assistance. Shall I reply and ask him to arrive a little earlier tomorrow?'

Marcus nodded. 'As for Mr Livingston, you'll be very pleased to know I've received two references vouching for his character and expertise – he seems renowned in his profession, and has been instrumental in launching several careers.' He paused, then added: 'That said, I do wish to remain prudent and wait for my third correspondent's reply before you write to him.'

'Of course.' She thought about what Richard had written and decided to share some of its contents. 'Richard has mentioned in his letter that Mr

Livingston also received high commendations from Lord Sutton.'

Kitty looked up from the paper again. 'Oh? Is Lord Sutton in Colchester?'

'Yes – Richard says Lord Sutton has been assisting the war effort in his own way.' She had been surprised to see Lord Sutton mentioned in Richard's letter, but the very act of speaking his name brought a peculiar fluttering to her stomach. A little distracted by her nerves, Ellie missed the look shared between her brother and sister-in-law.

'I'm sure the regiment welcomes any assistance it can get,' Marcus said evenly. 'And it speaks very highly of Mr Livingston that he also has Lord Sutton's good opinion.'

'Lord Sutton does seem familiar with the artistic circles,' Kitty offered enthusiastically. 'Perhaps he was the one who recommended you to Mr Livingston!'

'It's possible,' replied Marcus. 'But it would be quite forward of him, since we have only been recently acquainted. What do you think, Ellie?'

She thought about Lord Sutton's enviable collection, and then about his fallible confidence. 'I don't know,' she said honestly. 'But I don't think it matters much at all. In fact, what's important is Mr Livingston's opinion; any other speculations are rather unnecessary.'

'Well said, Miss Ashcroft,' her brother applauded. 'You are living proof that one can be both creative *and* sensible.'

Mr Curtis arrived exactly at four o'clock the following day

'My brother and sister went for a ride earlier today,' she said once they had exchanged pleasantries, 'but they were caught in the rain on the way back and are currently freshening up before dinner. They send their apologies and will join us later in the dining room.'

Mr Curtis nodded, and the two made their way to the Artist's Wing. Marcus had been hesitant about leaving them alone, but Kitty had pointed out that, as an educator, Mr Curtis was practically a chaperon himself.

Furthermore, the two men had developed a fast friendship over the past year, and didn't Marcus himself once compliment Mr Curtis's principles, and said he would trust Mr Curtis with his life?

It didn't take long for Marcus to concede to his wife.

As they walked, Ellie and Mr Curtis conversed a little about the weather, and she enquired about his recent visit to his family seat. Mr Curtis told Ellie about his plans to refurbish Penridge, his estate in Yorkshire, and the additions he wished to make to Bradley House's library, his home in Hertfordshire. When they reached her exhibition gallery, Ellie found she was not even mildly intimidated by Mr Curtis. Even his discerning gaze, which moved steadily from painting to painting, left Ellie unaffected; on the contrary, Ellie's fingers twitched with the desire to sketch his complex features: the strong set of his nose, his penetrating eyes, and the deep creases in his forehead that others might mistake for an ill temper, but Ellie now saw as mere concentration.

He stood, silent and observant, before drawing out a small notebook from his pocket. 'I have brought some suggestions. Perhaps we could start there.'

For a man who appeared so pristine and in control, Ellie was surprised to discover the handwriting was no more than a messy scrawl, bordering on illegible – it bore almost no resemblance to the orderly penmanship in his letters. Mr Curtis must have read her expression, for he exhaled sharply, caught between a scoff and a chuckle.

'I hope you'll pardon the shocking hand I use in private,' he said drily. 'My thoughts often present themselves faster than my ability to record them.'

'I suppose that's preferable to the alternative,' Ellie said softly.

To her surprise, Mr Curtis's lips curved into a small smile. 'Indeed. Now, shall I help you decipher those letters?'

She nodded, but found she could make out the first item of the list. '"Persephone's Promises"?'

'Ah, yes.' Mr Curtis walked towards the collection of flowers in vases, the contents and colours changing with the seasons. 'I thought that might be a fitting title for these. Are you familiar with the story of the Greek goddess

Persephone?'

'I know she ruled the underworld with Hades,' Ellie replied, embarrassed. 'I don't recall the rest.'

Mr Curtis gave her a reassuring smile. 'Spending more time with books would have detracted from your time with paints – a right shame, given your talents. Now, Persephone. She was the daughter of Zeus and Demeter, goddess of harvest and growth. After Hades abducted Persephone, Demeter fell into a great sorrow that brought famine to the world. Zeus intervened by speaking with Hades, who agreed to allow Persephone leave of the underworld for six months every year. When Persephone was reunited with Demeter, Demeter's joy made the earth bountiful again – the seasons of spring and summer. When Persephone returned to the underworld, Demeter's sorrow returned, darkening over the earth – giving us autumn and winter. Through it all, Persephone had little choice in the matter. She loved her mother and had grown to love her husband. She had made her promises to both, and each year, she was obliged to keep those promises – or at least, that's how I like to interpret the myth.'

Ellie was still in awe when she said: 'That was wonderful, Mr Curtis. You excel at story-telling – you're much better than my brother.'

The gentleman laughed, the sound deep and warm. 'I shan't share that with Mr Ashcroft, lest it wound his pride. Now, what do you think of the title?'

Enraptured during Mr Curtis's retelling, Ellie had all but forgotten the purpose of his tale. Now she looked at the collection with fresh eyes and was fond of the name. 'I like it. "Persephone's Promises" – it's very befitting.'

They consulted the notebook again after this first decision was made. Ellie struggled with the writing, but Mr Curtis was there to guide her. With the same patience as before, the gentleman read out and explained his choices, capturing the spirit of almost every work with a few words. The watercolour landscapes of the Earlwood gardens became 'The Dutch Quarter', with the hyacinths named 'Rebirth' and the tulips 'Brevity'. A moonlit nightingale became 'How Silver Sweet', while a pair of muddy boots left outside to greet the new day became 'As Dreams Are Made On'.

Another landscape, this time of Rowan's Edge where Richard lay under a tree with his horse grazing nearby, was paired with the suggestion 'A Gentleman's Retreat'. Here, Ellie spoke up, albeit quietly, about changing it to 'Rowan's Retreat'. She explained her attachment to the place, and Mr Curtis concurred with the new title, amending his list with a pencil.

They worked through the rest in a similar fashion, until the last painting was named and Mr Curtis's notebook full of additional notes.

Ellie was pleased with the progress they had made; the light in Mr Curtis's eyes suggested he felt the same. The mantle clock told them there was still some time until dinner would be announced, and, in a moment of courage, Ellie decided to share her secret sketches with the gentleman.

'I have taken up so much of your time already, but could you perhaps offer your opinion on a final matter – a piece currently in progress?'

'I can certainly do my best, Miss Ashcroft, but I possess neither the knowledge nor the vocabulary to discuss art at length.'

'You possess an extraordinarily keen aesthetic sense, which I greatly respect.'

Mr Curtis took this in stride, as he seemed to take many things. 'Very well.'

Ellie led him to the adjoining room that had become her studio, apologising for its mess. 'I don't often have visitors here.'

'Then I am quite honoured,' he said. He showed no revulsion or disapproval at the piles of sketches, the various vases and fruit bowls, the easels and half-formed canvases, the scattered paints and brushes. Then, rather gently, Mr Curtis added: 'You have been privy to my lacklustre penmanship – no process is without its peculiarities.'

Relieved, Ellie found the sketches in question and wordlessly gave them to Mr Curtis. There were about a dozen rough pages of the regimental scene she had put together from Richard's sketches, with the men in different numbers, angles, and places. When he had finished looking through them, Ellie presented a more complete drawing.

'This is the final sketch.' She gestured at a canvas with a larger replication of the same image. 'I'm still deciding on some of the colours and trying out different mixes.'

'I see.'

Ellie drew in a deep breath. 'I've never taken on such a serious subject before. The closest I've ventured would be a portrait of Richard before he left for the Army.'

Mr Curtis took his time to form his thoughts and words. 'I disagree. You may not have engaged with such a specific subject as the war, but all your paintings are serious and heartfelt. Your apprehensions are understandable, but you need not undermine your skills or belittle your accomplishments.'

Ellie nodded, feeling simultaneously scolded and inspired. 'Thank you, Mr Curtis. Your support means a great deal to me.'

'Your gratitude is unnecessary. I thoroughly enjoyed your exhibition, and I am fascinated by your creative process – each of these sketches are so finely crafted they can stand on their own, yet you have succeeded in using them to create a piece that surpasses them all. I am duly impressed, and quite eager to see how you will develop and grow as an artist.'

Ellie flushed with pleasure and swallowed the words of thanks that bubbled to the surface. She breathed deeply, trying to keep her voice even. 'Then I would be much obliged if you could kindly offer your opinion on this.'

Mr Curtis studied the sketches again, and then turned his attention to the canvas. When he spoke again, his rich baritone echoed the wisdom of millennia. '"We make war that we may live in peace."'

A steady warmth wrapped itself around Ellie's heart, and she saw Richard's uninhibited smile more clearly than ever. She needed a long moment to recover, and Mr Curtis stood by silently, respectfully, giving her all the time she needed.

'Thank you,' she repeated, when she could trust her voice. 'I think... I think Master Shakespeare could help us here again: "We Happy Few".'

'"We band of brothers."' Mr Curtis completed the line, approval in his voice. 'Very fitting, Miss Ashcroft.'

Before they left the Artist's Wing to join her family for dinner, Mr Curtis gave Ellie a gentle, fatherly smile. 'Knowing the end result is half the work.'

24

'I'VE OBTAINED PERMISSION from the Colonel for a week's leave of absence,' Ensign Richard Ashcroft told his friends the next day at luncheon. 'I've written to my brother and hope to set out at dawn on Saturday.'

'Capital!' Graham said, while Smith asked, 'How far is your family seat?'

'It's seventy miles to Thornleigh Abbey, but I'd like to stop by Harlow to find a little something for my sister.'

'How capital,' repeated Graham. 'What are you looking for?'

Richard smiled and ducked his head in a gesture that had become familiar to Sutton. 'My sister loves wildflowers – she likes how they have escaped cultivation but still retain their loveliness. We used to pick them every week when we were children – we managed to amass quite a collection!'

Sutton recalled Miss Ashcroft expressing her partiality for such flowers, and thought about Harlow's landscape. 'If memory serves,' he said, 'there is a cottage in the vicinity with some particularly fetching wild roses.'

'Oh, she would like that very much! Would you mind terribly if we stopped by, Sutton?'

'Not at all.'

Some confusion crossed Smith's face. 'Are you two setting out together?'

Richard beamed. 'Yes, indeed – Sutton is lending me one of his horses – it's extremely generous of him. We're heading to Thornleigh together – I daresay I'll welcome the company on the road.'

The bell rang for the end of luncheon, and Sutton promptly rose in time with the others.

'Soon you'll be punctual to *all* your engagements,' Graham said with a grin.

Sutton assumed his most unimpressed expression. 'Alas, I don't have the luxury to dally about – I've been tasked by a particular someone to visit a local distillery to sample and obtain some gin for Mr Earlwood.'

'Then I shall thank you on behalf of this mysterious someone,' Graham said with a flourished bow. 'I've got the evening off – since you'll undoubtedly need to cleanse your palate afterwards, would you like some company?'

'Oh? You possess a palate that requires cleansing? Well, if you insist, supper is at 8 o'clock.'

Graham doffed an imaginary hat. 'Till then, my friend.'

Sutton grumbled when he opened the door. 'One would think being in the Army ought to instil one with enough discipline to be on time.'

'Yes, but only when one's appointment relates to army business. I have afforded you special concessions.'

The butler took Graham's coat, and the two walked side by side to the dining room.

'Besides,' Graham continued, 'one would think the great 7th Viscount Sutton would have his butler open the door when welcoming an unruly soldier into his home.'

'Of course, one could be forgiven for one's mistake, since that might apply to the viscount when he is at his family seat. And perhaps the viscount might wish to ensure the unruly soldier would not be dragging muddy boots into his lordship's dwellings.'

'Touché.'

They reached the dining room and sat at opposite ends of the table. Since

Sutton often dined alone in the rented house, he had grown rather fond of the intimacy afforded by a table that seated no more than six or eight. Tonight, the size was perfect for the two friends.

The wine was poured after Sutton's nod. 'Hope you won't mind the claret – it's from 1798, I think.'

'It seems pointless to hold any grudges against fine wine, especially if they were made before the war.'

The viscount smiled. 'My thoughts precisely. How was your afternoon?'

'Tedious. My primary duty is training the subalterns and keeping my superiors updated about their progress, but sometimes, Colonel Watson consults the higher ranked officers about broader strategies. I honestly don't know how the Colonel can deal with so much administration.'

'Practice, perhaps. Or necessity.' Sutton raised his glass. 'To the hard-working men of the British Army.'

They drank, and Graham wore a contented look after his sip.

'Yes, I know – this is far superior to the ghastly "wine" you've been having,' Sutton said with a smile. 'It's fortunate you never cared for gambling – you reveal your every thought, and *I* would have ended up deep in debt from my futile attempt to assist you.'

Graham smiled sheepishly. 'Claret, you say?'

'Straight from Bordeaux – give or take twenty years. Thank the Lord – and my father – for keeping the Bellevue cellars well-stocked.'

His friend laughed and raised his glass again. 'To the British peerage and their superior tastes.'

'And their superior stockpiling,' Sutton said before he drank.

The first course was served after their impromptu toasts. Sutton couldn't help but be a little embarrassed at the sight of the simple soup and cold meats.

'The kitchen's been instructed to make use of the local produce,' he explained. 'My staff tells me some farmers are struggling. There isn't much variety, but I see no need to make purchases outside Colchester or Sussex.'

Graham set down his spoon. 'You are a noble and virtuous man, Aubrey. You should know that I, of all people, would never think ill of you for being so…noble and virtuous.'

Sutton shrugged, not quite meeting Graham's gaze. 'I know how highly you regard Bellevue's fare – and we both know you are ruled by your cavernous stomach.'

'"The sauce to meat is ceremony; meeting were bare without it."'

'Touché,' Sutton echoed, the pleasure warm in his voice.

Thereafter, Graham littered compliments throughout supper, whether praising flavours and textures or comparing them to the simple dishes that evoked fond childhood memories. When the savoury courses were over, Sutton sat back with satisfaction and opted for a little dessert, which he rarely took. The lieutenant, however, ate his with great enthusiasm and relish, and soon requested a second serving.

'One would mistake you for a starving boy,' Sutton teased.

'You know I can't afford sugar on my meagre wage. Besides, I suspect you requested a cake on account of my visit – I have no wish to insult your cook, or for a perfectly good treat to go to waste, since I know you won't be finishing it.'

Sutton chuckled and enjoyed a glass of port while waiting for Graham to finish. He felt a small pang for his friend, who did not have the luxury of a good meal – and might not for a long time yet. When Graham finally set down his napkin, the two men retired to the drawing room, which had fast become Sutton's favourite place in the house. The fire was warm and soothing, as was the brandy that cradled the back of his throat.

'I've retrieved the bottles for Mr Earlwood, as requested.'

'Thank you,' said Graham. 'It means a great deal to me.'

'I know.' Sutton chuckled as a thought occurred to him. 'It seems I'll be travelling this time with only *one* portmanteau and an entire *barrel* of Colchester's finest.'

Graham laughed. 'My goodness, if the press got hold of this!'

'Not to mention, I'll have a seventeen-year-old subaltern in tow,' Sutton said.

'What an age to be. I've no doubt he can manage on his own, but Ashcroft's never been on the Tour, and he's not half as worldly as you.'

'The times are changing, and being seventeen for us is the not same as it is for Ensign Richard.'

Graham noticed the address. 'I did not know you were on such familiar terms with the boy.'

Sutton shrugged. 'I can't bring myself to think of him as "Ashcroft", even in his brother's absence. He laughs too much.'

'And what of his sister? Have you had word about Mr Livingston's interest?'

'I have not.' His tone was more brusque than he'd intended. Immediately remorseful, Sutton supplied: 'He called my work "contrived" and "mediocre" – as much as I'd like to, I fear I'll never forget those words.'

'You're only five and twenty – there's time yet for you to forget those, and many other words.' Graham finished his brandy and stood to refill their glasses. When he sat down again, the lieutenant's voice was unusually severe. 'There's something you might wish to know about Ensign Richard Ashcroft. It is not precisely mine to share, but as you've formed a significant connection with the family and you'll be back in Darlington, I think it best for the knowledge to come from me rather than some busybody.'

'Go on.'

'I know you can be judgemental about these matters, and I implore you to keep your prejudices at bay on this occasion.'

Sutton glared at his friend, now anxious. 'Go on, James.'

'By natural rights, Richard is not an Ashcroft. He is an indiscretion of the late Mr Ashcroft.'

The knowledge hit him hard and fast, and Sutton set down his glass for fear of dropping it. That explained the young man's colouring, his placement in potential danger, his sister's trepidation at his mention, his absence from conversations amongst the Ashcrofts' companions. But it did not explain the Ashcrofts' genuine concern and regard for the boy's well-being, the unending stream of letters that came from his family, the portrait upon the fireplace…

Sutton felt a headache coming on, and he became twice as bitter. He, a viscount from one of England's most lauded families, had received less affection from his own parents than this boy – this *illegitimate* boy – had from the Ashcrofts.

The betrayal from his late parents pounded heavily against his heart. Sutton barely recognised himself when he uttered: 'The 6th Viscount Sutton was correct, then – the British Army is truly a home for bastards, drunks, and fools.'

He saw Graham's jaw tighten, but the lieutenant's voice was light. 'Pray tell, which am I?'

Sutton's stomach twisted. His hands were suddenly cold, and his quickening heartbeat pounded in his ears.

'James...'

He did not have the words, but that was no excuse. Graham remained silent, letting Sutton gather his thoughts. Their disagreements had always followed this pattern since they were children: Sutton lashed out; Graham waited for apologies. But Sutton had gone too far this time.

'James,' he repeated, his chest heavy. 'I'm sorry – that was... By God, that *wasn't* what I meant.'

'What *did* you mean?'

Sutton looked down, unable to meet his friend's gaze. 'I... I don't know. I don't understand any of this. But truly, I am sorry.'

Instead of accepting the apology, the lieutenant asked: 'Shall I advise Richard to find other means of transport?' *And inform Mr Ashcroft of your absence?* lingered the next, unspoken words.

Sutton considered the offer, knowing Graham had his best interests at heart. Here was a way out of his tangled, emotional mess, with very little inconvenience to Sutton himself. A coward's way.

Remembering Graham's earlier words, Sutton was gripped with a desire to become as noble and virtuous as the praise deserved. 'There is no need.' He took a deep breath, trying to make sense of his anger and betrayal. 'Is he close to his family?'

Graham nodded. 'He is. You've heard how he speaks of Miss Ashcroft, whom he adores. He speaks the same way of Mr Ashcroft, whom he loves and admires. The circumstances of his birth may have been an unfortunate chapter in their lives, but apart from the occasional unkindness from society itself, I daresay you won't find a happier family than the Ashcrofts.'

'Then why the army at such a perilous time? Why not the church? Why leave behind such a loving and accepting family?'

'For the same reason I joined,' replied Graham. 'I always felt overshadowed by my older brother, and Richard did too – albeit for different reasons. He has found a place where no one cares about his illegitimacy, where he is treated according to his merits, not his lineage.'

The words sliced through Sutton, leaving behind a deep aching. Graham's face softened.

'I didn't mean it like that. We have our different opinions about the aristocracy, but I would never disparage you or what you do.'

Sutton took this in stride. 'No – *I* am sorry for disparaging *your* vocation. Truly, I didn't mean it.' He paused again as a realisation settled over him. 'A quarter of my acquaintances result from extra-marital affairs, and the rest conduct them on a regular basis – deriding Richard for his "status" would be nothing short of hypocrisy. But I simply can't comprehend how there's such affection in a family with a socially questionable history, while someone who does everything *by the book* lacks the very same affection.'

The small room reverberated with his words, and Sutton felt all his trivial complaints turn inward until they met the deep, pitiful core. There, stripped of all other layers, he found himself longing for the sincerity of the Ashcrofts, for the unwavering, unconditional love he had never experienced himself. If left to his own devices, Sutton would have unleashed his anguish and longing in an uncouth manner – he had certainly behaved unwisely during his bouts of loneliness in the cold, hard stones of Bellevue Park.

But he wished to do better, *be* better. 'I am envious of Richard. He has a loving family that chose *him* over their reputation.'

He thought again of his own parents, who cared little for Sutton beyond his ability to carry on the family line. Even so, as the youngest of nine, he had been an afterthought for much of his childhood. At birth, he had simply been

'Aubrey', a tired attempt to refashion one of his mother's names; 'Charles' came much later, after his last brother was taken by illness and just before he lost his two sisters. Only then did his parents, both well into their fifties, realise the next Viscount Sutton would need a middle name.

As if reading his thoughts, Graham said, 'I think there are far fewer happy families than there are their counterpart. But if we are not born with such good fortune, we can still find where we belong, by ourselves and for ourselves.'

'Even in this, some are more fortunate than others.'

'Indeed.' Graham paused, giving the last bit of life to Sutton's earlier outburst. 'You know all too well the unpleasant facets of my own family, but where friendship is concerned, I consider myself the most fortunate.'

The forgiveness hurt, even as it began to heal Sutton's heart. 'As do I. Thank you, James.' Then, with a small huff and shake of his head: 'I can picture us as old men, drinking together and sharing our woes.'

'Perhaps you will mellow with age, and *I* will be the broody one.'

Sutton's eyebrow quirked. 'Impossible.'

'Not if you've found Lady Lavender,' Graham said softly.

Sutton decided not to respond. They sat in silence for a while, neither wishing to disturb a bond that ran deeper than words. Only when the fire started to recede and the clock chimed midnight did Sutton speak again, his voice a little hoarse.

'A full day tomorrow?'

'Quite.' Graham made no move to rise. 'Do you think you will be well enough to travel the day after?'

'Quite,' echoed Sutton. 'I might go for a ride in the morning – clear my thoughts a little.'

'If you need something to do, you could always help with the firewood.'

'And risk landing an axe on my foot?'

Graham smiled, and here was the real breaking of the silence, of the preceding moroseness. 'So long as you don't injure your family jewels – you'll need to keep those intact for the 8th Viscount Sutton.'

'If only you'd found yourself a wife… I would have bequeathed everything to your puppy-eyed, perpetually-happy, mud-cased progeny – but you just *had* to join the army.'

'Yes, quite a shame. I suppose it's now up to you and Lady Sutton.'

'Anyone worthy of that title would be far superior to me – I would need to become worthy of her first.' He'd surprised himself with his own admission, but Graham seemed pleased to hear this. 'How have you grown out of your temper tantrums, and how on earth am I going to do the same?'

'It helps not to have much of a temper in the first place,' Graham said lightly. 'But second to that: necessity. It does wonders for a man.'

Sutton was sceptical. 'Where shall I go to find such necessity?'

'Within tends to be the best place to start – I'm sure you have enough Seneca and Marcus Aurelius in your library to help with that.' Graham paused. 'Will you be alright tonight?'

'I suppose I must – necessity.' Then he added, reassuringly: 'I will. I think it's rather time to let go of some unpleasant memories and feelings.'

Graham nodded and finally rose. 'I'd say we're on the right path then.'

25

UNLIKE HER SIXTEENTH BIRTHDAY, which was marked with great aplomb in Ellie's very own debutante ball, her seventeenth celebration was a far more subdued affair. Apart from the Earlwoods, no one else had been invited to the intimate supper at Thornleigh, where only some special dishes were to mark the occasion. For Ellie, who neither wanted nor needed any festivities, the promise of her favourite culinary delights was more than enough.

The day itself, however, was greeted by the gloomy December weather that always weighed down Kitty's spirits, though she would endeavour to hide it for both Ellie and Marcus's sakes. Ellie's birthday – or, rather, the events surrounding her birth – had been the most bittersweet time of Marcus's life: within the span of a few days, he had lost a mother he had loved and gained a sister he would come to love. Time had helped soothe her brother's painful memories, but it had always been on her birthday that Ellie would see a hint of tears in his eyes.

While today would be no different, Ellie felt far more content than she could remember. She rose early, as was her habit, and was dressed in her Sunday best. The house would be quiet for a few hours yet, and Ellie relished the prospect of spending that time on her new work before her family left their rooms at midday. The Earlwoods would arrive in the late afternoon, but before then, she wished to sit with her family in the drawing room and share the quiet communion she so cherished.

But it was her latest painting that excited her the most, even beyond Mrs Nancy's ices and puddings. All apprehensions prior to sharing the sketches with Mr Curtis vanished after he'd offered his insights and support, and in the few days since their meeting, Ellie had worked on her new painting with single-minded intensity.

Presently, she walked through Thornleigh with a bounce in her step, pausing only to request some tea and toast, heading straight for her studio. She quickly donned an old apron, mixed the same colours she had used previously, picked up the same brush, and started painting. Although Ellie usually exercised extreme caution when setting paint to canvas – not least because the materials were rather dear – her newfound approach to painting was something else entirely: she was bold, decisive, and almost fierce. Ellie had read about artists who were so taken by their passions that they spent days on end in front of the easel, working instinctively and stopping only when they had finished. She was not quite so rash – but she *had* been less reserved than usual and more reliant on her own feelings. It was liberating – even a touch *exhilarating* – and regardless of this painting's result, Ellie treasured the process, the pure joy of embracing what she loved.

Ellie was so focused on her work – presently to finesse the features of a soldier whose sketch Richard had sent – that she had forgotten the requested toast and tea until a knock sounded at the open door. It was a perplexing disturbance; Maria knew to leave the tray silently on the designated table. Nonetheless, Ellie ignored the distraction until she finished her current strokes. Only then did she set down the brush and turn towards the door.

Ellie had enough sense to place down her brush gently and take two steps back from the still-wet canvas before she allowed her emotions to take hold.

'Richard!'

She crossed the room, and her brother barely had enough time to set down the tray before she was in his arms, clutching him tightly.

'Oh, Richard!'

She felt him chuckle as he held her close. 'My dear sister,' he said gently. 'I have missed you, too.'

Her face was wet with tears when they parted, and Ellie was mortified to see the stains on his shirt, not from her crying, but from the paint on her apron. 'I'm sorry, I've ruined your shirt! Those oils will never come out!'

Richard laughed, a familiar sound that made her heart soar. 'Then it's a good thing I didn't come in my livery – I have far fewer sets of those than I have plain shirts.' He offered her a handkerchief, which she gladly took. 'Still so prone to tears, my little sister. You've not changed these last few months.'

He placed both hands on her arms and took a step back, studying her intently while she did the same.

'That's not quite right – perhaps you *have* changed. Earlier, while you were painting, you were so very serious – I almost couldn't recognise you. Even now, you look…more assured.'

Ellie tilted her head, neither acknowledging nor refuting his comment. 'You seem different, too.' She raised her own arm, tentatively prodded an upper shoulder, and exclaimed in surprise. 'Oh Richard, you're a *real* soldier now!'

Grinning, Richard made a show of flexing his arms and adopting a variety of poses, much to Ellie's delight. Their months apart faded away in minutes, and Ellie embraced her brother again.

'I've really missed you,' she said softly. 'Thornleigh really isn't the same without you.'

'You survived all those years when I was at Cambridge,' Richard replied, stroking her back.

'That was different. You were always going to come back from Cambridge.'

She left the rest unspoken, but the implication hung in the air between them. This time, Ellie withdrew from the embrace gracefully and dabbed the handkerchief at her nose.

'How long will you be here?' she asked. 'Oh, you hadn't mentioned you were coming! How were your travels? Have you eaten? And you brought in the tea, too – shall we go into the morning room and have some breakfast?'

Richard held up his hands in mock terror. 'What an interrogation, Miss

Ashcroft! I shall only respond to your last question, with a resounding "yes" – I have it on Mrs Nancy's authority that you've stopped taking breakfast.'

Ellie took off her apron, folded it neatly, and set it next to her paints. 'I've been eating here whenever Marcus and Kitty decide to breakfast in their rooms – you know how I don't like taking large meals alone. Mind you, I'm always ravenous by luncheon, and afternoon tea is still my favourite time of the day.'

'Still harassing Mrs Nancy to satisfy your sweet tooth?'

She scrunched up her face. 'No more than you badgered her for those dreadful snails all those years ago.'

'You make it sound so unappetising – I'd have you know that *escargot* will one day become quite the delicacy.'

Ellie slid her arm into his and they left her studio. She saw Richard's curiosity about her current painting and was relieved when he did not enquire. Once they entered the adjoining exhibition room, however, Richard said:

'I couldn't help admiring these on my way in. I see some of your old paintings, but surely, you've not done so much while I was away!'

'The absence of a nagging brother can do wonders for one's productivity,' Ellie replied. 'Right now, I'm actually working on something that… Well, I'll show it to you when it's properly done.'

'I look forward to it.' They stopped by the set of flowers, and Richard studied it with a look of marvel. 'I thought these were just separate pieces, and yet… My dear sister is an artistic genius!'

'Oh, don't exaggerate so.' She playfully hit his arm, but smiled with pleasure. 'Mr Curtis – he and Marcus have become quite close, and he often dines here – Mr Curtis helped name these works: "Persephone's Promises".'

Richard's enthusiasm was palpable. 'That's brilliant! And you'll be able to share those names with Mr Livingston when he comes!'

'Yes, Mr Curtis is splendid with words. He's also looking into plaques to accompany the paintings – I don't know the details, but he's discussed them with Marcus.' Ellie paused to unclasp her neck chain. She removed the ring, holding it out to her brother. 'I believe this belongs to you.'

'Thank you, Ellie.' Richard slipped the ring onto his finger while Ellie tucked away the neck chain.

They left the art rooms and found their way to the morning room where a small fire was glowing. Richard tended to it while Ellie rang for some food, listing all of Richard's favourites. Soon, the room was ablaze with warmth, and fresh pots of tea arrived. The rain outside showed no signs of abating, but Ellie's good cheer only grew.

'Are you here for long?' she asked when they were seated.

'Three nights. I leave on Friday so I can return to Colchester by Sunday.'

'How fortunate your rooms were aired just yesterday.' When Richard didn't respond, Ellie processed the implications. 'Marcus knows you're here? Marcus knows you're here!'

Her brother smiled sheepishly. 'Surprise! And happy birthday!'

Their breakfast arrived, with plates of steaming eggs, sausages, and rashers, much to Richard's obvious delight. They helped themselves, with Richard devouring his hot breakfast while Ellie nibbled some toast.

'How I've missed Mrs Nancy's meals,' Richard said with a contented sigh as he helped himself to a second serving. 'Sutton has certainly done his best to improve the meals at the barracks – bless his soul – but Mrs Nancy is incomparable.'

Ellie glanced up at the name. 'Is Lord Sutton well?'

'He is. And on that note...' Richard cleared his throat. 'I completely understand if you would rather spend the day without him – he has found lodgings at the inn, and was kind enough to arrange a room for me last night – he's been nothing but kind, but it is *your* birthday – though perhaps when the Earlwoods arrive, if that's still the plan?'

Her brother had reverted to his boyish tendency to ramble, and though Ellie could only decipher half his meaning, it was enough for her to ask: 'Lord Sutton has accompanied you to Darlington, and you've let him stay at an inn? *You* were at an inn last night, instead of in your own rooms?'

Richard smiled sheepishly. 'It was well past midnight when we arrived, and we didn't wish to bother anyone at Thornleigh.'

'That, my dear brother, is sheer nonsense! Lord Sutton has been nothing but kind to us all, and he is welcome here at any time – I'm sure Marcus and Kitty would both agree! Oh, we must let Mrs Rowley know.'

'I didn't wish to presume,' Richard said quietly. 'And though he would never voice it, I'm quite certain Lord Sutton would never think to presume.'

'Presume what, precisely?'

'That you would welcome him.' He sighed at Ellie's confusion. 'Perhaps I'm the one presuming here…'

A movement behind Ellie caught his attention, and Richard's discomfort quickly turned into delight as he rose to his feet. 'Marcus!'

Turning around, Ellie saw Marcus and Kitty, both dressed for the day. With a warm smile that reached his eyes, her eldest brother replied, 'Richard.'

The two shook hands before Richard pulled Marcus into an embrace. When they parted, the Ashcroft patriarch said, 'My, Richard, you have indeed been training hard.'

As Richard went to greet Kitty, Marcus turned his attention to Ellie. 'It seems you've found your surprise gift. Happy birthday, dearest sister.'

'Thank you.' Tears welled in her eyes as she looked at her family, her complete, happy family, all gathered together. 'Thank you.'

The Earlwoods arrived a little after three, all exuding good cheer despite the on-going rain. Lettice, thrilled to be brought along, wore an exceptionally bright smile and looked quite a vision in her best dress. Upon arriving, she immediately made for Ellie.

'Happy birthday, Ellie! I hope you'll get all the cakes you could ever want!'

Everyone laughed at this, though Ellie coloured a little. 'Thank you, Lettice. And I hope that when the time comes, you will help me eat them!'

Soon after the Earlwoods were settled in the drawing room, Ellie saw the carriage bearing their final guest. Once Richard had explained their situation, confirming that the viscount had indeed accompanied him, Marcus sent a note to the inn post-haste. A guest suite had already been prepared in anticipation for his stay, and while Ellie remained curious about Richard's presumptions, she was looking forward to seeing Lord Sutton.

Wishing to correct the earlier misunderstanding – putting Lord Sutton up in an inn, after all his hospitality! – Ellie insisted on greeting him at the door. Marcus gave his approval and they walked to the main entrance together. The viscount's carriage had just stopped, and Ellie could see the two horses were soaked through. Though she knew the pair would soon be dried, warm, and well-fed, Ellie's heart still went out to them.

Her compassionate heart quickened to another rhythm when Lord Sutton stepped out of the carriage, nodded at the footman, and looked up straight at Ellie. He was exactly as she'd remembered: calm, poised, brimming with unrivalled intensity, heedless to the rain that slid down his hat and clung onto his overcoat. And yet, as he held her gaze, Ellie also saw what she remembered but could not place: surprise, uncertainty, a touch of tenderness.

The viscount crossed the courtyard, stopped at the threshold of the house, removed his hat, and gave them both a graceful bow. 'Good day, Mr Ashcroft, Miss Ashcroft. Thank you for your kindness and hospitality.'

The dark curls not under the protection of his hat were wet, and a drop of water trailed down his cheek. Ellie's mouth was suddenly dry.

'Welcome to Thornleigh Abbey,' her brother said. 'We are pleased to have you here, and are grateful you assisted Richard's journey from Colchester.'

'The pleasure is all mine,' Lord Sutton replied in a voice that sent a delicious shiver down Ellie's spine. He then fixed his singular attention to Ellie. 'I believe felicitations are due. Happy birthday, Miss Ashcroft.'

She managed a curtsy, and tried to find her voice. 'Thank you. I hope you will enjoy your stay.'

Lord Sutton's gaze lingered on Ellie before he turned to her brother.

'My men will show you to your rooms,' said Marcus. 'Perhaps you might wish to freshen up – given the weather, we're convening in the drawing room today.'

'Yes, I shall – thank you.' Despite this, Lord Sutton remained hesitant at the doorway, glancing down.

Her brother understood the meaning before she did, relaxing beside her. When Marcus spoke again, his voice was warm rather than merely polite.

'While your consideration is very much appreciated, please do not worry about such trivial matters. You've had a long journey, and despite their conveniences, I doubt the inns provided much comfort. Please, do come in – my valet will take care of the rest.'

Lord Sutton's lips curled into a genuine smile, like a child receiving the acceptance he so craved. He gingerly stepped into Thornleigh Abbey, his muddy boots leaving marks on the floor.

When Lord Sutton joined them in the drawing room, donning a pristine ensemble with a fetching purple waistcoat, the small party rose and greeted him enthusiastically, a gesture that seemed to take the viscount by great surprise. Always in high spirits, Mr Earlwood did not hold back on the account of decorum and gave Lord Sutton a quick but affectionate embrace, thanking him for his kindness to both Ellie and Richard. Ellie caught Lord Sutton's brief look of shock and hid her smile behind her hand; the viscount, however, sought her immediately, and gave her such an unadulterated look of exasperation and accusation that widened Ellie's smile. When Mr Earlwood finally released Lord Sutton, the viscount was more than a little rumpled.

Kitty waited until they were all seated before making an announcement.

'As we all know, today is our dear Ellie's seventeenth birthday. Last year, we held a rather stunning ball to mark the occasion, but when I asked what she would like this year, Ellie only wished to spend the day with her nearest and dearest. And an extra slice of her favourite cake.'

At Kitty's nod, a footman entered with a large cake, while two maids distributed and filled the teacups.

'Since some of our guests need to be back in the nursery' – she winked at Lettice, who was delighted to be singled out – 'and since our Ellie's favourite meal is decidedly afternoon tea, I'd like to make a toast now.'

Kitty lifted her teacup, and the others followed suit. 'To Ellie! We wish you the happiest of birthdays!'

A little embarrassed and entirely overwhelmed, Ellie could only nod at Kitty and take a sip of her own tea. She looked around the room, at her two beloved brothers, at her closest friends, at Lord Sutton, and she did indeed feel like the happiest person in the world.

Lettice made sure to set down her cup very carefully before getting to her feet in excitement. 'May we give Ellie her presents now? Oh please, Kitty, may we?'

The maids were cutting and serving the cake, giving Ellie an exceptionally large slice, but it seemed even the prospect of the sweet treat wasn't enough to quell the young girl. At Kitty's consent, Lettice scrambled behind her seat, and retrieved a parcel Ellie had not noticed.

'I thought we could hide all your presents behind the seats,' Lettice declared proudly. 'Mary thought it wouldn't be a good idea, but Harriet said you'd be too distracted to notice – and she was right!'

Ellie received the present gratefully and peeled back the wrapping to reveal a folder with several sketches. Still bubbling with energy, Lettice inched closer to provide her explanations and pointing at each in turn.

'This is you out on a walk. This is you at your debutante ball – Mary told me all about your dress, and Harriet helped. This is you when you're drawing. I made them all myself – except when Harriet helped.'

The pictures were a child's handiwork, but Ellie was touched by the effort and sentiment.

'Thank you, Lettice. I like these very much indeed.'

The girl beamed. 'I'm so pleased you do! Mary said it was silly to draw someone who is so great at drawing, but *I* told her if you're drawing other people all the time, then it's only polite for someone to draw pictures of *you*!'

Richard chuckled, saying: 'That's a very wise observation, Miss Lettice!'

Satisfied, Lettice returned to her seat, picking up her cake and eating it as neatly as she could.

While they all enjoyed their tea and cake, the party took turns in presenting Ellie with their gifts. The guests had indeed stowed away their presents behind or under the seats, which made Ellie look on with amusement every time a particular parcel was retrieved. She took great pleasure and care in opening each gift, and thanking everyone in turn. Ellie's artistic endeavours had not been far from everyone's minds, and, for the most part, the gifts were to encourage and assist Ellie accordingly: a beautiful book from the Earlwoods on aesthetics, a sturdy bonnet from Mary for outdoor sessions, an apron with such exquisite needlework from Harriet that Ellie couldn't bear the thought of smearing it with paint.

Unable to contain his own excitement, Richard then presented a small, leather-bound book, which contained the descriptions, locations, and pressed flowers he'd encountered in Colchester, and even some he'd picked on the way back to Thornleigh. She would peruse the book in her own time and treasure it for years to come, but for now, Ellie simply laid it down carefully and thanked her brother.

Soon after, Kitty smiled at Ellie with a mischievous glint, and gave her a parcel wrapped in familiar paper.

'This is from Marcus and me,' she said, her voice light with amusement. Ellie peeled back the wrapping and found a luxurious riding cloak from Mr Murray's, lined and trimmed with silk. The cloak was not very heavy, but she knew it would keep her warm in winter.

'It's beautiful,' Ellie murmured. 'Thank you both so much.'

Kitty smiled. 'Consider it a long overdue token – it must've been over a year ago.' Then, realising not everyone would be privy to its significance, Kitty explained: 'Shortly after my husband and I were first acquainted, I took Ellie for a spot of shopping, stopping by such fine establishments as Mr Murray's. A few days later, I received a stunning riding cloak from Ellie – which was really from Mr Ashcroft. I didn't know these siblings could be so conspiratorial!'

Marcus blushed at so public a declaration. 'Well, there was no harm done,' he commented.

'Quite the contrary,' Kitty replied.

Throughout these exchanges, Lord Sutton had remained silent on a seat beside Richard and, given the circular shape that had naturally formed amongst the group, seemed a little excluded from the present company. A quick glance at his plate told Ellie he had barely touched the cake, and she felt a twinge of sadness for him.

As if noticing her attention, Lord Sutton's gaze caught Ellie's, and he gave her a small, reassuring smile. Then he swallowed and cleared his throat.

'I also have something for Miss Ashcroft,' he said, directing his words at Marcus and continuing after his nod. 'I shall have it fetched – please excuse me for a moment.'

He rose and approached the footman waiting by the drawing room, speaking in hushed tones. Beside her, Richard leaned in and said, 'Oh, I had forgotten, and should have allowed him to present his gift instead of jumping in like a schoolboy… I hope he'll forgive my transgression.'

'I hope he'll forgive mine,' Ellie replied softly. 'I thought everyone enjoyed lemon drizzle cake.'

Richard smiled. 'It's not the cake – my guess would be his nerves. Our good viscount didn't eat much in the mess hall when he first arrived at the barracks, but now cleans up his plate like every other soldier.'

'Nerves? Whatever for?'

'You'll see,' Richard said right before Lord Sutton returned, this time with three footmen in tow.

'I hope it is not terribly presumptuous of me,' he said, sitting down. Behind him, the footmen each carried a blank canvas in three different sizes, with the smallest as wide as her arms-span, and the largest as tall as Lord Sutton himself. Their sizes far out-stripped anything she'd thus painted, their pristine whiteness challenging and encouraging Ellie to fill them with her imagination.

Then, he silently passed over a bundle wrapped in black cloth, and Ellie opened the folds to find a set of five sable-haired brushes, each secured in place by golden threads stitched into the fabric. She ran her fingertips up the smooth, wooden handles and across the soft bristles, finer than any brush she'd ever owned.

Her first instinct was to stammer the refusal of such an exquisite gift – the canvases themselves would have cost a small fortune – but when she looked up again, Ellie saw the uncertainty and the mildest apprehension behind the viscount's otherwise steady gaze.

She could feel the room's eyes on her, but at this moment, Ellie only had eyes for Lord Sutton.

'Thank you for your most generous and thoughtful gift,' she said. 'I will use them wisely.'

And that, it seemed, was all he needed to hear.

True to Richard's words, Ellie observed Lord Sutton relaxing progressively throughout the day until he enjoyed himself heartily at dinner. When she asked for a second helping of pudding, the viscount followed suit, and even smiled at her from across the table.

After supper, they returned to the drawing room, which had been rearranged in their absence to facilitate evening entertainments. The card table had been set up, and the pianoforte, which Ellie looked at guiltily for her own lack of practice, was open and ready to play.

As Ellie sat by the fireplace, she saw Richard gesturing at the firewood by the grate, saying, 'Fancy chopping some tomorrow morning?'

'Not in this weather,' was Lord Sutton's reply.

Ellie found the image of the viscount swinging an axe exceptionally amusing.

Meanwhile, Kitty and Mary had entered the room and made straight for the card table, cajoling Mr and Mrs Earlwood to join them in a game of whist. The other gentlemen seemed content to sit with some brandy, and Ellie and Harriet each ventured for a small glass of madeira.

Tilting her head at the instrument, Ellie asked Harriet, 'Have you played much recently?'

'Not as much as I'd like,' her friend replied. 'How about you?'

'I've long conceded that music is not my forte,' Ellie admitted. 'It's Richard who far excels in that area.'

Hearing this, Lord Sutton said, 'Is that so?'

'My dear sister exaggerates,' replied Richard. 'I merely enjoy making a great clamour.'

'It's been too long since I've heard your clamour,' Ellie said. 'Would you please play for us?'

Richard sighed with mock exasperation. 'Only for you, dear sister.'

He made a show of dragging himself to the instrument, which elicited the intended giggles from Ellie and Harriet, and sat down to play a mischievous Haydn sonata, one of his and Ellie's favourites. Some of the passages were uneven and some notes weren't quite right, but he remained good-natured throughout his performance and garnered a hearty round of applause when he finished.

'I'm afraid that's the only one I still remember,' he said, casting a mournful glance at the pile of music sheets beside the pianoforte. 'And you know how awful I am at reading music.'

'Do you have a preferred hand?' Harriet asked.

'The right.'

'Well, perhaps I could do the left and we could muddle our way through something.'

Richard brightened at this. 'A capital idea, Miss Harriet!'

Ellie watched as the two went through the sheets, deciding on a piece. The cards table had resumed their game after Richard's interlude, and Marcus took Harriet's vacated spot. Lord Sutton stood a little further off and seemed content to survey the scene before him. He smiled when the duo played the first chords of a Mozart sonata and closed his eyes.

Beside her, Marcus asked, 'How are you faring?'

'Very well indeed. It has been a wonderful day.' She looked at Richard, who was squinting at the music as he played. 'Thank you for this gift – I was none the wiser until I saw him this morning.'

'It's been our pleasure.' He paused, then added: 'Lord Sutton has played quite a part in conveying Richard here.'

'I've heard as much,' said Ellie. 'My dearest brother, thank you for allowing…the other gift.'

Marcus nodded, reading her thoughts. 'We will speak of this later.'

They turned their attention back to the musical duo, who, despite never having played together before, were coordinating rather well. Three quarters of the way through, Richard fumbled on a particularly difficult passage and couldn't help breaking into laughter.

'We're a sorry pair,' he said to Harriet, still laughing. 'Though the fault is all mine – you were doing brilliantly!'

The sudden lack of music – in the middle of a phrase, no less – felt strange to Ellie, a sentiment Lord Sutton seemed to share. He approached the pianoforte, glass still in hand.

'Forgive my intrusion, but I think Herr Mozart would be much offended to have his work abandoned when you are so close to the end. Mr Richard, may I attempt your part?'

'Yes, please do!' Richard stood, while Lord Sutton set down his brandy. The viscount bowed to Harriet before sitting on her right at a respectable distance. She counted them in, and they picked up from the interruption, Lord Sutton's fingers gliding across the keyboard with ease and grace. A little surprised at first, Harriet soon regained her composure and provided a steady accompaniment to Lord Sutton's melody.

Their combined performance was soon over, and Richard clapped enthusiastically. 'Why, Lord Sutton, you've been keeping your talents to yourself! May we have another?'

The viscount smiled and turned to Harriet on his left. 'Only if the lady wishes.'

Harriet chose another Mozart piece, and, after a quick exchange, the new duo switched places. Lord Sutton played his part effortlessly, providing a regular rhythm for Harriet in the jaunty tune. Harriet's delight was palpable, and the viscount seemed similarly happy. Before the recapitulation, he glanced up at Ellie, holding her gaze for almost three bars before he required the sheets again. It struck Ellie that he was trying to please her without making a show of it, and the thought warmed her to the bones.

As one piece led to another, the rest of the room continued in their soft chatter, with an occasionally louder remark from the card table. Harriet and Lord Sutton reached a happy accord in their playing and were now continuing through a series of sonatas in all their movements. Meanwhile, Richard settled on the other side of Marcus, and the two brothers spoke quietly. Ellie let the ambience wash over her, and she found herself very much content to remain where she was, surrounded by music, family, and friends.

There was a brief on the chaise while her two brothers changed seats. Now beside her, Richard laid a hand atop hers.

'My sweet sister, I don't think I've ever seen you so happy.'

'You've yourself to credit for that,' she replied.

'You honour me too much. You've grown so much since I saw you last.'

'But not *too* much, I'd hope.'

He smiled, a little sadly. 'Indeed. I'd hate to see you weary of the world.'

Then he looked away, studying the painting above the fireplace for a long moment. The firelight flickered across both the portrait and the man, and Ellie watched in fascination as the differences emerged. She had once thought the portrait a more serious version than her brother, but now, she saw the reverse was true.

Squeezing his hand lightly, Ellie asked, 'What troubles you?'

'They are my burdens to bear.' He closed his eyes. 'Perhaps I'll share them when you are eighteen.'

Ellie nodded, understanding the implication. 'Then I shall remind you next year.'

At the pianoforte, Harriet began to make considerably more mistakes, though they were working through an *andante* movement with few technical demands. When they'd played the final chord, Ellie heard Lord Sutton ask if Harriet wished to sing instead.

'My talent for singing is even less than my passable playing,' she responded. 'But I do know some accompaniments by heart and can play them reasonably well, if you'd like to sing.'

They agreed upon a Handel aria, and Lord Sutton stood, bowing at his small audience. Beside her, Richard straightened to attention, saying to his siblings, 'We've tried to get him to sing at the barracks, but he's always refused.'

The music started, with neither pianist nor singer requiring any sheets to guide them. Perhaps due to her familiarity with the song, Harriet played with more feeling and tenderness. The room quieted until the only sounds were the crackling of the fire and the notes from the pianoforte.

And then, in a clear, smooth baritone, rose Lord Sutton's voice, warm and rich and wrapping around Ellie's heart. She should have been surprised to hear such tenderness from this proud man – vaguely, she heard a sharp intake of breath from Kitty or Mary – but somehow, Ellie had known. The world knew of his status and cool composure, but she had been privy to his uncertainties, his rapture, his sensitivities. What she heard now was merely an extension of the man she had come to know.

His expression shifted in recognition, and Ellie's heart responded in kind. A smile grew on her lips, unbidden and unassuming, and though his own lips were preoccupied with the song, Lord Sutton's eyes deepened, focusing on her – and only her. He charmed and caressed Handel's words and music into his own, and gave them to her with all the intensity and sincerity of his very being, which she, in turn, welcomed and folded into herself. It became their song, their unspoken ownership and partnership, their untouchable music of the spheres.

The song came to its natural close, slowly and softly. A moment of silence ensued, before someone clapped and the others joined in. This time, it was Lord Sutton who looked away first, bowing to the audience and making a gracious gesture at Harriet, his own smile as wide and generous as Ellie had ever seen. Marcus rose from his seat to offer his compliments, and the two gentlemen shook hands before Marcus thanked their guests, signalling the end of the evening. Recovering her wits, Ellie also expressed her thanks, and the Ashcrofts walked the Earlwoods to the great hall and watched their carriage depart.

But through it all, Ellie's mind was elsewhere, recalling the sights and sounds of Lord Sutton's performance. There was no question now that they shared something beyond civility and a mutual appreciation for the arts – not when his eyes softened as they bid each other goodnight, nor when she felt his gaze upon her as she ascended the stairs, nor when, much later, she lay in bed, warmly wrapped in the echoes of his voice.

And through it all, Ellie was transformed – by memory, by knowledge, by the slow fire kindled within.

26

SUTTON AWOKE BEFORE dawn the following day, and knowing sleep would not return to him, he rose and rang for his valet. It took him a few, sleepy moments to realise he had brought none of his men to Thornleigh Abbey – by then, a servant had arrived, and Sutton politely asked if anyone was available to assist his toilette. Some minor confusion ensued until Mr Ashcroft's own valet arrived to attend on Sutton. The valet's initial surprise quickly settled into appreciation for the viscount's wardrobe, and they had a pleasant exchange on the subject. Although not a word was said about Mr Ashcroft himself, Sutton deduced with a smile that the Master of Thornleigh Abbey preferred to dress well after the sun had risen. The viscount was amused at the thought, but was otherwise unconcerned – after all, Sutton knew he was not alone in his penchant for mornings, and he would be quite happy indeed to spend some time in a particular lady's company.

There was a spring to his step as Sutton descended the stairs and was led to the parlour, where a full breakfast selection was already laid out. But his hopes were dashed when he saw only Richard Ashcroft, alone at the table and enjoying a hearty breakfast.

The viscount managed to school his features before Richard noticed his presence, and greeted the young man warmly. Richard rose from his seat, making quick work of his mouthful, and saying: 'Good morning, Lord Sutton! Please, do take a seat!'

Sutton obliged and, much to Richard's amusement, asked for some toast and tea.

'That's precisely what my sister prefers in the morning!'

'Is that so?' Sutton could see no evidence of crumbs anywhere on the table, and chose instead to focus on Richard's plate. 'I see you don't have the same preferences.'

Richard sat down and chuckled, a sound becoming as familiar and endearing to Sutton as Graham's own laughter. 'It's also Mrs Nancy's unparalleled skills. I've been dreaming of her breakfasts all these months, and I very much intend to make the most of my time back home!'

'You seem very fond of Mrs Nancy.'

'Oh yes, indeed. My sister and I are very close in age – we grew up under the combined care of both Mrs Nancy and our nurse. And while poor nurse was tasked with disciplining two wilful children, it was Mrs Nancy's mission to nourish and reward us.'

Sutton's tea and toast arrived, and he admired the golden hues of the bread. Noticing this, Richard said, 'And Mrs Nancy always makes the perfect toast. Ellie went through a period when all she would eat was buttered toast – I suspect Mrs Nancy can now turn out a batch in her sleep.'

'I daresay this might be superior to my own cook's handiwork.'

Richard sipped his own tea, smiling. 'Did you also grow up in the kitchens?'

Months ago, this impertinent question from a mere acquaintance would have made Sutton indignant, and he would have formulated a sarcastic reply while resolving to sever all ties with whoever dared voice such a presumption. Yet his time spent with the army – and, indeed, with Richard himself – had changed him so drastically that Sutton only chuckled, a gleam in his eyes.

'I was quite the insufferable child and thought I owned the kitchens. I even wiled away many a day believing I was in charge of the operations, commandeering all activities from my high chair.'

Richard laughed good-heartedly. 'And your cook didn't mind? Or your nurse, for that matter?'

'They were both too afraid to upset me, lest they lost their positions – though I do think they also felt rather sorry for me.'

Richard grew thoughtful at this. 'I commiserate with you. Although my brother did his best to bring up two siblings when he was barely a man himself, he did not always manage to shelter us from harm.'

Sutton nodded, considering his next words carefully. 'Graham has told me a little about your youth. He thought I'd take it better hearing it from him, rather than a gossip with questionable intentions.'

'And did you take it better?'

The young man had become incredibly still. Understanding Richard's trepidation, Sutton answered as gently as he could. 'I hope my being here speaks more loudly than words ever could.'

Richard relaxed. 'Thank you.'

'No need,' Sutton replied, waving a hand. 'We have no choice in how we come into this world – what matters is what we decide to do when we are here.'

'Why, Lord Sutton, you're starting to sound like a revolutionist.'

'Mind you, it's only' – he paused and pulled out his pocket watch – 'eight o'clock. I will have changed my mind thrice over by noon.'

Richard's amusement turned into delight as footsteps brought another arrival to the breakfast room. Following the younger man's gaze, Sutton saw a glowing Miss Ashcroft, her practical morning dress complemented by a smudge of paint across her left cheek. The two men stood in greeting and the lady curtsied in response.

'Good morning, Lord Sutton.' Her smile was shy but warm. She walked to her brother. 'Richard, I hope you've been looking after our guest.'

'Lord Sutton's not the sort that needs to be "looked after",' the young man replied, winking at Sutton. 'You've not been gone for long – are congratulations or commiserations in order?'

She kissed Richard's cheek and sat down beside him, opposite Sutton, and the two men took their seats again.

'A little of both.' She scrunched up her face, and Sutton decided he was rather partial to this playful side of her. 'I *think* I've managed to get all the colours right, but the composition doesn't feel right. I can't put a finger on *precisely* what's wrong, but staring at it was only making me cross-eyed.'

'You'll get there,' Richard said. 'Or you won't. Either way, I'll remain in awe of your talents.'

Sutton held back a chuckle at the mixture of patience and exasperation on Miss Ashcroft's face. Sensing his amusement, she addressed him directly: 'I love my brother dearly, but as you may have surmised, he's not particularly adept at offering artistic advice.'

'Nor do I claim it,' Richard replied. 'Lord Sutton is far more suited to the task.'

'You give me too much credit,' Sutton said. His heart felt curious at Miss Ashcroft's scrutiny, so he turned his attention to a slice of toast, spreading the butter liberally.

At this, Miss Ashcroft turned to her brother. 'Look at how you've neglected our guest! Your own plate is brimming while Lord Sutton has resorted to mere bread!'

'You're quite unlike yourself,' Richard said, at the same time Sutton said: 'Rest assured, ma'am – this is entirely my preference.'

Blushing a little, Miss Ashcroft drank her tea in silence. Although Sutton was quite preoccupied with his own novel feelings and the curious warmth in his chest, he now noticed the lady was out of sorts. Her hand reached for her collar, but there was nothing there. Sutton watched as her surprise eased into relief, and followed her gaze to find the emerald ring on Richard's right hand. It was, after all, a token from her brother – Sutton should have known.

'I'm afraid I don't have my sketchbook with me,' Richard said, oblivious to what had passed. 'There's nothing spectacular in it – I sent you all the good ones – but who knows when inspiration might strike.' The younger man turned to Sutton. 'Ellie's excellent at painting, but she hasn't travelled as much as me. I send her sketches whenever I go someplace new, and she turns them into all those magnificent paintings – we'll be collaborating like so for years.'

Sutton nodded, remembering this particular revelation too well. 'Ah yes – the only benefit of Mr Hill's "teachings".'

'Oh, you know all about Mr Hill! I'm sure Ellie painted him in a much more generous light than he was, that pretentious toad.'

'Richard!' admonished Miss Ashcroft, to which her brother only shrugged. 'Lord Sutton, how did you learn your painting?'

'From sycophantic instructors who cared more about their reputation than my education,' Sutton said before he could stop himself. The memory of Miss Ashcroft's kind compliments returned, and he shuffled in his seat. 'They spent too much time flattering my "genius", and had no time left to cultivate it.'

'Your tastes are impeccable,' Miss Ashcroft replied, much to Richard's agreement.

'Yet I do not possess the skills to *create.*' Sutton sighed a bit more loudly than necessary, hoping it would conceal his true disappointment. 'Alas, that is all but in the past.'

'Not necessarily,' said Richard, his voice suddenly excited. 'Why don't we all practise our sketching today? We could each take turns at modelling, and we'll convince Marcus and Kitty to join when they rise – no doubt Kitty would prefer an outdoor amusement, but the rain's not letting up any time soon. We'll all have a chance to improve – it'll be capital!'

Richard rang the bell, and before either Sutton or Miss Ashcroft could protest, they both found themselves swept up in the young man's enthusiasm.

By the time dinner was announced, Sutton had completed no fewer than twenty sketches of the Ashcroft family. True to his word, Richard had cajoled Mr and Mrs Ashcroft to partake in the exercise. While the Ashcroft patriarch refused to pick up a pencil himself, he indulged his siblings and passed the day as a model. Mrs Ashcroft, on the other hand, alternated between drawing and modelling – in the former, her sketches barely resembled her subjects, which alleviated Sutton's embarrassment about his own woeful attempts; in the latter, she was a stellar participant, eager to strike all manners of flamboyant poses.

The quintet compared sketches after each session, equally ready to praise strengths and acknowledge shortcomings. Richard and Miss Ashcroft were by far the most skilled with a pencil, but Sutton found that, with their gentle criticisms and encouragement, he was able to address his weaknesses. He would not go so far as to call the day's exercise transformative, but he did wonder what might have become of his art had his own tutors taken this approach.

Mrs Ashcroft had tired of sketching by the day's end, and announced during dessert her inclination to make merry with some music in the evening. Richard lauded the idea, and the matter was all but settled. Sutton was soon seated in a comfortable chaise in the drawing room with a glass of brandy, feeling a little out of place while Miss Ashcroft, Mrs Ashcroft, and Richard gathered around the pianoforte debating which songs to sing and which parts to distribute. Mr Ashcroft, who sat beside the viscount, gave him an amused look.

'As you can see, Lord Sutton, my family can be quite a handful.'

Hearing this, Mrs Ashcroft called out from the pianoforte: 'And to think we're on our best behaviour, too.'

'Let's do the Thomas Arne!' proclaimed Richard. '"Blow, Blow Thou Winter Wind" – how topical! Ellie, you take the right hand and I'll take the left. Kitty, you'll be our voice.'

'Oh dear, I haven't sung in quite some time...' She turned towards the two men on the chaise and said: 'We'll need a few practice runs – we'll pretend you're not here, and you should both do the same.'

With that, the trio started the worst rendition of Arne's Shakespearean songs Sutton had ever heard – and also the most charming.

'I hope you're not finding your evening too trying,' Mr Ashcroft said at his side. His voice was soft and would not be heard by the musicians. Sutton replied in kind.

'Not at all – though I admit it might take some acclimatising.'

Mr Ashcroft's eyes shone with amusement, and Sutton saw the resemblance with his siblings. 'You're a brave and honest man, Lord Sutton.'

Sutton turned to observe Miss Ashcroft, whose absolute concentration softened his heart. There was a certain warmth between him and Mr Ashcroft tonight, and Sutton thought it the most opportune time to make his intentions known.

Gathering his courage, Sutton looked back at Mr Ashcroft and said: 'And your sister is a remarkable woman. With your permission, I wish to court Miss Ashcroft.'

The two men were silent for a while, waiting for the musicians to finish one song and start another. A few bars into the next song, Mr Ashcroft spoke again, his voice as soft as before.

'My sister and I have never discussed the topic of her entering into matrimony – her situation in life is comfortable and secure. She has expressed her desire to excel in her craft, and I will do everything in my power to assist her. While she is under my care, my sister is given leave to do anything she wishes.'

If Sutton had admired Mr Ashcroft's principles before, they only increased after this latest discovery.

'Sir, I cannot claim we have much in common,' Sutton said, 'save one crucial exception: our regard for Miss Ashcroft's welfare and happiness. I am pleased to learn of your stalwart support of her wishes. She is very talented indeed, and, with the assistance of such influential figures as Mr Livingston, I have no doubt she will make her own indelible mark on the artistic world.'

He paused as the music stopped briefly, only continuing after it had resumed.

'But if you think I would somehow attempt to hinder Miss Ashcroft's progress or suppress her passions, then you are sorely mistaken. My intentions are quite the opposite: I only wish to encourage her work, challenge her mind, and support her every endeavour.'

'Well,' Mr Ashcroft said slowly, 'the bold birthday present you gave her does show as much.'

This concession sounded to Sutton like a small victory. 'On the note of her work, I think it would be quite beneficial for Miss Ashcroft to step a little out of her current boundaries. She has a unique perspective, which, while rare in itself, is doubly so when coupled with her extraordinary talents in expression. Allowing her to travel and explore the outside world would do wonders for her art.'

'I appreciate your advice,' Mr Ashcroft said, this time with a little steel, 'but do not overstep. As you have witnessed first-hand, my sister does not boast the hardiest constitution, and is much too fragile to handle your extravagant suggestions.'

It took effort to keep his voice low. 'I respectfully disagree. I believe Miss Ashcroft is much stronger than you give her credit.' He made the decision to lay down all his cards, and alleviate the last possible reservation Mr Ashcroft may hold. 'I have seen the bond she shares with Mr Richard as clearly as I have seen her sublime portrait of him in the drawing room. I have no doubt that Miss Ashcroft will love and defend her brother to the very ends of the earth, and that, in itself, is infinitely braver than the matter of pushing one's artistic boundaries.'

They sat through the next song without a word. When Mr Ashcroft spoke again, Sutton was prepared for what was to follow.

'You know about Richard.'

Remembering his embarrassing outburst to Graham, Sutton straightened, determined to be more dignified this time. 'I do. I also know he possesses a gentleman's best qualities and deserves to be treated as such.'

'And would your family share the same view?'

Sutton scoffed softly. 'I have no immediate family left in this world. My extended family consists of gentle souls, discontent with the *status quo* but too meek to challenge it, or cunning minds trying to beguile me into drawing up the entailment my father had intended but didn't quite manage before his passing.'

With the exception of Graham, Sutton had never shared such a stark truth with any of his acquaintances. But Sutton hoped he had read the gentleman correctly – after all, Mr Ashcroft loved and defended his half-brother, and had married Mrs Ashcroft, a woman with her own questionable qualities and relations.

It was enough to satisfy Mr Ashcroft. 'You have my permission to court my sister, though the final decision lies solely with her. In return, you must give me your word that you will not harm or distress her.'

'You have it.' Sutton extended a hand, which Mr Ashcroft promptly took. The gentlemen shook to bind their agreement.

Mrs Ashcroft had noticed the exchange, and asked after the song was over: 'Lord Sutton, what has my husband persuaded you to do?'

The viscount was irritated by this prying, particularly when Miss Ashcroft looked at them so inquisitively. To his relief, Mr Ashcroft calmly answered:

'Lord Sutton has agreed to a game of charades after you are finished with your songs.'

Mrs Ashcroft clapped her hands together in delight, while Miss Ashcroft brightened at the words. 'How marvellous! Let's do one last song then – and let's make it a good one!'

The pianoforte started again, and Lord Sutton turned to his companion. 'Thank you, Mr Ashcroft. I will happily keep score.'

'Could you be entreated to join a team?'

'I don't believe my talents lie in constructing silent impressions.'

'Neither did I,' replied Mr Ashcroft, 'but necessity dictated I learn the skill – a piece of well-meaning advice to a family friend.'

The music stumbled towards some particularly discordant bars, and Sutton smiled despite himself. 'Then I shall reconsider my stance.'

27

As Richard's impromptu visit drew to a close, Ellie's initial delight mellowed into the melancholy that accompanied having to part with her brother. The remaining days of his visit passed by quickly, and the eve of his departure arrived sooner than she would have liked.

After Richard's last dinner at Thornleigh – itself a lavish feast featuring the young man's favourite dishes – Ellie broke their habit of venturing into the drawing room, and instead invited Richard to her private studio. She was apologetic to the others for not extending her invitation, but they were happy to proceed to the drawing room first. Kitty and Marcus were both understanding, and even Lord Sutton, who had been exceptionally amiable during his stay, responded graciously to her, and then asked the remaining party if they wished to hear any music this evening. It was his first such offer since he'd surprised them with his playing and singing, and Ellie rather regretted missing out on another opportunity to hear his music.

The viscount, however, was nothing but astute. 'If Mr Richard is so inclined, perhaps we could make merry on the pianoforte later in the evening.'

'I am indeed – let's do so!'

She and Richard were well away from the dining room when her brother said, 'My dearest sister, have you and Lord Sutton reached an agreement of sorts?'

Ellie reddened. 'I don't know what you mean – I don't even know what such an "agreement" would entail!'

Her brother's grin only widened. 'I suspect some possibilities include the exchange of promises, of rings, of locks of hair – the latter would be particularly delightful, given Lord Sutton's endowments in that regard.'

'There has been no exchange of the sort!'

Having reached their destination, Ellie felt sufficiently justified in redirecting the conversation.

'I've been working on a new piece these past few weeks,' she said, leading him into what had become her most private place in the house. 'It's very different from anything I've attempted before, and it's not quite finished, but I wanted to show it to you nonetheless.'

The canvas was on its easel, just as she had left it this morning, but the room was enshrouded in darkness. Reaching for a candle, Ellie made quick work of lighting the room, keeping her attention on the task at hand. Her usual nerves from sharing a new work were now compounded by her uncertainty about the subject matter.

When the room was adequately lit, Ellie hazarded a glance at her brother, uncertain of what to expect. What she saw, however, stunned her; the jovial brother she had known her entire life was looking at the half-finished painting with uncharacteristic sadness.

'Oh, Ellie,' he said softly, 'I don't know what to say.' Then, in a thick voice: 'I wish to look away, for fear of crying if I don't, but I am also impelled to look upon it and allow the emotions to flow as they will. I've never doubted your talents before, but this... This is something altogether.'

Richard held out an arm, and Ellie ducked into it wordlessly, settling into her brother's embrace. She held on fiercely as her own throat choked with tears.

'Please, be safe.' And then, though she knew he would have no response for her next words, she let them slip past her. 'Please, promise to return safely.'

Richard wrapped his arms around her more completely, burying his face in her hair to hide his own tears.

It was with a heavy heart that Ellie rose the next day, the dreariness of winter finally weighing down on her. She took her time with her morning toilette, eventually choosing a yellow dress to help brighten their imminent farewell.

When she finally arrived in the breakfast room, Ellie was surprised to see Marcus and Kitty already seated despite the hour, engaging Richard in some lively conversation. Lord Sutton, whose early habits had become open knowledge, also sat at the table, nursing a cup of tea. He was the first to notice Ellie's arrival, and gave her the soft, gentle smile she so relished.

Then Richard looked up, and her heart constricted once more. 'Good morning, Ellie! You look so lovely in that dress!'

'Good morning, Richard,' she replied, giving her brother the most cheerful smile she could muster. 'Are you ready for your journey?'

'As ready as I'll ever be!'

Ellie exchanged greetings with the rest of the table and sat opposite Richard, noting how the morning room seating had shifted. For the most of her life, Marcus had sat at the head, flanked by Richard at the left and Ellie at the right. Soon after Kitty joined the family and Richard left for the army, the new Mrs Ashcroft took the honoured right side of the table, with Ellie taking the left – a seat she occupied until a few days ago, when Kitty moved to Marcus's left hand to make way for Lord Sutton as their esteemed guest. Richard and Ellie were left to sit beside Lord Sutton and Kitty respectively, and their distance from the head of the table made Ellie feel like a child once more.

Her musings were interrupted by Kitty, who read out Mary Earlwood's latest letter. The eldest Earlwood daughter expressed her father's gratitude for Lord Sutton's gift of gin, and, on behalf of the family, wished the viscount and ensign safe travels.

The rest of the conversation was stilted, and it seemed an age until the party rose to make for the main entrance where Lord Sutton's carriage awaited.

Richard fell into step with Ellie, linking their arms once more.

'Just so you know,' he said, 'I'll be sorely disappointed if you don't go straight to your studio after I've left. I'm most eager to see my completed painting.'

'*Your* painting?'

'Yes, of *course*.' He puffed up his chest, drawing laughter from Ellie. 'I henceforth expect nothing fewer than three paintings in my honour every year!'

Ellie gave her brother a stern look. 'I may put up with your newfound bossiness, but I doubt it'll capture other ladies' hearts!'

With a flourishing bow, he replied, 'Ah, but I've no need for *any* lady's heart, not when I've been blessed with the most wonderful sister – *and* sister-in-law – one could have!'

'Flatterer,' muttered Kitty. 'Try not to get into too much mischief.'

They had reached the entrance, where the open door brought in the early winter chill. Richard exchanged kisses with Ellie and Kitty, and then a firm handshake with Marcus. The two brothers never said much to each other; their determined jaws and eyes spoke more than words could. After a long moment, the two men parted, both as brothers and as equals.

Kitty turned to their other guest. 'Lord Sutton, are you certain we cannot entreat you to extend your stay? You've hardly been here a week, which is a travesty given the distances you've travelled!'

'I am touched by your hospitality and friendship,' replied he, 'but I confess, seeing the familiar comforts of Thornleigh after my time in Colchester has made me long for home. I shall accompany Ensign Richard part of the way to Essex, but I'm afraid we must go our separate ways after our second change.'

'Oh, that's not what I meant at all!' exclaimed Kitty, at the same time Marcus said, 'You have been exceedingly kind to us already.'

While Lord Sutton's departure had been overshadowed by Richard's, Ellie felt another twinge of sadness at having to say goodbye, this time twice over.

'Miss Ashcroft,' the viscount said, 'I wish you all the very best with your current and future works. I have no doubt you will impress Mr Livingston.'

'Thank you, Lord Sutton. And thank you for the gifts – I will cherish them.'

'Oh no – that will not do. Brushes and canvases are meant to be used – sometimes even abused. By all accounts, do *not* cherish them.'

As the viscount shook his head gravely to mark his point, Ellie noted his second waistcoat button was undone. This, along with his mock seriousness, elicited a smile and a nod.

'Then I shall use them well – and cherish their sentiment.'

The viscount gave them one last bow before crossing the threshold of Thornleigh Abbey once more, this time in his departure. Ellie, Kitty, and Marcus remained within as the two men climbed into the carriage. Once the horses were afoot, the trio moved to the parlour where there was a fair vantage of the carriage ring. Within moments, the chaise passed by, Richard braving the light drizzle to look out and wave goodbye. Ellie sat in her spot, unmoving, until the carriage was out of their sight.

Kitty laid a hand on her shoulder. 'We'll see him again. We'll see them *both* again.'

Ellie swallowed her tears, hoping beyond hope the words would prove true. 'It turns out I'm not very good at saying goodbye.'

'No one is,' replied Kitty gently. 'Have faith, dearest Ellie – we *will* see them again.'

28

THE TWO MEN looked out the window at the scenery around them, all too aware of their growing distance from Thornleigh Abbey. Richard remained uncharacteristically quiet, fidgeting with his hands. The emerald ring he had worn during the last few days was gone, presumably back on Miss Ashcroft's neck chain. In this absence of conversation, Sutton listened to the steady rhythm of hooves and wheels upon the road. It would be four hours until a brief rest and change of horses, and another four until they reached their second inn, whereupon they would go their separate ways.

Unlike their journey from Colchester, which, despite its length, was brightened by anticipation, the mere quarter of an hour on this first leg already felt far too long. Richard had closed his eyes and would have appeared at ease if not for the continual wringing of his hands. Sutton was loathe to intrude, and sat across in mutual silence.

Instead, the viscount satisfied himself with facts and memories alike: the facts of having gathered the courage to voice his intentions to Mr Ashcroft, of receiving the permission he'd sought from the patriarch, of admitting, irrefutably, his interest to the world; the memories of Miss Ashcroft, gentle, joyous, looking at him with quiet intensity. He had sketched every member of the Ashcroft family, and the Ashcroft family now had sketches of him. He had been treated as if one of their own.

It was a thought both exhilarating and terrifying.

The rain and road continued, leaving Sutton to contemplate these novel sensations.

Richard returned to his usual self during the last part of their journey together. Stretching their legs, inhaling the fresh country air, and warming their stomachs with hearty soup did wonders for the young man, whose bright eyes once again took in the world around him.

'I may have been lax in my expression of it,' he said to Sutton, 'for which I deeply apologise, but I am very thankful indeed for your companionship and assistance throughout the last week.'

Sutton did not try to keep the smile out of his reply. 'Of all the endless ways you might have broken your silence, you opted for something dull. I am much disappointed.'

Richard grinned. 'Well then, perhaps you might like to know you've missed a button on your waistcoat.'

Unfazed, Sutton looked down and remedied the situation. Since Mr Ashcroft arose early this morning, the gentleman's valet had assisted Sutton in most of the task before he was called away. The viscount finished dressing unaided, and must have failed to secure the button in question.

'Thank you.'

'You're quite welcome. Now that the required pleasantries are out of the way,' continued Richard, 'might I ask if you enjoyed your time at Thornleigh?'

'I did very much indeed. Your family is a little different from others of my acquaintance, if I may be honest, but they are more marvellous for it.'

Richard nodded in understanding. 'I think my brother was a lot more subdued before meeting his wife – she's brought much cheer to Thornleigh in the past year.'

'Perhaps she merely coaxed to the surface what had remained hidden,' said

Sutton. 'I imagine you and Miss Ashcroft had quite a colourful childhood.'

'We did,' Richard replied with amusement. 'Growing up, I'd thought my family perfectly typical – especially since my sister and I were quite sheltered. We had a range of tutors and instructors, and we never had much interaction with other children. I never went to boarding school, and never saw any need – it was Marcus who insisted I attend Cambridge like a proper gentleman. When I finally discovered the world beyond Thornleigh, it was quite a shock to realise *we* were the atypical ones!'

'Great Britain would be a much better place if its families resembled yours,' he said, 'particularly in the ways of love and affection, given without conditions, triumphing over circumstance.'

The moving carriage provided the sole sound for a moment.

'You make it sound so simple,' Richard finally said.

'It *is* simple – though it may not be easy. Nevertheless, one should not conflate the two.'

Richard formed his next words tentatively. 'You seem to have quite an opinion on the issue. Please forgive me – I do not mean to be rude – but are you perhaps speaking from any personal experiences?'

'Not quite – but in a way, yes.'

The admission opened Sutton to vulnerabilities he'd rather not acknowledge, but his compassion and admiration for the younger man, who had suffered infinitely more, overruled his anxiety.

'My great grandfather, a flamboyant man, was involved in a prominent scandal – itself exacerbated by unfortunate political connections – that almost destroyed the Sutton viscountcy during the early Hanoverian reign. My grandfather was so relieved to inherit the title and so protective of it thereafter that he did his utmost to ensure his children would never be guilty of such crimes. Fortunately for him, and for the viscountcy, his heir – my father – was most stalwart in returning to his Puritan roots. But unfortunately for my poor mother, none of my siblings survived past infancy.'

'You must have carried quite a burden,' Richard said quietly.

'We all have our crosses to bear – and it just so happens that yours and mine are as opposite as they can be. The golden mean would be highly advantageous here.' Sutton sighed. 'Still, I find my own complaints are unsubstantiated. I cannot possibly imagine what you've suffered in face of the very same unkindness condemned by the teachings of Christ, which the Church then becomes the first to condemn – and not the father for his sins, but you, for bearing the proof of them.'

'Or perhaps *you're* too hasty in dismissing your own suffering. My brother and sister have loved and accepted me every day of my life – it is their priceless gift that equips me to deal with the rest of the world. It is *I* who cannot imagine growing up without the comforts I have taken for granted.'

Sutton was touched by the consolation. 'Lieutenant Graham helped a great deal.'

'I don't doubt that one bit,' replied Richard, his expression softening.

The mention of Graham provided Sutton with a suitable segue away from one solemn subject to another. 'Are you eager to return to the barracks?'

'I am. I already miss my family – yes, I'm well aware it's not yet been a full day – but I *am* looking forward to making myself useful once more.'

'And that, my friend, is what continues to hold me in awe. I may boast my titles and estates, but hardly any other virtues.'

Richard chuckled. 'Well, you have made our meals more palatable. That is not an insignificant feat.'

They passed the rest of their journey in light conversation about their mutual companions, and, when they reached the next inn, Sutton was quite sorry to part with the young man.

It took a restless night at the inn and another long day before Sutton was finally home. The gates of Bellevue Park, somewhat imposing to visitors and passers-by, were nothing short of welcoming to their master, who, after the customary greetings to the butler and housekeeper upon his return, immediately ordered the two home comforts after a long journey: a bath and a hot meal.

It would take a quarter of an hour for the former to be ready, and another hour for the latter, but Sutton had no need of contending with his usual impatience. His time with Graham and the Ashcrofts had challenged and enlightened him – he had only himself to blame for his dissatisfactions, but it was also within his power to strive for his own happiness and peace.

His mind made up about one particular matter, Sutton asked for his steward and made for his private study with purpose and determination. He ignored the pile of correspondence on one side of his desk, reaching for his banknotes instead. When he'd counted out the required amount, the viscount pulled out a clean sheet of paper and dipped a readied pen in ink.

Dear Mrs Evans:

I enclose here a sum of one hundred pounds, with which I wish to cease our arrangement. I hope I have not caused offence with this seemingly hasty decision, and I wish to assure you I have nothing short of the deepest regard for you. Your assistance and discretion over the past few years have been invaluable both personally and professionally, and you have enriched my artwork and style considerably. It is only a change in my circumstances that have prompted this – though I would not insult your intelligence to assume you have been ignorant after our last engagement – and if we are to meet again, I hope we will do so as friends.

Yours, etc,

Aubrey Charles Beaumont, 7th Viscount Sutton

He had just signed off his name on the final banknote when his steward arrived. Sutton folded and sealed the letter.

'Please deliver this to Mrs Evans.'

'Immediately, my lord?'

Sutton took out his pocket watch – it was almost five in the afternoon. 'Yes, Allen. If she is otherwise engaged this evening, return first thing tomorrow morning.'

'Very good, my lord – I will see to it personally.'

The viscount listened to Allen's receding footsteps until they disappeared, and only the crackling of the fire accompanied Sutton's thoughts. His bath was no doubt ready, but the viscount was not – the stillness of his study sharpened his mind, where a clear vision had formed. He pulled out his sketches from Thornleigh and sorted the ones of Miss Ashcroft into a separate pile. Most of his depictions were wanting, but they provided a good start for revisions.

He had known long ago that his artistic attempts would not be perfect, but it was only recently that he recognised perfection was not the goal. What mattered in this moment was his patience and perseverance – and Sutton understood, without a shadow of doubt, that he had the capacity to find both.

A fresh sheet of paper, a sharpened pencil, a tender smile at his previous sketches – and with steady, certain strokes, Sutton began to capture the loveliness of Miss Ashcroft.

29

'GOOD DAY, MR LIVINGSTON,' Ellie said to the gentleman in the formal drawing room. 'It is my great pleasure to welcome you to Thornleigh Abbey. Might I offer you some tea and cakes?'

Mr Livingston, who was much shorter and less severe than Ellie had expected, bowed, straightened, and gave his hat and walking stick to Oliver. 'Ah, Miss Ashcroft – we finally meet. While I am tempted to accept your hospitality, I am far more eager to see your works, if you would permit.'

'Yes, of course,' replied Ellie with barely a stutter, though she had not expected the gentleman to be so enthusiastic. She gestured to Kitty, and said the words she'd practised for the past day: 'I hope you'll allow me to introduce my sister-in-law, Mrs Ashcroft. She will be accompanying us.'

Mr Livingston bowed to Kitty. 'A pleasure, Mrs Ashcroft. Are you also inclined towards the arts?'

'I'm afraid not – I'm far too impatient for such endeavours. But I promise I shan't intrude on any of your discussions with Miss Ashcroft.'

'I am much obliged,' replied he.

The women rose, with Ellie leading the party. 'Shall we?'

It was too short a distance to the Artist's Wing for any substantial conversation, but they were able to ascertain Mr Livingston had only arrived in Darlington this morning and he would be off again the next morning. Nonetheless, Ellie invited the gentleman to sup with them, which Mr Livingston gratefully accepted, all the while gazing upon the paintings, vases, and other decorations they passed, as if his attention was always elsewhere.

Although Ellie was rather baffled by the short, stocky, and unremarkably-dressed man, she reassessed her initial impression when they entered the exhibition room. Indeed, Ellie watched the gentleman's swift transformation with silent fascination: suddenly, his eyes sharpened and his posture straightened, his very presence amplified and intensified. Ellie had been preparing to meet this cool and collected professional, but now that he had revealed himself, she was more than a little intimidated.

Yet his tone, while clear and practised, still held its previous kindness as he said, 'Miss Ashcroft, you have produced quite an impressive collection. May I look at these individually?'

'Please, take all the time you wish – Mrs Ashcroft and I will wait here.'

He gave her a little smile, and with that, Mr Livingston returned his attention to the paintings while the ladies arranged themselves on a couch at one end of the room. The day after Richard and Lord Sutton's departure last week, Ellie had alternated between finishing her latest painting and rearranging her other works in preparation for this very moment. Mr Curtis had surprised them all with his immeasurable assistance: true to his word, he had the plaques engraved and prepared to his high standards, which he delivered in person to Thornleigh two days past. For the rest of the afternoon, Mr Curtis not only helped Ellie pair the plaques with the paintings, but also offered suggestions on arranging her works based on thematic fluidity, intellectual impact, and emotional effect.

To Ellie's relief and satisfaction, Mr Livingston was now embarking on the exact path Mr Curtis had cultivated. She had been afraid Mr Livingston might find a couple of pieces uninteresting; before she could express this, Mr Curtis had been adamant about removing some of her weaker pieces, leaving behind only the best she had to offer. Certainly, Mr Livingston spent more observing some paintings than others – a comment on his personal preferences – but on no occasion did the gentleman glance over any single work.

Beside her, Kitty was as silent and demure as promised, though Ellie saw her sister-in-law picking at a seam on her dress. Ellie herself was tempted to wring her hands, but she bit her lip instead. Mr Livingston, who had patiently considered about one fifth of the paintings, seemed intent on providing the same treatment to the rest.

Almost an hour had passed by the time he reached 'We Happy Few', the incomplete painting of soldiers at their encampment, the oils still wet. She had been reluctant about including a piece that was only a quarter done, but Mr Curtis had insisted, arguing for the importance of showing Mr Livingston her future direction. There were enough completed works to vouch for Ellie's ability to finish 'We Happy Few'. She had also wished to position it as the final painting of her small exhibition, partially to signify that all the previous works had led to her most recent and daring achievement. Again, Mr Curtis had other ideas, persuading her to place it *near* the end and following it with some of her quieter works to act as a soft *denouement*. He had explained the Greek philosophy of *catharsis*, one of the crucial elements at the end of a tragic play, and Ellie had listened to him, enthralled, a little desirous of attending the theatre.

Now, Mr Livingston had become exceptionally still in front of the wet paint and pencil work that constituted 'We Happy Few'. Several hours seemed to pass before the gentleman moved away from it and towards the three works trailing after the storm. There was 'Mind Your Manners', a bird bath with spring chicks and their mother; 'The Fourth Course', the aftermath of a picnic, when the food had been consumed and their diners had left; and, finally, 'As Dreams Are Made On', a pair of muddy boots greeting the dawn of a new day.

Mr Livingston viewed all these, taking his time as he had before. He remained fixed in place at the final painting, spending as long as he had with 'We Happy Few'. When he walked away from it, and from the selection of Ellie's finest works, a single, low hum sounded in his throat. He approached Ellie and Kitty, and seemed surprised at the fading light outside.

The ladies rose to their feet. 'I hope you've found some works to your satisfaction,' Ellie said, a little nervous.

The gentleman studied her for a long moment before his countenance resumed to his earlier, genial self. As if on cue, his stomach grumbled, breaking the tension in the room.

'My apologies, Miss Ashcroft. Perhaps some tea would not be amiss – and you had mentioned cakes, I believe?'

'Yes, indeed,' replied Ellie. 'Our cook has prepared some citrus cakes, which are among my personal favourites.'

'Excellent! I've often been admonished for enjoying far too many slices than I ought, but as I always say, it's far better to enjoy something than to abhor it.'

When Ellie hesitated at this, Kitty stepped in, gesturing towards the hallway.

'Shall we, Mr Livingston?' Leading them back to the parlour, Kitty then asked: 'When do you typically dine?'

'Around seven o'clock. Now that I think of it, I may have missed luncheon today – it's always so hard to keep track when one is travelling.'

'My, you must be famished!' replied Kitty. 'In that case, might I suggest we skip afternoon tea and proceed straight to dinner? We usually dine at five.'

'Ah, that would be most excellent – thank you, Mrs Ashcroft. Time always passes so quickly when I study certain works of art – I have skipped more meals than I should care to admit!'

The last two hours may have passed very quickly indeed for Mr Livingston, but Ellie found it had crawled by much too slowly for her liking – and all without a word of appraisal from the gentleman. Indeed, Ellie's curiosity only continued to grow as Marcus joined them and the tablecloths were changed during dinner, while Mr Livingston engaged in a large number of topics: the culinary delights at Thornleigh; the similarities and differences between country and city; his own experiences on the Continent; even a touch of war and politics. It was as if he had not spent a large portion of the afternoon looking at her paintings – by the end of the sweets course, Ellie thought of the petite gentleman more as a genial guest than one of the most influential and renowned art critics in all of Great Britain.

It was only when they were settled in the drawing room again that Mr Livingston returned to the purpose of his visit. The gentleman sipped his port, praised its quality, and then said: 'Miss Ashcroft, the gentleman whose likeness hangs above the fireplace must be an important figure in your life. Has he inspired any pieces not on display today?'

Unprepared for the query, Ellie stuttered a little as she replied, 'Yes – well, no, not quite. That is, I have some sketches, and mean to paint more on the subject.'

'Good. I look forward to seeing them, either in their incomplete states or when they are finished – preferably both, if I may be so forthright.' Then, without any further amble or explanation, he said, 'Miss Ashcroft, allow me to praise you on your achievements. I enjoyed your paintings, and applaud your ability to capture the various sentiments attached to each of your works. Well done.

'While I admired all your paintings, only a few truly impressed me. All the works in "Persephone's Promise" were skilfully and tenderly executed – and they have an excellent title, might I add. "Rowan's Retreat" is very admirable. "We Happy Few", though it is still in its early stages, holds a lot of potential – I wish to see it again when it's complete.'

She had not expected this response and was at a loss for words. To her relief, Marcus saved her the trouble of answering. 'Thank you for your interest, Mr Livingston, and for taking the time to visit.'

'Of course. I very much enjoy discovering unknown artists.'

Here was the unspoken compliment that delighted Ellie to the very core: without any unnecessary praise, the gentleman had stated his approval and appreciation of her art, and, more importantly, his belief in her ability to create more such works in the years to come. This morning, she had simply wished to demonstrate her artistic capabilities to a complete stranger; now, she had received encouragement from this influential expert.

Ellie straightened in her seat. 'Thank you, Mr Livingston,' she said. 'Your endorsement means so very, *very* much to me – *truly*.' Then, with a blush: 'Forgive me – I am not gifted with words.'

The gentleman gave her a warm smile. 'Your gift is in observing and capturing your unique perspective of the world – and that is no small feat. I hope you will continue to draw and paint.'

'I shall,' she replied earnestly. 'I cannot imagine any alternative.'

The next morning, Ellie rose to a cold and rainy dawn, the dark grey sky gradually brightening into a lighter shade. Outside, the rain fell in constant sheets, showing no sign of abating, drowning out the songbirds. Winter had truly set in.

While this season was perfectly suited to Ellie's present ambitions for 'We Happy Few', especially with fires merrily lit throughout Thornleigh, it had the opposite effect on Kitty, whose spirits only continued to sink. Unable to go on any extended rides, Ellie's sister-in-law spent more time in her rooms than ever.

Not a week after Mr Livingston's visit, Ellie was on her way to morning tea when she heard her brother and his wife arguing in the parlour. Their topic of contention was not new: Kitty wished to spend more time outdoors, either in Rowan's Edge or to call on her friends on horseback; Marcus, on the grounds of preserving her health during the coldest months of the year, forbade her from doing so and consigned her to the grounds of Thornleigh, or to their chaise and four.

'*Pardon* me?' Kitty's uncharacteristically shrill voice carried down the corridor. 'Pray, have I heard *incorrectly*? Surely you did not just attempt to *forbid* me from leaving?'

'I did indeed,' came Marcus's tight response.

Ellie dared not take another step towards lest her presence became known. She saw Kitty's large cat just outside the door, looking rather disapproving of the entire exchange.

'Oh, *indeed*?' Kitty continued, unaware of their audience. 'Then I shall make *you* aware that I do *not* consent to such *forbidding*.'

'And I shall assure *you* that you consented to precisely such a thing when you became *my wife.*'

The ensuing silence was deafening.

'Do not try me, Marcus.'

'Likewise, Katherine. I have given my orders to the groom, and that is final.'

He left the room, still furious when he entered the corridor. Ellie ducked her head, not wishing to see her brother in such a state. His approaching footsteps made Ellie look up again. He appeared barely able to contain his anger. She followed when he gestured for them to walk, and the two remained silent until they reached the drawing room. By then, Marcus's irritation had mellowed into resignation.

'I'm sorry you were privy to such an unhappy exchange,' said he. 'She has such a strong will.'

'Which you admire,' Ellie said softly.

Marcus sighed. 'Yes, I do admire her will. Sometimes, I do wish it weren't so...' He shook his head.

Ellie considered her next words carefully. 'I admire Kitty's strength, too. I have always admired it. And I think it's difficult for someone with so much spirit to be confined inside, rain or no.'

'It is ghastly outside! She could catch a chill – or worse!'

'I know. And I'm sure Kitty knows, too.' Ellie thought of how she differed from her sister-in-law, and how Marcus must be struggling with Kitty's vivacious disposition during their first winter as husband and wife. 'Perhaps Kitty would be more comfortable in Bath, or some other milder climate.'

'Bath... We have spoken of it, but...' Marcus hesitated. 'Would you be willing to put your paintings on hold and come with us?'

Ellie drew in a deep breath. 'No, I would not. It suits me to remain at home, drawing, reading, and enjoying Mrs Nancy's treats as much as I wish, taking frequent, short strolls around the garden, and visiting or receiving friends when the weather permits. But I am not Kitty – and I do not wish to impede her happiness.'

'You would not object to being left alone?'

'My dear brother, I am more than capable of providing my own entertainment – and I have a painting to finish. If you and Kitty wish to spend a portion of the year in Bath, or London, or anywhere else in Europe, then by all means, go.'

'Are you quite certain? We would be gone for months at a time, and the journey back would be long and unpredictable, should you require our assistance. And what of Christmas? We have always spent it together at Thornleigh.'

'Yes, we have – and always with Richard.' She grew quiet, then took her brother's hand. 'I think... I *know* I have become much stronger than in my youth, and I have certainly become much better at knowing when to rest – the incident at Bellevue Park notwithstanding. And I am not as alone as you might think: Mrs Nancy and Mrs Rowley have known me all my life, and Maria has been a wonderful maid – they have always taken great care of me. And we have made many friends around Darlington, my dear brother. We are not as alone as we were during my childhood. Given enough notice, I don't think our friends will object to my joining their seasonal festivities.'

'Yes – the Earlwoods have rather become like family.' He began exploring the idea aloud. 'The Winslows, too. And Mr Curtis – he keeps a physician in his employment at all times to tend to any ailment at his school.'

'Don't forget Mrs Norris – I doubt you would find a more attentive nurse.'

'Indeed.' Marcus smiled, then continued very slowly. 'I am a fool for having missed the precise moment, but you have become very wise, my sister.'

'You set an excellent example, my dear brother.' She squeezed his hand before letting it go. 'Do think on it. And do make amends with Kitty – you will both feel much better for it.'

'Yes, ma'am.'

Having done the best she could, Ellie rose and returned to her studio. She passed Kitty's large cat on the way, and had the strangest feeling he was watching her with approval.

The rifts were repaired by dinner. Soon after, the ladies made for the drawing room without Marcus, and were delighted to find the brown and white cat curled up in Kitty's spot. Kitty, now in much higher spirits, sat beside her cat and made sure he was amenable to being petted before turning to Ellie.

'Oh dearest Ellie, I'm so excited about Bath – and I have you to thank for it!' She lowered her voice after the cat gave her an admonishing look. 'Are you certain you won't mind staying here, over Christmas no less?'

'Quite certain – in fact, you know I prefer my home comforts.'

'Then I shall write to you every day and describe to you all the events and fashions in Bath.'

'So long as writing diminish your enjoyment of the place,' replied Ellie.

'It won't – and oh, it is all so exciting! Marcus is making arrangements at this very moment, and I think he means to set out as soon as possible.' When her cat stretched and gave Kitty another look, she added: 'Would you like to join us, m'lord? Yes, of *course* you're invited – Bath would be most fortunate to receive your patronage!'

Several days of incessant rain delayed their journey, but when it finally ceased, the clouds parted to reveal the rare beauty of the winter sun. After Ellie's repeated reassurances that she would remain happy and healthy in Thornleigh, and Marcus's own repeated reminders of whom to contact should any unexpected needs arise, Mr and Mrs Ashcroft – and their lordly feline – departed with several portmanteaux, leaving Ellie as the temporary mistress of the house.

The young lady breathed in the crisp morning air and decided to take advantage of the fair weather with a short stroll in the garden. She wore the new coat Marcus had gifted her, asked Maria for her company, and set down the familiar path.

Everywhere she looked – the blue sky, the brown stones of Thornleigh, the evergreens bright against the rest of the landscape – Ellie saw possibilities and promises. There was a shift in her perspective, small but significant, bringing to her notice the fine details that had inspired her to draw and paint so many years ago. She tried to pinpoint the cause, and was awash with a new sensation attributed to one thing: liberation.

For the first time in her life, Eleanor Frances Ashcroft was left to her own devices, without the supervision of an older brother, nurse, or governess; for the first time, she was free to do precisely as she wished.

Her smile, once it had grown, could not be tempered – nor did she wish it. The garden, though bereft of blossoms and blooms, offered her comfort and solitude. With a small start, Ellie realised she'd never painted her garden in its coldest, bleakest state. Her thought was accompanied by images only she could see, visions only she could bring to the world.

Despite its emergent presence, the sun was not enough to ward off the winter chill that clung to the earth. The cold air, having turned her nose and cheeks pink, began to seep through her coat. She gave the garden a final survey before turning back to the house.

Before she reached the threshold, Ellie had decided on two things: firstly, that she did indeed possess the skills, tools, and passion to finish her most ambitious painting yet before winter was over; and secondly, she wanted nothing more than to become a true artist, and would accept any offer Mr Livingston might make.

30

Since Graham was indisposed during the festive season, Mr and Mrs Ashcroft were away in Bath, and Miss Ashcroft was left without a chaperon in Thornleigh Abbey, Sutton spent Christmas Day alone in Bellevue Park, eating very little of the usual feast and all but ordering his staff to take the ham and twelve-bird roast home to their own families. He spent most of the day in his studio, making half-hearted attempts with pencil and paper. He had worked and reworked his sketches from Thornleigh Abbey, but the lack of a proper reference made it difficult for Sutton to capture Miss Ashcroft's true likeness. If Sutton were kinder to himself, he would have acknowledged his improving discipline as no small feat, but as it were, Sutton cursed his arrogance and passed the slow hours in isolation, sinking into despondency after setting aside yet another inadequate drawing.

His routine was interrupted in the second week of January by a letter from Mr de Lancie, who, along with his usual entourage, wished to spend the remainder of winter in Bellevue Park, and who, upon discovering the viscount's departure from Colchester, wished to provide Sutton with some company during the coldest time of the year. Grateful for the distraction, Sutton wrote back with an official invitation, relayed instructions to Mrs Jenning, and promptly went searching for the Beethoven sheets Mr de Lancie had sent last year.

With only a week until his friend's arrival, Sutton was determined to learn the sonata as best as he could – a feat that required at least three hours at the pianoforte every day. Unlike Mr de Lancie, who had a natural talent and could read music and play by ear equally well, Sutton relied primarily on his memory and often required extensive practice before he could remember the minute details and overall contours of any piece. Only Graham knew the truth about how he learnt his music; even Mr de Lancie, with whom Sutton had played and sung on numberless occasions, was oblivious to Sutton's faults, and often complimented Sutton's musical aptitude.

When he had achieved his task sufficiently well, Sutton then went to consult his valet about his wardrobe. This, too, required a great deal of time and consideration: Sutton was adamant that no item would be worn twice in the following weeks. Enough variation was required so it would not appear he was recycling outfits, but the variations themselves must not be too flagrant. This task took two days and included sending a man to London for some later ensembles, along with the explicit instruction of returning unnoticed. It would not do for Mr de Lancie or his party to think Sutton vain.

On the morning of the party's arrival, Sutton chose a deep blue ensemble with a crisp white shirt. He set about tying his cravat, and discarded the crumpled silk four times for a new one before he was fully satisfied with the knot.

It was thus impeccably attired that he greeted his guests at the main entrance. The four carriages bore Mr de Lancie's usual party: his three sisters, two brothers-in-law, a cousin, two friends, and their personal attendants. Lady Rochford, Mr de Lancie's widowed eldest sister, was the first to greet Sutton with a smile and a gloved hand.

He kissed it, saying, 'Lady Rochford, you look as stunning as ever.'

'And you are ever the flatterer, Lord Sutton. I've been anticipating this day since I last left Bellevue – pray tell, will I have the pleasure of accommodating the same apartment?'

'Naturally. We've become quite accustomed to calling them the Rochford rooms.'

Lady Rochford did not hide her delight, and took Sutton's offered arm. 'I can arrange a plaque to that effect if you ever mean to replace the existing one.'

Sutton walked her to the salon, where tea and sandwiches were already laid out. It was only after she was seated that Sutton greeted his other guests, who knew well enough to defer to Lady Rochford, respectful of both her seniority and title. The room quickly filled with the warmth of chatter and conversation. Despite the grievances he sometimes suffered with some members of his society, Sutton was altogether grateful for their company.

As Sutton had expected, his unrelenting study of the Beethoven sonata paid off. They had barely settled down for dinner when Mr de Lancie enquired: 'Lord Sutton, how are those sheets?'

'They contain some very fine tunes – thank you for taking the trouble of sending them.'

'My pleasure. Shall we try it out together after dinner?'

'Perhaps we should rehearse it together first – I've only looked at them briefly and don't think I can manage both without stumbling.'

'You are too humble,' said Mr de Lancie. 'If anything, *I'll* be the one to stumble – you know I never practise as much as I ought to.'

And so, after giving the ladies their customary half hour to themselves in the drawing room, the gentlemen joined them, with Mr de Lancie seeking the room's pardon for making use of the pianoforte.

'My dear,' Lady Rochford said, 'your false modesty is the primary reason you're still unmarried.'

'It's more stylish to be a bachelor in London,' replied the gentleman. 'Besides, it *has* been a while since Lord Sutton and I have played together – do bear with us in the first few bars, should we require some time to adjust.'

As foreseen, their initial attempts were rather wanting, with Sutton claiming fault for being unfamiliar with the piece sounding in all four parts. Mr de Lancie was very forgiving, and, on the third or fourth attempt, both the *primo* and *secondo* moved past the introductory bars.

Once they had established their rhythm, Sutton found few impediments in continuing. Indeed, his careful study of several difficult passages in the week prior resulted in his graceful and flawless playing, while, to Sutton's surprise, Mr de Lancie fumbled every now and then. Regaining his confidence, Sutton's fingers moved with practised ease, and by the time they'd reached the end of the exposition, the viscount found himself enjoying their rendition.

They paused briefly at the end of the first movement, turned sideways to each other, and, after Mr de Lancie nodded to indicate the new tempo, the two fell into perfect harmony at the start of the *Rondo Moderato*, which also served as the final movement. Sutton's *primo* sang elegantly while Mr de Lancie's *secondo* provided the gentle foundation for the melody. At one point, Sutton noticed his friend was tapping a foot to the beat, a discovery that made him smile. At their final chord, this smile broadened to a large grin before they both turned to their applauding audience.

'Absolutely delightful!' exclaimed Lady Rochford, who was otherwise clapping quite demurely.

They bowed before turning to each other, Mr de Lancie immediately shaking Sutton's outstretched hand.

'Always a pleasure, Mr de Lancie.'

'Likewise, Lord Sutton.'

Lady Rochford called for more music, but when no one offered to follow up on the four-hand duet, Mr de Lancie took it upon himself to play some more. Having done his part for the evening, and feeling mightily pleased with his performance, Sutton went to enquire after his friend's two other sisters and their husbands. Mrs Cavendish, the elder of the two, surpassed both her sisters in grace and intellect, and was well-matched with Mr Cavendish, a third cousin of the 6th Duke of Devonshire, and twenty-seventh in the line of succession. On the other hand, Mrs Dupont could not be any more different from her siblings, and, despite her surpassing Mr de Lancie by five years, possessed the immaturity of one five years his junior. While Sutton was not particularly fond of Mrs Dupont beyond her sartorial tastes and connections, he didn't mind the company of her husband, whose severity could often be mellowed with drink.

The tenuous relationship between Mr and Mrs Dupont, owing much to their incompatible dispositions, had been lately exacerbated by the events in France. Mr Dupont, who maintained close French relations amongst the aristocracy, had been nothing short of appalled by the Revolutionary Wars, and even more so by what he'd deemed 'Napoleon's warmongering' along the Iberian Peninsula; meanwhile, Mrs Dupont cared nothing for politics, but had her own reasons to be vocal about the war, much to the embarrassment and irritation of her husband.

Indeed, as soon as Sutton had exchanged greetings with the group and his guests had paid their general compliments about his hospitality, Mrs Dupont said: 'Lord Sutton, I must commend on your attire. However do you manage to be so well-dressed every season of every year?'

'You are much too kind,' replied Sutton. 'Most of the credit goes to the exceptional skills of my valet and tailor.'

'Oh, are those trimmings French? How fortunate it must be to choose and purchase your lace from wherever you wish. Mr Dupont has forbidden me to acquire anything from France – he seems to believe withdrawing his business with French lace-makers will starve out Napoleon's armies.'

Sutton refrained from glancing at Mr Dupont and simply replied, 'I acquire all my lace from Bruges.'

'Ah yes, of course – it is very fine work indeed!' She paused before further bemoaning her miseries. 'Nonetheless, I grow tired with this ongoing quibble with France. I have two sons – they're six and four now, and you really ought to visit, Lord Sutton – and they like nothing more than to fight all day. If only the boys of Great Britain and France – for who are men, but their mother's sons? – would have the sense to grow up and shake hands. That would certainly put an end to this unnecessary nonsense.'

Mr Dupont spoke at this. 'Please do forgive my wife, Lord Sutton – she's been in a sour mood about our country's "quibble" ever since being deprived of her preferred French perfume.'

'And pray tell, who was responsible for the said deprivation?' She pouted, a look that may have suited her at fifteen, not twice that age. 'Lord Sutton, you are a gentleman of great sense and style – perhaps you could speak up on my behalf?'

This was not the first time Sutton had been privy to Mrs Dupont's antics, but it *was* the first since Graham was deployed to the Colchester barracks, making sacrifices so that women like Mrs Dupont could have the luxury of complaining thus. But rather than turning to anger, Sutton only felt great pity for Mr Dupont.

He was still forming a response that would not insult his guest when Mrs Cavendish chided her sister.

'You forget yourself. Do you not remember Lord Sutton's childhood friend, Mr Graham?'

At Mrs Dupont's confusion, Sutton supplied, 'It's Lieutenant Graham now.'

'Oh!' Mrs Cavendish seemed genuinely happy at the news. 'Please pass along my congratulations.'

Meanwhile, Mrs Dupont's recollections had returned, and she immediately blushed. 'Yes, I remember now. How is he?'

The lady's contrition was enough of an apology for Sutton, who then went on to describe Graham's current state, positions, and duties. Perhaps his descriptions of their daily hardships were a touch unnecessary, given his current company, but, having experienced some of the work himself, Sutton was altogether keen to share them.

'I was obliged to pull my weight,' he was saying, 'and simply felt it was my duty to assist by chopping some of the firewood. I couldn't believe the state of my hands after the first day!'

'How ghastly!' exclaimed Mrs Dupont. 'Have your hands recovered?'

Sutton held out his hands, palms up. The remnants of a few calluses were still visible, pale and round against his darker skin.

'These were much worse in December,' he explained, 'but Lieutenant

Graham made it clear they were no injuries at all – he said at the very least, I hadn't slipped my hold and sent the axe elsewhere!'

Mrs Dupont gasped in horror while Mrs Cavendish thoughtfully said, 'And yet, your playing was so graceful earlier.'

'I was hardly bothered after the first week or two,' he said, somewhat truthfully. 'Now that they're healed, I hardly notice them.'

'Well, Lord Sutton,' said Mr Cavendish, 'I must commend you for your foray into such unfamiliar territory. I had a similar experience in my youth at one of our farms – my father impressed on me the virtues of knowing the land, and ordered me to spend a week as a tenanted hand every autumn. In retrospect, the work was quite simple, but my tender hands suffered tremendously.'

Having received a similar treatment, Sutton thought this extremely wise. 'Will you ask the same of your sons?'

'Without a doubt. Our eldest is not yet twelve, but as soon as he – and his brothers – turn fourteen, I'll take him out to a field, just as my father had before me.'

Mrs Cavendish was in agreement, but Mrs Dupont seemed shocked by the suggestion. 'Oh, but not our boys! I would never inflict such a cruel fate on my sweet angels!'

'A crueller fate would be to waste away one's life without any sense of responsibility,' replied her husband. 'I'm much inclined towards Mr Cavendish's methods.'

The conversation had become rather heated, made quite apparent when Mr de Lancie finished playing and there was no more music to cushion the words. The rest of the room began to take an interest, and, as host, Sutton felt it his duty to direct the topic elsewhere.

'I wonder,' he said a little loudly, 'what shall we do tomorrow? There are many amusements to be found outside if the weather holds.'

His words had the intended effect, and their large group began suggesting a variety of activities, such as shooting, hunting, and riding. Mr Dupont, who was more inclined to indoor pursuits, suggested putting on a theatrical, while

Mr de Lancie expanded on the idea and proposed an operetta. Mr de Lancie's and his cousin, Mr Firth, shared similar tastes, but his two bachelor friends, Mr Morton and Mr Gibbs, preferred outdoor sports, which Mr Cavendish championed. Sutton's previous experience with this particular party – and their general disagreement – led him to declare, once again, the solution of splitting them into two groups for the duration of their stay.

When they had exhausted all options, Lady Rochford said, 'How about a ball, Lord Sutton? We should take every advantage of the full moon in two weeks. I would gladly see to all the arrangements.'

These words gave Sutton pause. While Lady Rochford was an expert in overseeing balls both as the eldest Miss de Lancie and later the mistress of her late Baron husband's estate, and while she had indeed organised countless balls on behalf of her bachelor friends over the years, Sutton felt disinclined to allow anyone to take on a position he'd always left unoccupied.

'I am humbled by your most generous offer,' he said carefully, 'but Mrs Jennings has seen to Bellevue's balls thus far. Indeed, I have every faith in her that she will once again succeed in the upcoming Spring Ball, and I am certain she would personally welcome any suggestions you might have.'

Lady Rochford nodded in understanding. 'Ah, yes, your annual Spring Ball. I'm sorry to have missed it last year.'

'Then you must make up for it by dancing twice as much this year,' replied Sutton.

'I eagerly await your invitation.'

'Surely, the lack of a ball doesn't preclude dancing,' said Mr de Lancie. 'We could very easily have our own private occasion.'

Sutton smiled at his friend. 'Indeed. Perhaps three evenings hence? Would that be sufficient time to have recovered from your journey?'

There was general agreement, with an underlying buzz of excitement, which Sutton felt himself. He enjoyed dancing under the right circumstances, and often found himself inspired to draw afterwards.

With that settled, Sutton dared to venture onto the previous topic. 'And tomorrow? Have we reached an agreement there?'

The predicted flurry of conversation began again, and Sutton couldn't help but smile at this group's eccentricities.

Despite being occupied with entertaining his guests over the next few weeks, with the evenings often running into three or four o'clock in the morning, Sutton remained determined to work on his sketches. He had stopped attempting to capture the particulars of Miss Ashcroft's lovely face and instead set to work on other elements: her dresses, her figure, her posture. While the timing of his daily activities made it impossible to rise at his usual early hour, Sutton managed to find moments in the late morning, after one group had left to go hunting and before the other awoke in the late afternoon to rehearse their amateur theatrical of *The Winter's Tale*. He grew to treasure those few hours of solitude.

The viscount was also enjoying his guests' company far more than anticipated. While Sutton did not share the same history and intimacy with Mr de Lancie as he did with Graham, the Londoner proved to be a good companion, who, to his credit, understood the nuances of high society more thoroughly than Graham. They spent many hours discussing the latest in art and music, occasionally disagreeing on their preferences. Sutton also grew fond of Mr de Lancie's brothers-in-law and the sensible Mr Firth. The gentlemen often lingered in the dining room far longer than necessary after supper.

And thus, Sutton spent January in the company of his friends. The party had decided to stay till mid-February, which suited Sutton perfectly well since he intended to return to Colchester until Easter. The viscount had countless duties and responsibilities come spring and summer, but until they commenced, he wished to spend time with his friends in the army.

Sutton was in the middle of their last rehearsal for the theatrical, wherein they were perfecting it for their performance the next day, when Grove interrupted with his apologies.

'Pardon me, Lord Sutton – there is a rider here with an urgent letter from Lieutenant Graham.'

His heart pounding with dread, Sutton left his position on the makeshift stage and approached his butler with brisk steps. He nearly ripped the letter in his attempt to open it and read its contents with bated breath.

Dearest Aubrey:

I regret to interrupt what I suspect will be one of your last rehearsals for the theatrical, but I'm sure you will deliver your lines spectacularly. This morning, we received word from the Colonel that our battalion has been ordered for deployment to the Peninsula – we are to leave by Sunday. While this news seems to be in haste, it is not unexpected – the sole purpose of our assignment in Colchester was to train both ourselves and new recruits for this very task.

I may not see you before we leave, but I urge you not to be concerned by the news. Great Britain's need of the Fifth does not detract from Sicilia's need of Leontes.

I remain your ever loving friend,

James

He lowered the letter with trembling hands, prompting Grove's concern. 'Sir? Shall I fetch you some tea or brandy?'

'Yes, thank you – either.' His voice was numb, but his mind doubled its work. 'And fetch Allen – and Parsons also. I'll see them both in my study.' Then, remembering the butler's fondness of Graham since they were both boys, he added softly, 'Graham's battalion will soon be deployed. It is unpleasant news, and it will no doubt be the talk of both taverns and drawing rooms tonight.'

Sadness and understanding flashed across the butler's face before he composed himself. 'Yes, sir. Thank you, sir.'

Sutton took a deep breath before turning to his guests, whose expressions bore a mixture of concern and curiosity. He tried to ignore Mrs Dupont's inquisitive look and instead focused on Mr de Lancie, who had also left his rehearsal mark.

'I deeply regret this untimely interruption,' Sutton said, echoing the words he'd just read, 'but I have received some urgent news from Lieutenant Graham. Subsequently, I must attend to a few matters immediately.'

'Of course,' said Mr de Lancie. 'Shall we call off the performance?'

There was a disappointed sound behind him, undoubtedly from his sister, and Sutton almost replied in affirmation. But then he remembered Graham's words and realised it would be both impractical and impolite to set out for Colchester this evening. It would take the rest of his afternoon to arrange matters with both his house and estate stewards; he would remain for the rest of the evening and set out at the break of dawn.

His decision made, Sutton said, 'Would you all mind terribly if we moved our performance to tonight? I'm afraid I'll be indisposed tomorrow.'

Mr de Lancie's concern did not abate. Only at Sutton's small nod did the gentleman acquiesce. 'I'm sure we can manage this evening.'

'Thank you. Again, please do pardon my hasty departure.'

Sutton bowed and left the room, hearing Mr de Lancie say, 'Shall we go through the fourth act again? Mrs Dupont, you must endeavour to remember your lines – Perdita is no small role.'

It did not take long before Sutton reached his study where Allen was waiting. Grove stood at the entrance, and said, 'Sir, a horse has been sent for Mr Parsons, who is at one of the farms today. He should be here within half an hour.'

'Thank you, Grove.' He sat at his desk, and wasted no time. 'Allen, I'm sure Grove has informed you of the news I just received. Are the coats I ordered for the soldiers ready?'

'Almost,' replied the steward. 'We are about a dozen short, but I'm certain we could purchase some pre-made ones elsewhere, albeit at a premium.'

'That is a suitable solution. Take them to Colchester tonight – the coats must reach the barracks before the battalion leaves.'

'And if we are too late?'

'Then follow them to whichever port they intend to board their ships,' replied Sutton. 'Many soldiers cannot afford coats to protect them from the elements – since they are to fight for our country, they *must* receive these amenities. And for the love of God, Allen, spare no expenses.'

The steward nodded once more. 'I understand, sir. I will do everything in my power to see it done.'

'Thank you.'

After Allen left, Sutton found he could not remain seated, and started pacing the length of his study until Parsons' arrival. The estate steward was quite out of breath when he arrived.

'Parsons,' Sutton said without preamble, 'to your knowledge and expertise, does Bellevue Park have anything that could be of assistance to a battalion fighting in the Peninsula?'

'We have stores of grains and other foods, some of which may either spoil or be difficult to use when on the road. There is also the matter of weight to consider, sir. I have a brother in the army, and he has often written about forsaking fine and heavy luxuries when it came down to either those, or carrying artillery.'

Sutton hadn't considered this. 'My thoughts are with you and your brother.'

'Thank you,' replied Parsons. 'He has only sustained minor scrapes thus far, but we nonetheless await every piece of news from him – though he barely has the opportunity or means to write.'

'How do you mean?'

'He often spends long days marching, and when he stops for the night, he is too weary to do anything but rest for a few hours before another day begins. Writing supplies are also few and far between, as are the page boys to carry and deliver letters.'

Parsons paused, realising what Sutton had in mind. 'Sir, we do indeed have large quantities of pens and paper for your use, and for general uses around the estate. A new supply of paper would take some time to prepare, but we could set aside enough for your purposes and send off the rest. If each soldier is given a dozen sheets to carry on their person, the weight would be negligible.'

'Allen is currently arranging the transport of outerwear,' said Sutton. 'See to it that the stationery is also added.'

The estate steward bowed. Before he left, Sutton added, 'And Parsons, may your brother return safely.'

This time, when Sutton was alone again, he sat down at his desk, burying his face in his hands. He'd barely had time to untangle the thoughts and feelings that came with Graham's news, but now that he'd tended to the immediate arrangements, fear began to gnaw at his stomach.

His mind conjured an image of his friend, cold and still on the battlefield. Sutton suddenly felt sick.

There was a quiet knock on the door, and Sutton raised his head to see Grove, whose unguarded expression betrayed his own sorrow.

'I brought you a fresh pot of tea, sir.'

He entered the room and set down the tray, silently replacing the cold, untouched teapot. Then, as if reading Sutton's thoughts, the butler said, 'I believe Mr Allen and Mr Parsons are working in tandem to ensure the consignment leaves before sundown. In the interim, shall I arrange your own carriage to Colchester at first light?'

'Grove...' Sutton paused, holding back the emotions that would be an uncouth display, especially to one's servants. But Grove's family had worked for Sutton's for many generations, and the butler himself had been privy to the Beaumonts' joys and sorrows. 'I wish I could do more for Graham. These clothes and paper – they are mere triflings compared to what the men will suffer in the weeks to come.'

'I assure you, sir, neither Lieutenant Graham nor his fellow soldiers will think of your gifts as "mere triflings". And while you are not there on the battlefront, you, too, have duties and responsibilities, sir. Over the past month, your guests have been enjoying a range of activities that make us British, and over the next few months, you will be busy seeing to your numerous tenants, farms, and lands. While thousands of men are fighting abroad to defend the fabric of British society, you must remember that you, sir, are a crucial part of that fabric.'

Sutton nodded, grateful for the older man's words. He rose from his seat and straightened his clothing as best he could.

'My apologies, Grove,' he said, 'for you must contend with not one, but two pots of untouched tea. Alas, there is a dinner to host, a theatrical to perform, and further apologies to make.'

'I'm sure your guests will be more than understanding. And, if not, then it might be of consolation that three bottles of your father's claret is being decanted as we speak.'

Sutton gave a small smile, which Grove returned in kind. Then the two men left the study to contend with their respective duties.

VOLUME III

31

THE LETTER DROPPING from her hands, Ellie fought back her tears – fought, and failed. All her fears had materialised in Richard's words: her dear brother was going to the war.

Oliver, who had delivered the ill-fated news at breakfast, left and returned with reinforcements. Vaguely, Ellie was aware of footsteps and murmurs, of those privy to this dark hour. Someone asked a question, but it was drowned out by her own sobs.

And then a pair of strong arms was around her, pulling Ellie's small frame into a comforting embrace, rubbing small circles on her back. She inhaled the scents of the kitchen, of milk and yeast and butter, and ever so slowly, Ellie's crying subsided.

When she finally lifted her head and looked around, most of the staff had dispersed. Only Mrs Rowley, Mr Talbot, and Mrs Nancy remained, the three pillars of housekeeper, butler, and cook that defined every household.

Mrs Nancy, who held Ellie like her own daughter, produced a handkerchief and waited for Ellie to blow her nose. 'Miss Ellie, is this letter the source of your distress?' Ellie nodded. 'May I read it?'

Another nod, and Mrs Nancy picked up the paper. She read it quickly and silently, and, when finished, asked, 'May I ask Mr Talbot and Mrs Rowley to inform the rest of the household about this news?'

There were portions of Richard's letter that were private between the siblings, but Ellie trusted Mrs Nancy would only share the pertinent sections with the heads of the household. She nodded once more before another wave of tears gripped her.

'Let's get you somewhere more comfortable,' said Mrs Nancy. With those strong arms, the woman helped Ellie to her usual seat in front of the fire. 'Try to relax, Miss Ellie. I'll have a word with Mr Talbot and Mrs Rowley.'

Mrs Nancy went to confer with the housekeeper and butler. Ellie closed her eyes and counted to ten. She began anew when she reached the end, and kept counting until she wasn't sure if she'd reached the hundreds or thousands.

By the time Mrs Nancy returned, the tears were welling again.

'There's a nice cup of tea coming along,' said Mrs Nancy, sitting down beside her and taking her hand, 'and some pastries that were set for afternoon tea.'

Ellie tried to find her voice and had to swallow a few times. 'Thank you, Mrs Nancy,' she finally said weakly. 'But I don't wish to eat. I'm sorry.'

'I know you've no appetite, Miss Ellie, but I've been fiddling with the recipes again – it'll be a mighty help if you could tell me if they're any good. Just a small bite and your opinion – you'd be doing me a great favour.'

Ellie didn't respond and closed her eyes again. When Ellie fell into a bout of illness as a child, Mrs Nancy would use the same approach to coax her into eating. Ellie would only take the smallest bite or two, or find the food disagreeable, but it was more than eating nothing at all.

But Mrs Nancy never pushed Ellie beyond her wishes. Instead, still holding her hand, the older woman started telling Ellie about the process behind these pastries, listing their ingredients, quantities, ways of procurement and measurement, what needed to be done to them, and so on. These simple words calmed her, and by the time the tea and pastries arrived, Ellie did feel a little better.

The cook prepared the tea exactly the way Ellie liked it. She then selected a few pastries and loaded them on two plates, giving one to Ellie. Instead of imploring Ellie to try one, Mrs Nancy took a pastry and bit into it herself, nodding approval.

'My niece has been helping me in the kitchen – I'd say she's gotten the hang of baking these. Now, they are delicate little creatures – see how they're golden and flaky? That requires a lot of butter – but the difficulty with freshly-churned butter is how quickly it warms when you work with it. The butter must be rubbed into the flour and rolled out as quickly as possible before it melts and ruins the entire batch. But the dough sticks to the working surface, so you must make sure you've floured the right amount. If there's too much flour, you won't get the soft texture after it's baked – and that simply won't do.'

While Mrs Nancy explained the process, occasionally breaking off a piece in demonstration, Ellie started taking small bites as well. She had no capacity to distinguish the pastry from any of Mrs Nancy's previous recipes, but nonetheless, Ellie could appreciate the way it crumbled and melted in her mouth. She had always been fascinated by Mrs Nancy's descriptions and explanations of her craft, and as she listened, the heaviness in her stomach gradually left her.

'Now this,' the cook continued, picking up another delicacy, 'this has similar properties as the first, but the fillings introduce some more difficulties when it's cooking – sometimes, an extra "Hail Mary" can make a difference between a perfect and a ruined result.'

As the older woman continued, eating and explaining in equal measures, Ellie also ate, keeping her attention on the cook. By the time they'd reached the last item on their plates, Ellie realised she had eaten almost half a dozen of the small items, and that her stomach was now satiated.

Knowing all too well what Mrs Nancy had just done for her, Ellie finally said: 'Thank you, Mrs Nancy. I'm quite certain you haven't been trying a new recipe, but these are delicious all the same.'

'You are too kind, Miss Ellie. Now, is there anything at all I could do for you? Should we send word to Mr Ashcroft?'

Ellie shook her head. 'The news will reach Bath soon enough. Marcus and

Kitty aren't due back for another month, and I don't wish for them to return on my account – especially as it would do nothing to change Richard's current situation.'

Mrs Nancy nodded, and Ellie thought she detected a flash of pride in the older woman. 'Then maybe we'll send for Miss Harriet. I'm sure she'll be glad to see you.'

'Yes, please do. Thank you, Mrs Nancy.'

The older woman rose and barely had to ring the bell before Oliver entered, ready to be of service. His sad eyes told Ellie he had been informed of the situation, and she was glad she didn't have to break the news herself. But with Mrs Nancy's invaluable assistance, Ellie had regained her wits, knowing now she wouldn't need her smelling salts today.

'Send a carriage to Dunnistone,' Ellie said. 'Inform Mr and Mrs Earlwood of Richard's current situation, and kindly ask if they could be parted with Harriet for the next few days.'

Then, Ellie turned to Mrs Nancy. 'Thank you again. I am much recovered, and would like to be alone now.'

With an understanding smile, the cook withdrew Richard's letter from her apron pocket, then gathered the empty plates before leaving. Ellie gingerly touched the letter, carefully refolded. In her distress, Ellie had forgotten about the delicate paper, and, were it not for Mrs Nancy's quick thinking, Richard's words may have been smudged or ruined.

Now that she felt much steadier, and knowing Harriet would soon be here, Ellie reached for Richard's ring, back in its usual place around her neck. She took a few deep breaths, and re-read the letter.

My dearest sister:

You must know, first and foremost, that I love you with all my heart, and that I would do anything and everything in the world to ensure your safety and happiness for many years to come. When we were little and neither understood nor knew how to enunciate the polysyllabic "illegitimacy", we loved each other fiercely, not caring we had different mothers. As I write this today, at a time when we've grown into the understanding of that horrible word – and all its incarnations and connotations – I want to reiterate how much I love you, and how you are the truest, dearest, and best sister anyone could ever have.

I would do *anything* to protect you, dearest, sweetest Ellie – anything in my power. And while I deeply regret I cannot shield you from my next words, I am proud and eager to be able to fight for you; for it was announced this morning that our battalion will leave for the Peninsula before the week is over, and I will be on the frontlines, doing all I am able to keep you from harm.

Please do not be distraught, dearest, gentlest Ellie. You have a heart of gold, and it pains me to think this letter might break that beautiful heart. So please, gather all your courage and strength – and I know you possess both in abundance, for I have seen your bravery with my own eyes. Be brave, dearest Ellie – if not for yourself, then for me.

For, if I am to be honest, I do not know if I am ready for the task ahead. I am eager to serve my country and to protect the ones I love, and I believe my physical capabilities have been tried, tested, and expanded over the past few months of vigorous training – but I do not know if I truly have it within me to stand on the battlefield and face my enemies, enemies who also have mothers, fathers, brothers, and sisters. I realise, perhaps too late, that I may be too soft-hearted for my task ahead; but even with this realisation, I know I am steadfast in my desire to serve and to protect.

If there is one small consolation in my forthcoming, arduous journey, it is that I may finally meet the Marquis of Wellington himself. I have heard so much about him, and he, in turn, has held the 5th in the highest regard. It would be a great honour to fight under his command.

But that is an honour second to the honour of being your brother, my dearest sister. It has been a privilege growing up and looking after you, and it will be a privilege fighting for you. I know in my heart that we will be reunited one day, and I pray that day will come soon – and it will come here in this mortal world. Until then, know that I remain your ever loving brother,

Richard Ashcroft

32

COLCHESTER HAD CHANGED since Sutton left it in December. The roads to the barracks were busy with soldiers and civilians alike, and a great number of carriages took precedence, hurrying to and from the garrison. On several occasions, Sutton's carriage was required to make way for a more important one, and while he was impatient to see Graham, the viscount ordered his driver to stop by the side of the road as often as necessary.

When he finally disembarked at the main gates, Sutton made immediately for Colonel Watson's office. A young lieutenant informed him the Colonel would be indisposed for at least another half hour, but the viscount was welcome to wait until then. Sutton nodded, then spent the next forty minutes alternating between sitting restlessly and pacing across the length of the room.

Sutton stood to attention when the Colonel finally entered. The Colonel had aged a decade since Sutton saw him last: the sprightly man had amassed a number of lines and shadows on his face, transforming him from a man near the end of his prime to one approaching his twilight years.

The Colonel gave Sutton a wry smile, and said, 'If this war doesn't end me, then I'd be quite happy to retire after the campaign.'

Sutton bowed. 'You have my utmost respect, Colonel.'

'And you mine, Lord Sutton.' He gestured for Sutton to sit. 'The coats and stationery arrived yesterday morning and have been distributed to every officer. They are extremely grateful for your generosity, as am I. Often, it is not an enemy on the battlefield that becomes a soldier's downfall, but sickness of the body and soul. You have done a very fine thing, Lord Sutton.'

'It is nothing compared to your sacrifices,' he replied sincerely. 'If there is any other way I can provide any assistance, please, do let me know – I will see to it personally.'

The Colonel smiled. 'You have done more than you realise, Lord Sutton – perhaps it is time to do something for yourself. The first few squadrons have left for Dover, but I have kept Lieutenant Graham here as long as I could. I'm afraid we must all depart tomorrow, but he is in his quarters now, and I give him leave if you wish to dine together at your lodgings.'

'Thank you, Colonel.' Sutton's joy at discovering he could still speak with Graham was soon replaced by another thought. 'Colonel, I hope you'll forgive if I am too forward, but would you please also grant Ensign Ashcroft leave for this evening?'

Understanding flashed across the Colonel's face. 'Ah yes, I believe you are acquainted with his family, and accompanied the Ensign to Hertfordshire in December. Permission granted.'

'Thank you.'

Sutton stood, knowing the Colonel was already spread thin. But he also doubted he would see the Colonel again before the rest of the regiment left, so he gave the older man a deep, respectful bow.

'My prayers will be with you and the 5th every day,' he said. 'I look forward to your safe return – and to celebrating your retirement.'

With that, Sutton departed and went to find his friends.

Graham was in the courtyard, packing boxes of gunpowder with a dozen officers. Richard was among these soldiers, and it was he who saw Sutton first. The younger man ensured his box was secured before approaching Sutton.

'Sutton! The men who brought your wonderful gifts told us you weren't far behind them, but I was afraid we'd miss you nonetheless – I'm so glad you've made it!'

He extended his hand, dirtied with gunpowder, but Sutton did not hesitate before taking it for a handshake. Behind Richard, Graham nodded to Sutton with a wide smile before carefully finishing his tasks.

When his case of gunpowder was packed away, Graham covered the distance between them in brisk strides.

'We were afraid you wouldn't make it! Oh, and I've got some gunpowder on your coat – but heavens, are those *creases* I see? My friend, you have finally set foot outside without having every article of clothing laundered and pressed! I never thought I'd live to see the day!'

Sutton tried to give Graham one of his more imposing glares, but his attempt fell short and his expression was nothing but warm. 'I suppose it's high time I take a leaf out of your page,' he replied.

The other officers, including Smith and Fielding, greeted Sutton with bows and words of thanks for his gifts. Some shook his hand with enthusiasm, leaving Sutton rather humbled. Once they had exchanged greetings with him, the men returned to their business, devoting their singular attention to the careful handling of gunpowder.

Graham, who had lingered beside Sutton, turned to him regretfully. 'I would love to talk, but duty calls.'

'As a matter of fact,' said Sutton, 'I am here to relay Colonel Watson's message: both you and Ashcroft are relieved of your posts this evening. I've not had a chance to stop by the house, but I'd like it very much if you both join me for dinner – though I understand if you have more important business at hand, regardless of the Colonel's concessions.'

'Your friendship is the most important thing in the world,' said Graham softly. 'As you very well know, I care not about the food or drink, but about your company.'

Sutton smirked. 'And you tell me this on the eve of your departure – to think of all the twelve-bird roasts I've prepared in your honour!'

'Naturally, I had to eat all that I could – anything less would have been an insult to your hospitality.'

Sutton chuckled, then turned to Richard. 'What say you, Ashcroft? Are you prepared to consign yourself to an evening of questionable food and drink, but unparalleled company?'

'Since I defer to Graham in all matters and he clearly thinks very highly of you, I suppose I have no choice.'

'Indeed you do not,' replied Graham, looking at Richard with affection. 'Well then, perhaps we should take an excessive amount of time to clean up and change, just so Sutton can send his household into a panicked disarray about his lack of preparations.'

'A marvellous plan,' said Richard, eyes bright. 'How does an hour sound?'

Sutton smiled. 'Perfect. And with that, gentlemen, I shall take my leave and cause a suitable fuss elsewhere.'

To Sutton's approval and pleasure, the skeleton staff at his rented house had started preparing for guests as soon as they learnt of his impending arrival. Dinner consisted of two hearty courses with over a dozen dishes in total, and it was thoroughly enjoyed by the viscount and his two friends.

Afterwards, the three men enjoyed their gin and brandy in the drawing room. They spoke about various subjects, but shied away from that of the army's departure. As the night grew on, Sutton felt the increasing need to speak with Graham alone, though he did not wish to offend Richard.

It was to the viscount's great relief when, after their second refill, the younger man said: 'I have a favour to ask of you, Sutton, but I've left the objects in question at the barracks. Would you mind terribly if I went to fetch them?'

'I wouldn't mind at all. Would you like to take my horse?'

'Thank you, but it is only a short walk, and an agreeable one at that. I shan't be too long.'

With Richard gone, the two friends sat by the fireside, each in their usual places. They had found each other at an early age and had remained steadfast throughout the years, despite the changes brought on by time and circumstance.

Sutton pulled out a small pouch he'd prepared earlier and tossed it to his friend. The viscount swirled his glass while Graham opened it, chuckling at its contents.

'I took the liberty of getting you some new ones.'

'Thank you, Aubrey.' Graham chose a deep purple ribbon and tied it to his queue before removing the old ribbon from his hair. 'Now I'm ready for battle.'

'Be careful,' Sutton said softly, keeping his gaze on the crackling fire. Soon, the need for such warmth would start to subside throughout England, until the scent of summer seeped through every wall of every house. 'Do your duty, James, but for God's sake, be *careful*.'

His friend made no witty remark. 'I will.' Then, as if Sutton's entreaty had stirred something within Graham, he said: 'It has taken me many years to reach this conclusion – far too long, perhaps – but if I have learnt anything over the past few months, it is that our lives are far too precious, too short, and too full of difficulties to keep ourselves from seeking our own happiness. If you have indeed found Lady Lavender, do not let your own fears hold you back from what would make you happy – and for God's sake, do not presume that every marriage in England is as your parents' was.'

Sutton's lips curved into a small smile, and he looked over at his friend. He almost asked how Graham had learnt of his feelings for Miss Ashcroft, but realised his friend had always known him better than he did himself.

'You and your talk of "Lady Lavender",' he said instead. 'You know, I'd always imagined *you* would be the first to develop an attachment, and that *I* would be the one offering advice. Or rather, I'd either try to talk you out of the horrible match, or accidentally develop feelings for the same woman – in which case the only solution would be, naturally, a duel.'

Graham laughed. 'You mean like how we "duelled" as children by using those sticks as "swords", and intimidated your nurse's sons to be our "seconds"? In case you've forgotten, I gave you a right walloping back then' – he gestured at the scar above Sutton's eye – 'and I can do the same again now!'

Sutton ran a finger across his brow where his friend had struck him all those years ago. He pretended to think for a long moment, and finally declared with much pomp: 'Nothing and no one – not even Lady Lavender – will ever be worth our friendship. It applied then, and certainly applies now – and evermore.'

Sutton raised his left arm, lifting his glass at the end of this impromptu toast, and Graham responded with his right arm. With matching flicks of their wrists, the two men brought their glasses together with a short and clear clink, then sipped their drinks the way they've done so many times before.

Graham was solemn again when he said: 'From what I've learnt from both you and Ashcroft – and from what I know about you, my dear friend – you may have found your elusive lady. You have my best wishes, Aubrey.'

'Thank you.'

'And if I see you next—'

'*When* you see me next,' Sutton corrected.

Graham smiled at the insistence. 'Then I hope to be introduced to the esteemed lady.'

'It won't be my place to make such an introduction, but I've no doubts Ashcroft would insist on you visiting Thornleigh Abbey.' The mention of the young man was a clear reminder they did not have much time left together. 'When are you setting out?'

'Before dawn. We wish to make it to Dover and be boarded with time aplenty for the evening tide.' Graham looked at Sutton, studying his friend's features. 'You'd be best off resting – you honestly look a fright from here, with the shadows from the fire. There's no need to see us off.'

'Nonsense. You're to face my frightful visage first thing tomorrow, whether you like it or not.'

Graham neither agreed nor protested. Instead, he asked, 'Will you be terminating your lease here and return to Bellevue straight after?'

Sutton nodded, then winced upon remembering his hasty departure from his guests. 'If I'm fortunate, I will return to a home devoid of guests.'

'I thought you were fond of Mr de Lancie.'

'I am – but his sister, the one married to Mr Dupont... I quite pity the gentleman.'

Graham stifled a laugh, presumably at Sutton's tone. 'In either case, they'll be gone by Lent. Are you looking forward to beginning your rounds?'

The conversation moved onto more mundane matters, and it was not long before Richard returned from the barracks. The young man was a little flushed from his brisk walk, his eyes sharp and bright.

Graham rose. 'Do excuse me – nature calls,' he said. 'And the hour is late – perhaps we should reconvene at the front door.'

As soon as they were alone, Richard withdrew two letters and a small notebook from his coat.

'I have troubled you enough, Lord Sutton,' he said, reverting to titles once more, 'but I hope you would indulge me in one last favour. Please hold onto these two letters while I am away – and should anything befall me, please see that they reach my brother and sister.'

Speechless, Sutton stared at the letters in question, dread filling him at the thought of its contents and implications.

'I know I ask a great deal of you,' Richard continued. 'I know I do not have the right to burden you thus. But I trust you more than anyone else, and it is not because my friends are either long gone from my life, or marching with me into battle – it is because I have come to know you as a man of great honour and virtue. Please, Lord Sutton, your assistance would set my heart at ease.'

Sutton gingerly took the letters, handling them carefully as if they would tear or fall apart. 'I will place these in the deepest parts of my safe,' he said slowly, 'and I look forward to the day when we meet again in a room such as this, so that you can toss them into the fire.'

'Thank you,' Richard said simply. Then, with some hesitation, he held out the notebook. 'These are sketches for my sister. I've only sent her a handful of pages with my letters, as I'd hoped to fill the book before giving her the rest, but... She should have them now. Would you be so kind as to deliver it personally?'

Sutton considered this, then carefully took the book as well. 'I will keep your letters, and I will give your sketches to Miss Ashcroft. But you are bound to encounter many scenes when you are abroad, so I entreat you to continue your sketches and give the next collection to her yourself when you return. Do you have another pocketbook for such purposes?'

Richard shook his head, his expression a mixture of surprise and reverence. At this, Sutton reached into his own pockets, finding a small leather-bound item that would perfectly suit the young man's intentions, though it currently contained a few rough sketches he'd made of buildings, landscapes, and, most incriminatingly, Miss Ashcroft herself. With a warm face and as much care and precision as he could muster, Sutton tore away those first few pages, putting them back into his pocket before giving Richard the remaining book.

'Here. Fill this with all the architecture and landscapes you encounter across the waters, and return to delight your sister with its contents.'

His eyes bright with tears, Richard placed it in his pocket next to his heart. As they went to join Graham, Sutton ducked his head, allowing some of his hair to fall over his face and hide his own tears.

33

IT TOOK MARCUS AND KITTY two and a half long weeks before they finally returned to Thornleigh and were greeted by both Ellie and Harriet. The two ladies had fallen into a comfortable routine, their days filled with quiet activities, short strolls, and heartfelt conversations, but Ellie nonetheless welcomed the return of her family. Both Marcus and Kitty were heavy with worry, the news of Richard's deployment reaching them a little later than it had Ellie, but even so, Ellie noted the positive effect of Bath on their countenance.

'Your complexion is much improved,' she said to Kitty when they had all settled down for some afternoon refreshments. 'Did you enjoy taking the waters?'

Kitty's enthusiasm returned, though it was slightly dampened when compared to before. 'Yes, indeed – Bath was as splendid as I'd imagined. Admittedly, the society is a bit peculiar, but once we'd acclimatised to the penchant for promenade walks for the sole purpose of spying on others, the exercise became quite enjoyable.'

'We're sorry to have left,' Marcus added, 'but sorrier still to have left you alone to bear such terrible news.'

'I wasn't alone,' Ellie said, smiling at Harriet. 'I honestly don't know what I would've done without Harriet's companionship, or without the support from Mrs Nancy, and Mrs Rowley, and Mr Talbot – not to mention dear Maria. Everyone has looked after me exceptionally well.'

Marcus turned to Harriet. 'And how is your family, Miss Earlwood? I'm sure they've missed you dearly.'

'Lettice and our maid Anna visited twice, which I think was enough to appease my sister. She has begun to notice the more unpleasant parts of the world, but is still unable to comprehend them entirely.'

'She is fortunate to have both you and Miss Mary Earlwood for sisters,' said Marcus.

'No more than Miss Ashcroft is for having you and Mr Richard for brothers,' replied Harriet. 'Have you had more news about him, Mr Ashcroft?'

'Not from him directly, but I believe his regiment has safely crossed the Channel, and the men are on their way to the Peninsula. It must be a long and arduous journey.'

There was a brief silence before Ellie, having kept close to her heart the strength and courage Richard had lent her, spoke of other matters. 'A letter from Mr Livingston came yesterday – he wishes to call again next week to see the progress of "We Happy Few". I am not quite finished with the painting, but it's not far from completion. Since his request only came yesterday, and I knew you were due to return today, I've not yet responded.'

Ellie needn't have worried about her brother's reaction or permission. 'Yes, of course, do write to him – he is more than welcome to visit. Congratulations on your progress, Ellie.'

'Would you mind if I write to him now?' asked Ellie. 'I intend to be quick about it so Oliver can deliver it before the post box closes.'

'Yes, do go ahead,' said Kitty. 'I have much to relay to Harriet about Bath – though I suspect Mary won't be too happy if she discovers she's not the first to hear all the details. But oh, Harriet, you would have loved the various décor throughout the town! Some of the colours were magnificent, and the needlework flawless!'

Kitty's words dispelled some of the gloom that had enshrouded the house over the last few weeks, and as Ellie went to pen her response to Mr Livingston, she found her steps were not as heavy.

Harriet bade the Ashcrofts farewell the next morning after breakfast, exchanging a long embrace with Ellie before leaving.

'I'm only a short ride away, Ellie,' she said.

'As am I,' replied Ellie. 'You have been the most wonderful friend anyone can ask for, but I hope you'll remember I'm also here to share *your* burdens.'

Her friend's departure coincided with the arrival of the morning post, which Ellie had grown to anticipate on a daily basis. To her disappointment, there was nothing from Richard, but her spirits were lifted when Marcus announced there was a letter from Lord Sutton. The mere mention of the viscount's name sent flutters to Ellie's stomach.

'Lord Sutton will be in Darlington next week,' Marcus finally said, paraphrasing the letter, 'and he wonders if he might call on us. He apologises for not writing sooner, and writes he's been entrusted by Richard to deliver something in person. Kitty, Ellie, if you have no objections?'

In a mischievous tone, Kitty said, 'I would object *most* profusely if you do *not* invite him to stay. The journey from Bellevue Park is far too long for him to stop by for tea, and I, for one, shan't subject him to another evening at the inn.'

Meanwhile, Ellie asked, 'Has he given any dates?'

'Wednesday,' replied Marcus, before comprehension dawned. 'Ah, that is when Mr Livingston is here for his visit. They are acquainted, are they not? Perhaps they will enjoy each other's company.'

A vague memory brushed the edge of Ellie's mind, though she could not pinpoint the details. 'Perhaps we should inform Lord Sutton about our other guest – just as a precaution.'

'Quite right – I shall write to him soon.' He glanced at Kitty, and a look passed between them. 'Before that, we have a small announcement to make.'

Kitty, who never seemed to be affected by nerves, was now twisting the fabric of her morning dress, taking her time to meet Ellie's gaze. 'I would have told you sooner,' she said, mumbling a little with her head still down, 'but with Harriet here... Well, I wanted to keep this within our family for now.'

Ellie nodded, waiting for Kitty to gather her thoughts. After a long moment, Kitty lifted her head and declared: 'I am with child.'

'Oh,' replied Ellie. The meaning sank in, and she repeated more enthusiastically: 'Oh! Congratulations!'

With a small smile and a rather uncharacteristic blush, Kitty continued. 'We took our time returning from Bath due to my condition – I think I was first certain on the day Richard's news arrived, and... Well, we thought every precaution was necessary, though both Marcus and I were quite adamant I return to Thornleigh and remain here for the rest of the year.'

'We had wanted to inform you as soon as possible,' added Marcus, 'but these circumstances have been...trying.'

Ellie nodded again, her heart full of happiness for her brother and sister-in-law. She saw now the subtle changes in Kitty's behaviour – her reticence, her serenity, her frequent smiles and blushes.

'I understand,' Ellie said, 'and I'm only too pleased to learn of the news. Oh, how I look forward to meeting my niece or nephew!'

Marcus and Kitty shared another look, the love and joy clear on their faces. While Ellie usually looked away from such intimate moments, she studied their features this time, noting the way her brother's eyes crinkled, lips curving slightly, her sister-in-law's lashes softly brushing her cheek when she closed her eyes, a twin smile on her lips. It was a wonderful picture, and Ellie wished to capture the moment for posterity.

Rising, she said, 'I hope you won't mind if I spend the rest of the day in my studio.'

'Yes, of course,' said Marcus, the touch of husbandly and fatherly pride still lingering in his eyes. 'Take care not to overexert yourself.'

Ellie left her family, a small bounce in her steps as she walked to her workspace. But as she neared her corner, and as the glow from the happy news faded, Ellie felt the heaviness return. She saw the bittersweet providence of their situation: while Richard's life was in danger, new life, hope, and joy grew within Kitty; while the sons of Great Britain fell in battle, the Ashcroft family prayed for a healthy son and heir.

And now, though she still wished to draw her original idea of Mr and Mrs Ashcroft in love and in great happiness, a new idea formed in her mind: a companion piece to 'We Happy Few', a combination of the two fundamental yet opposing sides of life and death.

By the time night fell, Ellie had made enough progress on her painting to feel accomplished, though the activity had dampened her spirits with every stroke. In the half hour before she was required for dinner, Ellie gathered her despondency and penned a letter to Richard.

My dearest brother:

I don't know when – or if – you will receive this, but I felt the need to write. It has been almost a month since news arrived of your deployment to the battlefront, and you have been in my heart and mind every day. I have done my very best to heed the words from the last, precious letter I received from you, and have gotten on with what I must – though often, I find my drawings or paintings completely inconsequential when compared to the hardships you must be suffering. And so, I have refrained from writing to you, because I know you would frown upon my melancholy.

But my dearest brother, I have been so torn today, in a way that far exceeds my pains since the fateful day that brought your news. Marcus and Kitty declared after breakfast today that she is with child. A child, Richard! They so deserve this precious gift – it has been over a year since they wed, and though Kitty never speaks of it to me, I know in her heart she has been yearning for a child. To think their prayers have finally been answered! I will keep both mother and child in my prayers every day, for there are difficulties that lie ahead – difficulties that could be fatal.

Which brings me to this dreadful guilt I carry. I'm reminded of my own mother, whom Marcus adored and worshipped for seventeen years before I took her away from him. I cannot but feel the weight of my sin: the sin of surviving when my mother did not. And I write to you, my dearest brother, because I know you sometimes feel the same guilt about your own existence, and you bear the same burdens. We are neither responsible for the blows we have dealt, nor are we innocent of our crimes; we did not commit the original sins, but are the embodiment of them.

Oh Richard, how I miss you so. Thornleigh has felt empty without your constant laughter, and I keep imagining what you might be suffering. I've tried to dispel those unpleasant thoughts, but they return at the most unexpected moments to remind me, during a delicious meal or a cheerful conversation or a leisurely stroll, that you are fighting to preserve my happiness.

I remain your loving sister,

Ellie

34

WHAT A DIFFERENCE *a few short months make*, thought Sutton as Thornleigh loomed into view, the dark brown building bleak against the cloudy sky. When he last left this very house, Sutton was awash with the promising hopes of courtship with Miss Ashcroft. Now, as his carriage pulled into the driveway and he placed a hand upon the pocket where Richard's book was kept, Sutton lamented the purpose of his visit.

He kept himself neutral as he approached the front door, and was greeted by the butler, whose demeanour was markedly less enthusiastic than when Sutton had previously arrived with Richard. Back then, the butler had lit up with a smile, welcoming Richard back home with the most affectionate tone. Not for the first time, Sutton wondered where Richard and Graham were now, and if they were faring well.

As he entered the house, Sutton steeled himself for the imminent meeting with Mr Livingston, whom Mr Ashcroft had been thoughtful enough to mention in his invitation to Thornleigh. At the best of times, Sutton found it difficult to remain cordial to Mr Livingston. They had been well-acquainted before the incident, and Sutton had even considered the man one of his closer and more respected friends – which had made the betrayal more deplorable. Now, with his emotions already on a knife's edge, Sutton was afraid he might lose his threadbare control should Mr Livingston provide him with an opening.

Sutton was shown to the parlour, where he found Mr Ashcroft alone with a book. The gentleman stood as Sutton was announced and the two exchanged a firm handshake.

'Thank you again for your hospitality,' said Sutton, taking his seat. 'I understand this must be a difficult time for your family.'

Mr Ashcroft nodded. 'It has not been an easy time for Great Britain, but if God is willing, we will soon put this unease behind us. With the recent turn of tide in the campaign – if the reports can be trusted – we can only hope the Marquis of Wellington's reinforcements will be enough to gain a decisive victory.'

'Indeed. The Marquis is certainly not to be trifled with – a fact Napoleon has overlooked.'

'Are you acquainted with the Marquis?'

'A little. We have crossed paths a few times.'

'Is he as honourable as they say?'

'He is.' It occurred to Sutton the gentleman wished to know about the Marquis's attitude towards the men under his command, and whether he would take ruthless, unnecessary risks on his men's lives. 'If there's one thing to be said about Lord Wellington, it is that he is both a fine soldier and commander, a combination that, as I have been told on numerous occasions, is rare, admirable, and provides Great Britain with a great measure of success. There is perhaps no other man who possesses both an understanding of the soldier's plight and an astute eye for the battlefield at large.'

Mr Ashcroft nodded again. 'Thank you, Lord Sutton. Your words bring me much comfort.'

The men fell into silence. Sutton suspected he knew what the gentleman was thinking and feeling – he had been weighed by the same questions and concerns since Graham's deployment. Richard may have been Mr Ashcroft's brother by circumstance, but Graham was Sutton's by choice – and Sutton could not imagine a world without his dearest friend.

Wishing to direct the conversation elsewhere, Sutton asked, 'How are Mrs Ashcroft and Miss Ashcroft?'

'Quite well,' replied the gentleman. 'They are presently attending to some business with Mr Livingston – though I confess I never thought I'd utter such a sentence. I've found myself with not one, but two independent women.'

Sutton fought back a smile. 'Has Mr Livingston provided some helpful insights on Miss Ashcroft's work?'

'Very much so.' Mr Ashcroft considered his next words. 'I understand if you wish to remain anonymous – and you have my word that I will not share your answer with anyone – but were you perchance the one who introduced my sister's works to Mr Livingston?'

'I was not.' The question had taken Sutton by surprise, and his curiosity now grew as to who had facilitated their introduction. 'But if you wish, I could investigate the matter on your behalf.'

Mr Ashcroft seemed equally surprised by Sutton's response. 'Thank you, but that won't be necessary. While I was initially interested in learning who had informed Mr Livingston about my sister, my primary concern was with his reputation. I'm much more comfortable with him now that he has proven himself an expert and professional – despite his slight eccentricities.'

Sutton nodded, remembering with some fondness Mr Livingston's peculiarities, which the viscount had initially found endearing. But even more fascinating was how the genial, somewhat clumsy man transformed completely when he turned his attention to art. At some point before their altercation, Sutton had even considered painting a portrait of his former friend.

'Mr Livingston is both skilful and knowledgeable,' Sutton said instead. 'Miss Ashcroft is very fortunate to have his approval.'

He had barely finished his words when they were joined by Mrs Ashcroft, Miss Ashcroft, and Mr Livingston himself, who, years after their disagreement, looked at Sutton with curiosity. As the viscount rose in greeting, Sutton hoped the other gentleman hadn't heard his unmitigated praise.

Mrs Ashcroft, however, remained oblivious to what had passed between the two men, and instantly approached Sutton, extending her arm. 'Lord Sutton! It is wonderful to see you again!'

There was a glow about her, which, while contrary to the morose atmosphere Sutton had expected after Richard's deployment, suited Mrs Ashcroft perfectly. He kissed the offered hand, then turned his attention to Miss Ashcroft.

The young lady wore a lovely peach dress, and an even lovelier spot of colour on her cheeks. Her freckles had faded a little over winter, and Sutton wished nothing more than to count each remaining one.

She met Sutton's gaze with a shy smile and curtsied.

'Welcome back to Thornleigh, Lord Sutton.'

Then, with a hint of hesitation, she followed her sister-in-law's gesture, and offered her hand.

Sutton had kissed countless hands in his lifetime: hands that were slender or plump, soft or dry, pale or sun-kissed; hands belonging to gentlewomen, countesses, even princesses. Yet, as he carefully hooked his fingers underneath hers and lifted it to his lips, Sutton knew the small, cool, delicate hand he now held had become the most precious of them all. He pressed his lips softly, lightly, briefly, but when he withdrew, no more than a heartbeat or two later, he saw her dazed eyes and her breathless, parted lips, and Sutton felt the very same wonder that was painted so clearly on her small, charming face.

Their innocent exchange had sparked in him a desire that was lighter than air, smoother than wine. He watched as she went to take her seat, a stumble in her steps, a slight trembling in her hand. The soft impression of that same hand lingered on his lips, and it took Sutton all his willpower to look away from the lady and acknowledge Mr Livingston.

Here he was met with another dilemma. He did not wish to speak with Mr Livingston – had not wished to see the man at all – but his refusal would make the next half hour difficult for Miss Ashcroft. Sutton had not forgotten Mr Livingston's injurious comments, and had no intentions of forgiving him.

But Sutton was not here at his own leisure, or on his own behalf. He would do well to remember it.

His voice hoarse and his manner stiff, Sutton said: 'Mr Livingston. It has been several years.'

'Indeed, Lord Sutton,' replied the other man, almost casually.

They both sat down. Sutton found Mr Livingston's behaviour infuriating, but he tried to hide his disdain.

'What is your appraisal of Miss Ashcroft's work, Mr Livingston?'

'They are promising. Yes, indeed – Miss Ashcroft is a promising young artist. What of you, Lord Sutton? Still drawing?'

The quiet question from the otherwise unremarkable man did not fool Sutton. He heard the challenges in the words, delivered in the same, nonchalant tone as the scathing attack Livingston made all those years ago. *Your art is contrived at worst, mediocre at best.* The words had wounded Sutton time and time again.

But now, they belonged to another time entirely, before Graham's full commitment to the army, before Sutton's befriending of Richard, before Miss Ashcroft revealed her kind heart and gifted hands. His recent experiences had tempered and humbled him in ways he could not have imagined – and might not have noticed if not for this confrontation with Livingston.

So Sutton cast aside his pretences, crossed his left leg over his right, and said: 'I am. But my sketches are mere trifles compared to what Miss Ashcroft creates.'

'Oh?' The man's surprise seemed genuine. 'Well, that's very magnanimous of you, Lord Sutton.'

'Lord Sutton has been both humble and kind,' Miss Ashcroft said, her small voice confident. 'It was he who first encouraged and challenged me to explore subjects I would not have otherwise attempted. He has given me the most invaluable feedback, without which I doubt my work would be as it is now.'

Miss Ashcroft's impromptu defence was met with some surprised silence, and was only broken when Livingston commented, in his genial tone again, 'Well, that is very good to hear indeed.'

The next morning, after Livingston had left Thornleigh for London, Sutton retrieved the book Richard had entrusted to him and went downstairs to breakfast, hoping to find Miss Ashcroft alone. He fought back a smile when he saw only the young lady in the morning room, bright and fresh in her morning attire. He lingered at the doorway a little longer than necessary.

When he did make himself known, Sutton was inordinately pleased at how her surprise at the early morning interruption quickly changed into delight. 'Good morning, Lord Sutton,' she said. 'Would you like some toast?'

'Yes, please.'

He sat opposite her, but before they could make any small talk, Sutton thought it imperative to complete the most important task of his visit.

'Ensign Richard wished you to have this,' he said, solemnly giving the object to Miss Ashcroft. 'I'm sorry it took me so long to deliver it to its proper recipient, but I had some other pressing obligations and wished to see to this personally.'

The young woman took the book and ran her fingers across the cover. Her eyes were suddenly bright with tears, and Sutton found, once more, how he admired the woman's courage and strength.

'Thank you, Lord Sutton,' she said, a slight quiver in her voice. She withdrew a handkerchief and dabbed at her nose before continuing. 'Not only for delivering this, but also for being a wonderful friend to Richard. I'm so happy he's found his true friends in the army, and it brings me great comfort to know you are amongst them.'

He nodded and gave her the time and space to look through the book. It was a private moment, so Sutton turned away, gazing outside the window while she softly flipped through the pages.

Sutton turned his attention to his toast when it arrived. The slices were warm, golden, and perfectly cooked, and Sutton found great satisfaction in buttering them.

He had finished eating his first slice when Miss Ashcroft finally looked up at him, a tear slipping down her cheek. She brushed it away before it could reach her chin.

'Thank you,' she repeated. 'I take it from some of these landscapes that you obliged my brother in his venture on your last visit to Thornleigh?'

'Your brother was quite persistent about making a detour to stop by some fields. I remember the weather wasn't very compromising that day, but his insistence won out – and, if I am to be frank, convincing me to accompany him was quite an easy task.'

She gave him a watery smile and dabbed her nose again. 'Richard has mastered the effective combination of being both bossy and charming.'

'Indeed.' Then, tentatively, he added, 'But it was not Richard's persuasive talents that convinced me to make that particular detour.'

The lady stilled and swallowed, drawing his eyes to her bare, slender neck. 'Oh?'

'It was his insistence that you would find much joy in the wildflowers and sketches that crumbled my resolve.'

He let the words linger between them, watching her face carefully. To his relief and delight, she seemed nothing short of pleased, until another thought crossed her mind and brought a frown to her features.

'I must apologise for Mr Livingston's visit, and for his rudeness towards you,' she said quietly. 'If I had known of his animosity, I would have asked him to visit another time.'

'There is no need to apologise,' he said, a little pleased by her words. 'Mr Livingston and I have some unpleasant history, but the fault is not entirely his.'

'I cannot imagine you in the wrong, Lord Sutton.'

The simple admission warmed him and encouraged him to live to those words. 'Mr Livingston has an unparalleled eye for art, and a unique ability to advocate for the works he favours – he has been responsible for the careers of many successful artists, as you might already know. It just so happened that, after a few years of comfortable friendship, I made the error of asking for his professional opinion when I was ill-equipped to deal with any criticism.'

'Was he unreasonably harsh?'

'No more or less than I had deserved.' He could almost hear her silent question, and verbalised the words that had taunted him for far too long. '"Your art is contrived at worst, mediocre at best". Not the most encouraging feedback, but it was particularly hurtful to my proud, immature self.'

Miss Ashcroft paled. 'That is unkind, and hurtful, and certainly *not* true.'

'It was not unfounded,' he said honestly. 'It was not until recently that I have come to accept my own limitations. But more importantly,' he added with a smile, 'I must thank you for your staunch defence of me, undeserving as I am.'

At this, the fire he had seen in her yesterday resurfaced. 'For someone who is so assured of his talents, abilities, and knowledge, you, Lord Sutton, really ought to accept the credit and compliments as they are due.'

Sutton wondered if she was aware of how her passionate speech was effectively defending Sutton to himself, and he couldn't help but smile sheepishly.

'Besides,' she continued, more quietly but with the same conviction, 'there was truth in everything I said. You have given me more support and encouragement than perhaps you yourself realise.'

Then, a little hesitantly, she said, 'I would very much like to invite you to my studio. I have nearly completed a painting that has caught Mr Livingston's interest, and... Well, I would like you to see for yourself the exact reach of your influence.'

Her admission pleased and frightened him at the same time. He had grown to respect and admire Miss Ashcroft's works, but to bear the responsibility of shaping her art was another matter entirely. Yet he could deny Miss Ashcroft nothing, and they soon left the parlour for her studio.

When they reached the larger of the rooms, Sutton took a moment to appreciate the displayed paintings. While he recognised a number of works from her previous exhibition, the room had since been rearranged and now included a number of fresh paintings. He was struck anew by her perspectives and talents, and would have very much liked to study them at his leisure.

'Your exhibition looks more magnificent than ever. It is no wonder Mr Livingston has taken an interest.'

The young lady blushed prettily. 'I am fortunate enough to be assisted by many wonderful and insightful friends.'

She led him to an adjoining room that served as her workspace. The familiar scents of paint, which were soft and mellow in the exhibition room, rose to their full strength here. Sutton inhaled deeply, finding strange comfort in the bold smells. And somewhere beneath the paints, he caught the soft, subtle scent of Miss Ashcroft.

He suddenly realised their current situation: their proximity, intimacy, and lack of supervision. Granted, he had received permission from Mr Ashcroft to court the lady, and Sutton would be the perfect gentleman with Miss Ashcroft, but he also knew how their interaction could be misconstrued. He must behave carefully, and not bring Miss Ashcroft's reputation into question.

But then his attention was pulled by a large canvas, the centrepiece of the room. There, still wet from her progress, was a painting of uniformed soldiers at the eve of battle. One of the men was unquestionably Richard, and Sutton was astonished at how Miss Ashcroft had managed to capture both the young man's *joie de vivre* and duty to his country.

Beside the painting was a plaque, bearing the title 'We Happy Few'. He ran a finger across the smooth plate and the engraved letters, marvelling at the juxtaposition in the textures.

'I think you've been introduced to Mr Curtis,' she said softly. 'He holds a deep love of literature, and helped me name all the paintings. The plaques were also his idea.'

He gave her a small, intimate smile, and she responded in kind.

'I also thought you might recognise the canvas,' she added.

'I do indeed. I am immeasurably pleased and honoured you've made such a magnificent use of the gift.'

A little shyly, she gestured to a table close to the window. Upon it lay an array of sketches, some in pencil, others filled in watercolour, all depicting the various angles and perspectives of a battlefield. He recognised Richard's hand,

and admired how Miss Ashcroft improved on her brother's rough drawings. Sutton was partial to one depiction in particular, where the scene focused on the pensive features of a soldier standing on elevated ground, surveying the fray, the lines of his body taunt and ready to join the fighting. This man was unmistakably Richard, and, to his surprise, the one beside him, though slightly smaller and obscured from view, was none other than Graham.

A blank canvas stood beside the table of sketches, the large white space another of his gifts to her. He could almost picture her standing before the canvas, a pencil in hand, deliberating how to make the first mark.

Sutton gestured at the sketch he most preferred. 'I think this would make a spectacular painting,' he offered. 'Though, if you're still uncertain, perhaps you could work a little more on the ratios and perspectives, and perhaps on the map of the terrain itself. Have you ever been to the Iberian Peninsula?'

Miss Ashcroft shook her head, a little forlorn, and Sutton silently chided himself for the foolish question. 'Richard has sent me some landscapes I'd requested, and there are more in the book you have so kindly delivered. There's also a little bit of wilderness not far from Thornleigh, where you and Mr Earlwood stopped by last year – I know the place very well and have used it as inspiration.'

Sutton smiled, remembering their chance encounter and his envy at her skill that afternoon. But there was no envy now – only admiration. 'I have some illustrations that might be of further use. I'd be more than happy to send them to you, if you like.'

'I would very much like to consult them, if it's not too troublesome for you.'

'Of course.' Another thought struck him and he asked, 'Are you familiar with the works of Francisco Goya?'

She nodded innocently, oblivious to the rumours about the Spanish painter's other, far more salacious work behind closed doors. Sutton's voice was a little strained when he quickly added, 'I've heard he's in the final stages of two paintings centred on the events of May, 1808. I could enquire about its progress through some of my Continental contacts – though, given the current climate, I'm unable to make any promises.'

'Thank you,' she said, unaware of Sutton's slight predicament. 'I appreciate your offer, but please don't go to such trouble on my behalf.'

'I will write to my friends – it is no trouble at all.'

At her shy acquiescence, a realisation dawned upon him. All art always started through imitation, by recapturing the visions of predecessors – but at some point, a great artist must break away from the past and forge their own path. In all his years, Sutton had struggled to find his own vision, resulting in works deemed derivative and trite; yet Miss Ashcroft, despite her young age, had shown her capabilities to go beyond. She would take the world by storm, this delicate, unassuming lady with her soft gaze and compassionate heart – he was certain of it.

The emotions rose within him, and he could not deny their expression.

'Miss Ashcroft, I was wrong to have derided you as I did upon our first meeting. Your talents make you my superior – I suspect I felt this at the start, though it has taken me much longer to admit it. In time, I will make peace with my own deficiencies and limitations. I love art, and I will *always* love art – but I think it will be quite all right to spend my life devoted to appreciating it without excelling at it.'

She regarded him for a long time. Unable to hold her gaze, Sutton looked away. He felt foolish about revealing himself so thoroughly, and chastised himself for not keeping his sentiments in check.

He was finding an excuse to leave the room when Miss Ashcroft spoke, her voice like a gentle caress.

'Lord Sutton, you need not excel at any pursuits, artistic or otherwise, in order to be extraordinary.'

The words echoed in his heart long after they left the studio.

35

As usual, Ellie was content to spend a few hours listening to the conversation in the drawing room after dinner. Tonight, Ellie resumed embroidering a cushion cover she had abandoned some weeks ago. She was now concentrating on some leaves, and the bright green threads lightened her spirits.

Around her, Marcus and Lord Sutton were discussing the political situation in Great Britain and beyond, with Kitty occasionally interjecting. While the two gentlemen were undoubtedly both patriots, they differed on notions of culture and heritage. From what she gathered, Lord Sutton prioritised the protection of artefacts and paintings over that of land, and was rather vocal about expressing his opinion. Marcus, on the other hand, thought there was little value in such items if there wasn't any land left to work and to support the people.

Since she was impartial to the debate – which had become rather heated – Ellie saw the merit of both men's arguments. Nonetheless, she started a little when Lord Sutton made a particularly emphatic point, drawing on the words of Edmund Burke, almost causing her to make an error in her work.

Noticing her reaction – and betraying his attention on her despite his own conversation – Lord Sutton glanced at Ellie with a sheepish smile.

'I have rather lost control over my passions,' he said by way of apology. 'Mr Ashcroft, perhaps it's best we agree to disagree on the matter.'

The two men shook hands, and Ellie saw the geniality in both their expressions. She suspected they had both enjoyed their exchange of ideas, and it was the discussion itself, not the outcome, that they most valued.

When they were seated once more, Marcus said, 'Lord Sutton, I must thank you for delivering Richard's sketches. Are you certain we cannot persuade you to remain at Thornleigh for another week or two?'

Kitty joined in at this. 'It would be a shame to leave so soon after arriving. Mr Earlwood was very sorry not to have spent more time with you during your last visit – and the hunting season will soon be over. Though of course, we would understand if you wish to return to Bellevue Park. There is nothing quite like the comforts of one's own home, and the meals of one's own cook.'

'Ah, but Mrs Nancy is extraordinarily skilled,' replied the viscount. 'She can easily hold her own.'

His small smile disappeared as he deliberated the offer. Given what had transpired this morning, the prospect of Lord Sutton extending his stay filled Ellie with much anticipation. Instinct told her Lord Sutton would be happy to comply with the request if she made her thoughts known, so she lifted her gaze to meet his once more.

His eyes were dark and warm, and his ensuing reply was precisely what Ellie wished.

As winter began to thaw, so too did Thornleigh Abbey, partly aided by Lord Sutton's presence. The viscount, whom Ellie had once mistakenly thought as proud, proper, and superior to her in his knowledge of both art and the ways of the world, was now strolling through the corridors of Thornleigh with great ease, returning from his trips with Mr Earlwood with boyish grins and windswept hair, filling their evenings in the drawing room with his insightful and delightful comments.

One rainy afternoon, when Lord Sutton was prevented from his outdoor pursuits, Kitty commented on how much she had enjoyed their sketching exercises when Richard was in Thornleigh for Ellie's birthday. Ellie hid a smile at Kitty's seemingly off-hand remark – she suspected her sister-in-law was hoping to be the subject of several more sketches without carrying out any pencil work herself. A quick glance at Lord Sutton confirmed the viscount was open to the idea, and was perhaps even enthusiastic about it.

Marcus, who was never one to deny his wife, suggested moving to the library as it was both comfortable and well-lit at this time of day. Soon, the quartet was settled in their chairs, sketchbooks and pencils ready.

Kitty joined them for this first round, where Marcus was their subject, complete with a procured walking stick. Having played the part before during Ellie's youth, Marcus served as an excellent model, holding his poses without complaint.

It took a quarter of an hour for the first sketches to be completed. They compared these, much to Kitty's delight.

'Goodness me,' she managed between peels of laughter, 'I am not at all suited for the task! Oh, Marcus, I have wronged you terribly!'

Indeed, Kitty's picture barely resembled her husband. Her deficiencies would not have been so obvious had her sketch not been positioned beside Ellie and Lord Sutton's, which both held a considerable likeness to the subject.

'Oh Lord Sutton,' Kitty continued, the laughter still in her voice, '*your* drawing is wonderful. You've made my husband quite striking.'

'Thank you,' replied the viscount, 'though Miss Ashcroft's rendition is far superior. She has captured a level of detail I've always lacked.'

Ellie was warmed by his sincere compliment, but she also saw a distinctness in the viscount's style that had been absent during their previous sessions with Richard. 'Your strokes are much bolder,' she said. 'You've also done a great service to my brother's clothing – I daresay his waistcoat is better tailored in your drawing than on his person.'

'Quite right, Ellie,' remarked Kitty. 'Goodness, I'm constantly awed by your ability to articulate these things. Now, shall we draw you, Ellie? Do join us,

Marcus – it'll be great fun.'

Although Ellie disliked being on the other end of the sketchpad, refusing would have caused a terrible inconvenience. She had neither Marcus's confidence nor Richard's flamboyance, and could only be persuaded to sit by the window and peer out at the rain. Even that much felt pretentious.

Her aversion to modelling was now exacerbated by the knowledge that Lord Sutton was observing and drawing her features. As she grew hot with embarrassment, she was keenly aware that her freckles would become more pronounced.

The minutes grew longer. Ellie wished Richard were here, making the music of light conversation to complement the rhythm of scratching pencils. Modelling had not been so bad when Richard joined them in December. She wondered if he would ever join them again. Tears rose at the thought.

'I'm finished!' declared Kitty, who was usually the slowest of the party. At the men's agreement, Ellie dropped her pose, sagging back into her seat. She required a moment to compose herself, and hoped her melancholy had gone unnoticed.

When she looked up, Kitty and Marcus were studying the sketches, both smiling as Kitty dissected her shortcomings. But Lord Sutton wore no such smile. His lips were thin, his brow furrowed. He looked past her poised façade and saw everything: her fears, her insecurities, her loneliness. He saw *her* – and acknowledged it with a small nod, a slight curve of a smile.

The moment passed. Kitty and Marcus were now commending Lord Sutton on his portrayal, but Ellie herself was too afraid to afford his sketch more than a cursory glance. Instead, she sought pleasure in Marcus's rendition, which, while rudimentary, was quite charming.

'I very much enjoy your perspective,' she said to her brother. 'Perhaps you should pick up a pencil more often.'

Marcus laughed warmly. 'You are too kind, dear Ellie. My drawing days are over – and you shall not persuade me otherwise, Mrs Ashcroft.'

'A great shame,' Kitty replied with a wink at Ellie. 'I'm afraid I must put down my pencil as well. Oh, if only this rain would cease!'

With half the group keen to find amusement elsewhere, Ellie exhaled quietly and kept her disappointment to herself. She would have liked to draw Lord Sutton again, but there was no possibility of it now – Kitty had made several suggestions, and Ellie could only nod in agreement.

When they eventually settled on charades, Ellie had regained her composure once more. She looked at Lord Sutton and only saw the countenance of a polite guest. Try as she might, Ellie could not dismiss her frustration and sorrow at seeing his cool demeanour once more.

In the first week of March, Mr Curtis made his monthly visit to Thornleigh Abbey and became reacquainted with Lord Sutton. The two men had met briefly during Ellie's exhibition, and as they made themselves comfortable in the drawing room after dinner, Lord Sutton and Mr Curtis became absorbed in a discussion about the values of classical philosophy. Kitty was making her way through an early Mozart sonata with Marcus as her page-turner, and Ellie contented herself with finishing her cushion.

Ellie had set down her cushion and was admiring it when Mr Curtis said: 'Miss Ashcroft, your brother informed me about your completed painting. I believe congratulations are in order.'

'Thank you, Mr Curtis. You are more than welcome to view it, if you wish. I have also started on a companion piece – "We Band of Brothers".'

'An excellent choice. I shall procure a plaque for you.'

From the piano, Marcus said: 'Mr Curtis, you need not go to so much trouble. If you could kindly tell me whom to contact, I will do the rest.'

'Truly, it is no trouble. I require some additional plaques for Lampton Hall as it is.'

Marcus tried to protest, but his inattention had left Kitty neglected. 'Some help here please, Mr Ashcroft,' she said, and the matter of the plaques was all but settled.

When the page was turned and Kitty back on track again, Ellie asked: 'What are the latest developments in Lampton Hall?'

The gentleman turned to Lord Sutton and explained, 'Lampton Hall is a school I run for the less fortunate children in Darlington. I believe every child should have access to a good education, regardless of their social standing.'

'Yes, I remember – it is an admirable endeavour,' Lord Sutton replied. 'Though I imagine it's come with a fair share of difficulties and resistance.'

'Indeed. But the opinions of inferior minds do not bother me. To answer your question, Miss Ashcroft, you'll be pleased to know we've hired an art instructor for the students. The children enjoy these sessions a great deal, which has led us to consider other activities and instructors in the future.'

'That sounds delightful,' said Ellie. 'Richard and I were both seven when Marcus found our first art tutor, though he lasted about a month.'

'More fool he,' said Mr Curtis. 'Might I ask, what other instruction did you receive as a young girl? I feel quite confident about planning the boys' extracurriculars, but I confess, having no experience whatsoever in the area, I am a little lost as to what young ladies ought to be learning during their formative years.'

Ellie thought for a moment. 'Apart from art, I had music lessons at the pianoforte, though I was a very lacklustre pupil in that regard; voice lessons, which I enjoyed a little more, but it was nonetheless decided I was much better suited to listening to music; some dancing instruction with Richard, at which he rather excelled, and, thanks to his enthusiasm and continual encouragement, I managed to fumble my way through relatively well; needlework, which I enjoyed immensely; and French and Italian, though I confess that, despite the years of instruction, I can never say more than a few sentences in either.'

Mr Curtis nodded, deep in thought. 'Our pupils are learning French and Italian – and I've encouraged the headmaster to ensure both the girls *and* boys also pick up rudimentary Greek and Latin. I confess I've not given too much thought to music, dancing, and needlework – I don't wish to inundate the children with activities when they already have so much to contend with in their general studies.'

'If I may offer a suggestion,' Marcus said from the pianoforte, and continued at Mr Curtis's nod, 'perhaps you could give all your pupils an opportunity to learn those different areas and skills, and, after a few weeks or months, ascertain if they wish to continue in any specific subject. Richard was particularly opinionated about what he liked and disliked, and Ellie could be cajoled to express the same.'

'Yes – this is very helpful indeed,' said Mr Curtis. 'Thank you – I will think more on it and discuss it with Mr Simmons.' He turned to Kitty, who had finished the final movement. 'Mrs Ashcroft, I must commend the liveliness of your playing – Mozart himself would have been delighted. Which sonata is it? I may have to acquire the sheets.'

Mr Curtis never discovered the answer, for Mr Talbot chose that moment to knock and enter. Marcus stood at the butler's appearance.

'Sir, a special messenger has arrived with news from the Peninsula.'

Marcus crossed the room in no time and opened the letter. He scanned the contents, looked up at the concerned faces around him, and read:

We declare with much pleasure that, on the 27th of February in the year of our Lord 1814, the Anglo-Portuguese Army (which comprises of the 5th Regiment of Foot in the British Army) under the command of Field Marshal Arthur Wellesley, Marquess of Wellington, defeated the enemy army led by Marshal Nicolas Soult. This event shall be remembered as the Battle of Orthez. While the Anglo-Portuguese suffered a number of losses, Ensign Ashcroft was unharmed.

Yours, etc.

Postscript: The ensign insists on adding that Lieutenant Graham, also of the 5th Regiment, was also unharmed.

The relief hit Ellie without warning, making her dizzy. Her dear brother, whose fate had been uncertain for such a long time, was *safe*. She heard Kitty's relieved cries while Marcus consoled her, and Mr Curtis uttered comforting words. Ellie's own eyes filled with tears, and she reached for her handkerchief.

Remembering the postscript Richard had included, Ellie looked up at the viscount – and found him brusquely swiping his thumb across his cheeks. In that moment, in being privy to his vulnerability, Ellie's heart went out to him. She saw with astonishing clarity how she was infinitely more fortunate, even in her misfortunes: one of Ellie's brother had gone to war, but the other remained at home, loving and doting on Ellie as much as on Kitty. Despite the pains of their situation, the Ashcrofts had one another.

But Lord Sutton only had his best friend – and that same person was at war. Even now, the viscount was forgotten, left by the wayside while the Ashcrofts – and even Mr Curtis – celebrated the news.

Lord Sutton was alone – and only Ellie had noticed.

So she resolved, then and there, with all the quiet passion and gentle fierceness of her heart: he would be alone no more. *She* would be his companion, confidante, friend; she saw him, knew him, acknowledged him. *She* would be his anchor when Lieutenant Graham was away – and beyond.

When Lord Sutton's gaze met hers, his hazel eyes full of tears, Ellie held it, unwavering. She made it known to him her intention, her decision, her very being.

And his eyes softened, deepened – and Ellie knew he understood.

36

THIS TIME, SUTTON left Thornleigh Abbey with a lighter heart than when he arrived. It was not only the respite from his constant concerns about Graham, out in harm's way at the battlefront, nor was it the spring air that wound its way into his clothes and hair; no, it was the gentle, unspoken promises from Miss Ashcroft, who had let him know, in her unassuming way, that he was welcome in her life.

That morning, she wore a soft rose dress, fresh as dew at dawn, her hair neatly arranged, her hand untouched by paint. Mr Ashcroft had joined them for breakfast, though his wife made her apologies. But Mrs Ashcroft's absence went unnoticed – Sutton only had eyes for Miss Ashcroft.

'It has been wonderful having you here,' she said softly. 'Thornleigh won't be the same without you.'

'Quite right,' agreed her brother. 'We have enjoyed your company immensely.'

Sutton smiled, feeling a little sentimental and rather foolish. 'The pleasure was all mine. I hope you will consider visiting Bellevue again when spring has set in – it has been a family tradition to hold a ball every year after Easter, and I would be greatly honoured if you could all attend.'

'Thank you,' replied Mr Ashcroft. 'We would be delighted.'

The viscount hoped he could secure his name on Miss Ashcroft's dance card, but kept his tongue in check. Easter was still a fair while away, and so much could transpire in the next two months.

Instead, he smiled and said: 'There is but one condition: please persuade Mrs Nancy to contribute her lemon tarts. My valet has spoken of nothing else this past fortnight.'

Sutton was always ambivalent about visiting his various farms and tenants during Lent, and this year was no exception. His heart and mind were elsewhere, but his duties remained at Bellevue. His father had drilled into him the weight and responsibility of his position, where the community depended on him and his management of his estates. Yet, as with every year, his initial reticence gradually receded and was replaced with a sharp awareness of his heritage. Flanked by Allen and Parsons, both of whom had regarded Sutton with additional deference since his assistance to the Colchester barracks, the 7th Viscount Sutton committed himself to greet every one of the eight hundred souls who lived on his lands.

It was a time for him to meet the newest members of a tenant's family; a time for him to express his condolences for those who had passed on from sickness or from age; a time to thank his farmers for their decades – and often generations – of service. It was a time to oversee the tilling of the soil, the planting of wheat, the birthing of lambs, and, sometimes, for him to lend a hand at the expense of his own boots and shirtsleeves. Most of all, it was a time for him to reaffirm his connection to his lands, and to breathe in the unspoilt country air.

The long days of activity were tiring on his body, but Sutton's mind continued to whirl late into the night. While he had always paid attention to the goings-on in the Peninsula, Sutton had recently redoubled his efforts, asking various sources to inform him immediately of any changes. His solemnity was noticed by all the staff at Bellevue, but since most of them had known Graham as a little boy, they understood and even shared his pain.

He no longer found solace in the study, where Graham's empty chair reminded him too much of his friend's absence. Nor did he enjoy the formal drawing room, empty of guests to entertain. Instead, Sutton withdrew to his studio. Surrounded by the heady scents of oils, the viscount spent many evenings with all the candles lit, working and reworking the sketches he had made of Miss Ashcroft during his latest stay at Thornleigh Abbey. He struggled to improve on them, and after a week of frustration, Sutton resolved to change his studio completely.

It had been at least a decade since Sutton claimed this space for his artistic pursuits. In that time, he'd rarely removed anything from the room, but added to it the various equipments and instruments he had purchased for his craft. The staff knew not to interfere with the room, and it had not been properly cleaned since the viscount first inherited it. Thus, when Sutton finally decided to rearrange the room, he found himself facing the unenviable task of dealing with the paraphernalia amassed over many years.

He responded to this by deciding, not without some pain and difficulty, to purge the room of its inessentials. Dozens upon dozens of canvases at various stages of completion – some abandoned when King George III was still in good health – were ordered to be thrown out, much to the surprise of the younger footmen, and to the silent satisfaction of Mrs Jennings. Gone also were the various trinkets he had kept as subjects: Grecian urns, a full suit of armour, a pineapple that had seen *much* better days. He met his most challenging task when it was time to contend with his own works: sketches with pencil, charcoal, even some detailed with watercolour. But as he reminisced about the hours spent recreating Michelangelo or Vermeer, Sutton started making peace with his own limitations. He had acknowledged this in Miss Ashcroft's presence, but accepting it in his own time and space was far more arduous. He had spent twenty years striving for artistic greatness; it would take more than twenty days to dismantle his dreams.

But his determination had not been in vain. When the last unnecessary item was removed from his studio, Sutton felt a tremendous burden had been lifted. His studio, previously dark and musty with stagnant possessions, now appeared thrice the size. The curtains, which finally received a proper washing at the insistence of Mrs Jennings, were now drawn open, revealing the windows that had been scrubbed clean. There was fresh paper aplenty for him to start his next work, and none of the pressure to aim for grandeur and magnificence. He was light and liberated, and now entered his studio with anticipation rather than sombreness or dread.

No longer attempting to capture sublime mountains and oceans did wonders for Sutton's spirits. Instead, he worked on sketching and re-sketching different aspects of Miss Ashcroft. He found he did not mind spending numberless hours reworking the details, and rather relished the opportunity to examine his own feelings. When he was finally satisfied with one of the sketches, he moved onto the next with the same patience and sensitivity. It was slow and careful work, without any immediate triumphs, but Sutton found great pleasure and delight in the undertaking.

And so, the forty days of Lent passed by. He spent each of the six Sundays returning from the chapel, enjoying a roasted lunch on the feast day, and penning letters to Graham and Miss Ashcroft. In these letters, Sutton recalled the mundane events of his week and revealed his innermost feelings. Each Sunday evening, he locked away the letters in the same safe where he had placed Richard's letters. He allowed himself half an hour to nurse a glass of brandy in his study while staring into the fireplace. When the ritual was complete, Sutton would retire early in the evening, and pray for good news to arrive in the week to come.

37

DESPITE THE COLOURS and celebrations during Easter Sunday, which fell on a sufficiently pleasant day, Ellie felt none of its cheer. Even her recent completion of 'We Happy Few', which ought to have brought her much relief and pride, offered nothing but a reminder of Richard's absence. The single consolation was Kitty's recuperation from the bouts of morning sickness, after which she became more spirited than before. Since Kitty was no longer in any danger or discomfort, she and Marcus decided to announce the news after church, and received many congratulations in return.

Harriet, who had spent the past few weeks demonstrating embroidery at Lampton Hall, now approached Ellie. 'This is wonderful news,' she said. 'You will soon be an aunt!'

Ellie brightened at the thought. 'Yes, I will. Happy Easter, Harriet!'

'Happy Easter!'

They straightened and greeted Mrs Norris when she passed by. The older woman treated the ladies with her usual scrutiny, but she was clearly searching for someone else. When Mrs Norris was out of earshot, Ellie asked: 'How are you finding Lampton Hall?'

'Very well, thank you. As I'd suspected, some of the girls already have some skill with the needle, but there are many techniques they've not yet learnt. The other day, there were two boys who also wished to join, since their friend was in the group. Her name is Tabitha – you might've seen her around.'

'I think so.'

'She, Colin, and Peter were some of the first students Mr Curtis and Mr Simmons recruited. In any case, the boys had heard enough of Tabitha's talk about our needlework lessons, and wanted to try it themselves.'

'That's hardly conventional.'

Harriet smiled. 'I've come to appreciate that few things are conventional at Lampton Hall.'

'What did you decide?'

'I took up the matter with Mr Simmons, who, to my great surprise, advised me to allow the boys into the group. He lamented his own inability to wield needle and thread, which is of exceeding annoyance when a button requires immediate attention and there is no maid in sight.'

Ellie couldn't imagine Marcus needing to sew his own buttons, but at the thought of Richard fending for himself, Ellie decided Mr Simmons did indeed possess a sound logic.

'So I took his advice and allowed the boys to join – on the strict proviso they remain on their best behaviour. Peter is still finding a lot of the basics difficult, but Colin has taken to the needle surprisingly well. Ah, there's Mr Simmons himself.'

The schoolmaster approached them and bowed. 'Happy Easter, Miss Ashcroft, Miss Harriet.'

'Happy Easter,' the two ladies said in unison.

'Miss Ashcroft, congratulations on your family's happy news.'

They exchanged a few more pleasantries before the gentleman bowed again and excused himself.

That evening, despite the sumptuous Easter Sunday feast, complete with Mrs Nancy's customary custard, rich with milk and eggs, Ellie found her appetite had escaped her. She ate enough to satisfy her family and withdrew to her rooms shortly afterwards. She went to bed, tired and heartsick, haunted by dark and unwelcome visions.

Ellie awoke in a sweat, hours before dawn, her heart pounding in her ears. It took her some time to realise she was hearing the loud knocking at her door. Sick with worry, Ellie climbed out of her bed and opened the door.

There stood Maria, bleary-eyed and uncertain.

'I'm sorry to disturb you, miss, but there's a messenger who's ridden through the night, and Mrs Rowley didn't wish to awake Mr Ashcroft, who's in Mrs Ashcroft's rooms tonight, and there's Mrs Ashcroft's condition to consider, but it's only an hour or two from when you usually rise, so she sent me to fetch you.'

It took several long seconds for the meaning to register in Ellie's hazy mind. 'That's fine, Maria. It's a little chilly – please fetch my robe.'

Once she was sufficiently dressed, Ellie headed downstairs, keeping her footsteps as quiet as possible. When she reached the great hall, she was greeted by Mrs Rowley and Mr Talbot, both dressed for the day. In the butler's hand was a letter, which he promptly handed to Ellie.

It was addressed to Marcus, and Ellie almost decided to wait for him to rise. But there was urgent news contained within the letter, and Ellie was filled with a fierce need to know its tidings.

She reached for the ring around her neck and found it missing – she had not yet conducted her usual morning toilette. Instead, Ellie closed her eyes and counted to ten. When she opened them again, her fingers had stopped trembling enough for her to break the seal.

Dear Sir:

I am pleased to announce that due to Napoleon's abdication on this day, the 11th of April 1814, the British Allied Forces have declared victory in the Peninsular War. The Marquess of Wellington and our enemy commander Marshal Soult, who have continued their campaign in southern France, will be informed of this immediately, and begin the ceasefire negotiations.

I have no further intelligence on the well-being or whereabouts of Ensign

Richard Ashcroft, but will bring you news when it becomes available.

Yours etc,

Captain G. R. Kendall, on behalf of His Majesty's forces

Ellie exhaled a long breath before reading the letter once more to ensure she had not been mistaken. When she was finished the second time, she looked up at the housekeeper and butler.

'The Peninsular War is over,' she said. 'Napoleon has abdicated.'

Mrs Rowley let loose a small sound of relief before Ellie continued. 'But there is no news from the battlefront, or from Richard.'

'Such news will surely follow,' Mr Talbot reassured. His own relief was palpable, but the butler maintained his usual level of dignity. 'Miss Ashcroft, the messenger is still outside. I suspect he has many more deliveries to make.'

Doing her utmost to compose herself, Ellie straightened and folded away the letter. 'Mr Talbot, please see to it that the messenger receives a shilling for his troubles, and perhaps some bread and milk if he requires it.'

Ellie turned to the housekeeper next.

'Mrs Rowley, please send someone to attend to Mr Ashcroft's rooms, and, when he wakes, please inform him I request his presence immediately. Take care not to disturb Mrs Ashcroft.'

The housekeeper nodded. 'Is that all, miss?'

'Please also spread the news of Napoleon's abdication to the rest of the house,' Ellie said, realising that this was not just about the fate of her brother, but the fate of their country. 'There is no need to mention Mr Richard for the time being.'

'Yes, miss.'

Since she was still in her dressing gown, Ellie went back upstairs to conduct her proper toilette. As Maria helped Ellie with her clothes and arranged her hair, the morning birds sang their first songs of the day while the sky began to lighten. She wondered if Richard was greeting the same dawn in France, if he was listening to another variation of the same music.

The horizon was glowing with the first light by the time Ellie was fully attired. She walked downstairs again, her stays keeping her upright when she herself could not. When she finally reached the morning room, Ellie sank into the chaise by the fireplace and simply gazed out the window at the dawning of the day.

Morning grew, and the elusive English sun made her appearance, saluting Ellie with her gentle rays. The trees that lined the entrance to Thornleigh had regained their leaves, their first, tender greens caressed by the occasional breeze. She had created countless sketches of the window and what lay beyond. In a month, the gardens would be in various stages of bloom, boasting a range of shapes and colours that had been Ellie's most beloved inspiration during her formative years. She became wistful now for those early, carefree years, when the concept of war was as foreign as the country where it was fought. She and Richard and Marcus, happy to be in Thornleigh Abbey, grateful for one another's presence.

The fire, which had been built shortly before Ellie first sat down, was beginning to grow low once more. Had she sat for so long, after the delivery of such news? Had it been an hour, or two, or three? When had the birds stopped singing?

Footsteps approached, their sounds separate yet harmonious. The first set belonged to Oliver, who made quick work of reviving the fire; the second to Mrs Nancy, who wordlessly took a seat beside Ellie. Although the older woman did not carry a plate of food, as Ellie might've expected, she brought with her the warm and comforting smells of the kitchen, which Ellie breathed in deeply.

Oliver left as soon as he had completed his task. The fire burned merrily once more, lending its light and heat to Ellie.

'Has there been any more news?' she asked, though the butler had not brought her any. Mrs Nancy shook her head. 'Is my brother still abed?'

'Shall I send someone to rouse him?' the cook asked. 'It is just past ten o'clock – not a terrible hour, if Mrs Ashcroft were accidentally awakened.'

'That won't be necessary – let them enjoy as much rest as they can now.'

'You're a kind and considerate girl,' Mrs Nancy said gently. 'But you don't have to bear this burden alone. Even Mr Richard' – and there was a hitch here in the cook's voice – 'marched onto the battlefield with his comrades.'

The older woman's gentle understanding soothed Ellie, and stirred in her a thought that had only just occurred, much to her shame and guilt. With the return of her wits came the realisation that she was thirsty, and that she must look after herself during this trying time.

'Please bring my sketchbook and pencils, Mrs Nancy. And perhaps some tea and toast as well, please.'

Mrs Nancy rose to comply, leaving Ellie to her thoughts. The older woman's reminder that Ellie should not be alone was a stark reminder that there was indeed one person who was bearing this by himself, who could not seek the comfort of family, whose dearest friend was subject to the same uncertain fate as Richard. She could envision Lord Sutton alone, enshrouded in darkness, and her heart ached for him.

Marcus arose just after midday, entering the morning room in long, hurried strides. He sat beside her, full of concern and apology.

'You must've had a terribly frightful morning,' he said. 'I'm so sorry you've had to tend to everything alone. Talbot informed me about the abdication and the end of the war, but he mentioned nothing of Richard.'

Ellie gave him the letter she had kept on the small table beside her. 'I know it was addressed to you, but none of us wished to give Kitty a fright. I would not presume to open any of your correspondence under any other circumstance.'

'Of course – and I'm sorry you had to carry the burden.'

He quickly read the letter, then took Ellie's hand.

'Talbot said the letter arrived at four-thirty – have you been up since then?'

Ellie nodded. 'Oh Marcus, when do you think we will hear about Richard? Why is there still no news?'

All the tears she had fought back spilled forth as Ellie started to cry in earnest. Marcus held her until her sobs subsided.

'We'll have news soon enough,' he said, rubbing circles on her back. 'But what's important is that the war is over. Great Britain is safe, my dearest sister; we are safe.'

By the time Kitty dressed and arrived downstairs, the news about Napoleon's abdication had spread throughout Darlington and a number of guests came calling on the Ashcrofts. Mr Curtis was the first to arrive, his dour expression unchanged. He offered comforting words to Mr Ashcroft, obtained permission to wait with them for any news about Richard, and moved himself to an unobtrusive part of the room. Mr Digby soon followed, bringing with him Mrs Norris, whose loquacity more than made up for Mr Curtis's silence. Nonetheless, her relief about the end of the war, and her recollections about her own brother's sacrifices during the American Revolutionary Wars, helped spread the goodwill, which strengthened at the arrival of the Earlwoods, and then of the Winslows. It was not long until most of their friends in Darlington had called, bringing with them their goodwill.

Mrs Nancy had foreseen this gathering, and, apart from her brief interlude with Ellie, she had been busy in the kitchen all morning and afternoon. Their visitors congregated in the parlour with tea and refreshments, talking quietly amongst themselves as they awaited further news. As Ellie observed their friends and noted several absentees, she sent out a prayer for those with family in the army or navy, who were no doubt also waiting to hear about their loved ones.

When Marcus announced that dinner would soon be served for all who wished to remain and entreated everyone to dispense with the usual etiquette for evening attire, Ellie was resigned to suffer through an endless night of waiting. But just as Marcus had announced his invitation, Mr Talbot entered the room with undivided purpose.

'Sir,' he said, and their guests fell silent as he extended the letter tray to Marcus.

Her brother opened the letter and silently read its contents. All of a sudden, Ellie wished they were indeed alone, so that the three Ashcrofts in the house could deal with the news in whichever way required. For the slightest moment, she regretted not politely asking these well-wishers to leave after thanking them for their concern, and she became certain that the thin piece of paper in Marcus's hands would only bring her insurmountable grief.

But then he smiled, his eyes welling with tears, and declared: 'He's safe.'

The words echoed in the silence for a few heartbeats before the room sounded a collective sigh of relief, before slipping into hearty congratulations and celebrations. Ellie hadn't realised she was crying again until Harriet offered her a handkerchief.

'He's safe,' Ellie repeated to herself, and then to Harriet, and then to the world. 'He's *safe*.'

Her friend touched her arm briefly and Ellie nodded in thanks. Meanwhile, Kitty had recovered incredibly well, and was now leading their visitors to the dining room. Instead of following, Ellie made for her brother, the letter still in his hands.

'May I?'

Marcus obliged.

Dear Mr Ashcroft:

I write to you on the outcome of the battle at Toulouse between the Allied army under the Marquess of Wellington and the enemy French Armies, wherein a ceasefire was agreed upon discovering of Napoleon's abdication. Ensign Richard Ashcroft, of the 5th Regiment of Foot of the British Army, forming the 1st Brigade of the 3rd Division of the Marquess's Corps, is alive and well.

However, the Allied army has suffered a number of losses, with casualties totalling over 4,000 men. The exact figures and names will be made public as they become available.

The casualties were so large in number and so incomprehensible in thought that Ellie staggered, the exhaustion from the day finally catching up to her. Marcus steadied her and looked at her with concern.

'I'd like to retire to bed,' she said, feeling light-headed and incredibly weary. 'Would that be terribly offensive to our well-meaning guests?'

'Not at all,' Marcus replied. 'Would you like anyone to sit with you?'

She began to shake her head, but found that Harriet had followed her and heard their exchange. 'I'll be glad to go with her,' said her friend.

'Thank you, Miss Harriet,' said Marcus. 'I'll send some dinner upstairs. You have been so strong, dearest Ellie, but you must look after yourself – or Richard won't let either of us hear the end of it.'

As she and Harriet climbed the stairs, Ellie felt fear well in her stomach once more. Her relief at the news of Richard's safety had only been short-lived, for the rest of the letter, listing the number of casualties, only made it plain that not everyone had left the battlefield unscathed. She now hoped with all her heart that the letter for Lord Sutton mirrored theirs, and that Lieutenant Graham had also been spared.

When Ellie finally received a letter from Richard himself, almost a fortnight after the news of his safety, she cried tears of joy at the sight of his familiar handwriting.

My sweet and gentle sister:

I thank God every day that I am alive to see you once more; I thank Him now that I am able to write to you with this precious pen and paper. As I'm sure you've heard, I am very much alive, and Great Britain is safe from Napoleon's tyranny.

For tyranny it truly was, this warmonger who has deprived so many mothers of their sons, sisters of their brothers, wives of their husbands. He was the true enemy. The soldiers of France – the ones I fought, and who fought us – were no more than pawns of Napoleon, and of those who thirsted for glory at the expense of others.

I am alive, my dearest sister, and while I did not suffer any physical injuries, I cannot say the same for my soul. What Christian man with any semblance of conscience can look his fellow man in the eye, destroy the life housed within, and still call himself a Christian? How can a soul remain untarnished after seeing the cruelties of battle?

And the friends I have lost – to death, injury, and even madness. I fear at times I might be going mad myself. When my eyes are open, I see the shadows of men I am bound by oath to destroy; and when they are closed, I see the ghosts of far, far worse. Lieutenant Graham assures me I am only experiencing the natural aftershocks following my first bout of combat, and all this would soon come to pass – but do I wish it? Do I wish to devote my life to the Army, when I must give up my Soul in exchange?

Yet I cannot help but admire our generals, men like Colonel Watson and the Marquess of Wellington. The Marquess in particular deserves all my respect. When I recall his remarkable combination of martial intellect and his genuine regard for his soldiers, I am proud to have served under his command, to have carried out my duty for my country. News has spread that the Marquess will soon be honoured with two more titles for his achievements in the Peninsula: the Duke of Wellington and the Marquess of Douro. He is most deserving of both.

But his achievements do not mitigate our losses. Our casualties have numbered far too many – of the 50,000 men who fought in our Allied troops, the final count contains 593 dead and 5,024 wounded. These sufferings are far too great, and it is with my deepest sorrow that my friends are among those numbers. Lieutenant Hammond, who was one of the first to welcome me to the Regiment, is now with our Heavenly Father. Lieutenant Fielding, who joined the Regiment at the same time as me, has sustained some terrible injuries. And Lieutenant Graham, the man I've come to admire and respect above all others, was struck in his sword arm, and is in very poor condition. He, whose optimism knows no bounds, is uncertain about his fate. There are so many dangers that might present themselves on the journey back to England, and I am loathe to leave his side.

I do not know why I have been spared when my comrades have suffered, and are suffering as I write. I am endlessly grateful that I have survived, but I am nonetheless riddled with the torment of being unscathed. My only comfort is in knowing I will see you, Marcus, and Kitty again. I will count the days until our reunion, and remain your ever loving brother,

Richard

Ellie read the letter several times, savouring Richard's words even as she shed tears over his anguish. When her tears finally dried, Ellie made for her writing table, her heart set. Even as she began her letter, she knew how scandalous it was to write directly to Lord Sutton – but in light of what

Richard had experienced, Ellie dismissed such social scruples, and set to pour forth all her condolences and assurances.

38

THERE WAS NO HESITATION in Sutton's decisions. When he got word of Great Britain's victory and the army's return to England, the viscount prepared to welcome back the soldiers; when he discovered Graham's injuries, he enquired about the best physicians and the safest means of transport; and when he learnt of his friend's whereabouts, he sent money, men, and instructions. Sutton made it very clear that, given the end of the Peninsular War and Graham's war-time injuries, the lieutenant would take an indefinite leave of absence and convalesce at Bellevue Park.

It was not until three weeks after Britain's victory that Sutton heard from Graham directly. The viscount was at first taken aback at the unfamiliar hand, the elegant script so vastly removed from the lieutenant's rough writing, before the first few lines provided the explanation.

Dear Lord Sutton:

I am writing to you on behalf of Lieutenant Graham, whose injuries have hindered his ability to hold a pen. He has entreated me to act as his scribe and dictates the following:

My good friend, it seems I've survived the war after all, though many of our friends haven't been so fortunate. Lieutenant Hammond's loss, which you may have discovered by now, has struck me particularly hard. He was always such a simple and kind soul; I'd often wondered if he had the disposition for the army. Even when we were marching in the Peninsula, he lost none of his meticulous attention to detail. One morning, I saw him folding away his handkerchief into thirds and then halves before slipping it neatly into his pocket – the memory has stayed with me. I regret not being with him at the end, but from what I've learnt, his final moments were quick and he did not linger needlessly.

As for myself and my injury: I do not regret it at all, as it was sustained while shielding Ensign Smith from harm. He is barely sixteen – much too young to be on the battlefield. If he had perished in Toulouse when I had the power to prevent it, I would not have lived with myself. Now, Smith has a promising life ahead – and the gratitude from an unharmed James Smith is more than enough to compensate for an injured James Graham. So if you have worked yourself up into a concerned frenzy about my state, as I'm sure you have, then I entreat you to find peace with the situation. I wish to return to a joyous Aubrey, not a sullen and broody Aubrey – yes, that does include the dour expression you're currently wearing. Do please dispose of that before my arrival.

I am very much looking forward to returning to England, and to take up my apartments in Bellevue Park once more. I am moved by your efforts in arranging my transport and for welcoming Ashcroft as well. He has not left my side, and is intent on accompanying me through my entire journey, but he assures me he won't impose on you for more than a week, as he longs to return to his family. Apart from your generosity towards us, I do wish you would not burden yourself with any additional expenses on my behalf – once our country resumes its good relations with France, you'll need every last penny for yourself.

I have said much more than I'd intended – or perhaps not enough. Let's resume this when I see you next – I'm counting down the days and miles, my dear friend, and remain ever yours,

JG

While Graham's letter lifted Sutton's spirits, the unexpected missive from Miss Ashcroft was what soothed him. As per his instructions right after their first acquaintance, Sutton's steward brought Miss Ashcroft's correspondence immediately to his attention. He bore in mind the magnitude of recent events and tried not to form hasty conclusions about her directness. Nonetheless, Sutton was careful with the seal and used a particularly light touch when unfolding the letter.

Dear Lord Sutton:

I hope you will forgive me for being so forward in writing to you directly about such personal matters. If I have roused in you any suspicion about my character, or about my familiar behaviour with other members of society, then I entreat you to believe that I am writing to you in concern for your well-being, and that it is *not* in my nature to conduct any improper correspondences.

Indeed, after discovering the state of your friend Lieutenant Graham, I was impelled to write to you with my deepest condolences and my most sincere hopes for his recovery. I understand you and he share a bond that is stronger than that found in most families, and that you feel towards him the kind of brotherly love I have for my own brothers – which, I've come to learn, is not as common amongst our society as I would like to think. When I discovered Lieutenant Graham's injury – which my brother Richard informed me in his letters – I only thought of you, Lord Sutton. This declaration is neither prudent nor proper, but in this instance, I care not for propriety – for I wish you to know that in that hour, and in every hour since, the well-being of you and your friend have preoccupied my thoughts.

It is in this vein that I wish to put into writing my sentiments a month ago, right before you took leave of Thornleigh: you are not alone in this, Lord Sutton. If you feel the need to share your pain or unburden what weighs on you, then I wish you to know I am here for you, and I remain your ever faithful friend,

Eleanor Ashcroft

The tears that escaped dried quickly enough, but the glowing warmth in Sutton's heart remained for a long, long time.

'You look horrendous,' was the first thing Sutton said to Graham upon his arrival, but the viscount's tone was a little too shocked to pass off as playful. He barely recognised the soldier, whose long hair had been clumsily cut and

now hung limply around a face shadowed in pain.

Graham attempted a grin, but his eyes were hollow. 'And you look positively provincial. I'd bet my good arm your waistcoat is from *last* season.'

Although Sutton was concerned about his friend's health, he hid his alarm behind a dramatic huff. 'In case you've not noticed, Lieutenant Graham, there *are* things in life more important than fashion.'

'Noted, sir,' Graham said. He managed a stilted bow despite the contraption around his right arm, then brushed away the uneven hair that fell over his face. 'I hope your hospitality hasn't diminished along with your sartorial sense.'

'Now that, sir, is a barbaric accusation. I would never!'

'Careful now, Aubrey – we have Richard here as a witness.' The lieutenant winked at the young soldier, closed his eyes for a few, long moments, and walked unsteadily toward the manor.

Sutton exchanged a concerned look with Richard before leading them to the main library. The fire was burning merrily, extra cushions lay on Graham's usual chair, and there was a pile of carefully selected books on an adjacent table. But none of these preparations mattered, because Graham stumbled, fell onto Richard, and was partially carried to the nearest seat.

'I'm alright now,' Graham managed between his laboured breathing. 'Richard, take me to my apartments. Ah, Aubrey, show him the way.'

While Richard knelt beside the lieutenant, trying to soothe him in low tones, Sutton gestured to the two men waiting nearby and said: 'James, we'll do you one better – you can take the Dowager Apartments for now.'

'Dear Lord, I cannot – your late mother's spirit would haunt me to no end! It's just a small injury – see, I can walk. Aubrey, am I looking over the menu for you? Where's the dinner menu? Richard? Who are – you're not – Richard?'

Graham's words became indistinct as two men began assessing him.

Swallowing his growing fear, Sutton said, as calmly as he could: 'James, it's Aubrey. This is Mr Wright, a London physician who's very experienced with wounds like yours, and Mr Lewis, his assistant. You're at Bellevue, James. We're going to look after you.'

After inhaling Mr Wright's smelling salts, Graham straightened and blinked several times, his eyes clearing. 'Ah, Aubrey. Yes, of course, Aubrey. I'm just fatigued, but I'm alright. You needn't fret. I'm alright, Richard. You should get settled – it's been a long journey.'

At the physician's insistence that the room be vacated, Sutton and Richard left the library with no small degree of hesitation. To Sutton's knowledge, Graham had been treated by medics both on the field and during his journey back, but those sessions were superficial and brisk, aimed at saving a life without much thought for future recovery and prognosis. Now that Graham was here at Bellevue, Sutton would provide his friend with unparalleled medical care.

They had almost reached the double spiral staircase when Sutton said to Richard: 'Thank you for taking such good care of my friend. I understand you must be eager to return to Thornleigh Abbey, but you are most welcome to remain at or visit Bellevue as often as you wish.'

The younger man hesitated. 'The lieutenant rarely complained about his pain, but I helped dress his wounds during most of the journey. His injuries have worsened. I'm concerned his earlier collapse was not a sign of mere fatigue. I had intended to deliver Lieutenant Graham safely before setting out for Thornleigh, but... I do not wish to leave his side until he is well again.'

The younger man had formed the words with difficulty, but Sutton had no doubt about Richard's sincerity and devotion. The viscount did not fully understand what had passed between the soldiers in the Peninsula, but he admired Richard's determination.

'Very well. But your family must miss you dearly.' A thought occurred to Sutton. 'Perhaps you might wish to invite them here – they would be most welcome.'

Richard brightened a little. 'Yes – that's an excellent idea. Thank you, Lord Sutton – you really are most kind.'

A footman approached, bearing word from Mr Wright that Graham had settled into the Dowager Apartments without any further incident, and was presently devouring a large number of sandwiches while engaging Mr Lewis in an animated discussion.

Sutton relaxed while Richard smiled. 'Perhaps he *was* merely fatigued,' said the younger man. 'Or simply hungry. Well, I'll write to my family immediately. I've told them so much about the Lieutenant – to think they'll finally meet!'

Sutton nodded and watched as Richard was led upstairs. Only when he was out of sight did the viscount allow himself to smile at the thought of seeing Miss Ashcroft once more – and of introducing her to his oldest and dearest friend.

The joy of being reunited with Graham quickly subsided that evening when the lieutenant took another turn for the worse. Sutton and Richard remained in the library, respecting Graham's wishes not to be seen while in such a state. However, Sutton implored Mr Wright to be honest about Graham's condition. The physician obliged: the original wound was treated too hastily and had festered on the lieutenant's long journey back, perhaps beginning as soon as he boarded the ship back to England. A strong fever was raging in Graham's weakened body, and though the physician had applied the best poultice he had, only God knew his fate.

If Sutton found this news difficult to bear, Richard seemed doubly affected. The young man, whom Sutton had only seen lively and cheerful, became a shadow of his former self. He was pale and withdrawn, behaving as if a family member had been endangered, refusing to return to his rooms and insisting on remaining in the library.

Sutton himself retreated to his rooms, not for a lack of care, but because he knew he would require every ounce of his own strength if he were to assist his friend in any capacity – even if it included sending for the priest.

His sleep was shallow and broken that evening, and he rose well before dawn the next morning. Richard had not left the library, and greeted Sutton upon his arrival.

'Nothing has changed,' the younger man said, his shoulders slumped. 'The fever is persisting and he's barely conscious. Mr Wright's in the sickroom – he sent Mr Lewis to bring some supplies an hour ago.'

Sutton barely processed this. 'I want to see him.'

'Mr Wright barred me from entering.'

'I don't care – I *will* see him.'

Richard's relief at Sutton's authority only furthered the viscount's dismay. He opened the door to the adjoining chambers, the ensign not far behind him. Sutton strode in with certainty – and faltered at what he saw.

James Graham, Sutton's nearest and dearest friend, was rotting away. There was no other term for it. The lieutenant's face was sunken, his skin grey and stretched over his cheekbones. The bullet wound from his wrist had festered, spreading to his elbow, his flesh in the midst of decay. The fingers on that hand were blackened – there was no possibility of regaining their use. His other arm was pale except for the blood that dripped down into a metal pan. Sutton knew little about the humours, but no amount of bloodletting would save Graham's right arm – or perhaps even Graham himself.

Sutton choked out a sob, his throat clenching from the scent of death. Mr Wright, who was seated at a nearby desk, turned around at the sound. The physician looked no better than Sutton felt.

'Lord Sutton,' he said, struggling to stand up. 'You must not be here. The lieutenant needs to be alone.'

Sutton didn't try to mask his anger. 'He needs a physician to tend to him properly. He needs his friends. He needs…' Sutton heard Richard's quiet sobs, and found he could not continue.

The door opened and Mr Lewis entered with a large portmanteau. He nodded at Sutton and Richard before addressing the physician directly:

'Sir, I have brought the instruments.'

'Very good.' Mr Wright turned back to the desk and studied the book Sutton had not noticed earlier. Metallic clatters rang about the room as Mr Lewis laid out items on a table. Sutton glimpsed several knives and a long saw. His stomach clenched.

A long moment passed before the physician straightened and faced the viscount once more.

'Lord Sutton, I need two footmen – the strongest you have. No, three – I need more light, and linens, and brandy. I also need to work uninterrupted. I cannot do what I must if you are here, my lord.' Another long moment. 'Your priest. I need him to be ready. I need *you* to be ready, Lord Sutton.'

His anger disappeared as quickly as it had come. Sutton was thirteen again, afraid and uncertain at his father's deathbed.

'May I... May I say goodbye?'

The physician softened, nodding. Sutton approached the bed, barely aware of the activity around him. His only care was Graham: his friend, his confidante, his brother.

He was there. Graham was there – barely there. Sutton bent over Graham's body, pieces of his heart breaking away with every ragged breath and moan from the fading man. He brushed away the damp, limp locks from Graham's forehead.

'We'll need to do something about your hair after this is over,' he whispered. 'You can't be a dishevelled dog when you meet Lady Lavender – she might find you irresistibly charming.' Sutton tilted his head upwards, refusing to let the tears fall, refusing to let go. 'James... James. Not like this, James.'

Sutton rose, stumbling away from his friend, away from Richard and Wright and Lewis and the arriving footmen, away from the stench of death. He stumbled until he no longer knew where he was, could no longer fight against the anguish and grief and bile, until he collapsed on the cold hard floor, and was thoroughly sick.

39

If Ellie had thought Bellevue Park imposing and impressive in the autumn, she found it unspeakably beautiful in the spring. The trees were bright and fresh with new leaves, and the grey stones of the manor all but glittered underneath the sun. Ellie could only imagine what wonders the gardens held, and was keen on taking a few turns, a sketchpad in hand.

But it was the familiar figure who stood at the end of the carriageway, standing beside Lord Sutton, that made Ellie's heart leap with joy. She would suffer the tears and fears from the long, preceding months again and again, if she could be reunited with her brother thus. Like thousands of other women in Great Britain, Ellie cast aside decorum when the moment came, and, as soon as the carriage door opened, Ellie leapt out and into Richard's arms, laughing and crying as she held him.

'I've ruined your shirt again,' she said sheepishly when she finally lifted her head to look at her dear brother.

Her smile faded and she took a step back. A chill ran down her neck; the sun no longer felt so warm. 'Richard?'

It was Lord Sutton who answered, his voice hoarse.

'Do forgive the poor reception, Miss Ashcroft, Mr Ashcroft – our friend Lieutenant Graham… He is…' The viscount swallowed. 'He is not well.'

'I am sorry to hear it,' Marcus said at her side. 'We shan't impose on you at such a time – I'm certain we can find lodgings in Cambridge. Come now, Richard – we'll send for your belongings later.'

Ellie saw Lord Sutton's eyes darken, as if a tempest raged inside. There was so much she did not know about the viscount – yet, somehow, she felt she *understood* him.

'It is no imposition. Please, stay.'

It sounded like a plea – and Ellie's heart ached.

'My dear brother,' she said, barely recognising her own candour, 'we have had a terribly long journey. I'm certain Lord Sutton would not have invited us if he wished to be alone.'

'Yes, of course,' replied Marcus, a little surprised. 'Forgive my rashness.'

No more was said on the matter. They entered the manor as if in procession, their footsteps echoing through the large expanse of Bellevue House. Ellie's earlier courage faded away, leaving her unable to lift her eyes. The very air was heavy with grief.

She soon found herself in the Calliope Rooms once more, but Ellie paid little heed to the gentle sunlight streaming through the large windows and the vantage of the grand gardens. Even the bold painting in the drawing room, the Turner she had so admired, could not raise her spirits.

The hours until dinner were long, but the minutes at dinner were even longer. Their host was absent, leaving Marcus, Richard, and Ellie in a dining room much too large for its inhabitants. Richard, who had barely spoken a word since their reunion, ate no more than two spoons of soup, though he usually loved pease. When he made no inclination towards any of the other dishes, the Ashcroft patriarch gently said:

'Richard, tell us a little about the lieutenant.'

His brown eyes welled with tears. 'Lieutenant Graham is the best of us all. He is both kind and courageous, friendly and fierce. He was the first f-friend I made in the army, and the very best. He…he was injured while shielding Ensign Smith. He saved Smith's life.'

Marcus rose and moved his seat so it was beside Richard's, paying no heed to the heavy chair scraping against the floor or to the footmen's startled glances.

'He is fortunate to have your high opinion,' Marcus said, placing a hand on Richard's shoulder. 'We will pray for his recovery, Richard – and we will pray for the strength to face whatever may come.'

'Oh, Marcus! What if... What if...'

Ellie looked away, unable to witness her brother's despair. She had seen Richard scorned and shunned, but never had he seemed so helpless.

A movement from the doorway caught her eye – and then, without warning, Ellie was pulled into Lord Sutton's sorrow, sharp and strong against his soft curls. Her chest became too warm, too tight, her throat suddenly thick with rising tears.

'Lord Sutton,' she managed, her voice as broken as she felt. She saw a mask slip over the viscount as all eyes turned to him. 'How is the lieutenant?'

'There's been no improvement,' he said evenly, almost coolly. 'Mr Wright says tonight will be... He says we'll know in the morning.' Then, with only the slightest hesitation: 'The priest is here, should his services be required.'

Richard let loose a strangled sound, but before anyone could react, Lord Sutton continued: 'Mr Ashcroft, Miss Ashcroft, forgive me for not joining you at dinner. I hope the fare is satisfactory.'

'Yes, of course,' Marcus responded, bewildered by the viscount's cold courtesy. Then his jaw tightened, and Ellie saw her eldest brother's inner battle between sympathy and propriety. Marcus knew grief intimately, but he was also diffident about expressing his innermost feelings – a trait he shared with Lord Sutton, Ellie realised.

An idea blossomed. Strengthened by her newfound knowledge, Ellie fought her fears and followed her instincts.

'Dinner has been delightful, Lord Sutton,' she said, determined to hide her uncertainty, 'but might I trouble you to show me to some paints? I'd forgotten to bring my own.'

Ellie held her head high, avoiding her brothers' gaze in wake of her vulgar request and outright lie. Of the few times she did travel, Ellie was *never* without her paints – a fact known to both Marcus and Richard.

Lord Sutton's surprise was evident as he replied: 'Certainly, Miss Ashcroft – do forgive me for being neglectful. I'll see to it you are shown to the studio when you are finished with your meal.'

Her resolve was fading, as was the warmth in the viscount's eyes. If Ellie were to act, it must be now – regardless of consequences. She wondered if her sister-in-law had faced the same struggle when, over a year ago, Kitty abandoned decorum to confront Marcus, and refused to uncover Richard's whereabouts. Later, Kitty had admitted to following her instincts, and Ellie had listened in awe, unable to imagine doing the same herself.

But now, Lord Sutton was hurting, his closest friend slipping away from this world, leaving the viscount to contend with his grief alone.

It would not do.

Ellie set down her napkin. 'I am finished. Lord Sutton, I would be much obliged if you could show me to the studio presently.' Remembering Kitty's strength, Ellie turned to her brothers. 'Richard, Marcus, would you like to join us?'

Her eldest brother considered Ellie for a long moment, sending Ellie's heart pounding so strongly she was certain the entire house would hear it. Finally, Marcus said: 'I trust Lord Sutton knows infinitely more about paints than I do. We shall see you in the drawing room later.'

Ellie rose from her seat and closed the distance to the viscount before anyone could retract their offer – or their permission. 'Thank you, Lord Sutton. I have been wishing to explore your collection of paints at greater length for quite some time.'

'My pleasure,' said the viscount, though there was none in his voice.

They walked on in silence, but Ellie forbade herself from regretting her actions. She could not allow Lord Sutton to be alone at such a difficult time – she simply *would not.*

Instinct led her; compassion – and something more – drove her.

When they reached the viscount's studio, the scent of oils thick in the room, Ellie was relieved to see a number of blank canvases propped against one side of the room. She set up an easel, chose the largest canvas, and turned to the viscount.

'I would be obliged if you could mount this, Lord Sutton.'

Not waiting for the viscount's response, Ellie set about the paints themselves. She stamped down her excitement at the sheer variety – she would explore them later, if she were ever permitted to enter Bellevue again – selected the boldest colours and the largest brushes, and arranged them on a table beside the newly erected easel.

The heady scent of paints was starting to overwhelm her, but Ellie was prepared. She withdrew two of several handkerchiefs she always carried in spring, tied one over her nose, and gave the other to Lord Sutton. His expression remained unreadable.

All was ready. All that remained was for Ellie to pick up a brush, and make the first mark.

She did so with trepidation: a small upward stroke in coquelicot. She held back a shudder at having marred a perfectly good canvas so unthinkingly, and gave Lord Sutton a brush dipped in Pomona green.

The viscount stared at the brush in one hand, her handkerchief in the other, and, finally, at Ellie herself.

'Miss Ashcroft…' He trailed off, the first slip in his careful demeanour. 'I…'

Ellie met his gaze, her eyes warm. 'I find a certain liberty at painting without thought. Would you care to try it with me?'

For several unbearable heartbeats, Ellie thought the viscount would refuse and send her family back to Thornleigh. But then, with as much uncertainty as Ellie herself felt, Lord Sutton made a downward green stroke within a few inches of her red.

Wordlessly, Ellie drew a circle the size of an apple. The viscount hesitated, then followed with a larger circle beside hers. She dipped her brush in more paint, and, in one certain stroke, drew a vertical line from the top to the base of the canvas.

Something shifted in Lord Sutton. He responded with a horizontal line, then another, then another, until the top third of the canvas was covered with green. At this, Ellie changed her brush and dipped it in primrose, adding a diagonal stroke in bright yellow. The viscount followed suit, but did not pause for another brush; soon, lines of yellow streaked with green were added to the canvas. They continued, covering the canvas with mismatched colours and shapes, adding layers upon chaotic layers of paint without rhyme or reason, until Ellie's strokes became indistinguishable from the viscount's. Only then did Ellie dare to glance at Lord Sutton – and only then did she release the hold on her own tears.

Gone was the viscount; only the man remained. His strong jaw, which she had admired from the secret corners of her heart, was now trembling, twisting his lips into agonised lines. His eyes, darkened from the torments of the last few days, now shone with untold passions. And his hand, his sleek, striking hand that held his brush with the confidence of one who used it often, was now white from gripping the handle so fiercely she was afraid something might break.

Then, as swiftly as he had started, Lord Sutton stopped, dropping his brush to the floor with a defeated echo. He stumbled towards a chair and sat, his back slumped, his shoulders shaking. Now, he seemed so small, so vulnerable, so certain of his own loneliness.

Ever so gently, Ellie laid down her brush and removed the handkerchief from across her nose, wiping the wet paint off her fingers and ruining the delicate silk. Then, for the second time that evening, Ellie closed the distance between them.

And ever so gently, Ellie laid a hand on his shoulder.

His sobs stilled for a moment. Then, they continued with renewed vigour, until his cries echoed in the expanse of the room.

40

AUBREY CHARLES BEAUMONT, the 7th Viscount Sutton, gave in to the comforting touch, and wept. He wept for James, who might never rise to see another day; he wept for Hammond and Fielding, who would never know what their sacrifices had achieved; he wept for himself, who had never wept thus before, who had never *allowed* himself to weep thus. He had a reputation to uphold – a reputation he'd spent a lifetime creating and finessing – a reputation of being the superior man in every situation, who scoffed at the sentimental and the foolish, which he considered one and the same.

Yet Sutton wept – and he relished it. He found it difficult to breathe and his entire body shook with every wave of tears, yet he was finally free. In this private sanctum, under Miss Ashcroft's steady hand, Sutton allowed himself to grieve for all that he'd lost.

Slowly, his tears began to subside. He fumbled for a handkerchief, and gratefully accepted one Miss Ashcroft offered, not quite ready to meet the young woman's gaze. Instead, Sutton took his time wiping his face and blowing his nose. When his nose cleared enough that he could almost smell the turpentine again, Sutton took several deep breaths. Only then did Miss Ashcroft remove her hand from his shoulder.

He missed her warm touch immediately.

Sutton looked up at the young lady, noting the redness around her eyes and nose. In their proximity, Sutton could see every last freckle sprinkled across her cheeks.

Suddenly speechless, Sutton swallowed, his body tensing once more. But Miss Ashcroft, who had seen and accepted him at his most vulnerable, needed no words.

She smiled at him, softly and sweetly, and waited until he was ready to rise. Then they walked back to the drawing room, accompanied by the new understanding that blossomed between them.

For years to come, Sutton would not remember his stilted conversation with the Ashcrofts in the drawing room, or the long, sleepless night that followed. All that remained with him were the memory of Miss Ashcroft's small, dear hand, then Mr Wright's haggard smile as he left the sickroom, then Richard's relieved cries, then, finally, the realisation that a new day had come, and James Graham still lived.

It was another two days before Sutton was permitted to enter the sickroom. Graham tried to rise when he saw the viscount, but the effort was too much – Sutton rushed in to assist, propping up his friend with half a dozen pillows.

The viscount sat at the bedside chair and looked for the right words. His search was in vain, for Graham spoke first, his voice coarse.

'Don't look so glum, my dear Aubrey – it won't do you any favours with the ladies.'

Sutton struggled to keep his voice even. 'Barely recovered, and already talking about the ladies.'

'I could talk about the gentlemen as well, though I doubt you'd be as interested.' Graham paused and studied Sutton carefully. 'I can see how your gloomy disposition might be appealing to some. I stand corrected.'

The viscount laughed despite himself. 'Welcome back to the living, my friend.'

'Oh? I didn't think I'd ever left.' Graham suddenly tensed, undercutting his own words. He closed his eyes and took a while to regain himself. 'The pain... It hits without warning. Could you...' The lieutenant paused, uncertainty crossing his already harrowed face. 'Could you be so kind as to ring for some tea?'

Sutton jumped up and was pulling the cord before Graham finished his request. 'Of course. And don't be so bloody polite – there's no shame in asking for anything. I am at your bidding.'

'Ah, Aubrey... I have waited many years to hear those words. I accept you in my service.'

The viscount smiled again, shaking his head at his friend's antics. He relayed quick instructions and asked for some sandwiches and cakes along with the tea.

'Excellent idea!' Graham said. 'I'm actually quite peckish.'

'I see your appetite is returning. I'd thought you'd be morose after...what happened. I can hardly believe your high spirits.'

'What's not to believe?' asked Graham, his voice softening. 'I have my life, my friends, my dignity. I am a truly blessed man.'

'But your arm...'

The lieutenant shifted to a more comfortable position, then used his left hand to fumble with the sleeve and reveal what remained of his right arm. Mr Wright had removed the forearm and a little of the upper arm, which had been carefully bandaged. Sutton had arranged the measuring and making of a prosthetic, but it would be several weeks before Graham healed enough for its use.

'It's not so bad,' Graham said, looking at the bandaged stump. 'It's a little irksome when I forget and reach for something, but I'll get used to it soon enough.'

'"Irksome"?' Sutton shook his head. 'What a thing to say.'

'I won't be joining another campaign, so the arm is no great loss.'

Sutton's fears from the past week began to rise, but he masked it with irritation. 'What of…everyday activities?'

'There's nothing I can't learn to do with my left hand.'

'The piano. You won't be able to play again.'

'There are certain duets,' replied Graham. 'And I was never any good – I'd much rather sing while you or Richard play.'

'And what of writing? How would you pen your letters?'

'I could learn with my left hand. Besides, my penmanship was always shocking – *you've* criticised it quite passionately. And Richard was an excellent scribe – perhaps I could ensnare him into my service as well.'

Sutton shook his head once more, unable to comprehend his friend's easy acceptance. 'You've lost so much.'

'I've lost nothing important.' Graham sighed when Sutton looked on in disbelief. 'Aubrey, this is *my* burden to bear – and I'm making my peace with it. Am I in pain? Yes. Am I suffering? More than you can imagine. But am I going to allow this' – he jerked his right shoulder to move what remained of his arm – 'to destroy what's left of my life? I bloody well am *not.*'

His frustrations melted away, leaving Sutton quite ashamed. 'Oh James, I've been making this more difficult for you.'

'You have,' replied Graham, his voice gentle. 'But it's only because you care. And that, my friend, *is* one of your charms. Besides, what I mourn most is my luxurious hair – it was removed during field surgery and entirely without my consent!'

'Thank heavens for small mercies,' Sutton said wryly. 'Now I can finally look at you, free of that outdated hairstyle, and say: James Graham, welcome to the eighteen hundreds.'

Graham looked too mournful to be taken seriously. 'I liked the last century better. Well, never you mind – I'll just grow it out again.'

Sutton hid a smile. Their refreshments arrived, and he helped his friend with the tea and cakes.

'Now, Aubrey, we are suitably equipped to discuss a merrier subject. I hear

Richard and I are not the only visitors at Bellevue. When are you introducing me to Miss Ashcroft?'

Sutton hesitated. 'You're still convalescing. We both know how excitable you can get.'

'Nonsense!' Graham paused when he realised his response *was* rather zealous. 'Well then, I shall await Mr Wright's permission to leave the room – and I've trusted Richard to bring me all news of the outside world, so I'll *know* if you try to intimidate my physician into ordering more bed rest.'

Content with his friend's acquiescence, Sutton feigned innocence, a skill he learnt from Graham but had yet to master. 'I'm *never* intimidating. I simply make suggestions.'

⁕⁂⁑

Sutton stood as the Ashcrofts were announced into the library and clasped his hands behind his back to prevent any fidgeting. 'Miss Ashcroft, Mr Ashcroft,' the viscount said, 'I am delighted to introduce my dear friend, Lieutenant James Graham.'

The lieutenant nodded. 'Miss Ashcroft, Mr Ashcroft,' he said lightly, 'it is an unspeakable pleasure to meet you both. Forgive me for not rising – I am a little indisposed.'

'The pleasure is all ours,' said Mr Ashcroft. 'We are indebted to you for welcoming Richard when he first joined the army, and for the sacrifices you have made for our country.'

'Thank you, Mr Ashcroft. Please, do take a seat, Miss Ashcroft. Tea is on its way.'

Miss Ashcroft smiled and complied. As Sutton sat down, he noticed the lady's hands were clenched. He had a vague recollection of Miss Ashcroft's discomfit during her exhibition the previous year, and wondered how he could have ever thought her spoilt and conceited.

Before Sutton could intervene, Graham, who had the rare talent of making anyone feel at ease, spoke:

'Now, shall we ring for some cakes or pastries as well? I heard you have quite a sweet tooth, Miss Ashcroft – something we have in common.'

'Yes please, if it's not too much trouble.'

'Not at all,' the lieutenant replied a little mischievously. 'At least, *you* are not the one causing trouble – if anything, it seems a certain viscount has forgotten his manners around *his* guests.'

Sutton's lips twitched as he kept a straight face. 'Far from forgetting my manners,' said he, 'I'm remembering with great fondness how much you enjoy playing host. It would be most inconsiderate of me to deprive you of such pleasures, my friend.'

'Then I thank you most fervently for granting me such pleasures, sir.'

Graham winked at Miss Ashcroft before he made his requests, and Sutton saw the lady relax in her seat.

'Now, Miss Ashcroft,' Graham said, 'both Richard and Sutton have spoken highly of your artistic work. Might I one day be privy to your talent?'

The young lady blushed at the praise. 'I've actually brought a few small works, including a watercolour I wish to deliver to the Dean of Ely Cathedral, if we might venture there again.' She glanced up at Sutton, who nodded. 'But given your long acquaintance with Lord Sutton, I assume you've seen far better works than I could ever hope to produce.'

Graham waved a hand in dismissal. 'Sutton here has accused me of being a philistine on more than one occasion, and perhaps rightly so – many works by the "Masters" elude me. I'm much more interested in the depictions of people and places I know.'

'Forgive my friend,' the viscount interjected. 'He cares not about certain histories.'

'With the exception of military history,' replied the lieutenant. 'Hastings, Agincourt, Bosworth – paintings of *those* I would like to see! Otherwise, I'm guilty as charged. I'd much rather marvel over Miss Ashcroft's watercolour of Ely Cathedral than some Dutchman's portrayal of fruit.'

Miss Ashcroft tried to hide her smile, but Sutton caught it nonetheless. 'In that case, I have no choice but to oblige.'

Mr Ashcroft took this opportunity to enquire further on the lieutenant's health. 'I hope you're recovering well from your injuries.'

'Thank you. My apologies for sending the house into a frenzy when you had just arrived.'

Graham had said this lightly, but Sutton saw Richard stiffen. 'The lieutenant makes light of the "frenzy".'

'Well, I know Sutton has come to expect a semblance of excitement whenever I'm around, and I didn't wish to disappoint. Ah, but here are the tea and cakes. What perfect timing!'

Sutton helped his friend while refreshments were served. Graham's smile slipped a little, revealing the gaunt lines of his face. When Graham finally managed to fumble with his pastry unaided, his right sleeve shifted several times through air.

Miss Ashcroft set down her teacup just loudly enough for Sutton to notice. She had been apprised of Graham's general condition, but Sutton understood that seeing it was another matter entirely.

With just a trace of hesitation, she asked: 'Lieutenant Graham, are you quite comfortable? Are you sure we're not disturbing your rest?'

'Please, Miss Ashcroft, you are too kind,' was Graham's reply. 'I will excuse myself soon, but not before I've consumed my fair share of meringues. They are simply delectable! Ah, but it's been a while since I've seen those tartlets – Sutton only bothers with them for special occasions!'

Sutton leaned back into this chair as Graham and Miss Ashcroft set to enjoy the delicacies. The small group praised the pastries, then turned to recollections of other fine foods they had sampled. When Graham excused himself not ten minutes later, Sutton saw to his satisfaction that Miss Ashcroft's hands were gently resting on her lap.

41

After dinner, which Lieutenant Graham was unable to attend, Richard and Ellie separated from Marcus and Lord Sutton and went to the drawing room. There was much to be shared between the siblings after their tumultuous time apart, and the rest of the party was happy to give them some privacy before joining them later in the evening.

As soon as they were seated, Richard pulled out two envelopes from his pocket.

'I wrote these before I left England,' he said. 'I didn't know if I would ever see you again. When Lord Sutton bade us farewell in Colchester, I entrusted these to his care, asking him to deliver them if I did not return.'

'But you have returned.'

'I have.' Richard's expression became wistful. 'I have seen things – many things that will remain with me for as long as I live. Before I left England, I had thought it nobler to keep some matters to myself. I wrote these letters because you and Marcus would have only read them had I not survived. I now know I was being cowardly.'

Ellie knew not what he meant, but she disagreed with his assessment. 'You are anything but cowardly, my dear brother.'

'And you are my most devoted supporter, dear sister.' He ran his thumb along the edge of a sealed letter. 'What I wish to tell you now is simple: you deserve every happiness in the world.'

Ellie opened her mouth to protest, but Richard held up his hand.

'When I thought I might not return, I wrote to you my encouragement and blessings for your happiness. I asked you to accept the affection and hand of Lord Sutton – or any other man you deem worthy – regardless of what happened to me. I do not wish to prevent you from your happiness.'

'Nor do I wish to prevent you from yours,' Ellie replied, blushing at the mention of the viscount. 'But I don't understand – why this, why now?'

Richard gave her a small smile. 'Dearest Ellie, I've seen how Lord Sutton looks at you. But beyond that, I think it's important for you to know: I've realised I do not wish to marry. I know Marcus has worked so hard to ensure I could inherit Thornleigh if the need arose, but he has found Kitty. The Ashcrofts will have heirs aplenty. There will no longer be a need for me to marry – so I will not marry.'

'I don't understand,' Ellie repeated.

'Perhaps one day you will – and when you do, I hope you will forgive me my selfishness.'

Ellie's fierceness returned at this. 'You may have reasons I don't understand, but having them does *not* make you selfish.' She let Richard's words sink in. 'You don't wish to marry?'

'I don't.' Having made his intentions known, Richard now drew out Ellie's mother's ring. 'I have kept this as a talisman these past few months, but it's time I returned it.'

Ellie looked at the ring, the emeralds and diamonds glowing in the low light. Her late father had commissioned it during the first years of their marriage, and her mother had intended it for her second child. The late Mrs Ashcroft may not have approved of what Ellie now wished to do, but the young woman was ready to make her own decision.

'Keep it,' she said. 'If it has protected you in the Peninsula, then I hope it will continue to protect you in the future.'

Richard did not hide his surprise. 'I cannot – it is not mine by right.'

'It is *mine*,' Ellie said firmly, 'and I wish for *you* to have it.' She unclasped her neck chain and removed Richard's ring. 'This is yours, too.'

'Heavens, I can't possibly have *both* rings!'

Ellie placed her father's ring in Richard's palm. 'You can, and you *shall*. The two were made as a set, after all.'

'Ellie…'

She remained undeterred. 'I insist. Besides, I would feel much better if you had them in your possession.'

Richard shook his head with a smile. 'You *have* grown. Very well. I will take them both. But now they're *mine*, it's my prerogative how I choose to gift them in the future – the recipient may very well be *your* children.'

Ellie blushed again, not knowing how to respond. Then another thought occurred to her. 'You said you'd written another letter to Marcus.'

'Yes. I will speak with him about it another time.'

She nodded, respecting Richard's privacy. She watched as her brother put away his letters and rings before withdrawing a small book.

'On the same evening I gave those letters to Lord Sutton, he gave me this notebook to fill with sketches for you from beyond the Channel. Some of these are very rough, but you might be able to make use of them.'

Ellie opened the pages, marvelling at the landscapes and buildings he had managed to capture. It was as if her brother knew precisely which vantages she needed to complete her paintings. As she carefully turned the pages, Ellie saw several other potential works she might pursue.

'Oh, Richard… These are simply wonderful. Thank you.' She wrapped her arms around him again. 'It's wonderful to have you back.'

Since Ellie had foreknowledge of a private conversation between her brothers, she was a little nervous when they excused themselves briefly the next afternoon, and – a little uncharacteristically of Marcus – left her in the company of Lord Sutton and Lieutenant Graham in the library. While the viscount became restless after Ellie was left without a chaperone, the lieutenant seemed none the wiser, and continued his enquiries about her childhood in Thornleigh. He had passed the Abbey several times during his time at Darlington, but had never called on its inhabitants. When Ellie had nothing more to say about her upbringing, Lieutenant Graham offered his own tales about growing up in a small house just outside Bellevue's borders. Within half an hour, he had painted such an odd image of Lord Sutton as a boy that Ellie couldn't help but laugh – much to the viscount's grumbling.

When her brothers returned to the library, she knew for certain something irreversible had passed between them. Marcus wore a tight expression that did not bode well, but the slight nod he gave Ellie was an indication that whatever had transpired, and however much Marcus had disapproved, all would be well given enough time. Ellie wished her sister-in-law was here to soften Marcus's displeasure, and suspected her brother felt the same.

A few days later when they were being shown the gardens, Ellie saw Marcus place a hand on Richard's back – and knew they had resolved whatever had come between them.

She looked away to hide her smile, and caught Lord Sutton's own smile instead. Her heart soared with unadulterated joy. Under the spring sky, surrounded by her loved ones, Ellie was free and happy.

It took almost three weeks after Ellie's arrival for Lieutenant Graham to receive permission from the physician to move back to his usual quarters upstairs, and to engage in some light walking. When they re-entered Bellevue House after a light afternoon stroll, Ellie stood in awe, once again, at the expansive space that had become so warm and inviting. In the autumn, she'd noticed the glass windows at the top of the double spiral staircase and was glad for the light it provided. Now, the sun cast its rays down and amongst the stairs, bathing the entirety of the double spirals until the structure glowed like the heart of the house. She paused to take in the sight, and found her fingers itching for a pencil so she could try to capture the intricate displays of light.

She thought her behaviour had gone unnoticed, but as Lord Sutton led them on, the viscount said, 'I've tried to paint the staircase on a number of occasions, albeit with unsatisfactory results. Miss Ashcroft, you're welcome to try if you wish – I'm sure you will have much more success.'

That evening, Lord Sutton poured the men a celebratory brandy in the drawing room, and a sweet sherry for Ellie.

'To our lieutenant's continued recovery,' he toasted.

Lieutenant Graham had a generous sip before setting down his glass. 'Now, Lord Sutton, it's time we discuss the most important matter: you no longer have an excuse to delay your annual spring ball!'

Ellie saw the viscount struggle to hide his concern. 'You've only just moved back to your quarters – let's give it a few more weeks before hosting a ball.'

'Ah, but *I* won't be doing any hosting,' replied Lieutenant Graham. 'I will simply be one of your merry guests. I've had about thirty letters on the subject, and then there's your usual hundred or so friends – we're all impatient about our invitations!'

Lord Sutton seemed ready to voice an objection when Richard said: 'Forgive my ignorance, but how long does it take to prepare a ball of this magnitude?'

'Three weeks should do it,' Lord Sutton said reluctantly. 'Mrs Jennings, my veritable housekeeper, has assumed the daunting task since my mother's passing. No doubt there is a great deal to oversee, but she has perfected the process over the last decade – even when accounting for the guests who wish to arrive a week or two before the ball and stay for much longer afterwards.'

'How many guests typically sojourn at Bellevue?' asked Richard, fascinated by the notion.

'At least twenty to thirty – it depends on the year.'

Richard's surprise was evident. 'My goodness! How many rooms do you have in total?' Looking a little sheepish, he added: 'If you don't mind my asking, of course – I didn't mean to pry.'

'I don't mind at all,' replied Sutton, a hint of pride in his manner. 'There are over seventy apartments in Bellevue, spread over five floors. About fifty are suitable for guests.'

'Not to mention the State Rooms,' added Lieutenant Graham, who seemed as knowledgeable about Bellevue as the viscount, 'and Lord Sutton's own chambers. Oh, and the Lavender Rooms – one mustn't forget those! Shall we go on a tour later?'

Richard and Marcus assented, and Ellie's own excitement grew.

'It's settled then,' the lieutenant said, his eyes twinkling. 'A tour in the morrow, and the spring ball in three weeks.'

'Very well,' Lord Sutton replied. 'Mr Ashcroft, could I persuade you and your family to remain in Bellevue until the ball?'

Under other circumstances, Ellie would entreat her eldest brother to reply in the affirmative, but the thought of Kitty quick with child kept Ellie silent. She was relieved when Richard spoke up.

'Brother, I would be delighted to remain here with our sister until after the ball. You could return to Thornleigh and Kitty at any time you choose, and Ellie and I will bring back the stories and descriptions for her if she wishes to hear them.'

'Which she undoubtedly will,' Marcus said with a smile. 'I think she'll be quite disappointed to miss out on this occasion.'

'Bellevue's spring ball is an annual occurrence,' Lord Sutton said, gracious as ever, 'and Mrs Ashcroft is welcome to attend next year if she wishes.'

'Thank you – I think she'd like that very much indeed.'

This easy acceptance between the two men set Ellie's heart at ease. Regardless of what might transpire between Lord Sutton and herself, her family had established a friendship with the viscount. She was even more pleased when Marcus announced his decision.

'In that case, I'll entrust my siblings to you, Lord Sutton, and return to Thornleigh in the next few days. I hope they won't be an imposition.'

'They're quite the opposite, Mr Ashcroft.' The viscount smiled, mirroring Ellie's own feelings as he relaxed in his seat. It was soon decided that the Ashcrofts would receive a tour of Bellevue Park the next day, visit Ely

Cathedral the following day, and bid Marcus farewell on the third.

When Lieutenant Graham led the Ashcrofts on a tour of the house, Ellie was initially puzzled that Lord Sutton remained silent among the guests. Upon seeing how much the lieutenant relished playing the part, however, Ellie understood why Lord Sutton relinquished his role. Although he moved at a sensible pace, the lieutenant's voice was full of energy as he took them first to the vast State Rooms on the ground floor.

'These were built by the 1st Viscount Sutton, who had gained favour with King William the Third. I believe it was last refurbished by the 4th Viscount Sutton.'

'The 3rd,' Lord Sutton corrected, a little drily. 'Behold the extravagance of my ancestors.'

'Extravagant' was indeed apt. All the State Rooms contained high fresco ceilings recounting Grecian myths and characters, the colours rich and vivid. The State Bedchamber contained a four-poster bed gilded with gold, while the neatly arranged cutlery in the State Dining Room sparkled with opulence. Their footsteps and voices echoed amongst the marble and stone.

Yet, despite the care and craftsmanship that had gone into these State Rooms, Ellie could not help but feel uncomfortable in these grand rooms. They were *too* extravagant, and, to her humble opinion, a touch distasteful. There seemed only one common thread throughout the décor: that of excessive wealth. She understood the need for such rooms, but she was disappointed at the lack of elegance and subtlety.

'The bed alone cost over two thousand pounds back in the early 1700s,' Lieutenant Graham was saying, much to Richard's awe. 'The 3rd Viscount Sutton certainly aimed to please.'

'Have these rooms even been used?' asked Marcus, who was as practical as he was impressed.

The lieutenant chuckled. 'Very good question, Mr Ashcroft. I don't believe so – though rumour has it Queen Anne almost made it to Bellevue. Come to think of it, when we were younger and Lord Sutton simply the Earl of Beaumont, we had decided to use the State Rooms ourselves once he'd become a viscount. Whatever happened to that?'

'Oh?' replied Lord Sutton. 'I don't recall such a conversation.'

'I'm pretty sure it was the winter when you were nine, and we were bored of being snowed in.'

The viscount shrugged, though Ellie could see the humour in his eyes. 'Well, I guess we don't have it in writing.'

'Whatever happened to the gentleman's handshake?' the lieutenant muttered.

'We certainly did *not* shake on it,' replied Lord Sutton calmly. 'You'd burnt your hand in the kitchen earlier that day.'

Lieutenant Graham shook his head. 'I have been foiled once more. I shall be more successful next time.'

Ellie left the State Rooms with much higher spirits. Their next destination was on the first floor, and required taking the beautiful double spiral staircase. The lieutenant seemed a little out of breath after his climb, but he recovered after a moment's pause.

'Right,' he said cheerfully, 'let's take a look at Lord Sutton's rooms.'

Ellie walked through the private suite, smiling in appreciation at the décor. The carpets were plush, the wallpaper delightful, the curtains strong yet complementary. Although the colour palettes of each room differed, Ellie noticed the use of a vibrant indigo throughout.

'These are lovely,' Richard said, voicing Ellie's sentiments. 'Lord Sutton, I much prefer your rooms to the State ones!'

The viscount graciously accepted the compliment, while the lieutenant remarked: 'He redesigned them himself a while back, with some assistance from yours truly. I shudder to think of the old wallpaper – a ghastly puce that resembled squashed fleas in every part.'

'It was a popular shade during my great-grandfather's time,' Lord Sutton explained. 'Our family coat of arms contains purple and gold, and puce was once a fashionable choice. No doubt *my* refurbishments will seem outdated to future generations.'

'The aesthetics are very pleasing,' said Marcus, who had overseen several refurbishments in Thornleigh. 'When did you carry out these changes?'

'About a decade ago. My mother had just passed, and I had been Viscount Sutton for a full three years. It seemed like the right time for a fresh start.'

They followed Lieutenant Graham, who gradually led them to the opposite end of the house, near the Calliope where Ellie stayed. 'Lord Sutton also redid these: the Lavender Rooms.'

Unlike the bold colours of the viscount's rooms, the Lavender Rooms were soft and gentle, the furnishings elegant and refined. Yet, amongst the subdued décor, Ellie recognised a vivacious touch in the sitting room: the chaises were upholstered in a deep wine, the lampshades were a bright daffodil, and several cushions were embroidered with gold. Various paintings covered the walls, but the space above the fireplace was empty, waiting to be filled.

She was drawn to these rooms, and wished to convey her appreciation. 'This is a delightful apartment,' she said. 'I daresay I favour it above all the others in Bellevue Park.' Her words sounded childish to her own ears, but Lord Sutton's smile soothed her nerves.

'It is,' agreed Lieutenant Graham. His voice had softened, and there was a peculiar look in his eyes. 'Lord Sutton and I have talked about these rooms since we were children – they are for Lady Lavender.'

'Lady Lavender?' echoed Richard.

For the first time since starting the tour, the lieutenant hesitated before responding. He looked at Lord Sutton, who gave a small nod.

'When we were children,' Lieutenant Graham said, his words slow and considered, 'we would speculate and jest about our future. Even at a tender age, Lord Sutton took quite a fancy to some of the ladies. Since "Lady Sutton" was his mother and since he was fond of lavenders, we decided to name his future wife "Lady Lavender". The Lavender Rooms are intended for the mistress of Bellevue Park, and they have been uninhabited these last ten years.'

The weight of this revelation made Ellie uneasy; the lieutenant's avoidance of her gaze during his explanation exacerbated her discomfort. As the ensuing silence stretched, Ellie felt too much unwanted attention on herself. She had declared her appreciation for the rooms before she understood their meaning; her well-intended statement could not have been more ill-advised, or more embarrassing.

She was grateful when Richard broke the tension after what felt like an eternity. 'Thank you for the tour,' he said, his voice a little too cheery. 'I'm suddenly quite famished – shall we go for some tea?'

There was a general murmur of assent, and the party left the Lavender Rooms for the parlour. For the rest of the afternoon and evening, Ellie could barely look at Lord Sutton, too afraid of being seen, and of what she might see.

42

SUTTON WAS UNEASY about Miss Ashcroft's reticence after the incident in the Lavender Rooms, but he was unable to address the issue. That evening, he attempted a conversation about her artwork, but her embarrassment was still too fresh. He was in no position to offer the young lady any comfort, and he was anxious about their planned excursion to Ely Cathedral. The most he could do as he lay awake in his chambers was hope that some fresh air would lift the lady's spirits the following day.

As Graham was still recovering, and as Sutton still remembered Miss Ashcroft's fainting spell on their last visit, the small party took an open carriage through the countryside. Much to Sutton's relief, Miss Ashcroft began to relax as they left the confines of Bellevue Park. Within the first quarter of their forty-minute journey, surrounded by the pleasant landscape, the young lady seemed to revert to her previous self.

The conversation naturally inclined towards the lands and farms within Bellevue's estate, which both Sutton and Graham took turns in pointing out as they passed each area of note. When they rode past a small cottage, Graham found great joy in relaying a story of their shared childhood.

'And here is where Lord Sutton and I – at a time when we were simply Aubrey and James – engaged in our first armed combat.'

Richard perked up with interest and said to his siblings, 'The lieutenant with a weapon is quite a sight to behold.'

'Indeed – and I, at the tender age of seven, was fearless with my trusty pointed stick.'

Sutton was caught between amusement and sorrow – Graham would never hold a sword again.

'If I recall correctly,' Graham continued, oblivious to Sutton's mood, 'our Lord Sutton here was equally fearless – though his stick was much longer than mine.'

'I'd say they were of roughly equal lengths.'

His friend smiled. 'Nonetheless, I emerged quite victorious.'

'And I have suffered every day since,' replied Sutton solemnly.

'However so?' asked Richard.

Sutton turned to the ensign and placed his fingers upon the brow that bore his injury. 'Alas, Lieutenant Graham has scarred me for life.'

He also shared this with Mr Ashcroft and Miss Ashcroft, the latter who showed no surprise at seeing the small scar, but looked only as if one of her questions had just been answered.

Richard, however, was much more vocal. 'Goodness me, the lieutenant must have done quite a bit of damage for it to leave such a mark! And how dangerously close to your eye!'

'Don't encourage him,' commented Graham. 'The good viscount takes great care in reminding me of his brush with blindness at every opportunity.'

'And rightly so,' Sutton said. 'To think of all the beautiful art that could have been taken away from me!'

'What instigated the incident?' asked Mr Ashcroft. The words made Graham chuckle, while Sutton felt his cheeks warm – and not due to the sun overhead.

'We were practising our dance steps with some of the young ladies in the village,' he said. 'By a stroke of ill fate, both the lieutenant and I had lost our hearts to the same lady, and hoped she would become our sole dancing partner in our practice sessions. Needless to say, we decided to settle the matter as gentlemen, and the near deadly duel ensued.'

'Although I had technically won the duel,' Graham added, 'the girl was so distraught by my actions that she never spoke to me afterwards. Lord Sutton was appalled by her behaviour – after all, we both knew *I* had won the right to her hand – and, while pressing his handkerchief to his injured brow, declared in his most lordly tone that she was ignoble. And thus began our everlasting friendship.'

Sutton dared a glance at Miss Ashcroft, whose amusement was tinged with nerves. She seemed to have an opinion or a question about the matter but lacked the courage to speak up.

It was Mr Ashcroft who commented: 'I find it hard to imagine you would duel over the affections of a girl.'

'It was the only time,' replied Sutton, turning his attention to Mr Ashcroft while still remaining aware of his sister. 'That day, I learnt that no friendship is worth losing over a lady – and no lady worth loving would wish to come between our friendship.'

These thoughtful words lingered amongst them for a moment before Sutton shook off his peculiar state with a quip.

'Besides, my dabbling in duels ended up destroying my favourite waistcoat at the time. Few things are more precious than a well-fitting and pleasing waistcoat.'

Miss Ashcroft's smile, when it eventually spread across her face like the rising dawn, was one of those few things.

To Sutton's enormous relief, they all returned to Bellevue that evening without incident. Indeed, the two people about which he was most concerned could not be in better spirits: Graham, from his first leisurely excursion since losing his arm, and Miss Ashcroft, from the warm welcome and praise she'd received at the Cathedral.

Yet, despite their successful outing, Sutton was agitated. He had excused himself to finalise invitations in the two hours before dinner, but now that he was in his study, he cared little for tending to the ball. If not for Graham's insistence, Sutton would have broken the annual tradition altogether.

During these troubled times, Sutton only did what was natural: he sought the company of his friend.

To his surprise, Sutton found Graham was not alone. There, in Sutton's usual place before the fire, was Richard, a chessboard between the two men, their laughter warming the room.

He had turned and was leaving when Graham called out: 'Aubrey! You've signed all those invitations already?' When Sutton made no reply, Graham said: 'Richard, I'm a bit peckish – could you investigate what the pastry chef's been up to and bring back a plate? You know what I like.'

The younger Ashcroft complied, but his smile at Sutton seemed a little anxious.

'Now, Aubrey,' Graham said once they were alone, 'do come in and take a seat. I'm not inclined to get up, and I'll crane my neck if you keep standing like that.'

Sutton obliged, concern warring with curiosity. A glance at the chessboard revealed a game that could not have been started in the last fifteen minutes.

'Ah yes, I've been trying to beat Richard for the past week. He's quite the opponent.'

It was a difficult choice, but concern won – for now. 'James, we've had quite a trip today. Should you not be resting?'

'Five miles in your luxurious carriage is hardly "quite a trip", my friend. You were there when Mr Wright assured us I'm out of the woods. You needn't fret so.'

The viscount gave a wry smile. 'Yes, but you've also been conducting tours and arranging balls. It won't do if you exhaust yourself into an early grave.'

'I quite enjoy being amongst the living, if you haven't noticed.' Graham paused for a moment. 'Besides, Richard has been indispensable, helping me to bed or bringing me a blanket when I tire. I assure you, Aubrey, I'm well looked after.'

Sutton's curiosity took hold, but Graham had other ideas.

'What brings you here?' the lieutenant asked. 'Does it pertain to...Lady Lavender?'

And Sutton understood – understood what he had known all along. He would not have suspected it last September, when he first met Miss Ashcroft, nor in December, when he helped celebrate her birthday. But February, when he'd delivered Richard's sketches; April, when he'd received her heartfelt letter; May, when she'd painted with him and cried with him; now, on the cusp of June, when she expressed, in her sincere, unassuming manner, her preference for the Lavender Rooms...

He *understood.*

'Aubrey,' Graham continued, 'when I was...slipping in and out of consciousness that wretched week... I couldn't speak, but I heard what you said. About meeting Lady Lavender.'

Sutton looked up at his friend. They would never mention this again – now was the time to gather his courage. In a small voice, he asked:

'What do you think of her?'

Graham smiled. 'I think she's splendid.'

'Do you think... She was so distraught after praising the Rooms, but do you think she might...'

'That, my friend, only the lady herself can answer.' Chuckling at Sutton's expression, Graham added: 'You should ask her. Anyone who can reduce the venerable 7th Viscount Sutton to a bumbling boy deserves to be asked if she returns his affections.'

Sutton swallowed the requests for reassurance he longed to voice – he was determined to leave with a shred of his dignity. Instead, Sutton studied the chessboard again. 'You've been playing with the ensign for the past week?'

'A bit longer than that, actually.' Graham's tone was a little stilted. 'You're not the only one who's enamoured with an Ashcroft.'

Sutton hadn't expected *this* particular revelation.

'He and I have been through a lot together.' Graham's words were more rushed than usual. 'I'd thought it wrong to have such feelings, but...then I saw my comrades die, almost died myself, and lost an arm. If I'll be damned, then so be it.' He paused, taking in a deep breath. 'I see you have questions. Go on – ask them before I lose my nerve.'

'Does his family know?'

'Richard has informed his brother of his proclivities, but he's made no mention of me. And he's told his sister he's not inclined to marry – we don't want to scandalise her just yet.'

'What of Miss Amelia Thorpe? You were betrothed for so long, and seeing her marry Francis almost destroyed you.'

They'd had no occasion to speak of Graham's past fiancée or his late brother for years – it had become a separate tale altogether. 'I did love her,' Graham said eventually, 'and I have been fond of other women. But I've also been fond of men. One's sex makes no difference to me.'

While Sutton processed this, Graham asked: 'Am I still welcome at Bellevue?'

The viscount's gaze was as fierce as his tone. 'Don't ever spout such nonsense again, James. I won't insult you by claiming to understand your preferences – both men *and* women? Honestly, James, as if you weren't spoilt for choice as it were!' He paused while the lieutenant chuckled. 'And I can't speak for our acquaintances, who would deem your choices sinful if they were so aware. But *I* am the final authority at Bellevue, and you will *always* have a home here. These are *your* rooms, James, and they will be until my final breath.'

'Thank you, Aubrey,' his friend said quietly. 'Really – thank you.'

Sutton waved his hand nonchalantly. 'Now, is it time for you to rest? I'll make your apologies if you can't go down for dinner.'

'Don't fuss over me,' was Graham's reply. '*You* need to seek out Mr Ashcroft before his departure.'

Sutton helped make his friend comfortable, and went searching for Mr Ashcroft.

A few days after Mr Ashcroft's departure brought the arrival of Mr de Lancie and his usual entourage. When the introductions were made, Mr de Lancie took and kissed Miss Ashcroft's hand. The young lady blushed prettily at the exchange, and an uncomfortable and unfamiliar feeling surged within him. Sutton had never wondered or cared much about his friend's flirtations, and now was decidedly *not* a time to start. He reminded himself of Mr de Lancie's general character, of the Londoner's affectionate behaviour towards all women, partly due to being the sole son in a family of three sisters. While these flourishes towards Miss Ashcroft did not sit well with Sutton due to *his* own affections, they never bordered on inappropriate.

He was the 7th Viscount Sutton – it was beneath him to bristle at every friendly gesture towards Miss Ashcroft. As far as his guests were concerned, she was simply the sister of Ensign Ashcroft, who had served alongside Lieutenant Graham at the Peninsular War. No one questioned her connection to the lord of the manor; her pristine reputation remained intact.

As preparations for the ball continued and several guests arrived in Bellevue Park, Sutton attended to his friends and often only saw Miss Ashcroft at dinner. Many visitors chose to hunt or fish during the day, and while Sutton welcomed the exercise and fresh air, he lamented no longer spending hours with Graham and Miss Ashcroft in the library or among his art collection. To Sutton's relief, the young lady had established a happy rapport with his dearest friend. Sutton only wished he could neglect his other guests for their company.

He found her alone in the library one morning, when the house was still quiet and Sutton wanted to nurse a hangover in peace. The previous evening's entertainment had carried on well into the morning, with wine flowing freely around the card tables. Miss Ashcroft had excused herself early, but Sutton had only gotten two or three hours of rest and now felt the effects of his long night.

Miss Ashcroft was seated by the window, immersed in her sketchbook. Her morning dress, a gentle mint with silver trimming, had rumpled a little and gathered to one side, showing a slender ankle. A cup of tea and a plate of half-eaten toast lay on a side table. She was perfectly at ease, as if in her own home. His heart swelled once more, and Sutton considered asking for her hand in this rare, snatched morning.

He cleared his throat, and saw the recognition and delight at his presence before they turned into apprehension. He watched as she rose, smoothing down her dress before curtsying.

'Good morning, Lord Sutton.' She studied him and her anxiety melted into concern. 'Are you quite well?'

He was a little ashamed of how he must have looked. 'I am, thank you. I'm a little tired from all these activities.'

'I have learnt the hard way the importance of not exceeding my limits,' she replied. 'Are you looking for Lieutenant Graham?'

He had been hoping to escape his other guests for the morning, but it didn't seem right to admit this. It was more than a pleasant surprise to find Miss Ashcroft alone in the library – but it wouldn't do to admit that, either.

'I was hoping for some quiet time,' Sutton said instead. He gestured at the unoccupied chair where Graham usually sat. 'May I join you?'

The lady hesitated, and Sutton cursed his candour. Headache or no, his impulsiveness was doing them no favours. His half-formed idea of proposing left him – she deserved much more, when he had much more to offer.

'Of course,' she eventually said. 'You hardly need to ask in your own home.'

He gave her a rather forced smile and rang the bell to request a light breakfast and his sketching material. He settled in his seat while Miss Ashcroft politely set aside her work.

'By all means, don't mind me,' he said. 'There's no need to stop your work on my account.'

'Are you quite certain?'

Sutton nodded and gave her a smile he hoped was reassuring. 'I've been meaning to practise my sketching – I haven't done any since Thornleigh.'

'That's quite a shame,' replied Miss Ashcroft. 'I remember your sketch of Marcus – it was very elegant.'

He thanked her for the compliment while inwardly berating his behaviour.

To his relief, two footmen soon entered with the requested trays of tea and art supplies.

'You see, I'll be well-occupied here,' the viscount said once his tea had been poured. 'Please, do continue with your sketches.'

When Miss Ashcroft still seemed a little uncertain, Sutton sipped his tea and flipped through his sketchbook, assessing his work from several months ago. He stopped at a sketch of Mr Ashcroft and added a few more details to the attire, scratching away with his pencil. A few minutes later, Miss Ashcroft's pencil resumed its work. The viscount relaxed at the sound and dared to glance up again, careful to keep his own pencil moving.

She was still a little tense, but was concentrating on her task at hand. Her neatly coiffed hair shone under the light of the early morning, a few curls framing her delicate features and bringing out her endearing freckles. Her grey eyes were focused, and her lips were parted ever so slightly.

With a slow and deep breath, Sutton turned to a fresh page, and began to sketch the lady before him.

The first guests for the ball arrived at 6 o'clock, after which a steady stream of ladies and gentlemen entered Bellevue Park. By 8 o'clock, the grand ballroom was filled with guests waiting to hear the host's customary speech. Clad in a deep purple ensemble embroidered with gold, the viscount stepped onto the raised platform next to the dancing master and looked down at the hundreds of faces in a sea of colour.

'It is my immense pleasure to welcome friends old and new to Bellevue Park's annual spring ball. Many of you have commented on the unconventional timing this year, which is due to some events over the Channel – events concluding with Great Britain's victory. I am particularly grateful that my dear friend, Lieutenant Graham, is back on British soil after his participation in the war.

'However, many of his friends – and some of your acquaintances – were not

327

so fortunate. Before we begin tonight's festivities, I hope you will all join me in a moment of silence to pray for the dearly departed.'

There was neither a murmur nor whisper amongst his numerous guests despite their various political and philosophical beliefs. The silence stretched into a long, respectful moment, and by the time Sutton spoke again, he noticed some dabbing at their eyes.

'It is with those sacrifices that we stand here today. And in this spirit of celebration and commemoration, I wish to toast those who have served.'

Those who were familiar with the proceedings already had a glass in hand, and Sutton waited for the few without to be provided with one. When everyone was ready, Sutton raised his glass.

'To those who have served.'

'To those who have served,' the room echoed in one unified voice, sending a shiver down Sutton's spine.

'And now, I shall leave you in the capable hands of our dancing master!'

A small smattering of clapping led to a more prolonged applause as Sutton stepped towards his first dancing partner of the evening. Bellevue's tradition dictated the unmarried host dance the first set with the most honoured female guest of the evening, a privilege that fell to the Countess Grey, who was here tonight with the 2nd Earl Grey.

The countess wore a loose gown due to her current condition, and she was as spirited as ever when she and Sutton met in the centre of the ballroom. The music started and they fell easily into their steps and conversation.

'Lord Sutton, you must have had quite a difficult year.'

'It has not been without its joys,' replied Sutton. 'What of you, Countess? I've grown quite accustomed to your appearances, but some of my more recent friends are quite shocked by your condition.'

The woman laughed. 'Perhaps they'll be shocked even more when discovering I ceased my confinements after my fifth, and this will be my fifteenth, I think. It does become hard to keep track, you know.'

The dance continued thus, and Sutton found himself enjoying the simple and familiar pleasures of music, steps, and good company. After the final notes were struck, Sutton gave his partner a deep, respectful bow.

'Thank you for the pleasure once again,' she said, a little breathless. 'I think I shall sit out the rest of the dances.'

Sutton smiled. 'I'm sure you'll enjoy circuiting the card tables far more than the dances.'

As the countess departed, Sutton caught sight of Miss Ashcroft. She wore an ivory gown with dark purple trimmings that matched his ensemble. Her smile was tentative, but full of promises.

43

ELLIE HAD LOVED the delicate evening gown when she first unwrapped the package and its accompanying note from Marcus and Kitty, and she loved it even more now that Lord Sutton regarded her with a mixture of intensity and intimacy. For a few heartbeats, Ellie had quite forgotten her recent bouts of nerves when in the viscount's presence, or even that they were surrounded by hundreds of his guests. It seemed they were the only two people in the room.

She was gently brought back to her senses by Richard, who was asking if she wished to remain standing for the next dance or to join Lieutenant Graham in one of the adjoining rooms. Lord Sutton, whose attention was also demanded elsewhere, gave Ellie a small nod before looking away.

'Yes, let's join the lieutenant,' she replied. 'Though I doubt he'll be short of company.'

Her brother chuckled as they made their way through the ballroom towards the side rooms where the lieutenant had headed earlier. When they found him, Ellie's words proved to be true: the lieutenant was seated in a plush chair and joined by almost a dozen men and women, including Mr de Lancie. Lieutenant Graham's smile brightened when he saw Ellie and Richard approach, and he quickly facilitated the introductions before making room for the newcomers to sit, with Ellie next to the lieutenant, and Richard on a chair that was presently brought in.

Richard took to the company like a fish in water, narrating some of the more cheerful tales from the army. Meanwhile, Ellie sat by, happy to listen and happier still to see her brother in such high spirits. The group paid little heed to her, and Ellie was perfectly content.

When the conversation turned away from Richard and to Mr de Lancie's account of a recent London scandal, the lieutenant said quietly: 'I hope you're faring well, Miss Ashcroft. These gatherings can be…overwhelming.'

'It's not as bad as I thought it would be,' she said automatically, then blushed at her implication. 'That is, I do not mean I thought it would be "bad", only… Well, there are just so *many* people.'

The lieutenant smiled kindly. 'Balls are not to everyone's tastes. I was a little intimidated at first, but I have grown fond of them.'

Ellie relaxed a little. 'I know Lord Sutton has many acquaintances, but I'm a little astounded by the precise number.'

'Oh, this is but a small portion of them,' the lieutenant replied. 'I believe our friend keeps several compendiums of names and addresses, listing all those he knows.'

'Goodness gracious me. Are you well-acquainted with them all?'

Lieutenant Graham gave a boyish grin. 'I know many of them by name, and I've been in the company of some others over the years, such as Mr de Lancie and his family. But for the most part, Lord Sutton and I maintain different circles, and I don't see the great majority of them outside gatherings such as these. He and I have such different interests that sometimes I honestly wonder how we're still friends.'

Ellie nodded as uncertainty took hold once more. In a sea of elegant and refined ladies, Ellie suddenly felt very young, and very lost.

'Is something troubling you?' the lieutenant asked gently, noticing her apprehension. 'We have not been acquainted for long, but you may keep me in your strictest confidence.'

'Thank you,' Ellie replied. 'I don't quite know how to explain it. It's not just the sheer *number* of these people, but… Well, Lord Sutton is different when he's with us.'

The lieutenant's eyes softened, as did his voice. 'Miss Ashcroft, between you and me... It is with *them* that he is different. I promise you, he is the most himself when with us.'

He then changed the topic deftly with a nod towards the ballroom. 'Are you fond of dancing, Miss Ashcroft?'

'My brother Richard is far more suited to dancing than I am.'

The lieutenant laughed. 'I don't doubt that.'

Before the lieutenant could continue, Ellie was met with a familiar and unexpected face.

'Mr Livingston,' she said, a little loudly, 'what a pleasant surprise.'

'Indeed, Miss Ashcroft.' The shorter gentleman bowed to the group but declined the offer for a seat. 'Miss Ashcroft, if your dance card still permits and if you are so inclined, would you honour me with the next quadrille?'

Ellie could hardly refuse such a public offer. She withdrew her dance card, found the next listed quadrille, and pencilled in Mr Livingston's name.

'Excellent,' the gentleman said when all this was done. He bowed again and left, making his way towards a refreshments table.

'What a curious man,' Mr de Lancie commented. 'Impeccable taste in art, though. Hasn't it been years since he last attended one of Lord Sutton's gatherings?'

Another gentleman provided his speculations, while Ellie turned towards Lieutenant Graham, who said in a low voice:

'My goodness, I thought I'd never see Livingston again – Sutton doesn't have the most forgiving nature, and I know all about their disagreement. I wonder why he's changed his mind.'

Blushing, Ellie managed to reply: 'Mr Livingston was appraising my art at Thornleigh, and met Lord Sutton there a few months ago.'

'Ah!' Lieutenant Graham's surprise smoothed into understanding. 'Yes, of course. I hope you will enjoy the dance, Miss Ashcroft.'

When the current dance was drawing to a close, Ellie rose from her seat and excused herself from the company. She found Mr Livingston waiting at the edge of the room. Ellie took the gentleman's arm and followed him into the ballroom, where they lined up for the quadrille.

The music began and they fell into their steps. Ellie noted they were well-matched as dancing partners, both being neither too awkward nor flamboyant. After a few turns, Mr Livingston spoke.

'I am relieved Ensign Ashcroft has returned safely. I must say, your likeness was remarkable.'

Ellie smiled shyly, and could only express her thanks.

'I've just come from London,' he said mildly. 'I've been tasked with offering you a place at the Royal Academy.'

She stumbled in surprise and required a few moments to concentrate on her steps. Mr Livingston waited for her composure to return before continuing.

'Mr Ashcroft informed me last month that you had completed "We Happy Few" and invited me to see it in person. I understand he has been at Bellevue until recently, so I was only able to see it last week.'

Marcus had not mentioned Mr Livingston in person or in any of his letters, and while she knew her brother only wanted the very best for her, Ellie did not like that he had issued the invitation without consulting her first. After all, it was *her* painting, and it should be Ellie's choice – and Ellie's choice alone – when she wanted to share it.

Oblivious to Ellie's thoughts, Mr Livingston continued. 'I admired the completed painting very much indeed. I also saw the start of a companion piece – very promising, too. I had quite a discussion with your brother, which resulted in an audience with the Academy members. You are talented, Miss Ashcroft, but there is still much for you to learn. Under my recommendation and with the staunch support of Miss Mary Moser, the Academy is offering you a provisional place of study for the coming year. I believe the written offer has been sent to Thornleigh, so it may be a while until you receive the papers.'

Ellie missed another few steps of the dance, her heart soaring as she came to understand the magnitude of the offer. Mr Livingston had spoken with the Academy members, and procured the support of *the* Miss Moser, had obtained for Ellie a place to study at the *Royal* Academy – it was beyond any of her dreams, and more than she could have dared to hope for!

'Now, what have you been doing in Bellevue Park?' the gentleman asked when they were in step again. 'I suppose you've seen Lord Sutton's collection.'

'I have,' Ellie finally managed. 'He possesses many masterpieces.'

'Lord Sutton may not be the most talented with a brush, but his taste is faultless.'

Even with her joy at the recent news, Ellie felt a swell of defiance, remembering too well Lord Sutton's dejection when he recounted Mr Livingston's harsh criticism. This, in addition to her previous irritation at Marcus, took Ellie by surprise. She was never one to let her temper get the better of her, and she did not wish to start now.

Instead, Ellie smiled and said: 'I'm pleased you and Lord Sutton have made amends, and that you are here tonight.'

Mr Livingston nodded. 'I believe I should thank you for that courtesy. He mentioned in his invitation you might enjoy the company.'

Lord Sutton's consideration of her feelings, which he had decided as more important than his own, filled Ellie with warmth and affection, and took away her capacity for speech. Fortunately, Mr Livingston wasn't expecting a response.

'"Persephone's Promise", indeed,' the gentlemen said instead. 'And the Shakespeare – most excellent. Mr Curtis certainly has a way with words.'

Ellie missed yet another step. 'You are acquainted with Mr Curtis?'

'Yes – for many years now. He wrote to me last year insisting I visit your exhibition, and arranged all my visits to Thornleigh Abbey – didn't he mention it?' He shook his head, smiling in amusement and disbelief. 'Oh, but he wouldn't – always the silent benefactor.'

He bowed at the end of the dance while Ellie fumbled a curtsy. Of *course* it was Mr Curtis who had recommended her – a silent benefactor, indeed!

As the evening continued, Ellie's delight at receiving Mr Livingston's news and Marcus's blessing began to subside. She wanted nothing more than to accept the offer, but she understood a woman's duties too well to hold onto such fancies. A year ago, she would have cajoled Marcus to enrol her post-haste, lest the Academy's members changed their mind. But a year ago, she would not have produced "We Happy Few", or had the courage to experiment with larger canvases, or met Lord Sutton…

Ellie kept these thoughts to herself as she stumbled through a dance with Richard, and one with Mr de Lancie, and another still with Mr Dupont. Whenever there was a break in conversation, Ellie would survey the room before her, noting the array of fashions and searching for their host. Several times she saw him either in conversation or dancing with another lady. But while their paths did not cross, the viscount had met her gaze a few times and given her a small smile from where he was.

When the hour grew later still, Ellie retreated to the gardens, thankful for the cool night air and the delicate scents of flowers. She closed her eyes and inhaled deeply. There were lilies, and roses, and the faintest hint of orange blossoms.

Soft footsteps approached and stopped beside her.

She opened her eyes to see Lord Sutton, his smile soft and gentle.

44

SHE WAS A VISION in the night, her smile soft, and shy, and a little sad. She curtsied, a small and graceful dip, and he felt his heart beat in time to her movements.

'Lord Sutton,' she said, her voice quiet and radiant under the moonlight. 'It has been a splendid evening. Thank you.'

Her gratitude was genuine, but he detected the melancholy in her words.

'I simply signed and stamped the invitations – it is Mrs Jennings who deserves all the credit.'

'Even so… Given the flourishes in your penmanship, I, at least, am grateful for your sacrifice.'

He chuckled at her boldness, while a blush blossomed on her cheeks. Her lips parted slightly, and Sutton felt a longing to brush them with his fingers.

'Lord Sutton…' Her small, breathless voice sent his heart pounding. 'What… What was your mother like?'

'My mother?' Seeing her withdraw at his startled response, Sutton quickly amended: 'It's been a long time since anyone has asked about her so directly. My mother was typical, I suppose. She knew her duties and carried them out as well as expected: she obeyed her husband, produced her children, ran her household. A typical countess.'

If anything, his response unnerved her. Before Sutton could ask about her growing distress, Miss Ashcroft said: 'I never knew my mother. I don't know what is considered "typical" – I only have Kitty's example to go on.'

Sutton chuckled despite himself. 'I would not call Mrs Ashcroft "typical" in any sense of the word, but I assure you, she will make a better mother than mine did.'

That elicited a small smile from her; it was enough to give him courage.

'Miss Ashcroft, might you honour me with the next dance?'

Her hesitation returned, and with it, Sutton saw her slumped shoulders and weary posture. The day had been long, the evening longer, and Miss Ashcroft's constitution, though much improved since last autumn, was much more delicate than his. They had both drunk enough punch to forget the unspoken distance between them, but her reticence reminded him afresh of the incident in the Lavender Rooms. He felt a prickle of disappointment in his own conduct.

'Forgive me for speaking out of turn – you are under no obligation to indulge me. Do you wish to be accompanied back inside, or to remain in your own counsel?'

The young woman studied him, her grey eyes luminous and knowing. Sutton's mouth turned dry under her gaze, and he wondered how much she saw, how much she would accept.

'I would very much like to dance with you, Lord Sutton,' she finally said, 'though I suspect it will be my final turn of the evening. I fear I may need to retire shortly after.'

'Of course.'

Sutton offered his arm, which she took in the quiet, unassuming way that warmed him. As they walked through the garden, passing the men and women who had also come for a stroll, Sutton revelled in the peace of the night air, of walking side by side with Miss Ashcroft. He had left the ballroom for a moment of solitude, only to realise now that he was seeking companionship.

They reached the threshold, where the music and conversation spilled out like heady wine. Sutton took a deep, steady breath, resuming his role of a viscount subject to social scrutiny, one who was responsible for protecting a lady's reputation. He felt Miss Ashcroft's own transformation beside him, and, when he turned to her, Sutton saw a poised young woman who knew his heart as well as her own.

Her hand tightened on his arm ever so slightly as they walked back inside. They would speak more tomorrow – he was sure of it, and saw in her smile the same promise.

'Those flourishes on your invitations,' she said, her eyes already dancing, 'while delightful, are quite unnecessary. Your penmanship is the most beautiful at its simplest.'

His laughter was drowned out by the music, but he saw in her radiant smile that she had heard.

And through the dance, through the music that enveloped them and the steps that flowed through his body, he let himself drown in the fleeting scent of fresh flowers he caught when they were close, the freckled constellation brightening her features, the feel of her gloved hands in his, her silence, her contentment, her companionship.

The rest of the evening went by in a typical fashion, with Sutton playing his part well. After Miss Ashcroft and Graham both left for their respective quarters, Sutton stood for several more dances, complimenting the ladies on their exquisite eveningwear and enquiring after their children. When the music dwindled, Sutton joined the card tables for a game of whist, offering in turn his opinion on the fate of France and on Brummell's latest sartorial developments. It wasn't until the refreshments were brought in, just after two, that Sutton saw Richard's departure and felt his own weariness.

He barely had time to contemplate his own exit when Livingston approached him with a bow.

'Lord Sutton,' the gentleman said, 'I must thank you again for your invitation. It was unexpected, but not unwelcome.'

Sutton scoffed at Livingston's honesty. 'You have been generous with assisting Miss Ashcroft – inviting you was the least I could do.'

'My generosity is not on *your* behalf, Lord Sutton. You ought not take credit where you have no claim.'

The words incensed Sutton, and he was further affronted when Livingston held up a hand.

'I am not here to quarrel. Earlier this evening, I took the liberty of relaying to Miss Ashcroft an offer from the Academy to study there in the coming year. I now take the liberty of relaying the same news to you in the hope of preventing Miss Ashcroft from having to make an impossible decision.'

It took Sutton a few moments to understand the revelation, and a few more for Sutton's temper to rise. 'How dare you!' He lowered his voice when some nearby guests looked their way, but his eyes remained furious. 'How dare you suggest that I would ask Miss Ashcroft to *choose!*'

'The situation isn't unprecedented,' Livingston said mildly, as if talking about the weather. 'I've seen too much talent go to waste when a young lady contends with divided duties.'

'This has nothing to do with *other* situations; this is—'

The words dissipated along with his anger. Sutton had been too preoccupied with his wounded pride – with *himself* – to realise Livingston had been doing him a favour.

'Divided duties, indeed,' he muttered, now understanding Miss Ashcroft's earlier trepidation. 'I've been a right fool, when you only meant well.' He thought back to what had transpired with Livingston all those years ago, and shook his head with a sigh. 'Just as you only meant well that night. My art *is* contrived at worst, mediocre at best. I've been a fool to blame *you* for telling me the truth.'

The gentleman looked a little remorseful. 'Is that what I said? Well, I could have been a bit gentler.'

Sutton remembered how Miss Ashcroft had attempted to soften her own appraisals of his art, and his mood lifted. 'I doubt I would've taken your criticism to heart. I was wrong to lose my temper then, and I was wrong just now. Thank you for telling me about the Academy's offer.'

He extended a hand, which Livingston immediately took.

'You've changed, Sutton.'

The viscount smiled at the familiar address. 'I certainly hope so. I wouldn't be deserving otherwise.'

The two men shook hands and both sat down at the card table when Mr de Lancie insisted on another game. Sutton played on, enjoying the company of his friends, sound in the knowledge of what he must do in the morrow. As the night lengthened into daybreak, the viscount felt, for the first time at a ball, enthusiasm about the day to follow.

45

SHE SAW HIM on their final turn about the flower garden. His eyes, bright and intense, softened when he noticed her. In the warmth of his smile, she could feel the heat between their gloved hands as they danced, the unspoken promise of something more. When they had closed their distance, Ellie felt a weakness in her legs that had nothing to do with her afternoon walk.

'Have you had an eventful morning?' he asked, after greetings had been exchanged.

'It was very informative,' replied Richard. 'Lieutenant Graham gave us another tour, this time of the labyrinth and orangery, and regaled us with several more tales.'

'Is that so?' There was a hint of amusement in the viscount's tone. 'Then I'm sorry to have missed it – if only to corroborate the lieutenant's tales.'

Lieutenant Graham, who had indeed been a fine companion all morning, smiled in response. 'Shall we walk back to the house together then? We will pass several places where Lord Sutton's first attempts at "duelling" took place.'

'If my reputation is to be challenged,' Lord Sutton replied lightly, 'then it might as well be by your hand, Lieutenant. Lead on.'

The viscount waited for the gentlemen to pass, and fell in step with Ellie at the rear of the group.

'Did you rest well, Miss Ashcroft?'

'I did, thank you.' She struggled with her next words, though she had been turning them in her head since the previous evening. 'It must have been incredibly difficult for you to invite Mr Livingston, and to welcome him into your home. I am much obliged to your kindness and generosity.'

'It was not so trying as I had imagined, all things considered. I noticed the two of you dancing – you seemed to fluctuate between being perplexed and pleased.'

The memory of Mr Livingston's words made her anxious once more.

Lord Sutton continued: 'The gentleman sought me out after you had retired. He shared the news with me – congratulations, Miss Ashcroft.'

'I... Thank you.' Ellie dared a glance at the viscount, and saw he was nothing but pleased. She asked in a small voice: 'You don't mind?'

'What a preposterous thing to ask! Well, perhaps your concern is warranted, given my poor behaviour in the past. No, Miss Ashcroft, I do not mind at all. My aspirations have taken another shape, and they are completely unrelated to the Academy.'

The two walked in silence behind Richard and Lieutenant Graham until they'd left the flower garden and Ellie's heartbeat had settled a little.

'What are those aspirations, Lord Sutton?' she finally asked.

'Well, my townhouse – does your brother have one?'

Ellie shook her head. 'Marcus has never been fond of London. His trips are never long, and he can always find comfortable lodgings when he is in town.'

'That won't do – my townhouse is always open to him, and to your family. I intend to carry out some refurbishments for a particular apartment. Now that I think on it, the Academy is involved, though it does not compare to another, far more important consideration.'

The viscount's words were rushed, and, even as Ellie blushed at his implications, she noticed the colour on his own cheeks. She barely had time to react when Lord Sutton said, loudly enough to be heard by their party:

'I've been meaning to share a particular vantage of Bellevue that might interest you. Miss Ashcroft, would you do me the honour of obliging me?'

Ellie looked up at Richard, who nodded. It was all the permission – and encouragement – she needed.

'I would be delighted, Lord Sutton.'

Parting from their company, Ellie followed Lord Sutton as he led her through a side door into the house. She found herself in the viscount's most private rooms, strong with the scent of paint. When she was last here, Ellie had touched Lord Sutton on the shoulder while he wept. Her blush deepened at the memory.

They reached a small staircase and Lord Sutton gestured for her to enter. 'We'll have to take these right to the top,' he said, 'but we may rest whenever you wish.'

'Thank you.' Ellie gingerly lifted her skirts just so and began to climb. The viscount followed at a respectful distance of two or three steps behind. After four or five flights – she had lost count – Ellie required a small recess.

'Would you like to sit down for a moment?' asked Lord Sutton. 'We're right beside the nursery.'

Ellie shook her head. 'I just need to catch my breath.'

Lord Sutton waited patiently until she was ready. When they finally reached the top of the stairs, the viscount led her through a long hallway towards their destination.

Ellie gasped at the sight before her, below her, above her.

They were in the heart of Bellevue, above where the double spiral staircase ended and below where the vaulted ceiling began. She looked down and saw the striking asymmetry of the twin staircases, circling each other yet never meeting; she looked up and saw every distinct and chiselled stone that held the roof together.

'Oh, Lord Sutton, this is spectacular! If only I had brought my sketchbook! Might I come back another time? I would like to so very, very much!'

When Ellie finally tore her gaze away from the magnificent architecture, she saw the viscount gesture at a nearby desk. Only now did she notice the drawing instruments, the chairs, the empty canvases, the small easel. The realisation sank in slowly, sweetly, as soft and tender as his next words.

'Nothing would make me happier than to be at your disposal.'

When she looked up at him again, Ellie could not stop the tears that welled in her eyes.

'Miss Ashcroft,' he said, his voice breaking between the two syllables of her name. 'You are, quite simply put, extraordinary. You deserve nothing short of my love, devotion, and support. Draw the staircases, go to the Academy, show the world how extraordinary you are – do all that you desire, and more.' He swallowed, his eyes bright. 'And, if you so desire, you need not do it alone. Will you... Will you allow me the honour of accompanying you on your journey? Will you accept my hand in marriage?'

She looked at the man before her, the man she had unexpectedly come to know, love, and admire, and who understood and accepted everything she was.

Her gaze lowered to his own hands, large and beautiful, full of warmth, strength, and the occasional callouses that spoke of his willingness to work. One day, Ellie would draw those hands, or kiss them as he had hers, or, still, succumb to the delight and desire they would bring her. One day, she would stand before her family and friends as he slipped a ring onto her finger, promising to wed, worship, and endow.

But for now, Ellie smiled at Lord Sutton, and placed her hand in his.

MAPS & FAMILY TREES

Ground floor

Chapel

Conservatory
Studio
Private garden
Formal study
Dowager apartments

Long gallery
Dining

Library
Drawing room
Music room

Fountain
Formal gardens
Ballroom
Grand staircase
Salon
Main dining

Apartments

Formal galleries
Curiosities
State apartments

First floor

Study

Master suite

Prospero suite

Parlour

Highlands suite

Edward rooms

Staircase

Augusta parlour

Parlour

Nairn rooms

Lavender rooms

Cressy's room

Arabella suite

Calliope suite

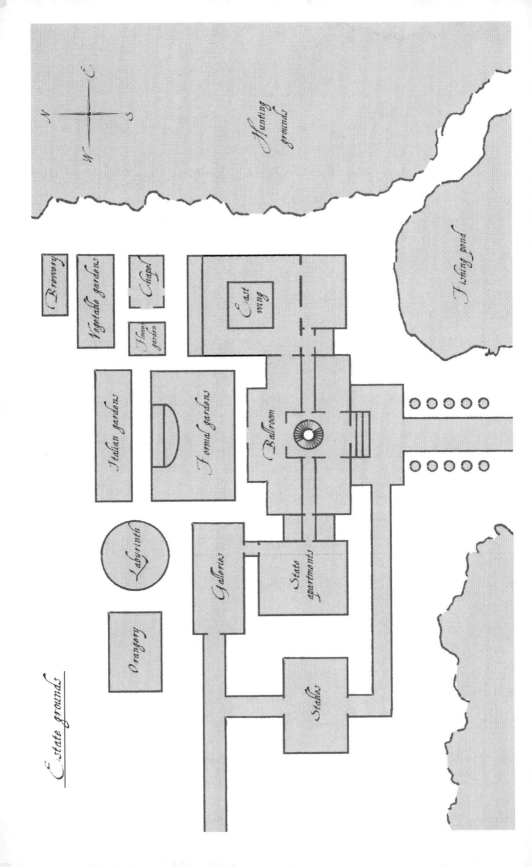

Main entrance

Conservatory

Beaumonts of Bellevue

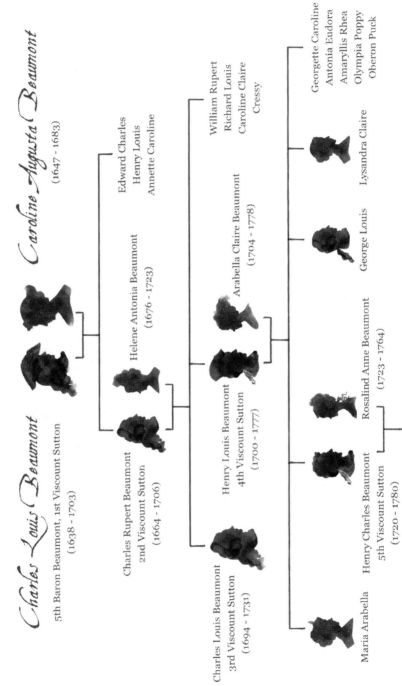

Charles Louis Beaumont
5th Baron Beaumont, 1st Viscount Sutton
(1638 - 1703)

Caroline Augusta Beaumont
(1647 - 1683)

Edward Charles
Henry Louis
Annette Caroline

Helene Antonia Beaumont
(1676 - 1723)

Charles Rupert Beaumont
2nd Viscount Sutton
(1664 - 1706)

William Rupert
Richard Louis
Caroline Claire
Cressy

Arabella Claire Beaumont
(1704 - 1778)

Henry Louis Beaumont
4th Viscount Sutton
(1700 - 1777)

Charles Louis Beaumont
3rd Viscount Sutton
(1694 - 1731)

Georgette Caroline
Antonia Eudora
Amaryllis Rhea
Olympia Poppy
Oberon Puck

Lysandra Claire

George Louis

Rosalind Anne Beaumont
(1723 - 1764)

Maria Arabella

Henry Charles Beaumont
5th Viscount Sutton
(1720 - 1780)

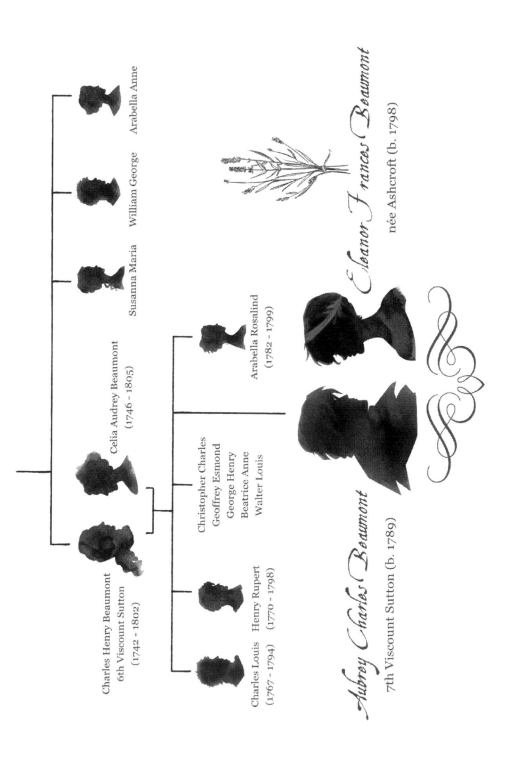

Charles Henry Beaumont
6th Viscount Sutton
(1742 - 1802)

Celia Audrey Beaumont
(1746 - 1805)

Susanna Maria

William George

Arabella Anne

Charles Louis
(1767 - 1794)

Henry Rupert
(1770 - 1798)

Christopher Charles
Geoffrey Esmond
George Henry
Beatrice Anne
Walter Louis

Arabella Rosalind
(1782 - 1799)

Aubrey Charles Beaumont
7th Viscount Sutton (b. 1789)

Eleanor Frances Beaumont
née Ashcroft (b. 1798)

AFTERWORD

Kickstarter Supporters

Abigail Holloway

Adia

Adrienne Tuatara Foster

aiko24601

Aimee Briley

Alex H

Alex Jackson

Ana Silva

Angelique Wille

Anna De Cicco

Anna L

Anna Li

Anna Maria L

Anna Tran

Anna Wojda

Ashley

Audie Austen

Bethany

Bonnie Rutledge

Caitlin Conlon

Caitlin Mortimer

Cassandra Young

Chelby Mather

The Creative Fund by BackerKit

CSD

D. Wilson

Danielle Jones

Dar Rivkin

David Yeager

Dawn Kaye

Donna Bevan Herren

Durrah

Elly McG

Ely Stilburn

em winters

Emmeline B

Engel_Dreizehn

eriberri

Erica Nelson

Erika Paul

Evelyne

Fallon

Fiona Morton

Gaby Spartz

Germa Barragán

Gioia Pappalardo

Guest 173789955

Guest 1885080474

Guest 407741892

Guest 432296112

Irene Langford

Jamie

Javiera Pincheira

Jenn Evans

Jenna Lindeke Heavenrich

Jenny Larson

Jessica Johansen

Jessica Kizer

Jina T

Joanne Renaud

Joy Counts

Julie Christensen

Julie Shasta MacTire

K. Gavenman

Karalynn

Karen L

Kasper

Kat Let

Katarina Scoleri

Kate

Kathryb

Katie Hamilton

Kelsey

Kelsey R. Marquart

Kim Nguyen

Kimia Shabahang

Kristen

Ktchan24

Kylie Mallett

Kyttynjirr

Lærke W. Thomsen

Lara Owsley

Lara Worsley

Laura

Laura

Laura B

Laura Doherty

Lauren Clinnick

Layla H

Lili

Linda Fitzpatrick

Lindsey Appell

Lorelei Nguyen

Lori F.

Luna

Dr M. A. Crippen

M. C. A. Hogarth

Maaria Posti

Mahida

Mariah Driggs

Marie Whelan

marilu

Mary Osborn

Megan Greenan

Michelle W

Monica Altx

Monica Singh

nancie

PV

QueenKaticus

Rachel

rayne0goddess

ReHa

Rhia

Rosie Crossley

Ruth Bonser

S. R. Dreamholde

Saga Albright

Samantha Richards

Sarah Fowerbaugh

Sarah Kingdred

Savannah Camacho

Shannon O. McGinnis

Shannon Symonds

Shelly Counts

Sian Eleri Jenkins

Silke Akkermans

Siyang Zhang

Sophia

Sophie

Stephanie Fitts

Stephanie Mason

Stephanie Robinson

Taree

Taylor Harrison

Tellina Liu

Teneia

Tomey

Tori Hebdon

Vicki Crockett

Xiri R

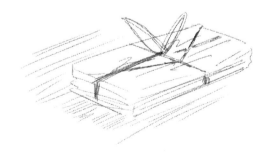

ACKNOWLEDGEMENTS

First and foremost, I'd like to thank all the incredible Regency Lovers for their love and support over the last six years. All your comments, messages, and emails have made this labour of love less laborious and infinitely more lovely. Without you, there would have been no *Regency Love* expansion or *Lady Lavender*. I'm especially grateful to everyone who backed this project on Kickstarter – who would've thought a little spin-off novel would get so much love!

To my co-conspirators at Tea For Three Studios: thank you for putting up with all my crazy ideas, over-excitement, impulsiveness, verbal vomiting, and the endless streams of innuendos at every meeting. Jen, thank you for taking the time out of your busy schedule to create the gorgeous cover art that had me drooling even *after* I'd finished my Bubble Nini. Mel, thank you for all your patience, encouragement, feedback, reading and re-reading (and re-re-reading) various drafts, and steadfast support. You always find a way to temper my exuberance with the perfect balance of kindness and good sense. Thank you also for the beautiful family tree and floor plans. I'm sorry-not-sorry about the double spiral staircase, but I now owe you a trip to Chambord.

As an indie game-development group, we rely on others to help spread the word about *Regency Love*. On behalf of the team, I am grateful to everyone who featured or reviewed *Regency Love*, including – in no particular order – Tracey Lien (back in her Polygon days), Amanda (from SBTB), Kelsey (from Nerdy But Flirty), Ashley (from Robo♥beat), Dawn Ire (from Otome Otaku Girl), Marc Mierowsky (from BSECS), Alex and Lauren (from Big Red Barrel), Diana and Michael Gray (from GameCola), and Emily Short. From Tumblr, we are particularly grateful to the following accounts: studyinstyle, arkadycosplay, englishotomegames, myladylydia, and dreamholde. A special mention goes to Laura Bee/dissipatience for her continued contributions to the *Regency Love* Wikia. Two more mentions go to Dawn Kaye and Erica Zeschke for correctly guessing the main *Lady Lavender* pairing. This is by no means an exhaustive list, but we hope you know we are only here today because of your continued support!

I have been fortunate enough to receive the support of amazing and gracious folks on Twitter, some of whom have become dear friends. My gratitude goes to Jon Ingold and Joseph Humfrey at inkle (it was so lovely to meet you both in Cambridge!), Bree Bridges and Donna Herren (the dream team behind Kit Rocha), Patrick Weekes, Aiko, and Drunk Austen (who'd be pleased to know I'm having a whisk[e]y right now). Lauren Clinnick has been a particularly bright (or shall I say '*luminous*'?) star – I'm so happy we spent that week together in New Orleans, and I look forward to more Melbourne adventures!

Massive thanks to my beta-readers, who provided me with the necessary constructive criticism to improve *Lady Lavender*. Beatrice Carr, thank you for your feedback on one of the earlier drafts – I hope this final one is much more to your liking! Wendy Lin, thank you for reminding me of the good old days when I used to kill off main characters. Also, please replace at least a portion of the ice cream you've stolen. To Erin, Kath, Jess, and Yarna, the amazing ladies of the Sydney Romance Book Club: thank you for welcoming me to your fold and critiquing my manuscript. Our monthly meetings bring me immense joy – I'm so glad I found you! Savannah 'Some chick from Boston' Camacho, thank you for the last-minute beta-reading, your help with the physical proofs, and your Minako-esque cheerleading!

My wonderful friends – near and far – who have supported me through various stages of this journey, regardless of how much they knew about *Regency Love* and *Lady Lavender*. Ruby Yee, Jenna J. Lindeke, Shannon Symonds, Costy Scarpa, and Yang Yang Zhang. Ardrian Hardjono and Charmian Tam (in London) and Maaria Posti (in Finland!): thank you for letting me crash at yours when *Lady Lavender* was still just the 'Sutton novel'. Emma Critchley, thank you for having me at your gorgeous wedding, which provided ample inspiration for the manuscript. Stephany Hiew, thank you for your friendship and text spams. I have fiercely guarded our matcha ice cream from Wendy, so we really ought to dig in again sometime.

My love and gratitude to Alexander, who cooked, laundered, cleaned, and ran Shakespeare Academy so I could spend countless hours 'doing Sutton'. I couldn't ask for a better househusband-in-training.

And finally, to Maria: you are the James to my Aubrey. This book is for you.

REGENCY LOVE

Lady Lavender is a spin-off novel of *Regency Love*, an RPG for iOS. In *Regency Love*, you play a character who could potentially end up being Mrs Ashcroft – or not. You can learn more about Ellie, Marcus, Mr Curtis, Mr Graham (as he was then known), Lord Sutton, and a range of other characters featured in *Lady Lavender*.

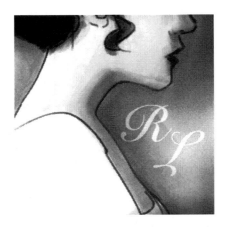

To find out more about *Regency Love*, check out our website (http://teaforthreestudios.com/regency-love) or search for 'Regency Love' on the App Store.

For more goodies on *Lady Lavender*, including playlists and character profiles, check out http://teaforthreestudios.com/category/lady-lavender/

TEA FOR THREE STUDIOS

Tea For Three Studios is an independent games-development group based in Sydney, Australia. The studio consists of:

Jenny Tan: Lead artist, visual development, illustrator, visual branding
Melody Wang: Code wrangler, UI warden, groomer of game mechanics
Samantha Lin: Lead writer, blogger, social media spammer, all the words

The group has been working together since 2011, and enjoys brewing tea and stories alike.

teaforthreestudios.com

Facebook: @TeaForThreeStudios
Twitter: @TeaForThreeTime
Tumblr: @teaforthreestudios

ABOUT THE AUTHOR

Samantha Lin lives in Sydney, Australia, with her extensive collection of Shakespeare and Sailormoon shinies.

www.samantha-lin.com

Facebook: @SamanthaLinWriter
Twitter: @samanthalin
Instagram: @sxylin

Made in the USA
Columbia, SC
06 December 2021

50524141R00200